READER'S COMMENTS

Adults

C.S. Lewis writes, "Ideally, we should like to define a good book as one which 'permits, invites or compels' good reading." Jenny L. Cote has done all that and more with *The Amazing Tales of Max and Liz.*

—**Karen Tenkate,** Australia, age 22

FABULOUS!!!! What fun to catch up with Max, Liz, and the gang as they are called to fulfill an intriguing mission in Egypt. Jenny L. Cote has woven threads of adventure, history, humor, and biblical truths into a tale as colorful as Joseph's coat. I really love the Max and Liz series, and I am ready for book 3!

—**Tasha Holliday**, Assistant Principal,
First Presbyterian Day School, Jackson, MS

With biblical truths and life lessons woven throughout, this is a must read for children and adults alike.

—**Jenny Keeton,** Mount Pisgah Christian School Teacher,
Alpharetta, GA

Enchanting! The interaction between the animals was delightful and carried the story from scene to scene, portraying the battle between good and evil. The story related the biblical account of Joseph with truth, clarity, and whimsical intrigue. I appreciated the way Nigel instructed Liz in Egyptian culture and language.

—**Karen Upton**, Principal,
Norfolk Christian Lower School, Norfolk, VA

Jenny L. Cote has served up another great adventure that's packed with humor, palace, and pyramid intrigue, plenty of all things Egypt, and of course a creative, can't put it down look at how it all might have happened during the life of the great patriarch, Joseph.

—**Claire Roberts Foltz**, Author, Focus on the Family's
Clubhouse, Jr. Magazine, and *The Mutt Tales*, Atlanta, GA

Jenny L. Cote engages and entertains as she addresses important life lessons—this time: forgiveness, trust, forbearance. With continued strong sales for *The Ark, The Reed, and The Fire Cloud* we anticipate another enthusiastic reception for this, her second book. We have already received inquiries from her many local fans!

—**Yvonne Rogers,** Children's Book Buyer/Manager,
Lemuria Book Store, Jackson, MS

Kids

I loved *The Ark, the Reed, and the Fire Cloud,* but I love *The Dreamer, the Schemer, and the Robe* even more. The stories are like the classics that C.S. Lewis made. *The Dreamer, the Schemer, and the Robe* is completely original from every other book there is. No other author could write a book like Mrs. Cote.

—**Charlotte Davis**, Homeschool 3rd grade,
Richmond, VA, age 8

Amazing! The perfect blend of humor, adventure, and gospel. A treat worth reading!

—**Stephen Brentlinger**, Homeschool 6th grade,
Williamson, GA, age 11

The adventures in this book are amazing and the characters are so cute. I especially liked Nigel. Who wouldn't like a little mouse with glasses?!

—**Renee Hogan**, Homeschool 5th grade,
Williamsburg, VA, age 10

Outstanding! Fantastic! A book that *everyone* should read. My favorite character is Nigel P. Monaco, a British Egyptologist. It is a great sequel to the first book. I do not want to give away too much of the story, so read the book for yourself!

—**Luke W.,** Providence Classical School, 5th grade,
Williamsburg, VA, age 11

The Dreamer, The Schemer and The Robe is a unique and heartwarming book, showing love between the animals and a way of life for Joseph. It's great!

—**Jake Tipton**, Madison Station Elementary, 5th grade,
Madison, MS, age 11

A thrilling story with twists and a menagerie of different characters filled with suspense. Once I picked up the book I couldn't put it down.

—**Braden Sanders**, Calvary Christian School, 7th grade,
Columbus, GA, age 13

When Joseph had a dream it made you feel like you were floating in the dream with him. I like how Jenny L. Cote gave a specific amount of robes, dreams and schemes to keep you reading. I also like the hieroglyphic code in the end to give a hint of what is coming in the next book.

—**Grace Calkins,** Providence Classic School,
4th grade, Williamsburg, VA, age 9

The best book I have ever read. I liked it because there was something always happening in the book so you couldn't stop reading.

—**Wes Crockett**, Jackson Academy, 7th grade, Jackson, MS, age 13

The way Jenny L. Cote has interwoven the fictional animal characters (Max, Liz, Al, and Kate) with the story of Joseph is great! This book has adventure and excitement and would appeal to elementary and middle school kids.

—**Brianna Posch,** Norfolk Christian Middle School, 8th grade, Norfolk, VA, age 14

This book taught me a lot about the Egyptian culture and God.

—**Megan Taylor,** Mt. Vernon Presbyterian School, 5th grade, Atlanta, GA, age 9

I love the Max and Liz stories. They always take you on an exciting adventure. I wish that they would never end. I can't wait to read the next book.

—**Mary Katherine Duncan**, Calvary Christian School, 3rd grade, Columbus, GA, age 8

Every time I've read Jenny L. Cote's books I've had a brand new favorite book, but this time I'm serious. This is my favorite book! Never stop shouting, Osahar!

—**Charis Thompson**, Austin Elementary School, 4th grade, Dunwoody, GA, age 10

Great read! I loved learning about Egypt. I enjoyed all the places they visited: the pyramids, the Sphinx, Pharaoh's palace, etc. Al was my favorite character because he is really funny!

—**John Washburne**, Fellowship Christian School, 2nd grade, Milton, GA, age 8

This book is even better than the first, which is hard to beat! It gave me a whole new perspective on the story of Joseph. It proves that no matter where we are, or how bad our situation is, God is always there to help us. We just have to listen and trust in Him.

—**Katie Greenough**, Kennedy Middle School, 8th grade, Germantown, WI, age 14

Reading this book was a great experience. I read the entire book in two days because I couldn't wait to find out what happened next!

—**Sarah Love Frey**, First Presbyterian Day School, 5th grade, Jackson, MS, age 11

Wow! This book popped out of its pages with great descriptions of both mystery and adventure. Most importantly, it reminded me that God has a perfect plan for our lives. I highly recommend it!

—**Lucy Waller**, Jackson Academy, 6th grade, Jackson, MS, age 11

This book got me hooked right away, so I read it in two days. I loved learning about Ancient Egypt. I also liked how Mrs. Cote put the Egyptian symbols under the chapter titles.

—**Wesley Roberson**, First Presbyterian Day School,
4th grade, Jackson, MS, age 10

I love the way Mrs. Cote takes Bible stories I've heard all my life and brings them to life in fun and exciting ways! Nigel is my new favorite character. I can't wait for all my friends to read this book!

—**Jessica Roberts**, Wesleyan School, 4th grade, Atlanta, GA age 10

The Dreamer, the Schemer and the Robe is my favorite book! Jenny L. Cote took a Bible story and made it more fun and easy to get into. Thanks Mrs. Jenny! It rocked!

—**Alex Thompson**, Kittredge Magnet School,
6th grade, Atlanta, GA, age 12

Never give up no matter what comes your way in life because if you always trust and love God, He will bring good out of it. *The Dreamer, the Schemer, and the Robe* taught me that with God we are more than just survivors—our dreams really can come true!

—**Georgia Sims**, Jackson Academy, 7th grade, Jackson, MS, age 12

I think that *The Dreamer, the Schemer, and the Robe* is a great book that many people will LOVE. It's one of those books you just can't put down. I read it in six days!

—**Jimmy Die**, Atlantic Shores Christian School, 5th grade,
Virginia Beach, VA, age 11

The Dreamer, the Schemer, & the Robe

Jenny L. Cote

Living Ink Books
An Imprint of AMG Publishers, Inc.
Chattanooga, Tennessee

The Amazing Tales of Max and Liz™
The Dreamer, the Schemer, and the Robe

Published by Living Ink Books, an imprint of AMG Publishers
6815 Shallowford Rd.
Chattanooga, Tennessee 37421

The author was aided by three Bible sources when writing this book. They are as follows:

The Message by Eugene H. Peterson, copyright © 1993, 1994, 1995, 1996, 2000, 2001, 2002. Used by permission of NavPress Publishing Group. All rights reserved.

Sanctuary: A Devotional Bible for Women, New Living Translation. New York: Tyndale House, 2006.

Hebrew-Greek Key Word Study Bible, New American Standard Bible edition. Edited by Spiros Zodhiates and Warren Baker. Chattanooga, TN: AMG Publishers, 2008.

ISBN: 9780899571997
Second Printing—October 2009

THE AMAZING TALES OF MAX AND LIZ is a trademark of AMG Publishers.

Cover designed by Daryle Beam, Bright Boy Design Inc., Chattanooga, Tennessee

Illustrations by Rob Moffitt, Atlanta, Georgia

Interior design and typesetting by Reider Publishing Services, West Hollywood, California

Edited and proofread by Rich Cairnes, Christy Graeber, and Rick Steele

Printed in the United States of America
19 20 21 22 23 –B– 9 8 7 6 5

The **AMAZING TALES OF MAX & LIZ®** collection
by **Jenny L. Cote**:

The Ark, the Reed, & the Fire Cloud

ISBN-13: 978-089957198-0

A magical adventure of animals traveling worldwide to Noah's ark. Max, a brave Scottish Terrier meets Liz, a brilliant French cat, on the way to the ark, along with a whimsical team of animal sojourners. Max and Liz become the brave leaders for the humorous and often perilous journey. Once aboard they help other animals through the flood and the long voyage, but also must foil a plot by a stowaway who is out to kill Noah and stop his mission of saving the animal kingdom as well as the human race.

The Dreamer, the Schemer, & the Robe

ISBN-13: 978-089957199-7

A thrilling adventure to uncover the captivating story of Joseph in mysterious Egypt. They've waited for centuries for their first mission as God's envoys in history, but Max and Liz finally get to work behind the scenes in the life of Joseph. All looks hopeless for the young teenager as his brothers sell him into slavery in Egypt. Max and Liz must combat the forces of evil that are out to thwart their plans, leading them into mysterious adventures with pyramids and mummies. If they fail in this mission, all of Egypt and surrounding nations will suffer from famine, and the Hebrew nation will never be born.

Look for future titles in this exciting series!
Published by Living Ink Books, an imprint of AMG Publishers
www.maxandlizseries.com • www.livinginkbooks.com
www.amgpublishers.com
800-266-4977

Joe,

You were the first Joseph I ever knew, and as you were named for the original Joseph, it's only fitting that I dedicate this book to you. As my big brother, you have modeled for me the same integrity, character, and faith in God that I see in the original Joe.*

Love,
Jenny

**Except for that incident with my Jot doll, back in the day when you wore the vertically striped pants of many colors. But I'm not bitter . . . really.*

This is a work of fiction based on truth.
For the true story, read Genesis 37–50.

Contents

Acknowledgments xv
Prologue: A Living Nightmare xix

PART ONE
The Dreamer

Chapter 1: The Sphinx 3
Chapter 2: The Joseph Assignment 12
Chapter 3: The Favorite 20
Chapter 4: Going against the Grain 27
Chapter 5: The Caravan 34
Chapter 6: God Hears Me 43
Chapter 7: A Scheme of Brothers 49
Chapter 8: Refusing to Be Comforted 57
Chapter 9: The Road to Egypt 66

PART TWO
The Slave

Chapter 10: The Market 77
Chapter 11: Of Mouse and Men 84
Chapter 12: Potiphar and Bastet 90
Chapter 13: In the House of Potiphar 96
Chapter 14: A Cat Fit for a King 105
Chapter 15: Potiphar's Vineyard 110
Chapter 16: Hapy in the Palace 115
Chapter 17: The Prison 123
Chapter 18: Rock, Papyrus, Scissors 129
Chapter 19: Egyptology 101 136
Chapter 20: The Third Day 143
Chapter 21: The Hunt 153
Chapter 22: Pyramid Progress and Passages 162
Chapter 23: A Triangle of Secrets 168
Chapter 24: Nigel's Secret Weapon 174
Chapter 25: The Favor of Potiphar 179

PART THREE
The Lord

Chapter 26: Kate and Benjamin 193
Chapter 27: The Dream Book 201
Chapter 28: A Woman Scorned 211
Chapter 29: Potiphar's Decision 217
Chapter 30: The Secret Passage 223
Chapter 31: Blind Faith 230
Chapter 32: *The Book of the Dead* 235
Chapter 33: Through a Glass, Brightly 241
Chapter 34: Joseph, the Jailer, and Jabari 248
Chapter 35: Heart Strings 255
Chapter 36: A Hair-Raising Morning 263
Chapter 37: The Baker and the Cupbearer 269

Chapter 38: The Tunnel 275
Chapter 39: The Banana Key 282
Chapter 40: What Dreams May Bring 288
Chapter 41: Pharaoh's Birthday 294
Chapter 42: Very Superstitious 303
Chapter 43: Sleepless in the Palace 311
Chapter 44: Never in Your Wildest Dreams 317

PART FOUR
The Revealer of Secrets

Chapter 45: Death of a Jailer 327
Chapter 46: The Blind Harpist 334
Chapter 47: Seven Years of Plenty 344
Chapter 48: Death of the Nile 353
Chapter 49: Brothers and Spies 359
Chapter 50: The Awakening 369
Chapter 51: Not This One 376

PART FIVE
The Hidden One

Chapter 52: A Necessary Cup 385
Chapter 53: Opener of the Ways 395
Chapter 54: The Temple of Anubis 405
Chapter 55: Redemption 416
Chapter 56: The Final Robe 426
Chapter 57: The Schemer's Dream 431
Chapter 58: Reunion 438
Chapter 59: The Hidden One 444

A Word from the Author 453
Bibliography 459
Glossary 461

Acknowledgments

Acknowledgments

I wish there was an Egyptian hieroglyph symbol of a smiley face to go in this book. I could post it here and say, "This ancient symbol is as enduring as will be my thanks to the following people." Just imagine one anyway.

Thank You God, the one true God, for giving me the words in this book. You inspired it and You wrote it. I merely took dictation, so it's all Yours.

For my wonderful family! To my guys Casey and Alex, thank you for your love and support while I was in my writing cave for three months. Thanks for letting me travel and tell the world about Max and Liz. For my other live-in "family" from Australia, Mike and Karen Tenkate—*thanks heaps* for your constant encouragement and website support. And certainly for two of the most important family members, Max and Liz—much love, me wee ones.

To my dear friend and brother in Christ, Michael P. Monaco—you inspired my new little star for this book, "Nigel P. Monaco"! I thank you for allowing me to use your name, and for teaching me to play the harp "by heart." Your inspiration and support made my writing take off and soar. Many *happy flying returns*, Mousie!

Warm thanks to a special reader, Stephen Brentlinger. God allowed your terrible leg accident to be used for good in this book about God using terrible circumstances for the good of Joseph. Thank you for allowing me to use your story for the chapter on Kate and Benjamin. Your faith amazes me, and I expect to see big things from you some day, dear boy. You have touched my heart, my mind, and my pen.

My research on Joseph and Egypt was extensive. Many thanks for insights from Dr. Peter Lacovara, Senior Curator of Ancient Egyptian, Nubian, and Near Eastern Art at the Michael C. Carlos Museum at Emory University. I highly recommend a visit to this excellent Egyptian Museum in Atlanta.

For my harp research, I appreciate Sandra Wilson Harris, "The Celebration Harpist" in Atlanta. Sandra allowed me to visit her full collection of harps and even gave me a mini-lesson. I'm not ready to play Carnegie Hall yet, so I'll leave that to you professionals!

I must personally thank two men whose commentaries on Joseph gave me invaluable insights and spiritual truths. *Their* ideas are woven throughout the pages of this book, and I give full credit to them for nearly every spiritual insight in *The Dreamer*. The first is F. B. Meyer, a British pastor born in 1847. His book *The Life of Joseph* became my primary text beyond Genesis. I used it so much that most every sentence in his book is highlighted or underlined! Also thanks to Dr. Charles R. Swindoll and his amazing book *Joseph*. Dr. Swindoll has always been one of my favorite Christian writers, and he has had a huge impact on my spiritual growth. Please never stop writing!

Thanks to Dr. Jim Johnson, senior pastor of Preston Trail Community Church, Frisco, TX, for his sermon series on Joseph that inspired me over a decade ago! Thanks for your sermon notes and ideas that helped me bring Joseph alive.

My undying appreciation to all the players involved on the production team who transformed *The Dreamer* into the beautiful book you hold in your hands. My literary agent, Mary Busha, my publisher; AMG (Dan Penwell, Dale Anderson, Rick Steele, Trevor Overcash, Warren Baker, Mike Oldham, Gin Chasteen, Amanda Donnahoe, Donna Coker, and the support staff); my editor, Rich Cairnes; my illustrator, Rob Moffit; my cover designer, Daryle Beam; my interior designer, Andrea Reider; and my proofreader, Christy Graeber. Thank you all!

My critique team is simply amazing and journeyed with me through every chapter written and through every writer's block moment: Lori Marett, Lisa Hockman, Paul and Janice Mims, Michael P. Monaco, Claire Roberts Foltz, Mary Busha, Bernard Kearse, and Patricia Burney. Thank you for bearing with my endless emails and requests!

To all those family members, Dunwoody Baptist Church, and friends who pray for me, encourage me, and love me through this gr-r-rand adventure of writing, thank you.

Finally, to the most important ones of all: THE KIDS! You guys rock and keep me going with your enthusiastic responses to Max and Liz. Thanks to my fans, my advance readers, and to all the awesome schools who welcome me to visit and chat about creative writing. Much love to you all and keep those emails coming!

I'm all smiles just thinking about every one of you.

PROLOGUE

A Living Nightmare

Weightless. He felt utterly weightless. Joseph stretched his arms out wide, feeling at one with the vast expanse surrounding him. He closed his eyes and lost all sense of orientation. There was complete silence. Suddenly he felt warmth on his back and a gentle breeze blowing the hem of his multicolored robe. It was soothing and inviting. He slowly turned without effort to see the source of the warm breeze. It was the sun, shining in all its glory. Wisps of fire escaped the turbulent ball of red and orange. Strange. How small it looked! He felt close enough to reach out and cup it in the palm of his hand.

Out of the corner of his eye came another source of light. But there was no warmth, only soft light. He turned his head to see a full moon drifting slowly over to position itself next to the sun. Compared with the small sun, the moon appeared tiny.

Joseph hovered there in the silence, the sun warming him and the moon reflecting soft light before him. It was a beautiful sight to behold. As he reached his hand out to touch the moon, out from behind the moon came a trail of stars! Each one, smaller still than the moon, glittered as it took up its position under the sun and the moon. Eleven. There were eleven stars in all, lined up in perfect order, hovering there before him.

The sun began to move. It tipped forward, and then rotated back. As the fireball repeated this tipping movement, the moon began to do the same. Soon the stars joined them. Joseph slowly realized these celestial objects were bowing before him. He acknowledged the gesture with a smile and a slight nod of the head, holding his hands out over them as if to bless them.

Weightlessness. Silence. Warmth. Light. Honor. Tribute. It was an unreal, glorious moment. All was perfect, majestic, and as it should be.

But then came a noise that began to penetrate his dream. The stars, all but the smallest one, jumped, startled by the sound. They began to tremble as the noise grew louder. The noise was ugly. It was the sound of metal scraping across stone. The sound took on an added dimension of heaviness. Joseph's hands drifted up to his neck, where he felt something cold and hard binding him there, weighing him down.

The celestial bodies ceased their bowing. The stars suddenly scattered as the noise grew louder. The smallest star hovered behind for a moment, but then it, too, fled into the blackness, following the others. The moon drifted away from the sun, and the light accordingly faded from its surface. After a moment, the moon could hardly be seen in the distance.

Only the sun remained, yet even it started moving away, taking the warmth with it.

Joseph reached out to grab hold of the sun, willing it to stay with him, crying, "No! Don't go! Stay with me! Don't leave me here alone!" But the sun moved away into the blackness, taking all remaining light and warmth with it as the ugly noise grew to an ear-shattering pitch.

Heavy. Loud. Dark. Alone. And now he felt cold. Joseph shivered and tried to scream, but the object around his neck restrained him. Where was his robe? It, too, was now gone, and left his skin exposed to the cold. Then he felt something wet around his ankles. The sensation was at first warm, but grew cold as air hit his moist, exposed skin. Yet somehow it felt soft and oddly comforting.

Joseph was being pulled away from a scene that a moment ago had been so good and safe and happy. He didn't want to leave. But the sun, the moon, and the stars were all gone, and the noise and the cold intensified. He kept his eyes closed and shook his head from side to side in protest of the turn of events. The oddly comforting, warm, moist sensation stopped, and something started to nudge him. He winced with pain as his body moved. Something cut into his wrists and ankles with every nudge. He didn't want to, but he knew he must open his eyes to see what was happening.

Slowly he allowed his eyelids to barely part, and a dim light met his gaze. It was a flame. Had the sun returned? His eyes adjusted and he saw that the flame came not from the glorious sun, but from a torch anchored to a dark, slimy wall above him.

Another nudge to his ribs. His hands slowly drifted to find the source of the nudge and he felt something soft and furry. Reality came crashing back into his mind as Joseph awoke with a start. He heard harsh voices shouting and the clanging of chains. He closed his eyes again and tried to lick his lips. His mouth was parched. Another nudge.

"Okay, boy. I feel you. I'm waking up," he told the furry animal next to him in a broken, dry voice. Joseph opened his eyes to the horror of the scene around him. No, he wasn't in the heavens, floating weightlessly and wearing a colorful robe of prestige and honor. He was lying in a dark, dank prison, wearing rags and bound in irons hand and foot, with a collar locked around his neck, its chains draped across his bare chest.

The other prisoners crowded in the small, confining space were pushing and shoving to reach the solitary opening of the pit, lifting their wooden bowls as scraps of food were carelessly tossed in to them. One prisoner shoved from behind and caused another to spill his bowl. "You'll pay for that, you worm!" shouted the angry prisoner. "Oh, yeah? We'll see who the worm is after you're dead!" the pushy prisoner replied. A nasty fight broke out between the embittered inmates.

A lump grew in Joseph's throat as he sat up and rested his head on the cold stone wall, observing the chaos around him. He felt another insistent nudge. He looked down to see a small, black Scottish terrier gazing up at him with the most soulful eyes Joseph had ever seen. It was the dog who had been licking his wounds where the iron shackles tore the flesh around his ankles. Now his canine friend was trying to get him up to receive the only food that would arrive today. If Joseph didn't get moving, it would be twenty-four hours before he could eat.

Joseph sighed heavily yet smiled at the little dog. "Thank you, my small friend. You are my only source of physical comfort here. How glad I am the jailer bought you that day for this place."

He rubbed the dog under his chin, causing him to scratch with his back leg. "I had the dream again, the one with the sun, the moon, and the stars," he said to the dog with a sad chuckle. "Ah, my silly dreams. What could possibly ever come of them now? I'd better get used to what is real." Joseph watched the fighting prisoners clamoring for their daily rations of spoiled meat and hard, stale bread. "I'm in a living nightmare. Why am I here? I did the right thing, Jabari. *The right thing!* But it landed me in prison."

He shouldn't be here. And as he gazed into the soft, warm eyes of this little dog sitting next to him, somehow he felt the dog agreed. Joseph shook his head and put his hands on the cold stone floor to push himself up. A roach scurried over his hand, but he didn't react. He was used to the bugs. He was used to the cold. He was used to the smell and the noise. But he could never seem to get used to the reason behind it all.

Joseph slowly stood, wincing with the pain of the irons. He shuffled his feet and joined the noisy, shoving, filthy prisoners.

The little dog furrowed his brow while he watched Joseph. A low grumble rose in his throat as he gazed at the injustice before him. *Aye, why indeed are ye here, laddie? 'Tis wr-r-rong!* Max murmured to himself. *I jest dunnot understand it!*

A small mouse came scurrying by and stopped at Max's feet. His nose twitched as he sat up on his hind legs and looked around. "Word is to be patient. That's what she said," whispered the mouse before he darted off into the dark corner of the dungeon.

"Patient," Max mumbled. "Only thr-r-ree dr-r-reams so far. Looks like we're in for another long spell of waitin' then. I hope I kin stand it." He looked sadly over at Joseph.

"Aye, an' I hope the *laddie* kin."

PART ONE

THE DREAMER

CHAPTER 1

The Sphinx

SIX YEARS EARLIER

"Are ye completely daft, kitty?! Wha' do ye mean it doesn't look like a bull?" Max grumbled at the big orange cat next to him, who sat rubbing his paw under his chin as if in deep thought.

"Sure and it's missin' somethin'," Al replied in his thick Irish accent, now circling his paw in the air with a gesture of uncertainty.

Max and Al stood over the picture Max had made in the sand. It was a beast with four legs, long pointed horns, and a scowl on its face. But even Max had to admit to himself it did lack something.

"I've got it, lad!" Al suddenly said with a laugh and a paw in the air. He popped out a claw and went over to scribble on Max's drawing. After a minute or two he stood to the side so Max could see his addition. Al wore a big goofy grin on his face as he wiped the sand off his paws.

Max burst out laughing. "Aye, Big Al! Ye done made it look like a r-r-real bull. It's Don Pedro hisself! I see wha' were missin' before—the r-r-reason for his scowl!"

Al had drawn a big hen sitting on top of the bull. The hen's mouth was open and her arms were spread out as if she were giving orders. Max and Al had met their Spanish bull friend, Don Pedro, on the journey to Noah's ark. The bull had suffered from anger issues and would go off on wild chases, disturbing their group of animal travelers. As the intellectual leader of the group, Liz the cat had assigned her French friend, Henriette the hen, to assist the bull in anger management. Don Pedro had been miserable with Henriette's obnoxious, bossy attitude and grating voice. Max and Al couldn't help but laugh as they remembered their poor friend Don Pedro.

"It seems forever ago we met Don Pedro, Henriette, and all those animal beasties on the way to the Ark," Al said thoughtfully. He looked around at the pictures he and Max had drawn in the sand: giraffes, seagulls, beavers, monkeys, and even wolves. A huge drawing of a whale surrounded them, and a majestic mountain goat was sketched in the center.

"Aye, it *has* been forever ago," Max replied as he gazed at the drawing of the mountain goat, a likeness of his good friend and mentor, Gillamon. "Liz said it's been aboot 2,000 years since the Gr-r-reat Flood. That lass of yers is like a walkin' timepiece, she is!"

Al grinned. "Ah, Liz, me beautiful lass—she gets smarter by the decade. And I think I've learned a thing or two in the past few centuries then . . ." He was interrupted by Liz calling him.

"Albert! You two come back and join us. I have something you must see, no?" Liz called with a beautiful French accent from high atop a stone wall above them.

Al waved and nodded his head. "Be right there, love!" He turned to Max. "As I were sayin', I've learned a lot o' things over the centuries—one bein' never to keep the lass waitin' when she's givin' a lecture."

"Aye, let's join our lassies," Max said. The two friends bounded up the stone blocks leading to the wall where sat Liz, a petite black cat, and Kate, a white West Highland terrier.

"Max, ye missed Liz's description of how this pyramid were built. Liz, please tell the boys again if ye don't mind," Kate pleaded, her tail wagging excitedly.

"Of course, *mon amie*," Liz casually replied. "But first, do tell me what you two were doing down there, Albert."

Al jumped up and kissed Liz on the cheek. "Sorry we missed yer lecture, love. Max and me were tryin' our paws at drawin' hieroglyphs like we been seein' at the pyramids. It's the most fun part o' the tour to me," Al said with a shy grin. "I like pictures."

Liz smiled at her mate. Al did not possess Liz's supreme intellect, but he did have a big heart and such lovability about him, which she found irresistible.

"Aye! Ye should have seen the picture Al here drew of Henriette," Max said with a chuckle. "He didn't think Don Pedro's portrait were complete without that bossy hen sittin' on top of the poor lad!"

Al gave a weak, nervous grin at Liz and tried to hide behind Max. Liz frowned at Max and Al. They never could remember her friend without some sort of a jab. Still, as much as she disliked their fun at Henriette's expense, the truth of the matter was that they were essentially right.

"Ah-hem," Liz cleared her throat to change the subject. "As I was explaining to Kate, you have already seen the pyramids of Pharaoh Snefru and Pharaoh Khufu . . ."

Al sat there with a blank expression on his face. He clearly didn't remember who these pharaohs were. Liz was ever observant of creature behavior, making it her habit to continually watch the expressions and body language of others to determine what they were thinking and feeling.

"Perhaps I should review what we've seen so far on our tour of Egypt, no?" Liz said, drawing a smile from Al. "The first pyramid was built by Pharaoh Djoser hundreds of years ago. It was the largest building of its time and stood at 204 feet, but it was a step shape, not like later pyramids. Following Djoser came Pharaoh Snefru, who made three attempts before he achieved the true pyramid shape with the Red Pyramid."

Liz stopped to see if her audience was still with her. They were all listening attentively, especially Kate, who was ever eager to learn from Liz. This trip to the pyramids was entirely Liz's idea. She had heard of the engineering marvels made in Egypt and just had to come study them for herself. Liz was aware her love for science and architecture was not shared by others. But at least for now Max, Kate, and Al were fascinated as well by these ancient engineering marvels.

"But it was Snefru's son, Khufu, who made the largest pyramid ever built, which we see there in the distance: the Great Pyramid. *C'est magnifique*! Four-hundred eighty-one feet high, consisting of more than two million stone blocks—some weighing nine tons each. It took twenty-three years to build this pyramid, with a block moved every five minutes. Impossible! *Ooh-la-la!*" Liz exclaimed. Only she could get so excited about things like building blocks.

Max furrowed his brow as he and the others looked out over the Giza plateau at the Great Pyramid. "An' why do the Egyptian laddies build such gr-r-rand pyramids?"

"The pyramids are actually elaborate burial chambers," Liz replied, eyeing the magnificent structure.

Al gave a chuckle. "Ye mean they bury *gold* in these big triangles?! Sure, and I'm surprised a rainbow doesn't hover over them as over a pot o' gold!"

"Aye! We kin get r-r-rich, big Al. I'll dig out the gold meself," Max chimed in, drawing a stern look from Liz. She was not amused.

"*Of course* there is gold in the pyramids, but the burial chambers are for burying the bodies of dead pharaohs," Liz explained matter-of-factly.

Al gasped, putting his paws up to his mouth. "Ye mean there are dead laddies in these big triangles?" He nervously looked up at the pyramid that towered over him, stepping away from it a bit.

"*Oui*, Albert. Pharaoh Kahfre is inside this pyramid," Liz explained as she tapped a massive stone block with her dainty paw. "But it is fascinating how they preserve the bodies, called 'mummies.'"

"*Mummies*? Now there's a funny name, lass! That's wha' I called me mum back in Scotland. Why would they be namin' dead laddies after their mums?" Max asked.

Liz slowly slapped her tail on the ground. Sometimes Al and Max made lecturing a bit tedious. "No, no, no. Listen, *mon ami*. The process the Egyptians use to preserve the bodies is called *mummification*. It has nothing to do with their 'mums.'"

"But why do the Egyptians make mummies?" Kate chimed in.

"Well, they believe that when the pharaoh dies, he becomes Osiris, king of the dead. The new pharaoh becomes Horus, god of the heavens and protector of the sun god. So you see it is like the cycle of the setting and rising sun," Liz explained.

"But there's only *one* God, lassie!" Max protested.

"*Oui*, Max, of course there is, but you must understand that many of these cultures we visit do not believe in the one, true God. The Egyptians believe in many, many gods," Liz replied.

"Oh, me," Kate sighed. "Humans have drifted from the Maker jest like in Noah's day."

Liz shrugged her shoulders. "*Oui*, it is what happens to some humans. The Maker gives them free will, *n'est ce pas*?"

"So wha' else do they believe then aboot all these *'gods'* an' death?" Max asked sarcastically.

"They believe that if the body is not properly preserved, then the old pharaoh cannot carry out his new duties as king of the dead. If this happens, the cycle is broken and Egypt will face disaster," Liz explained. "So this is why they mummify the bodies and put things in their tombs they would need in the afterlife, such as boats and other vessels, gold, furniture, food, even servant look-a-likes. *Comprenez-vous?*"

Al's ears perked up at the mention of food. "Food? What kind o' food?" His stomach growled. "And where do they put the mummy so he can get to all his foo—I mean, stuff?"

Liz smiled at Al, who loved to eat but never seemed to get full. "Sometimes they place the mummy in multiple nesting coffins, all painted to resemble the pharaoh."

Max and Al looked at each other for a moment of silence before big grins broke out on their faces.

Al shook his head. "I may not be very bright, but it seems to me the old pharaoh couldn't get to his stuff if he's locked up, much less dead!" He leaned over and whispered to Max, "'Tis a shame to think o' all that food goin' to waste."

"Aye! An' jest how is the mummy supposed ta take his boat for a sail, then?" Max added. "This is the driest land ever I laid eyes on . . . not that the laddie could get out anyway. An' the Maker said he's done with floodin' the world so I wouldn't be hopin' for the Nile waters ta come here like they did ta float the Ark!"

Kate, although sweet, could turn her fiery Scottish temper on in an instant, and she did just that. "Now ye two laddies listen ta me! We may not agree with wha' the Egyptians do, but ye need ta be rememberin' these are beautiful, ingenious people. They're God's creation, too, so don't be disrespectin' them."

Max and Al slowly settled down, and Max took on a more serious tone. "I'm sorry, lass. I jest have a hard time understandin' why they would believe such things. I've seen the power of the Maker before an' after death, an' it's *r-r-real.* All this . . . sun god an' king of the dead afterlife stuff is jest hard ta take when ye lived—an' died—the tr-r-ruth."

Max indeed knew about the power of the Maker and the reality of death. After Noah's ark landed, he and Liz faced death at the hands of Charlatan, the original impostor from the Garden of Eden. But God had overturned death and made Max, Liz, and their mates Kate and Al immortal. So Max knew very well about the one, true God, whom they had agreed to serve on special missions to help humans. But they had been waiting for centuries for their first assignment.

Kate softened. "Aye, me love. How glad I am the Maker brought ye back ta me. Jest be kind an' patient with those who believe different than ye do." She placed her paw on Max's shoulder. "Show the truth in how ye treat them."

Max winked at Kate. "Aye, lass, ye're r-r-right. I'll do me best."

"Me, too," Al said, his stomach growling again. "Now if one o' the Egyptians' gods were a big cat, I might not be snickerin' so!"

Liz grinned and slowly curled her tail up and down. "Is that so, *mon cher*?" Liz said as she daintily walked on top of the stone wall away from the group.

Al, Max, and Kate looked curiously at each other for a moment, then followed Liz around the base of the enormous pyramid. Max felt very small as he gazed up at layer upon layer of massive stone blocks. Liz did have a point. It was incredible how the Egyptians had done this.

As they turned the corner, Max stopped in his tracks and hit Al in the chest with his burly paw. "Get r-r-ready ta not snicker any more then, laddie."

Al's jaw dropped. There before them was a massive statue—a human-headed lion wearing the headdress of a pharaoh. Its long legs were majestically stretched out in front. It looked like the king of the beasts sitting on a big rock overlooking the savanna of Africa.

"And I thought *I* were big," Al said in awe of the big cat figure.

"You were saying, Albert dear?" Liz teased as she gestured up to the enormous structure. "This statue is called the Sphinx. Pharaoh Khafre built this complex with his pyramid, the Sphinx, and all these statues. *Magnifique!*" It truly was an amazing sight. Numerous stone figures surrounded them, standing tall and proud.

Kate cocked her head to the side. "Why a big cat then, Liz?"

Liz kept her gaze on the Sphinx and stared intently at its sharp, angled face. "Cats are respected more than any other creature in Egypt. They call we felines 'miw' here in Egypt."

Max spoke up, "Well, that seems a simple way ta call the kitty beasties—by how they sound! Do they call dogs 'bark' then?" He was a little jealous of the Egyptians' preference for cats.

Liz rolled her eyes. "I wish to study this culture more to understand their long-standing love affair with cats." Liz paused and then said, "I have heard that cats are an important part of interpreting dreams in Egypt. If a man sees a cat in a dream, it means he will have a good harvest."

"Not if Al is the cat doin' the harvestin'," Max joked. "He'll gobble up the poor laddie's whole crop!"

Suddenly there came a gust of wind that began to blow wispy sheets of sand across the ground like streams of smoke. The wispy sand encircled the animals and the statues as the wind picked up speed. Sand kicked up in their faces, forcing the animals to close their eyes. Max put his paw up to shield his eyes and squinted to see what was happening. Just below where they stood he saw the sand create a whirlwind, twisting ten feet above the ground.

Max took two steps toward the whirlwind, and saw an unknown shape forming in the center. It was all he could do to keep his gaze on the mysterious spectacle. The sand shape began to grow.

"What is happening?" Liz shouted above the roar of the wind, her eyes closed.

Max strained to see. "It's . . . hard ta tell. Somethin' is takin' shape in that dust devil." A low growl entered his throat; his guard was up. "Whatever it is, I'm r-r-ready for it!"

The solid sand structure grew to four feet tall. It now had not only form, but also movement. Max was able to barely make out a creature with four legs and a large head moving side to side.

"Max, don't go near it!" Kate pleaded with eyes closed, putting her paw out against the sand storm to feel for Max.

"The lassie's right! No need to be goin' off bein' a hero, Max! Come back!" Al shouted, spitting out the sand that blew into his open mouth. He was scared to death and held tightly to Liz.

Suddenly, Max's alarm was replaced with a feeling he had not felt in centuries. His heart started to pound wildly in his chest. He shook his head in disbelief and squinted harder against the blowing sand.

"There's nothin' ta fear!" Max shouted, now moving urgently against the wind toward the object. "I'd know that silhouette anywhere."

He moved in closer to the creature, who now looked right at him—and smiled. Tears quickened in Max's eyes.

"It's Gillamon!"

CHAPTER 2

The Joseph Assignment

The wind instantly ceased. The blowing sand settled all around the group of dazed animals. Al wiped the sand off his fur with both paws while spitting sand out of his mouth; Kate shook from the tip of her ears to the tip of her tail, and Liz sat in stunned silence, watching the scene unfold before them.

Max ran up to Gillamon, almost knocking the tall mountain goat over with his enthusiastic embrace. "GILLAMON! I kin't believe it. It's r-r-really ye yer-r-rself. Tell me I'm not dr-r-reamin'!" Max exclaimed, half crying and half laughing.

Gillamon warmly chuckled and placed his head over Max's small frame, returning his embrace. "Hello, Maximillian. You're not dreaming, lad. It's your old friend. I'm so glad to see you again after such a long time."

"Aye! Ye kin say that again!" Max replied. "When the Maker said ye'd be the one ta give us our next mission, I were expectin' ye ta come a little sooner than a couple of thousand years then."

"The Maker certainly has a different concept of time than the earthbound," Gillamon said with a twinkle in his eye. "Time is meaningless for the great I AM. But I do understand with the rising and setting suns here on earth, time becomes much more definitive." How happy he was to be reunited with his small friend. After living a timeless existence in heaven, Gillamon remembered that indeed, he had been a long time apart from this one he had raised and loved as his own back in Scotland.

Liz walked up behind Max, bowing her head in respect, saying, "*Monsieur* Gillamon. It is indeed an honor to finally meet you. Max has not stopped talking about you since the day we met. I am Lizette. Lizette Brilliante Aloysius."

Gillamon smiled and bowed low to Liz in return. "*Enchanté*, Liz. The honor is all mine. I have enjoyed watching you from a distance, and might I say how very impressed I am with your supreme intellect."

"*Merci*, Gillamon," Liz replied with her shy smile. "So I am eager to learn our mission, as I assume this is why you have come. Is there a mystery to solve?"

"Aye! Wha' does the Maker want us ta do?" Max chimed in eagerly. "Are there some mean beasties I need ta r-r-round up then?"

Gillamon looked at Kate and Al, who sat behind Max and Liz, and smiled warmly. "In a moment. First, allow me to meet your mates." Gillamon walked over to Kate and Al.

"I must extend my gratitude to you for your faithful support of Max and Liz. The Maker is greatly pleased with you," Gillamon said.

Al was still rattled by Gillamon's mysterious appearance in the whirlwind. "Are . . . are y-y-ye a g-g-ghost?" Al said, crouching behind Kate.

Gillamon chuckled. "No, lad, there are no such things as ghosts. Spirits, yes, but ghosts, no. I am as real as when I trod this solid earth twenty centuries ago. Go ahead, touch my goatee."

Al sheepishly looked at Kate and stepped out to walk up to Gillamon, who towered over him. He reached his shaky paw up and grabbed a clump of Gillamon's white double-bearded goatee and pulled, making the goat wince and give a low grunt.

"AL! Don't be hurtin' Gillamon then!" Kate said as she rushed up to push Al out of the way. "Me apologies, Gillamon! Al sometimes doesn't use his head (wha' little there is). I hope he didn't hurt ye." She frowned at Al, who crouched behind her again, and then returned her smiling gaze to Max's mentor. "How happy I am ta finally meet the one who saved Max as a pup."

Gillamon lowered his head to nudge Kate. "No harm done, dear Kate. I'm a tough old goat. You should see the wee cherubs who do that to me all the time," he said with a wink. "My, what a bonnie lass you are! I couldn't have been more proud of Max's choice for a mate."

While Kate blushed, Max and Liz joined the group, and Max bopped Al on the head with his burly paw. "Daft kitty!"

"Ah-hem, perhaps now Gillamon can tell us about the mission?" Liz said, diverting everyone's attention from Al's faux pas.

"Yes, I think you will find this assignment challenging, but also very rewarding. This will be quite different from Noah's ark, so listen well. First, since you now know you are on assignment from the Maker, you will be given specific—although limited—instructions in advance," Gillamon explained.

"But *Monsieur*, why limited instructions?" Liz protested. If there was anything Liz craved most, it was information.

"The Maker in His wisdom balances the unfolding of His plans in the world with the free will of His creation. He could make anything happen that He wishes, of course, but He chooses to allow the course of events to unfold based on the decisions and choices of the humans and animals involved. The element of faith will always play a role if you choose to be on mission for the Maker. And how you choose to exercise your faith will affect the outcome of this mission," Gillamon explained, looking Liz directly in the eye.

"*Oui. Je comprends.* This is how it should be, no?" Liz replied.

Max smiled at Liz. He had watched her grow in faith from one who had to have everything intellectually explained, to one whose budding faith made life full with meaning. While she still pursued the logical explanation for things, she was now more inclined to trust the workings of the Maker—even when they did not always make sense at first.

"Max and Liz, to answer your questions, there will indeed be a mystery to solve and some mean beasties to round up, but that is not all. You also have a life to change. And how well you do with this single, solitary life will determine if an entire nation is born," Gillamon explained.

While Max wrinkled his brow with the gravity of their mission, Liz's eyes lit up with excitement. Al looked worried, so Kate put her reassuring paw on Al's back.

"Before I continue, I need to know if you accept this assignment," Gillamon said, looking each animal in the eye.

Max looked up quickly and asked, "Ye mean we have a say ta do this thing or not?"

Gillamon smiled. "Of course, Max. You always have a choice. But if you choose to move forward, there is no turning back."

"Aye, jest like cr-r-rossin' cr-r-reeks," Max mumbled to himself.

"Gillamon, what will happen if we do not accept this assignment?" Liz asked.

"The Maker has unlimited resources to accomplish His purposes. He is not dependent on any one human or creature—this you must always remember. To be able to choose to serve Him is a *privilege*," Gillamon explained.

"Aye! Count us in then!" Max shouted proudly. The others echoed their agreement.

"Good, good. Very well, here is the assignment. Your prime objective is a young man named Joseph. He is one of twelve sons of the man Jacob. God has chosen this special family to create a new nation—the Hebrew nation—beginning with Abraham,

Jacob's grandfather. God promised Abraham his descendants would be as numerous as the stars in the sky and the grains of sand on the seashore," Gillamon said with a smile.

"Sure, and that's an awful lot o' mouths to feed," Al whispered to Kate. She rolled her eyes at the ever-hungry Al.

"Here is your mystery. This mission will involve a series of eight dreams, three schemes, and four robes. When you see these things come to pass, you will know that your mission is complete," Gillamon explained.

Liz felt a rush of excitement go through her. "*C'est bon!* How I love a good mystery!"

"So who is dr-r-reamin' an' schemin' then?" Max asked, a low growl in his throat.

"More than one," is all Gillamon replied. "Also, there will be a test given by the Revealer of Secrets. It may appear at first to be a scheme, but you will see that it is actually a test to reveal true character and a change of heart."

"Gillamon, ye're r-r-really str-r-retchin' me mind then, lad! How are we supposed ta figure this all out?!" Max protested.

Liz smiled and held up her dainty paw. "Never fear, *mon ami.* I will help us figure everything out." Liz wasn't bragging; everyone knew she was, of course, the brains of the outfit.

"While this is true, Liz, there is another difference between this mission and the Ark. For this mission, you all will be in different locations with different jobs to do," Gillamon said.

"What? Ye mean I won't be with me lass, Liz?" Al protested, clutching Liz a bit too tightly.

Gillamon bent his head low to look Al in the eye. "Sometimes we must be parted from those we love to accomplish things for the Maker. But you will not be far from Liz. In fact, you will see each other quite often." Then, motioning toward Kate and Max, he added, "I'm afraid the two who will be most apart will be your friends here."

Kate looked up in alarm, nudging Max with her head. "Oh, me love, I hate ta be apart from ye even for an instant!"

"Aye, but remember we've got a lifetime together, lass. 'Tis jest a short while, I'm sure. Right, Gillamon?"

Gillamon looked thoughtfully at the pair of dogs, knowing this assignment would be hard on them. "Well, it will be more than twenty years apart, I'm sorry to say. But remember, in the scheme of time, this is no time at all."

"Oh!" was all Kate could say as she closed her eyes and nuzzled Max. Then she looked up at Gillamon. "Aye, but I'll do it for the Maker. He knows wha' is best."

"That's me girl, lass. Ah, Kate, I dunnot know how I kin be apart from ye for so long, but the Maker will help us," Max said, comforting Kate.

Liz sat and stared intensely at Max and Kate. What remarkable faith they had! "Gillamon, what will be our specific assignments?" she inquired.

"The mission will begin with the four of you together on a caravan headed to the center of power in Egypt. It is quite convenient you were already in this part of the world," Gillamon pointed out as he turned and gave Liz a knowing look. "Isn't it amazing how you had this sudden urge to come study the pyramids, Liz?"

Liz smiled and paused to consider how the Maker had gotten them to the right place at the right time by instilling in her a desire to see Egypt. Just when she thought she was in charge of her own movements, she was reminded, as always, of who was really in charge.

"You and your caravan will encounter Joseph and his brothers. Kate, you will then depart the caravan and go with Joseph's brothers to live with Jacob. Max, Liz, and Al, you will travel on with Joseph to the city of Avaris. There you must get Joseph to the right place. Liz, your assignment is Potiphar, chief officer of Pharaoh's bodyguard. As this unfolds you will need your quick wit about you," Gillamon explained.

"Ah, *oui*, I will be ready, *Monsieur*," Liz humbly replied.

"An' jest where will I go then?" Max asked.

"That will depend on what happens in the marketplace. And Max, you may not like your station at first, but be patient. It will all be worth it," Gillamon responded with the reassuring voice he had always used with the little dog.

"Sure, and where will I be, Gillamon?" Al asked.

"You, lad, will be living in the finery of Pharaoh's palace—where you will be regarded as a god," Gillamon said.

Al blinked hard in disbelief at Gillamon before breaking out in a broad grin. "A god ye say? Like this Sphinx kitty here?"

"You will be treated with the finest care and given all the food you could ever desire," replied Gillamon.

"Now this sounds like a good assignment for me! What could be better than for me to do what I love to do? EAT!" chuckled Al. "Life jest keeps gettin' better—first I were a noble, famous warrior for the Ark, and now a god in Egypt!"

Max frowned at Al's gloating and his seemingly easy assignment. "Don't go off bein' a big- as well as empty-headed laddie! Especially on the god thing then. Weren't we jest talkin' aboot how there's only one God?"

Gillamon nodded in agreement. "Max is right, Al. And a word of caution to you. Don't confuse good with easy. You can be assured there will be challenges in your assignment that will require you to be that noble, famous warrior you are. In fact, your assignment may end up being the hardest of them all."

Al's smile faded and he gulped. "Sure, and I'll do me best. Sorry for gloatin' then."

"Gillamon, when does our mission begin?" Liz asked, ready to get started.

"It begins right now. You are to head east across the desert until you see the caravan traveling south to Dothan, in the land of Canaan," Gillamon replied.

"How will we know which caravan is the correct one to join?" Liz questioned.

"You will know it when you hear it," Gillamon mysteriously replied with a grin.

Max walked over to Gillamon. "But Gillamon, does this mean I have ta tell ye good-bye again so soon? I thought I might have at least a wee bit of time with ye."

Gillamon looked Max right in the eye. "We will be seeing one another, Max. It just may not be in the way you expect. Always look for the Hidden One."

Max cocked his head to the side. "Aye, ye never stop with yer r-r-riddles then! Ah, well enough, it's good ta see ye, me old friend. An' I'll try ta keep an eye out, whatever that means."

Gillamon looked back at the coming wind that had once again sprung up behind him. "Farewell, my friends. Remember what I've always told Max. Know that you are loved and that you are able. I will see you again . . . soon."

With that Max, Al, Kate, and Liz had to stand back as another whirlwind enveloped Gillamon. The foursome covered their eyes as Gillamon disappeared into the wind as quickly as he had come. When the sand settled they looked at one another in awe.

"I told ye he'd come. Well, we'd best be on our way," Max said as he started trotting east on the Giza plateau. Kate and Al followed along.

But Liz sat there a moment, slapping her tail on the ground, thinking about all Gillamon had said. Questions were swirling in her mind as furiously as had the sand around them. Who exactly were the Revealer of Secrets and the Hidden One? And there would be more than one dreamer and one schemer? So many questions. So many things to uncover.

"Liz, me love, are ye comin' then?" Al called back to Liz.

"*Oui*, Albert. I'm coming," Liz said as she jumped down from the stone block wall and glanced back at the Sphinx. Out of the corner of her eye she thought she saw movement behind the huge catlike figure. No matter. She shrugged her shoulders and followed after Al, Max, and Kate.

Three pairs of eyes peered from behind the Sphinx, staring at the foursome as they headed out toward the desert.

They looked at one another and began to laugh—wickedly.

CHAPTER 3

The Favorite

"I hate him," seethed Naphtali as he watched Joseph walk away from their campfire, now gone cold from neglect.

The fire in the pit had almost gone out, but a hot fire now blazed in the eyes of these four brothers of Joseph. Naphtali forcefully jabbed his shepherd staff into the rocks surrounding the cooling embers until finally it broke. He threw it to the ground in disgust.

"Did you see the way he looked at us when we told him our headcount for the spring flock?" Dan asked.

"Yeah, with his perfect little journal and reed in hand, taking notes?" grumbled Asher.

Gad spit on the ground. "Father's little pretty boy scribe. I bet he knew we should have more ewes in the headcount, given the healthy females we have."

"Do you think there's any way he could know we sold some off to that last caravan coming through?" Naphtali asked.

Dan thought a moment and threw a rock in the direction Joseph walked, although he was now a long way off on the far hillside. "I don't see how he could know of our secret deal with the Ishmaelites. He's never been around when they come. He's too perfect to lower himself to be in their company. No, I think he just suspects our numbers are off from what he projected."

"I'm sure he's running home to Papa so he can tell on us," Asher said as he kicked up the dust, causing a cloud to cover his short, brown tunic. "He probably gave our other brothers a more favorable report, just because they are the sons of Leah. I get so sick of how we're compared all the time in this family."

The sheep in the flock started bleating nervously. Naphtali grabbed Gad's staff that was leaning on the rocks and ran over to the unsettled sheep, calling over his shoulder, "Hurry! Now our brother has made us lose watch over the flock. That wolf is back."

"Give me my staff!" yelled Gad, running after Naphtali.

Dan and Asher left the cold campfire behind as they too ran out into the fields and after the wolf that sought to snatch a young ewe from the fold. That's all these four brothers needed—more sheep missing from their numbers. Joseph would be sure to take note.

Jacob smiled from under the canopy where he sat in the shade, the strong breeze making the canvas flap back and forth. He saw Joseph coming in the distance and held up his hand in greeting. As he stood to tie back the flaps, he squinted in the sunshine and enjoyed the warmth it brought to his skin. The lines on his face and his salt-and-pepper hair showed the years he had lived in this harsh land. Jacob breathed in deeply, issuing a prayer of thanks to God for the safe return of his beloved son Joseph.

Jacob always worried whenever Joseph was away from home. It was no secret that of his twelve sons, Joseph—his eleventh—was his favorite. Born to him late in life by his most beloved wife, Rachel, Joseph held a place deep in Jacob's heart no other offspring could ever take. And each of Joseph's siblings felt the pain of that favoritism deep within his own heart. The brothers knew that the most favored blessing of their father would ever be reserved for Joseph.

This was an ugly family pattern that had started with Jacob's grandfather, Abraham. Abraham was the Patriarch, the one God first spoke to in promise that his descendants would be more numerous than the stars in the sky or the sand on the shore. But Abraham got tired of waiting for the promise to be fulfilled and took matters into his own hands. He had a son, Ishmael, not by his wife Sarah, but by her servant Hagar. Abraham later cast Ishmael aside, showing favor and greater love for his second-born, Isaac, born of Sarah, when God's plan finally unfolded. A seed of hatred was planted between Isaac and Ishmael that would grow into a tangled web of fighting between their descendants from generation to generation. And the root of that hatred was a fight over their father's blessing. The power of a father's blessing—or lack of it—changed the course of history.

Following the familial pattern, Isaac in turn loved second-born Jacob more than firstborn Esau. Such favoritism led to deception and the breakup of Jacob's family. This generational curse was now seeping into the house of Jacob.

Rachel had also given Jacob his youngest son, Benjamin, but had died in his childbirth. This loss shook Jacob's world. The wife he most loved was taken from him just as they were coming back to live in the land of his father, Isaac. It had been years since her death, but Jacob grieved for her still. And that pain was transferred to the thought of ever losing Rachel's firstborn, Joseph. Jacob would make sure no harm ever came to Joseph.

Jacob could hardly contain his excitement as Joseph entered the outskirts of their camp. Little Benjamin and the other young children went running up to him to welcome him home, giggling as Joseph picked them up in the air. They each waited their turn for Joseph to make them "fly" with his strong, tanned arms outstretched under them.

Joseph's muscular physique and handsome appearance naturally drew people to him. His light brown locks of hair fell back onto his shoulders, he smiled with perfect teeth, and his bright blue eyes gazed up at the children he held. Even among Jacob's grandchildren, Joseph was the favorite uncle. The little ones felt safe in his presence because he was so gentle and kind. And he always took time to give them the attention they so longed for, but rarely received, from their own fathers. Even though he was only seventeen and still unmarried, Joseph saw the value of children. Perhaps he took the meaning of his name seriously, for Rachel had borne Joseph after many years of waiting to have children, and named him "add to me" or "give me another son."

Joseph took Benjamin zooming through the sky as he ran up to Jacob's tent, the other children racing and laughing along beside him. "Hi, Father, looks like all is well here," he said as he put the little boy down. He took some pistachios from his sack to give the children, who then scurried off to enjoy their treat. "I wish I could say the same for the fields."

Jacob frowned and waved his hand to dismiss any negativity as he embraced Joseph. He held onto him for a few moments, closing his eyes and once again sighing with relief that his boy was home. He released Joseph and then put a hand to Joseph's shoulder. "Later. I have something for you. Stay here."

Joseph went over to dip his hands in a basin of water as Jacob ducked inside the tent. He brought the water up to his face, caked with the blowing sand and sweat from his long walk. Ah, how cool and refreshing to feel the water on his tired skin! He took a soft linen cloth and held it up to his eyes for a moment, smelling the scent of home. As he lowered the cloth from his face and opened his eyes, there stood Jacob, grinning and holding out a long, beautiful robe.

"What's this?" Joseph asked.

"A gift—for you," Jacob chuckled as he held out the sleeves in a gesture for Joseph to put it on.

"But why, Father? This is not the robe of a shepherd," Joseph said, not moving toward the coat.

"Exactly," Jacob grinned, moving insistently toward his son. "You are not to toil in the fields like your brothers. You no longer need to wade through the muck of the herd, fight the beasts of the field, or scrape up hillsides in search of lost sheep to carry on your shoulders. You have proven yourself worthy of this robe because of your good work in managing my affairs and overseeing your brothers. Put it on."

Joseph looked doubtfully at his father, but he was ever obedient to this man whom he deeply respected. The robe was indeed beautiful. It was long, white, and richly adorned with stripes of many colors around the edges of the sleeves and ankle-length hem. This was a robe reserved only for the noble, the royal, and others who needed not toil for a living. It was certainly not the robe of a shepherd. A shepherd's robe had short sleeves and length to allow ease of movement, and was woven with dark-colored, rough fabric so as not to show stains.

The fabric of this robe was the highest quality linen. Joseph had never before seen anything of such finery. It felt good to his skin, but felt uncomfortable to his heart. Jacob's smile dropped as he noticed the frown on Joseph's face.

"What's wrong, son? Don't you like it? Does it not fit you well? I spared no expense and had the best seamstress make it specifically for you," said Jacob, fussing over the robe to see if the measurements were right.

"It's . . . it's beautiful, Father. It's the finest garment I've ever seen. It's just that I don't feel right wearing this when my older brothers must wear such lowly garments. And it's not just the look of the robe, the meaning behind it is more important," Joseph explained.

Jacob again waved his hand and shook his head to dismiss Joseph's argument. "I am the father of this house, and my word is law. I determine who has what, and that is all that matters. You *will* wear it. Joseph, you have given me nothing but joy, while your brothers have given me nothing but grief with their mischief and poor choices. This robe suits you," Jacob insisted as he stood back, gazing at Joseph with adoration.

Joseph lowered his head and submitted to his father's will. He wrapped his arms around his body to feel the caress of the luxurious fabric and allowed his gaze to study the incredible embellishment on the sleeves. He looked up at Jacob, a smile now on his face. "Thank you, Father. I will do as you say. Thank you for such a beautiful gift," Joseph said as he reached over to embrace his father. While Jacob, beaming with pride and joy, hugged Joseph, Joseph's smile faded as he gazed out over his father's shoulder to the fields. He could only imagine the response he would get when his brothers returned home.

Reuben pulled the donkey along behind him, tugging at the leather harness he held in his rough, calloused hands. The donkey was stubbornly resisting his lead, tired from walking and wanting to rest. "I don't care you are tired. Do you think I'm not tired as well? Come! We're almost there," Reuben gruffly snorted at the beast of burden.

Five of Reuben's other brothers followed on the road behind him and the stubborn donkey. They were relieved to finally be going home to Hebron, herding their sheep along to graze in familiar fields near the tents of Jacob. Reuben looked over to see the other four brothers coming with their flocks from the west. He wondered if their experience with Joseph's report had been bad again. As the oldest, Reuben knew his half-brothers were up to no good.

Judah called up to Reuben, "I see Dan's group. What do you suppose Joseph told Father this time?" He laughed and shook his head. He knew what an irritant Joseph had been to his brothers, and he took delight in rubbing it in.

"I was just wondering that myself," Reuben replied. "I'm sure we'll have some heated discussions with Father again."

The brothers all met up at the fork in the road before reaching Jacob's camp. Judah chewed a blade of straw in his teeth and mischievously teased Dan, "So, how's your ewe count look according to our favorite brother?"

Dan just glared at Judah and shot back, "None of your business, Judah. You keep watch of your own flocks. You wouldn't want to find any missing now, would you?"

The tension among these ten brothers never ceased. But when they looked up as they neared Jacob's tent, the tension was redirected at their mutual antagonist. Joseph stood there waving at them and wearing his new, colorful robe.

"Will you look at that?" exclaimed Simeon with disgust.

"Looks like pretty boy got a new robe," said Naphtali.

"I bet Father thought his tattling was worth such a prize," said Levi, expressing the jealousy all the brothers felt inside.

As the dirty, smelly brothers approached Joseph, clean and finely dressed, he smiled and went to greet them—but was met with silent, icy stares. No one spoke a word to him. They stared at him up and down, gazing at the object of their father's affection. Gad spit on the ground near Joseph's feet. The brothers turned from Joseph and went to their own tents to greet their families, leaving Joseph standing alone in the road.

Joseph stood there watching his older brothers walking away and thought, *They can't say one kind word to me.*

Little Benjamin came up to Joseph, tugging on his sleeve and saying, "I like your robe, Joseph. It makes you look like a king!"

Joseph looked down at sweet Benjamin, whose penetrating deep blue eyes met his gaze with nothing but love and admiration. He cupped the young boy's chin in his hand. "Thank you, dear little brother. I'll let you try it on later," he said with a wink. Benjamin smiled back and went running along to play, his curly locks of brown hair bouncing as he skipped.

The family curse was nipping at Joseph's feet. Yet the coming night would take the curse to a whole new level.

CHAPTER 4

Going against the Grain

Joseph's soft, strong hands gently tied the twine around his bundle of grain. What a good crop this year! The color was so rich and golden, and the heads of grain were full and fat. His mouth watered as he thought of all the delicious bread and honey cakes they would enjoy from this grain. He looked up at his brothers, who also were tying up bundles of grain all around him. Soon they had a full dozen bundles of healthy, delicious grain in a complete circle. Yes, it was a good year for grain.

As Joseph reached his arms up to give a big stretch for his back, he saw his bundle of grain suddenly stand upright. He stepped back in surprise, for he had left his bundle lying on the ground by his feet. His brothers all shouted in surprise as their bundles also suddenly stood upright. Then the most amazing thing of all happened.

The eleven bundles surrounding Joseph's bundle circled in close and started bowing down to it. Joseph stared in amazement as the grain bundles repeatedly bowed lower and lower before his bundle, as if paying homage. He looked up and into the eyes of his brothers, and awoke with a start.

Joseph was sweating. He sat up in bed and put his hand on his stomach as it growled with hunger. *What a crazy dream!* he thought. *That's what I get for not eating dinner. I'm starving. My empty stomach must have made me dream. I wonder if there are any honey cakes left.*

Joseph got up from his mat and went to the food tent in search of some bread. He sat down at the wooden table and lit a single oil lamp. He found what he was after and tore off a piece of the sweet bread, chewing it slowly as he pondered his dream. He had been so troubled by the reaction of his brothers that day, he hadn't felt like eating dinner with them and had given an excuse to turn in early. Maybe tomorrow he could tell his brothers about the dream to make himself appear a bit foolish and give them a laugh. Maybe it would ease the tension a bit. It certainly couldn't make things worse.

Or so he thought.

"So you think you're going to be our *king* as well as our little brother, is that what you think?" Judah roared at Joseph.

The other brothers echoed Judah's anger in response to Joseph telling them about his dream of their bundles of grain bowing down to his bundle.

"Yeah, so it's not enough that you already are Father's favorite and have the privilege of not working like us out in the field?" Issachar said, slamming his fist on the table, knocking some dates out of the bowl.

"Are you sure you got the dream right, Joseph? You shouldn't have been tying up the grain bundle anyway. You might get your precious new robe dirty," Zebulun smirked. He brushed some crumbs off the scratchy, stained robe covering his large belly.

"I was just telling you about my dream! I didn't eat dinner last night, so I figured my empty stomach made me dream such craziness. I didn't mean anything by it! How could it mean anything?" argued Joseph, realizing he was sinking further with his brothers.

They all got up and walked away, leaving Joseph alone at the breakfast table. Joseph started to get angry. He was tired of not being able to do anything right as far as his brothers were concerned. He had done no wrong. He tried to be kind to them, but remained true to God, to his father, and to himself by telling the truth about them. They were the ones at fault with their shady behavior with the flocks.

And Joseph was right. His older brothers had dishonored the family name more than once, causing Jacob to move the family away from Shechem, where the family name was hated. If Joseph was Jacob's favorite, well, it was for good reason, and it wasn't Joseph's fault.

Joseph stood up from the table and looked out over the camp with his arms folded across his chest, his jaw clenching and unclenching. He felt the colorful linen robe blowing at his ankles with the breeze. All he knew to do was be who he was. He was Joseph. And his brothers would just have to accept him as he was, robe or no robe, dream or no dream.

Weightless. He felt utterly weightless. Joseph stretched his arms out wide, feeling at one with the vast expanse surrounding him. He closed his eyes and lost all sense of orientation. There was complete silence. Suddenly he felt warmth on his back and a gentle breeze blowing the hem of his multicolored robe. It was soothing and inviting. He slowly turned without effort to see the source of the warm breeze. It was the sun, shining in all its glory. Wisps of fire escaped the turbulent ball of red and orange. Strange. How small it looked, yet he felt close enough to reach out and cup it in the palm of his hand!

Out of the corner of his eye he saw another source of light. But there was no warmth, only soft light. He turned his head to see a full moon drifting slowly over to position itself next to the sun. Compared with the small sun, the moon appeared tiny.

Joseph hovered there in the silence, the sun warming him and the moon reflecting soft light before him. It was a beautiful sight to behold. As he reached his hand out to touch the moon, out from behind it came a trail of stars! Each one, smaller still than the moon, glittered as it took up its position under the sun and the moon.

Eleven. There were eleven stars in all, lined up in perfect order, hovering there before him.

The sun began to move. It tipped forward, and then rotated back. As the fireball repeated this tipping movement, the moon began to do the same. Soon the stars joined them. Joseph slowly realized these celestial objects were bowing before him. He acknowledged the gesture with a smile and a slight nod of the head, holding his hands out over them as if to bless them.

"THESE DREAMS ARE FROM ME, JOSEPH. THEY ARE NOT MEANINGLESS. THESE DREAMS ARE FROM ME."

Joseph awoke with a start, trying to get his bearings. A voice had penetrated his dream with such majesty it had a physical effect on his body, electrifying his nerves from his head to his feet. He was breathless from the sheer power of the voice.

He got up and stepped outside his tent. Joseph gazed up at the night sky filled with stars too numerous to count. He knew the voice could only have been that of the God of his fathers, Abraham, Isaac, and Jacob. He clutched his hand over his heart, which was beating hard from the rush of adrenaline. "Oh, God, I am Your servant Joseph. If these dreams are from You, please, tell me what they mean."

The only reply was the echo in Joseph's mind, "THESE DREAMS ARE FROM ME."

Joseph sat down in the sand and lay back on the ground to look up at the stars and the full moon shining down on him.

He thought he saw a face on the surface of the moon. Was it his mother, gazing down at him with love? Oh, how he missed the tender love of his mother. His mind was racing, trying to understand his dream. For now, it appeared all the voice wanted him to understand was the source of the dreams. After a while, Joseph drifted off to sleep, the stars and the moon keeping watch over him.

Jacob gently shook Joseph's shoulder, whispering, "Wake up, Joseph. Wake up."

Joseph opened his eyes to see the kind eyes of his father gazing at him, a puzzled look on the old man's face. He sat up and rubbed his eyes. "Good morning, Father."

Jacob furrowed his brow and brushed the sand off Joseph's back and hair, asking, "Why were you sleeping out here?"

The brothers noisily came up from behind, having already eaten and wanting to see what was going on with Joseph. "Did you fall down, brother?" Judah quipped.

Jacob turned and frowned at Judah. "My son was sleeping out here, and he must have had good reason, Judah. He most certainly did not fall down."

Joseph winced at the way Jacob spoke to his older brothers. He had to give an explanation, so why not tell them all what had happened? What did it matter what they thought? The brothers couldn't hate him any more than they already did. And perhaps his father would validate Joseph's dream, and that it was from God.

"Actually, I had another dream last night," Joseph started, drawing grunts and smirks from his brothers.

"Another dream? What about, my son?" Jacob asked. He had not even heard about the first dream, so this was all new for him.

"Well, I was floating up in the heavens and the sun, the moon, and eleven stars all came up and surrounded me. Then they started bowing down low before me," Joseph explained.

"What kind of a dream is that?!" Jacob snapped at Joseph, who was taken aback by his father's response. Jacob stood and towered over Joseph, who remained seated in the sand. "Will your mother and I and your brothers actually come and bow to the ground before you?"

The ten brothers smiled with malice and punched each other in the ribs. This was delicious. For once the favorite son was getting scolded by their father. What a nice change to see Joseph on the receiving end of Jacob's disfavor!

Joseph didn't know what to say. What *could* he say? And how was it that his father so quickly gave an interpretation of the dream? Is that what the dream meant? How could it, for his mother was dead?

Joseph lowered his head and looked down at the ground as Jacob straightened up and walked away, shoving Reuben out of his way as he passed. The brothers also turned, and laughed as they followed their father, leaving Joseph sitting there alone. But behind the robes of the last brother to leave stood little Benjamin. He rushed up to Joseph and put his arms around his big brother's neck and whispered in his ear.

"I thought it was a pretty dream," Benjamin said softly. He kissed Joseph on the cheek and went running away as he was called to breakfast by his aunt Leah.

Joseph put his hand up to his cheek where the soft kiss of Benjamin left a moist mark. He silently thanked God for giving his mother Rachel another son, this precious little one who believed in him. He looked at Jacob walking away in the distance and hoarsely whispered, "But then, Father, God spoke to me and said these dreams were from Him."

Jacob opened the flap of his tent and sat down with a frustrated grunt. He put his head in his hands, upset that he had scolded Joseph for just honestly speaking his mind and explaining what had happened. Jacob had spit out the first thought that entered his mind about the dream. *What if the dream really meant what I said? How could that be? What could this possibly mean?* Jacob got up and pulled the tent flap back to feel the rising sun warming his face. *Was I the sun? If so, how could I be so cold to Joseph?*

Jacob and Joseph kept their distance that day, each quietly pondering what had happened. And each feeling the ache in their hearts of a wedge driven between them.

CHAPTER 5

The Caravan

Liz sat gazing up at the moon, so full and bright it cast a silvery sheen over the rippled sand, making it look like an ocean. She studied what looked like a face on the moon and smiled. *It looks like a man in the moon*, she thought. *I wonder if man could ever actually go to the moon. How I would love to gaze back at the earth from up there!* She laughed at herself for thinking such silly things. Her brilliant mind frequently led her to places she could only dream of going. *Well, it is a lovely dream.*

Al was snoring and Liz's mind was so full of questions about their mission she couldn't sleep. Their group had been traveling for three weeks, encountering some caravans but not *the* caravan. They had to stay clear of humans who might seek to bring them home, so the foursome would hide when the desert dwellers came by on the road. They wanted to be sure they only went with the right caravan of humans, as instructed.

Liz looked over at Kate sleeping soundly next to Max. Her heart ached at the thought of not seeing Kate for twenty years. Liz and Kate were close friends. And Kate always watched over Al, although she tried to keep him in line when he misbehaved. Oh, but Max! She could only imagine how Max must feel. This could be their last night together for a long time. Being separated from a loved one was a heartbreaking thing to consider. But she knew Kate and Max would accomplish their mission for the Maker with courage and selflessness.

"Ah, *Monsieur* Maker, please be with my friends and help them as they are apart for so very long. I am grateful Albert and I will be close," Liz began to pray silently. "My mind is puzzled with the limited information Gillamon gave us. I am not complaining, but please, reveal to me what I am to understand so I can direct our group. Why is Joseph leaving his family and going to Egypt? And what about this caravan? How will we 'hear' the right caravan? What does that mean? Please make it so very clear to me I could not miss it even if I tried."

Liz remained awake for a while longer, praying to the Maker. While she did not receive a specific answer, her heart was filled with the peace that the answer would indeed come. And she felt it would be unmistakable.

"HEY! LOOK AT ME! MY COAT IS FALLING OFF! HEY, DID YOU HEAR WHAT I SAID? MY COAT IS FALLING OFF!" shouted the camel with the twin humps.

The one-humped dromedaries rolled their eyes and muttered among themselves, "That has to be the most obnoxious beast I have ever seen in my entire life!"

"Tell me about it. He can't even speak with a normal voice. All he does is shout."

"And that two-humper looks disgusting. His hair looks like it's peeling off in sheets."

"I think the humans are growing sick of him, too. One of them woke up yesterday with his tent half eaten by this beast!"

"And when the human tried to pull the tent out of the two-humper's mouth, that camel spit this gooey, smelly, green slime all over him. Not that I mind the humans getting a taste of their own nastiness, but I even felt sorry for the human."

The dromedaries were gathered in a circle, their backs to that other camel as they gossiped about him. He was an outsider. There were no other beasts like him in the caravan, or anywhere in Canaan or Egypt for that matter. The traders had bought him from an exotic merchant from the east, thinking he would turn a good profit in Egypt.

"HEY, DID YOU HEAR ME? I SAID MY COAT IS FALLING OFF! SHOULD WE ALERT THE HUMANS OR SOMETHING? THIS LOOKS SERIOUS!" the camel bellowed.

The oldest dromedary of the group turned to address their traveling companion, whose shouting had now awakened the entire camp. The humans were grunting with frustration as even *they* looked at the camel with fresh disgust.

"Osahar, I'm sure what is happening to you is normal. Didn't you say you were from a cold climate? Well, maybe now that you are in a hot climate you *should* shed your coat. Look at us. We don't need heavy coats because our climate is hot. Maybe you'll even look a little more like us . . . except for that second hump of yours," the dromedary said with a sneer. "Now stop all your shouting. You've awakened everyone in the camp."

"BUT I'M USED TO LONG FUR. HOW WILL I LOOK WITH NO FUR? AND WHAT IF ONE OF MY HUMPS FALLS OFF, TOO?" Osahar anxiously replied.

The camel standing there was indeed quite a mess. He was seven feet tall and his two humps were not gently rounded like the dromedaries', but rather pointy. His shaggy, sandy, grey-brown coat fell off in clumps with every passing breeze. He still held a clump of long hair on the top of his head and underneath his chin, making him look like he was wearing a wig and a goatee. His bushy eyebrows were heavy and dark, and his extra long eyelashes blinked away the sand that blew in his face this morning. This camel was hairy (or had been) all over, including his ears and crooked, pouty lips. He snorted through his thin, long nostrils as he looked at his backside with growing concern.

Despite his messy appearance, his face was quite sweet and endearing, almost naive, for this camel was only a year old. He had been taken from his parents by the eastern traders before he understood the ways of camel life. So he truly didn't understand all that was happening to him.

"HEY! THIS IS GROSS, I TELL YA, GROSS! HOW CAN I GO OUT AND BE SEEN LIKE THIS?" Osahar continued to shout.

"That's it! I've had it with this beast!" shouted the human. "I think we've been had by that strange trader with the slanted eyes. Who would want this obnoxious beast around all the time? I say we let him loose here in the desert," the young Ishmaelite Abu fussed.

Abu's father yawned and stretched long and hard as he studied the camel. "Well, we'll see if he turns a profit at the market. If not, we'll release him to the desert and cut our losses. For now, we're stuck with him."

The dromedaries and humans all looked with frowns upon this young, molting camel, who felt quite alone in the world. Osahar looked away toward the desert sands. He knew he didn't fit in here. He missed home and his family. He just wanted to feel normal again. Tears welled up in his big brown eyes as he walked over to a scrubby bush and pulled off a branch. The thorns didn't matter to his tough tongue and palate. He needed to eat whatever he could find, whether a thorny bush or a tent. The humans never gave him anything. He was on his own. He sniffed because of that reality and felt another clump blow off his back. *I feel like I'm falling apart. I hope we get to Egypt soon. Maybe someone there will want me.*

"'Tis a bonnie day, Kate. Wake up, me love," Max said as he whispered in Kate's ear. He was mindful of their short time together, and didn't want to waste a minute of it.

Kate fluttered her eyes open and smiled. "Good mornin', Love."

"Ah, *bon*, you are up. We should be on our way before the sun is up too high. Did you sleep well, *mes amis*?" Liz asked.

Kate stretched and yawned with a high yelp. "Good mornin' ta ye, Liz. I'm ready."

Al still lay there sleeping, with drool coming from the side of his mouth. Max had lost count of how many mornings he had awakened Al over the centuries. But it was always a chore. This big orange cat could sleep through almost anything. Max enjoyed coming up with new, entertaining ways of waking his feline friend. Today he decided a scorpion would be great fun. He instructed the scorpion not to strike his friend, but just to give him a little "encouragement" to wake up.

Max carefully placed the big brown arachnid on top of Al's nose and yelled in his ear, "AL! 'TIS A STINGIN' BEASTIE AFTER YE!"

Al woke and crossed his eyes as he stared up at the brown scorpion, whose tail looked coiled and irritated, as if its owner were ready to strike.

"AHHHHHHHHH!" Al shouted, knocking the scorpion off his nose as he jumped up and went rolling down a sloping hill, the sand falling in sheets around him. He landed with his big belly and legs stretched out, covered in sand. Al looked up to see Max chuckling at him.

"Mornin' ta ye, laddie!" Max called.

"Top o' the mornin' ta ye, Max. Did ye see how I handled that beastie?" Al asked, trying to act as if he had bravely escaped the clutches of certain death.

"Oh, aye, Big Al. Ye scared the brown beastie away. He won't be messin' with ye anymore then," Max said with a grin.

Max, Al, Kate, and Liz once again set out on the road in search of the caravan.

"Liz, where do ye suppose we are now?" Kate asked.

"Well, I overheard the last two men we hid from mention we are south of a place called Dothan," Liz replied.

"Dothan? Well, maybe that'll be where we can finally meet up with the caravan," Al remarked, jumping up and down on small boulders along the way.

Kate and Max looked at one another with burdened eyes. They knew what that would mean. It would be time to say good-bye.

"Joseph, didn't your brothers say they were taking the herds north to Shechem?" Jacob asked. "They've been gone awhile now."

It had been more than two weeks with no word from them. This worried Jacob. The people of Shechem hated his sons for what they had done to their city in an act of revenge. Some men of Shechem had forcibly taken the brothers' sister Dinah to their village. Simeon and Levi had then gone in and tricked the men and wiped them out, bringing their sister back home. The rest of the brothers went in and plundered the entire city, taking the herds, donkeys, all the livestock, and all the possessions and wealth they could get their hands on. The situation was so bad that Jacob had moved the entire family away from the area to the valley of Hebron to escape the wrath of the people. Now his boys were back shepherding near the town. No telling what could happen.

Jacob thought a moment and decided he'd better send Joseph to check on them. This was a tough decision because Joseph would be exposed to certain danger on this sixty-mile journey. There were always robbers, wild beasts, and possible injury on such a journey. But if trouble broke out in Shechem, Jacob's family could be virtually wiped out. It would mean a sacrifice of his peace of mind, but Jacob had no choice. He had to send Joseph.

"Joseph, get ready. I want you to go to Shechem and look for your brothers," Jacob said, a look of strain all over his face from this tough decision.

Joseph immediately stood up and replied, "I'm ready to go, Father."

"Go and see how your brothers are doing and how the flocks are getting along. Then come back and tell me what you find out," Jacob instructed.

Joseph ran to his tent, gathered his knapsack, and packed some things he would need for his journey. He slipped the robe over his head and looked around his tent to see if he had everything. He didn't want to carry too much since he wouldn't be gone that long. He went back to Jacob to bid him farewell.

"I'm off, Father. I'll do as you have asked and be back soon," Joseph said as he and Jacob embraced.

Jacob held Joseph by the shoulders and looked him solidly in the eye. "You come back to me."

"I will, Father. Don't worry," Joseph said with a warm smile, clasping his father's hand with his own.

Little Benjamin came running up and grabbed Joseph by the legs. "Bye, Joseph! Will you be back soon?"

Joseph picked up Benjamin and made him "fly" once more before he gave him a big hug. He whispered in his ear, "I'll see you before you know it."

Benjamin giggled and stood by Jacob, holding the old man's hand as they watched Joseph walk away. Benjamin looked up at Jacob, who obviously was distressed. "Don't be sad, Father. Joseph said we'd see him soon. And my brother always keeps his word."

Jacob looked down at sweet Benjamin, his youngest son and now the only one of his sons with him here in Hebron. "I'm sure you're right, Benjamin," Jacob said as his gaze drifted back to Joseph waving a final farewell in the distance. "I'm sure you're right."

"HEY! THERE GOES ANOTHER CLUMP!" Osahar shouted from the back of the caravan moving steadily along the road. "YOU BETTER KEEP AN EYE ON ME FROM UP THERE. YOU MAY TURN AROUND AND FIND THERE'S NOTHING LEFT OF ME SOON!"

"Did you hear that?" Liz gasped as she stopped in her tracks, her ears moving like antennae to pick up the sound. Max, Kate, and Al all stopped to listen.

"Aye. Sounded like a dyin' beastie groanin' his last," Max said, his brow furrowed.

Liz jumped up on a group of tall boulders on the side of the road and strained her eyes to see if she could locate the source of the sound. Her heart leaped as a long caravan of men, donkeys, dromedaries, and one lone Bactrian camel came into view. Some of the men appeared to be bound by the wrists and tied together, walking in a line. Evidently the sound came from the camel at the back of the line. He was swaying his head back and forth, shouting.

Gillamon's voice echoed in Liz's mind: "*You will know it when you hear it.*" Liz knew in her spirit this must be the caravan. She turned to face the others.

"*Mes amis*, I believe the caravan we have been searching for is coming down the road. But we must be wise and make certain this is the one. There is a shouting camel in the back of the caravan, which I believe is our signal. He is rather loud, no? We will hide behind these rocks and follow the caravan from a distance when it passes. When it stops for the night we will discuss their destination with the animals in the caravan," Liz instructed.

Max and Kate nuzzled together behind the rocks and Max licked a tear from Kate's cheek. "Steady, lass."

As the caravan drew near, the animal friends watched each passing human and beast of burden in the line. They all looked miserable due to the noisy camel constantly shouting from behind.

Liz smiled. This *had* to be the caravan. She couldn't have missed it if she tried. Liz whispered a *merci* to the Maker. Now their mission could really begin.

CHAPTER 6

God Hears Me

Joseph winced and bent down to remove a sand spur stuck to his sandal and piercing his foot. He noticed how filthy his feet were after walking so far. Maybe he could find a creek to wash up and rest a bit. He stood and gazed around the countryside of Shechem. His brothers should be here. Freshly grazed vegetation was evidence they had been here, but neither the flocks nor the brothers were anywhere in sight. Joseph wondered if they could have been run off by competing shepherds. Or worse, maybe they had encountered an angry mob seeking revenge.

A voice called from behind him, "What are you looking for?"

Joseph turned to see an old man standing in the field. He was rather tall, and had a long, flowing white beard and hair. His eyes were kind and he appeared friendly. Joseph walked over to the old man who seemed to have just come out of nowhere.

"I'm looking for my ten brothers. They were coming here to pasture our flocks. Have you seen them? Do you know where they would have taken the sheep?" Joseph asked.

The old man nodded. "Yes, I know them. Quite an unruly bunch," he said with a chuckle. "I heard them say, 'Let's go to Dothan.' So I would travel about twenty miles north. I'm sure you'll find them there."

"Thank you," Joseph said with a smile and a hand to the old man's shoulder.

The old man smiled with a twinkle in his eye as he lowered his gaze and looked Joseph straight in the eye. "You're welcome, Joseph. I wish you well on your journey." His beard blew in the brisk wind that encircled them.

Joseph nodded and walked away. He was thinking about his brothers moving on to Dothan as he walked up the hill. Then it dawned on him he had not told the old man his name. *How did he know my name?* thought Joseph. *Did he hear my brothers talking about me?* Joseph turned back around to look at him.

The old man was gone.

The fire crackled with sparks flying upward as the wood popped from the heat. The Ishmaelites, dirty and worn out from their journey, were huddled around the blaze, cooking their dinner.

Liz peeked out from around their tent to make sure they were all occupied. She instructed Max, Kate, and Al to remain hidden while she investigated the caravan. She then went to talk with the dromedaries kneeling down together in a circle. She noticed that the loud camel was off by himself, obviously not welcomed by this group.

"Bonsoir. May I inquire as to where this caravan is headed?" Liz asked as she daintily walked to the center of the group.

The dromedaries looked at her as they chewed grass. *"Bonsoir?* What kind of talk is that?" asked one of the beasts.

"Pardon, it means good evening," Liz explained. "It appears you have been traveling a long distance. And that you have a rather loud traveling companion."

"You don't know the half of it!" one of the dromedaries replied. "To answer your question, we are heading down to Egypt. These traders are going to the market there with slaves and spices. The humans have loaded each of us down with a couple of hundred pounds of gum, balm, and resin to sell."

"That resin is really smelly," another added. "I hate resin. But not as much as I hate that loud camel's shouting. Believe you me, I'd head on down the road away from us if I were you."

"Ah, *oui*, resin. But it is a fascinating substance, no? As a hydrocarbon secretion of many plants, particularly coniferous trees, it has many wonderful uses. I've heard that frankincense and myrrh are especially wonderful forms of resin. And it is logical that these natural aromatic products are in demand in Egypt," Liz said excitedly. "I am sure they need them for embalming the mummies."

The dromedaries sat silently staring at Liz, blank expressions on their faces. All that was heard was the chirp of crickets in the background. Liz realized she had immediately lost her audience with her analysis of resin. This intelligent cat adored the study of many facets of the natural world, particularly flora. But she rarely found anyone on the same intellectual level with whom she could discuss her discoveries. And these dromedaries weren't anywhere near capable of such a discussion.

"OH, MAN, NOW MY BEARD FELL OFF!" they heard Osahar shout from the edge of the camp.

Liz was relieved to have a change of subject and asked, "What is the situation with the two-humped camel?"

"He's an oddball, that one. The traders picked him up as we left Gilead and it's been miserable the entire trip," complained a dromedary. "He's all upset because his coat is falling off. He NEVER stops shouting!"

"Perhaps he is unable to stop shouting," Liz replied, her tail slapping the ground up and down as she thought out loud.

"What do you mean, he *can't* stop shouting?" asked the older dromedary.

Liz stared at Osahar and said, "He may suffer from klazomania."

More silence and crickets chirping. And more blank stares.

Liz rolled her eyes. Didn't these desert animals know anything? "Klazomania is a condition of compulsive shouting. The camel may not be able to control himself. And if he is suffering an unexpected physical condition with his molting, as you have stated, then it is logical his klazomania would intensify."

"Uh-huh," was all a dromedary replied. "Well . . . why don't you go check him out yourself?"

Liz decided to do just that. "*Merci* for the information."

Osahar was sitting down on the ground, his head hung low. Liz came up from behind and stood eye to eye in front of him, a coy smile on her face. "Good evening—Osahar, is it?"

The camel looked up, startled to see the petite black cat suddenly there before him. "WHO ARE YOU? AND HOW DID YOU KNOW MY NAME?"

As he shouted, Liz's ears and whiskers went back as a gust of Osahar's smelly breath blew over her. She coughed and cleared her throat, but kept her smile. "My name is Liz. I am part of a group of four animals, two dogs and two cats. We have been looking for your caravan. I would like to thank you for helping us locate it."

Osahar looked behind him as if Liz could be talking to someone else. "ME? HOW DID I HELP?"

Liz chuckled. *But this is obvious, no?* she thought to herself. "We were told to look for a caravan heading to Egypt, and that we would know it was the right one when we heard it."

The camel looked self-conscious. "OH. WELL, YOU'RE WELCOME. I HAVE A PROBLEM WITH SHOUTING. I CAN'T SEEM TO CONTROL MYSELF."

"Ah, *oui*, I believe you suffer from klazomania, which is a condition of compulsive shouting," Liz explained. She put her soft paw up to the camel's cheek in sympathy. "You cannot help this, *mon ami.*" When she pulled her paw away, a big clump of camel hair stuck to her claws. She smiled weakly and furiously tried to flick it off.

"SO NOW I HAVE TWO PROBLEMS. I'M A COMPULSIVE SHOUTER AND MY COAT IS FALLING OFF. WHAT GOOD AM I TO ANYBODY?" Osahar asked, looking discouraged.

"*Au contraire*, Osahar. There are wonderful things you must understand. Do you know what your name means?" Liz asked. One of Liz's hobbies was name origin and interpretation.

"NO," Osahar replied.

"Osahar means 'God hears me,'" she told him. "So you see, you have been gifted with a name that I must say is very appropriate. Everyone hears you, as we did from afar, but God also hears you. And He used your problem of shouting to lead us here. We are actually on mission from the Maker to help a young man named Joseph. The fate of an entire nation depends on our mission, so you see, your shouting has served a very important purpose," Liz said with a compassionate look of acceptance on her face.

Osahar's big brown eyes blinked back the tears. "YOU ARE THE ONLY ONE WHO HAS EVER SPOKEN A KIND WORD TO ME IN THIS LAND. THANKS, LIZ. AND THE MAKER SENT YOU? THE MAKER HIMSELF?" The camel could hardly believe what Liz had told him. "God hears me," he said, speaking with a quieter tone for the first time, surprising himself and Liz. He smiled, and his heart experienced warmth and the joy of being not only accepted, but appreciated for who he was.

"And do not worry about this molting. It is natural, no? It is what you Bactrian camels do. The Maker equipped your body with the ability to withstand below-freezing temperatures in cold, snowy climates in Asia and excessive heat in the hot desert. It is now late spring and you are in a hot climate, so it is time for you to shed your coat. But do not worry, you will only lose your long coat, not all your hair," Liz explained.

Relief flooded Osahar. "THANK GOODNESS! I THOUGHT I WAS FALLING APART. AND THE DROMEDARIES AND THE HUMANS DON'T LIKE ME VERY MUCH." The camel paused and shouted, "I'M GLAD YOU'RE HERE, LIZ."

The camel and cat shared a moment of joy with the beginning of a new friendship.

"I'm glad to be here as well. I look forward to introducing you to my friends," Liz said with a smile. "And do not worry about those dromedaries. They suffer from, how do you say, 'elective ignorance.'"

Osahar nodded and hesitated for a moment. "LIZ, CAN I ASK YOU SOMETHING SINCE YOU'RE SUCH A SMART CAT?"

"But of course, *mon ami*," Liz replied.

"MY HUMPS WON'T FALL OFF, WILL THEY?" Osahar asked.

CHAPTER 7

A Scheme of Brothers

"Here comes that dreamer," Simeon said when he spotted Joseph coming on the distant horizon.

The brothers all quickly got up and stood to see for themselves. The tension of pent-up jealousy and hatred rose just as quickly.

"I say we take the lord of the dreams and kill him," Gad sneered as he spit on the ground. The brothers all murmured in agreement, except Reuben.

"Yes, let's do it! We're out here far from home. Now is our chance to rid ourselves of this menace," Asher encouraged.

Issachar offered a suggestion: "We can throw his body into one of these cisterns and it will look like he fell in there himself."

"We can tell Father a wild animal ate him," said Dan. "Then we'll see what comes of his dreams!"

"No!" Reuben interrupted. His mind was racing for a way out of this for Joseph. "Let's not kill him. Why should we shed innocent blood and have that on our hands? Let's just throw him in the cistern as Issachar suggested, but alive."

The brothers looked at each other with wicked grins and agreed to Reuben's plan. While Reuben was secretly planning to get Joseph out of the pit later and restore him to their father, the others had a different outcome in mind. As far as they were concerned, they would abandon Joseph in the cistern, so he was as good as dead.

The caravan was on the move again. Max, Kate, Liz, and Al followed at the end of the line with Osahar. Not only was it safer back here where no one else wanted to be, Liz had introduced the lonely camel to her friends and felt they could help keep him company. The traders would see the foursome soon enough. It might be they would put them up front or make them ride along on a dromedary.

"So ye come from the cold mountains of Central Asia then?" Max asked Osahar.

"Liz said ye were a long way from home," Kate added with her sweet smile. "I know how ye feel, lad. We're a long way from home ourselves."

The camel looked down at his small companions, treading carefully so as not to step on them. "YEAH, I'M A LONG WAY FROM HOME."

"Ye don't have to shout!" said Al, stopping to put his paws over his ears.

"ACTUALLY, I DO," Osahar replied matter-of-factly.

The animals spent all morning getting to know each other. Liz encouraged the others to be patient with their new friend. She reasoned that the more he felt at ease and got over his molting, the more likely his klazomania would calm down a bit. They could only hope.

The sky was staggeringly blue over the green fields of the glen in Dothan. Joseph looked up to see the jagged, tall cliffs towering above the fields, holding his hand up to shield his eyes from the bright sun. This was indeed beautiful country. Joseph then looked across the valley of the Jordan and saw his brothers in the distance. He took in a deep breath of relief. Joseph had been determined to pursue his brothers until he found them safe and sound. Their backs were turned as he walked up to their tents.

"Hello, brothers! I've been looking for you everywhere. Father sent me . . ." Joseph started to say. The brothers turned, all with hatred and anger oozing from their faces. He immediately knew something wasn't right.

"Of *course* he did," Naphtali said as he grabbed Joseph's knapsack and pushed him to the ground. Joseph was taken aback, startled by this fierce reception. His young face showed the surprise and alarm he felt.

Levi, Zebulun, Gad, and Asher grabbed Joseph from all sides, pulling on his robe. "This is the first thing to go!" shouted Levi.

The brothers ripped Joseph's robe off his back, tearing it to shreds. The robe, symbol of their father's love and favoritism, was cast aside on the dusty ground while Joseph cried out for pity.

"Please! Please! What are you doing?" he screamed as the brothers roughly picked him up.

Tears streamed down Joseph's face as he realized what was happening. The hatred of his brothers had escalated to a point of no return. They were going to kill him. Panic gripped his heart and he immediately thought of his father and the pain this would cause him. Joseph was pulled roughly across the stony ground and suffered scrapes along his back and legs. He pleaded with his brothers to stop. But they egged each other on, picking Joseph up and throwing him down into the empty cistern. He landed hard, hitting his head on the rough stone. He was cut and bleeding, kneeling on the floor of the cistern, gazing up at the small opening to the sky above.

"I beg you! Don't do this! Please! Don't you realize what you are doing? This will kill our Father! You are my *brothers!* How could you do this? Please, please, don't do this!" Joseph begged as he bitterly wept and cried out in anguish.

The brothers all peered over the edge of the cistern with hardened hearts and without concern for Joseph's cries. "Who's doing the bowing now? Certainly not us." The dreamer was cast into a nightmare, and his brothers were reveling in it. They smirked and all walked away, ignoring Joseph's cries for mercy. They wiped their hands off on their drab tunics.

After all, it was midday and time to eat. The brothers sat down to break bread.

Word was passed down the long line of the caravan that they were arriving in Dothan. They would be stopping to draw water from the cisterns there. Liz looked back and saw Max and Kate walking closely together. Max was whispering in her ear as Kate's tears flowed. A lump grew in Liz's throat as she witnessed the final minutes for this pair before they parted. She looked over to Al, tears quickening in her eyes for her friends. Al's big green eyes were full of compassion as he nudged Liz and said, "I know, me love. It breaks me heart, too."

Before them, across the vast plain, they could see the road that led to the Mediterranean coast. This busy road led many travelers away from Jordan and on into Egypt.

"HEY! DID YOU HEAR THAT? WE GET TO STOP UP HERE. GOOD THING. I NEED A BREAK," Osahar said, not realizing he was interrupting a somber moment for the four friends.

The brothers' ears perked up at the sound of the camel, and they looked over to see the long line of dromedaries in the caravan heading their way. They stood from their meal to determine what the caravan carried.

"Ishmaelite traders," Dan said. He knew their type well.

"No doubt heading to Egypt to sell a load of spices," Naphtali added.

Judah stood up. "And slaves."

The brothers watched Judah walk over to view the caravan. He turned to them and said, "What good does it do us to kill Joseph and cover up his blood? I say we sell him to the Ishmaelites. That way his blood isn't on our hands, and we can make a little profit while we're at it. Good for them, good for us." Judah wore a false look of compassion as he told them, "Joseph is our brother, after all. Our flesh and blood."

Earlier Reuben had left the group to take his turn watching the flock, so he was not part of the decision. But the remaining eight brothers eagerly agreed with Judah. This made complete sense to them. Selling Joseph would take away any spilled blood from their hands and any guilt they could possibly feel from their conscience. Most importantly, it would take their problem far away, where they would never have to deal with him again.

As the caravan neared the brothers' tents, Judah waved them over. "Come, there is plenty of water here for you and your animals."

Abu and his father were at the front of the caravan and directed everyone to follow them to the man who welcomed them there. Although these two groups of men would conduct business, the long-standing hatred between the Isaac and Ishmael family lines made them emotionally keep their distance. They would interact only as much as necessary and then be gone.

Judah walked up to them and held up his hand in greeting. "We have a business proposition for you. We have a strong young man who would bring you a good profit at the slave market in Egypt. Are you interested?"

Abu and his father nodded, followed Judah over to the cistern, and peered down at Joseph. Abu whispered in his father's ear, "This slave could help offset the loss of that camel if we can't sell it."

The father nodded. "Twenty pieces of silver is all I'll pay," the father said to Judah. "Take it or leave it."

Judah turned to his brothers to discuss the sale of Joseph. "He's only offering us the going rate for a crippled slave."

"Father's favorite son isn't worth very much after all, is he? Just a few pieces of silver," smirked Levi.

The brothers laughed at Joseph's expense and agreed on the price.

Judah turned to Abu and his father and replied, "Done."

Abu ran back to their donkey to get the money sack. He brought it back to his father, who in turn handed the silver pieces over to Judah. "Blood money, is it?" he said with a dark laugh.

Judah smiled and took the money, clutching it tightly in his hand. He instructed his brothers, "Pull Joseph out of the pit."

The brothers threw the end of a rope into the cistern and it hit Joseph in the head. He looked up and his mind filled with relief. He was getting out of the pit! His brothers must have had a change of heart. Joseph felt a surge of hope and quickly tied the rope around his waist and held on to it as his brothers lifted him to the top. He fell onto the dusty ground, the sand caking with the blood from his still-fresh wounds.

The Ishmaelites and the brothers stood over Joseph as he sat up and said, "I knew you couldn't leave me there. I'm glad you've changed your minds." He held up his hand for his brother to help him stand. But it was the Ishmaelite who gruffly pulled Joseph up and felt the muscles in Joseph's arms and back.

The brothers all stood back with arms crossed, smug looks on their faces. Joseph suddenly realized what was happening. "No! No! Not this!" he screamed.

Max's ears went up as he heard Joseph, and a growl rose in his throat. He impulsively ran over to see what was going on. Kate followed closely behind. When they got to the brothers, Max noticed Joseph cut and bleeding. And next to him on the ground was a multicolored robe, looking just as discarded as its owner.

Abu's father looked Joseph over and remarked, "Yes, he is a strong boy. He'll be easy to sell." He felt like he had offered too little for the sale of this well-built young man. Suddenly he felt Max and Kate at his feet. "What's this?"

Abu spoke up, "These stray dogs have been following us all day, Father. I think I saw a couple of cats with them, too. They must have followed the smell of our food."

The older man rubbed his chin with his chubby hand, his fingernails grimy. "Cats, too?" He realized he now had additional items to sell in Egypt. Cats were always in demand in Egypt. He picked Kate up and held her out to Judah. "Here, I'll throw in this dog as well since I clearly got the better end of this deal."

Max whined but restrained himself. His heart was breaking as he saw Kate handed over to this stranger, but he knew this was part of their mission. It was all part of the Maker's plan. He had to let her go.

Kate looked down at Max and softly whined, "Good-bye, me love. Until we meet again. I'll keep ye ever in me heart."

Judah looked at the beautiful little white dog and remarked to his brothers, "A dog for a dog, huh? I think we got the better end of the deal."

Joseph couldn't believe what was happening. How could his brothers so easily sell out their own flesh and blood? He was speechless and held his head in anguish from such betrayal. A large Ishmaelite man came up carrying a set of chains. Joseph heard the clank of irons and swallowed hard as the man harshly pulled Joseph's arms out to clamp the chains around his wrists. As he led Joseph away to join the caravan, Joseph looked back at his brothers, who still stood by watching him. His eyes pleaded for mercy but there was none to be found in theirs.

"Farewell, dreamer," the brothers called as they turned to walk back to their lunch.

Kate looked over Judah's shoulder at Max as the man held her close to make sure she didn't run off. She and Max shared one final parting glance. Max unsuccessfully tried to hold back the tears as he walked to the back of the caravan to Liz, Al, and Osahar.

Al came up and put his arm over Max's back. "We're here for ye, lad."

Liz held her dainty paw up to Max's chin and they shared a moment of tearful grief. She kissed him on the nose, then found her voice and said, "Remember what Gillamon said, Maximillian. 'Know that you are loved . . . and that you are able.'"

"HEY! WHAT'S WRONG? WHAT'S GOING ON?" Osahar asked as he observed that Kate wasn't returning and that Max was clearly upset.

Liz looked at Joseph as the rough trader bound him in shackles with the other slaves in the line, knowing many hearts were being broken by this transaction. She looked up at this young camel, who no doubt had unknowingly just played a part in the affair with the attention he brought to the caravan.

"Hard things, Osahar. Hard things are going on," Liz said as her gaze turned to Kate in the distance. "But necessary things."

Liz realized the first scheme in their mission had just unfolded. A brother sold into slavery by jealous brothers. And they had called him "dreamer." Liz looked at the young man and doubted he had dreamed this would ever happen to him.

CHAPTER 8

Refusing to Be Comforted

It was dusk when Reuben returned to their camp. He rested his shepherd's staff on the side of the full cistern where he stopped to water his donkey and to get a drink himself. He sipped the cool water that refreshed his parched tongue. It tasted good, and he drank so fast that water dribbled down his chin. He wiped his mouth with the back of his arm and looked down into the rippling water of the cistern. His mind was racing with how best to get Joseph out of the other, empty cistern and to handle the opposition of his brothers.

Being the oldest, Reuben knew he could try to impose his authority to return Joseph to their father, and that would be that. But with this rebellious group of brothers, nothing was guaranteed. They had, of course, listened to Reuben's suggestion to throw Joseph into the empty cistern, but even Reuben knew they had no intention of ever letting him out of the pit. He would just have to see how it went and deal with their response.

Things seemed rather quiet around the camp. *Good.* Reuben quickly made his way over to the empty cistern where they had thrown Joseph early that morning. He leaned over and looked inside, but the shadows of the early evening made it dark at the bottom of the pit.

"Joseph? Are you okay?" Reuben hoarsely whispered.

There was no reply.

"Joseph? JOSEPH! Answer me!" Reuben shouted, now worried that perhaps the fall had harmed him. His shouts were met with silence. He strained his eyes to see down into the pit, but could not see his brother. Maybe he just couldn't see well enough with the shadows. Reuben ran back down the trail leading to the camp's fire. He needed a torch to light up the cistern.

Kate sat quietly in the shadows, watching Reuben. After listening to the brothers laughing and mocking Joseph all day after the caravan left their camp, she was surprised to find this one brother showing some sort of concern over his brother. It gave her a tiny ray of hope there might be some goodness in the confines of this camp.

"I'd keep my distance from the bad ones," the donkey called to Kate. "They're nothing but trouble."

Kate walked over to the small female donkey. She was Reuben's donkey, and he indeed worked her hard. "Wha' is yer name?" Kate asked.

"I'm Dodi," the donkey replied. "What a strange accent you have. Where did you come from?"

"I guess ye weren't here earlier today when I arrived. I'm Kate. Some caravan traders gave me ta the brothers in exchange for Joseph," she replied, tears welling up again. It had been a hard day. "I had ta part from me mate an' me friends today."

Dodi looked at Kate and her eyes softened. "I'm sorry, Kate. These humans are so cruel to us animals."

"Aye, methinks they're cruel ta each other as well," Kate replied as she considered Joseph's fate. "It appears they were cruel ta me, but I've actually been sent here by the Maker," Kate explained. "I'm not here at the hands of the humans."

"The Maker Himself? I've never known anyone on such a mission. Are you sure He called you to do this?" Dodi asked. "Not that I doubt you, but how could you know something like that for sure?"

Kate smiled. If Dodi only knew how Kate and the others had been called for this mission! Wouldn't she be surprised to know how old Kate really was? Kate decided to not reveal her immortality to Dodi. "Oh, I know it for sure, lass. Trust me," she said, now grinning.

"Anything I can do to help?" Dodi asked.

"Jest be me friend, an' help me ta understand the background an' ways of these brothers," Kate replied, grateful to have a companion here in this place.

The donkey brayed with a laugh. "Understand the brothers?! How much time do you have?"

Kate smiled, "All the time in the world."

Reuben ran back past Kate and Dodi with a torch in hand, and leaned over into the cistern. The light from the flames bounced off the grey stone walls of the pit and revealed that it was completely empty—no water and no Joseph. "JOSEPH!" Reuben cried as he threw the torch to the ground and fell to his knees in the dust. He tore his garment and cried out, "My brother is gone!"

Kate frowned. She kept her distance but decided to follow Reuben to see what would happen.

The other brothers heard Reuben's cries in the distance as they sat in their tent. Soon Reuben came and found the brothers. They immediately saw how distraught he was. He fell to the ground before them and exclaimed, "Joseph is gone! What am I going to do?" He may have been the oldest of the brothers, but for now he was lost and needed direction. How strange. He wasn't there when the deed was done. But he was the only one crying out for what to do about it.

"He's not here," Judah explained without emotion. "We sold him to the Ishmaelite traders." With that, he tossed Joseph's robe at Reuben's feet.

Reuben picked up Joseph's robe, clutching it in his hands as he hung his head low. If only he had been bold enough to stand up and do the right thing when the anger of the brothers had been unleashed on Joseph, none of this would have happened. His brothers had sold Joseph, but as the oldest, Reuben realized that ultimately this was his fault. His mind didn't have to go very far to wonder how their father would react. And that was almost more than Reuben could bear. What could he possibly tell Jacob?

A goat was bleating in the distance. Reuben looked at Joseph's robe in his hand, and then at the brothers. He doubted that, in their act of hatred, they had even thought about what they would tell their father. They never thought very far ahead, but always let their emotions drive their actions. Reuben had also been guilty of acting on impulse in the past, so he certainly couldn't condemn them. As he felt the soft, fine linen of Joseph's robe in his hands, and allowed his fingers to brush the ornamentation on the sleeves, an idea came to his mind. It was deceptive, but it seemed more merciful than the truth.

"Bring that goat here," Reuben instructed.

Issachar and Asher ran to get the goat. Reuben then turned to Levi.

"And give me your knife."

Benjamin squealed with delight, "Father! Father! They're back!" He saw the group of brothers with their flocks coming down the road to Jacob's camp.

Jacob's heart jumped as he heard Benjamin's call. He ran out of the tent and immediately began to scan the horizon for his sons. The women and children of the camp went running down the path to greet the men, and it was a joyous scene. It had been weeks since they had seen each other.

As Jacob looked over the group he realized Joseph was not with them. Although concerned, Jacob assumed his sons had just missed crossing paths with Joseph somewhere on the way. He was sure Joseph would return home as soon as he realized the brothers had left Shechem. Oh, the relief that flooded Jacob to know that nothing bad had happened there.

Reuben saw Jacob in the distance and felt sick to his stomach. He was dreading this encounter. He didn't know what he dreaded more—the fact that he was going to tell his father a bald-faced lie, or how his father would respond to news of Joseph's "death." Both thoughts were painful to Reuben. He decided he'd best get on with it, and picked up his pace, yanking on Dodi's harness.

Kate picked up her speed, too. She knew this would somehow be a crucial part of her mission, to witness the heartbreak of Jacob. She didn't really know what her role would be, but realized she needed to be in the middle of the coming events.

Jacob raised his hand in greeting to Reuben, who nodded in reply. Reuben handed Dodi off to his wife after removing his knapsack from the donkey. "Take Benjamin with you," he instructed his wife. He didn't want their youngest brother to be part of this. Reuben then motioned for his nine brothers to join him. Together they walked up to the tent of Jacob.

"Father," Reuben said in greeting as he went and kissed his father on the cheek. Jacob embraced him and stood back to look his son in the eye.

"Reuben, I'm glad you and your brothers are home. I trust you had a good journey," he said. "Come, sit down, and rest." Jacob gestured for Reuben and the brothers to recline in his tent. Jacob's daughters hurriedly brought in some dates, bread, and water for the tired men, and then left. Kate snuck into the tent but stayed hidden.

The brothers were all very quiet. A feeling of discomfort filled the air as they looked from each other to their father, and then away. Jacob knew that something was wrong. His boys were always boisterous, especially when returning from a month in the fields. They would cut up and share stories of how they chased away the beasts that sought to harm their flocks. They enjoyed boasting over who had the greater kill of a wild wolf or lion, and usually had a trophy of some sort to bring home—a symbol of their manliness.

Jacob took a couple of dates from the bowl and reclined back on his elbow, watching the strange behavior of his sons. He looked them over, one by one. "What, no stories for me? I want to hear who had the greatest kill on this last journey! Dan, was it you? Or Judah, perhaps? Tell your father about the time in the fields. Who has a trophy to show me?" he said.

No one said a word.

"I sent Joseph after you in Shechem, but I assume you didn't see him," added Jacob.

Reuben saw his opportunity,. He cleared his throat and opened his knapsack, looking nervously at his brothers. Judah nodded in affirmation of Reuben. The orchestrator of Joseph's fate, Judah, was too much of a coward to own up to what he had done.

"Father?" Reuben said softly. "Father, we have something to show you."

Reuben slowly pulled Joseph's blood-covered robe from his knapsack. As Jacob's gaze drifted to the robe—and to the blood—he dropped the dates on the ground and began to tremble.

"Father, we . . . we found this. Please examine it to see whether it is your son's robe," Reuben said softly as he gently placed Joseph's robe in Jacob's lap.

Kate peeked out to see Jacob's reaction, and her heart sank. The look on his face would forever be burned into her memory.

Jacob's trembling hands took Joseph's robe and he held it out as he had that day Joseph first tried it on. His heart was beating out of his chest. *It looks like Joseph's robe, but how could it be? This . . . can't be my son's robe,* Jacob thought.

The brothers nervously watched their father, their eyes darting back and forth to each other. Now the realization of their cowardice came crashing into their minds. Their trophy this time was not the skin of a wild animal. No, it was the robe of their brother, dipped in goat's blood to cover their wicked act of betrayal. For the first time, their consciences were pricked as they looked at Jacob.

Kate studied the brothers and anger welled up within her. *Ten grown men ganged up on a teenage boy an' sold him into slavery because they were jealous of their father's affection. They are puny, selfish cowards! An' now their father is in agony, thinkin' his son is dead. Wha' kind of men be they?* she thought. *How could the Maker possibly see any value in usin' men such as these ta start a nation of His people?*

Jacob was in shock. He looked numbly at Reuben and said, "This is my son's robe. A wild beast has certainly devoured him." He paused and then began to shake uncontrollably.

Jacob stood and staggered backwards. "Joseph! Joseph has . . . been torn to pieces!" he shouted. With that Jacob tore his clothes, crying out in anguish, "LEAVE ME!"

Jacob clutched Joseph's robe to his face and wept bitterly, his shoulders shaking from deep sobs. Reuben looked at his brothers, who were looking to him for their cue of what to do, of how to respond. Reuben stood.

"I'm so sorry, Father," was all he could say. What else was there to say? He could gush more lies, such as, "He was our beloved brother," or "We loved him," but nothing would help. Nothing could set any of this right. Reuben couldn't bear additional guilt beyond what he felt right now so he decided to keep quiet and do as his father requested. He directed the brothers to leave their father's tent.

As the brothers filed out, Reuben lingered, looking at his poor father sobbing uncontrollably, rocking back and forth as he held

Joseph's robe up to his face. It was all he had left of his beloved son. What had they done? Reuben's shame was unbearable, but he knew this misery was of his own making. He quietly left the tent, wishing he had been the one his father lost.

Kate sat watching Jacob, sharing his pain but feeling anger at the same time. *This isn't right! Joseph is not dead! Oh, if only Jacob knew the truth! Aye, a wild beast did devour Joseph, but it were not a beast of the field. It were a beast of jealousy under this poor man's roof.* "Oh, Maker, please help me ta know wha' ta do ta help this dear soul," she prayed silently.

"JUST BE WITH HIM, KATE. FOR NOW, JUST BE WITH HIM."

Kate went over to Jacob, now curled up holding Joseph's robe, his legs pulled underneath him in the fetal position on his mat. She gently lay down next to him, giving him her warmth and her presence. She would do as the Maker instructed. How she wished she could do more.

As she lay there next to the weeping patriarch of this family, Kate gained an insight as to how the Maker must feel when any of his creatures suffers heartbreak from the blows of life. He could always see the full picture of what was going on, while only a sliver of the true reality of the situation was revealed to His creation. How hard it must be for Him to know there was more to reveal, but for the mysterious sake of His plan, to keep it hidden.

Kate wondered what Max must be experiencing now with Joseph. Relief came to her mind as she remembered the reality of this situation. Joseph was not dead. He was alive. And ten brothers knew that solid truth. But would Jacob ever know it? She closed her eyes and willed Jacob to feel her warmth and her love. And somehow, to feel the truth.

In the coming days, Jacob wore only sackcloth and covered himself in ashes, mourning over Joseph. Jacob chose to wear that which was the complete opposite of Joseph's robe—the lowliest, scratchiest, most degrading fabric. All of Jacob's sons and daughters tried to comfort him, but no one could reach him.

"I will go down to the depths of death itself in my grief over Joseph," he wailed.

Jacob reached down and felt the small dog at his side. His hand caressed her softly, as if she were a handle of hope, a lifeline to hold onto. He knew not where she came from. It didn't matter. She was there, and he welcomed her presence.

Jacob refused to be comforted by his sons, daughters, and wives. Nothing they said or did could relieve his pain.

The only one he allowed to remain by his side was Kate.

CHAPTER 9

The Road to Egypt

HEY! WATCH IT UP THERE!" Osahar shouted at Al, who, along with Liz, was enjoying a ride on top of the camel. "YOUR CLAWS ARE DIGGING INTO MY NECK!"

Al didn't respond as he continued his long, drawn-out stretch with a big yawn. Liz looked over at Al and noticed he had stuffed camel hair into his ears. She reached over and unplugged his ear. "Osahar has requested you stop clawing him, Albert."

"Sorry aboot that," Al called into the camel's ears. Al watched Liz as she tried to flick the camel hair off her claw and whispered, "I got tired o' the beastie's shoutin'."

"Well, now, I am certain he is likewise tired of your clawing, no?" Liz said with a frown as she flicked her paw repeatedly in the air. Finally the camel hair blew away.

"I'm starvin'," Al said.

"WHAT'S NEW? YOU SAID THAT TWO HOURS AGO," Osahar replied.

"Get used ta it, camel. Al's appetite is aboot as powerful as yer voice then," Max said as he trotted alongside the camel, trying to stay in the shade of his humps. "Too bad *ye* don't have humps on yer back ta store food an' water, Big Al."

Al pulled the clump of camel hair out of his other ear and stared at Osahar's humps. "Ye mean ta tell me there's food in these humps? I thought they looked like the pyramids, but I didn't know there were treasure inside."

"DON'T EVEN THINK ABOUT IT!" the camel shouted.

"Albert, dear, there are indeed water and nutrients stored in Osahar's humps, but nothing he could share," Liz explained.

"I've never wanted water so much in me life," Max said, chuckling inside, for he had always tried to avoid being around water. He couldn't swim. "Me tongue is hangin' out from bein' so thirsty. I could use some water aboot now, an' would even jump into a lake if I had the chance."

This journey was hard on all of them. At least Liz and Al were able to conserve their energy by riding on the camel. Max was certainly having a more tiring journey as he trotted along the road. Liz looked down at Joseph as he walked in front of them and thought no one could be having a more difficult time than he. She could only imagine what was going through his mind. She looked at his bare back, scraped from the rough treatment from his brothers, and frowned. No longer did he have a fine robe to protect him from the burning sun.

Sweat poured from Joseph's brow. He attempted to glance up and see the position of the sun in the sky overhead but could only endure a passing glance of the blinding fireball. How large the sun now looked, much different from his dream! His thoughts turned to Jacob.

A tear fell from Joseph's eye, mingling with the sweat on his face. His father must have been told something by now about his disappearance. Oh, if only he could have given his father a last word before he was carted away to Egypt! He knew his brothers would come up with a story to cover their scheme. Or they would tell their father nothing at all, claiming ignorance. Joseph couldn't think of any option that would bring less pain than another.

The line of shackled slaves shuffled their feet in the hot sand as they struggled in the desert heat. They walked along in the back of the caravan, behind the line of dromedaries laden with valuable spices. There was a teenage boy in front of Joseph who appeared to be two or three years younger than he. Joseph watched him go from hanging his head to holding it back to relieve the tension in his neck. Suddenly the boy stumbled and caused the line of slaves to falter as well. Joseph caught himself before he landed on top of the young boy. He stood over him and reached down his manacled hand.

"Here, let me help you," Joseph said to the boy, whose eyes were filled with nothing but despair. Their irons clanked together as the two slaves touched.

"Thanks," the boy said, his lip trembling. "I'm so hot. I feel like I'm going to faint if I don't get some water."

Joseph studied the young boy, whose face reminded him so much of Benjamin. He had dark, curly locks of hair. His eyes were deep brown, not dark blue like his little brother's. But there was a penetrating depth to his eyes that reminded him of Benjamin's gaze, which probed deep into Joseph's heart. He wondered how long ago these eyes, now filled with despair, had abandoned the sweet innocence of childhood.

Joseph called up to the trader who was handling the slaves, "Can we get some water? This boy is about to faint."

The trader glanced back at the slaves with little or no concern. "Keep moving!"

The young boy hung his head. Joseph knew he had to get some water or the boy would not make it much farther. "I know you want this slave in good shape for sale at the market. But you won't have this slave to sell if he doesn't get some water soon," Joseph boldly called up to the trader.

The rough-looking trader put his hand up to halt the caravan and walked back to Joseph and the boy. "You won't be in good shape for the market either if you don't get your friend here to move."

At that moment Max noticed a Bedouin wanderer coming down the road. He wore a white turban that covered the back of his neck, shielding him from the sun. His donkey was laden with heavy leather pouches draped across its back. Max looked closely and saw that one of the pouches was dripping.

"Aye! Water!" Max said as he took off running and barking at the desert dweller.

The man stopped and looked at Max, who ran up to him, his panting tongue hanging out of his mouth. The man smiled at Max and reached down to pet him. "Hello, little friend," he said as he gently stroked Max's fur. "Are you thirsty?"

His brown face was wrinkled from the scorching sun and the sands of time. He stood and took a cup from his satchel and tipped over one of the water pouches. He knelt down and allowed the dog to lap up the cool water, smiling as he watched Max eagerly splash it all over his fur.

Joseph looked up as he heard the dog barking and saw what was happening. "Please, sir, allow us to get some water from this man. You won't need to use your supply. I'm sure he will help us."

The trader looked at the man and his donkey and then back at Joseph and the young, struggling boy. He grunted and called the man over. "You! We need water for these dogs as well."

When Max finished the water, he noticed the man grinning at him with a twinkle in his eye. "You will always be given what you need, just when you need it."

Max wagged his tail in appreciation and trotted back over to the others. *Sounds like somethin' Gillamon would say*, Max thought to himself.

Liz smiled and said, "Well done, *mon ami.* It appears you have provided Joseph the opportunity for water as well."

"Aye, the Maker provided the water, lass. But I'm glad I could help the lad," Max replied, happy to be able to do something to give aid. Max had been struggling with watching the injustice of Joseph being sold by his brothers and not being able to do anything about it. Still, he knew that what was happening to Joseph was part of the plan, however mysterious. He knew he would have to continue to watch some difficult events unfold in the process.

The man turned his gaze to the trader who now called him over, and he led the donkey up to the slaves. He refilled the cup of water and gave it to the young boy who was struggling to stand. The boy's shaking hands took the cup and he quickly drank it down, not stopping to take a breath. He handed the cup back to the man, thanking him.

The man refilled the cup and gave it to Joseph, who also gulped down the refreshing water. "Thank you, kind sir."

"You are most welcome. Cups of cold water go a long way," the man said with a nod to Joseph. He went down the line of slaves, offering cups of cold water to each one. Finally he turned and pulled on the donkey's harness, clicking his tongue to signal for the beast to start walking. He held up his hand in a gesture of farewell.

"You've had your water. Now get moving," the trader said with a shove to Joseph's shoulder.

Joseph and the boy picked up their feet, now with renewed energy to go on.

"I'm Joseph. What is your name?" Joseph asked from behind.

"Benipe," he answered.

Joseph was taken aback. He was delighted that the boy had a name similar to Benjamin, but was curious as to his origin. "You are Egyptian? How is it you are out here on this caravan heading *to* Egypt?"

"My parents died when I was young and I took off with some traders as a scavenger. I left Egypt behind. There was nothing for me there," Benipe explained.

"And now you are headed back to Egypt," Joseph observed. "What happened?"

"I crossed the wrong people. They saw more value in me for the money they could get," Benipe said sadly. "I'm not worth much to anyone. I don't have any skills."

Joseph felt immediate compassion for this hurting boy. "You're wrong. You're worth far more than anyone could ever sell you for. Your true worth isn't measured in pieces of silver. Your value is in the eyes of God, who made you," Joseph encouraged. "And I know He gifted you with skills to use. You just haven't discovered them yet."

Benipe looked doubtfully at the ground as he listened to Joseph from behind. He was glad Joseph couldn't see his face. *How could a god's eyes value such a wretch like me? I'm not worth looking at.* He gave a forced laugh. "Which god, Joseph?" the boy asked. "There are many in Egypt. And I'll tell you they are far too busy to trouble themselves with me. Besides, now I'll never know what skills I have. I'll be *told* what skills to have as a slave."

Joseph thought a moment before he responded. He realized this boy didn't have a source of faith in the one, true God from which to draw strength. Joseph was grateful his father had raised him to know the God of Abraham, Isaac, and Jacob. God Himself had spoken to Joseph the night of his dream. He knew God was real and active in his life, even as this horrific event was unfolding. Joseph didn't understand all this. But he couldn't look to his circumstances for the truth. He had to look to God alone, who held Joseph's future tightly in His grip.

"Benipe, you'll be told what to do, but not what to be," Joseph encouraged. "Don't allow anyone to write the story of your life but you."

"How can you say that? Look at us! Look at *you*! We are headed to Egypt to be *slaves.* When we get to the market, whoever buys us will write our life story and that will be the end of it. Nothing I say or do will change that. Nothing will matter," Benipe lamented.

"You will always have a choice in how you respond, no matter who owns you and what you are made to do. And how you respond will determine your character, Benipe," Joseph said. "Nothing will matter more than that."

As they walked on, the young boy grew silent, thinking about Joseph's words. It was too hot and uncomfortable to talk anymore.

Liz intensely listened to every word Joseph said. She liked Joseph immediately, and saw why the Maker had chosen him to do something so important as to help a nation come into being. He was remarkable, and seemed wise beyond his years. He persistently reasoned with the trader, using the argument of the salability of the young slave to secure the needed water for the young man.

More amazingly, Joseph was not lashing out against his circumstances. He was looking ahead to his choices and how he would positively respond to his situation. His words didn't sound angry and hopeless like those of his new friend. And he was offering help to another in the midst of his own suffering. Yes, Joseph was remarkable indeed.

But this journey was just beginning. She would be eager to see if Joseph retained this philosophy of taking responsibility for one's character as time went on. How was she supposed to help him in the process? So many questions remained unanswered. But at least they were finally on the road to Egypt.

Liz looked down at Max and over to Al. Each would be playing his part in the story of Joseph soon. Gillamon had told her to have her quick wits about her when they arrived in Egypt. She would need to be ready to make some swift decisions in the marketplace. After centuries of waiting, the Maker was ready for these animals to help set in motion the events that would determine the fate of a nation. And once they arrived, things would unfold quickly.

Liz reviewed their mission again in her mind and made a mental checklist: eight dreams, three schemes, and four robes. One scheme and one robe had passed so far on this mission. They knew nothing of specific dreams yet, but Liz was certain some dreams had transpired to cause the jealous brothers to label Joseph "Dreamer." In the Hebrew language, 'dreamer' meant 'lord of the dreams.' She wondered what was in those dreams to anger the brothers so.

Dreamers are always a threat, for their dreams seek to put an end to the status quo, Liz reasoned. *Dreamers bring about change. And schemers are always waiting in the shadows to fight that change.*

As the caravan made a turn in the road, the first of the pyramids came into view. Liz continued her analysis. *Schemers are the last ones willing to bow down to a lord.*

Liz stared intently at Joseph. What changes would this dreamer bring to Egypt? What schemers would be ready and waiting for him once he arrived?

And who would be lord over whom?

PART TWO

THE SLAVE

CHAPTER 10

The Market

The market was buzzing with activity. Merchants of all sorts packed their booths full with wares for sale. There were sellers of fruits and vegetables, meat and fish, ceramic pots, sandals and fabric, baskets, cosmetics and perfumes, papyrus and paints, farming tools, animals, and, of course, men. Colorful striped canopies hung from the sides of the unfired clay brick buildings, giving shade to the merchants who lined the wide passageway of the market. Roads from all directions flowed into the market of Avaris, located on the outskirts of the middle-class quarter of town.

The aroma of burning incense hung in the air, and the shouting of the buyers and sellers reached a feverish pitch. The chorus of animals bleating and squawking added to the noise, not to mention the smell, of the marketplace. A group of older men sat on colorful mats in a circle, discussing the events of the day, hoping to hear news from distant lands and the latest developments at the rich Nubian gold and copper mines in the southern region of Egypt. They sat next to a booth with baskets filled to the brim with papyrus scrolls.

The scrolls contained architectural designs belonging to a local group of architects known for their masterful building plans of pyramids, temples, magnificent homes, and even middle-class dwellings. Several tables were lined up with some scrolls unrolled as the men looked over potential building projects. This booth was located at the end of a row that opened up to the wide area where caravan traders unloaded their goods.

"HEY! I DON'T SEE ANY OTHER CAMELS HERE! DO YOU THINK I'M THE ONLY ONE FOR SALE?" Osahar shouted as he looked around the busy market.

Liz patted Osahar softly on his neck. *"Oui, mon ami.* You are the only one of your kind."

"Ye kin say that again," Max muttered under his breath.

Al's face was beaming. He was overcome by the joy of the scene before him. "Food!" he said as he jumped off Osahar's back and onto to a striped canopy where he slid down to land on a table filled with bowls of figs, dates, and pistachios. Luckily, the merchant woman's back was turned, so she didn't see Al "swimming" in her pistachios.

"Daft kitty! Al, don't be wander-r-rin' off an' destr-r-royin' the mar-r-rket with yer cr-r-razy pouncin'! We've got a mission her-r-re," Max growled. "An' get out of the pistachios befor-r-re ye get us all in tr-r-rouble then!"

Visions ran through Max's mind of the destruction Al had unleashed on Liz's garden when they first met in France. Starving from their sea crossing, Al stumbled into Liz's garden, nibbled on the first thing he found (catnip) and went on a rampage. His feeding frenzy turned a beautiful, perfectly manicured garden into an ugly mess in a matter of minutes. Max could only imagine what could happen here in the market if Al were to find some catnip.

Al sheepishly grinned and scurried off the table before he was seen. The merchant woman looked around and saw the bowl teetering on the edge. She steadied the bowl with her hand and frowned as she slowly picked cat hair out of the figs.

Liz decided to let Max control Al while she scanned the marketplace to assess their situation. She jumped off Osahar's back onto a tower of empty crates stacked up next to the camel. She had to locate Potiphar, chief of Pharaoh's guard of executioners, as Gillamon had instructed. He clearly would be a nobleman and would be surrounded by servants. But there were so many buyers at the market today! How could she know which one was Potiphar? This might require some local help.

The traders were greeted by a slender, dark, Egyptian man, the market overseer. He wore a short white linen loincloth and a blue-and-yellow-striped headdress. He also wore a wide gold bangle on his lower arm, and on his feet were brown leather, strapped sandals. He was followed by a scribe who held a writing reed, a scroll, and an ink palate. Abu and his father led the overseer and the scribe to review their supply of goods for sale. The Egyptian examined the resin closely and nodded his head in approval, motioning for the scribe to make notes.

"Ah, I knew I could count on you to return with the finest myrrh and spices. These items will sell well today, as there have been requests from the temple priests for a higher grade of this resin," the overseer said. "The embalmers are ever seeking to improve the mummification process."

"Of course, of course! We are happy to bring you the finest resin anywhere. But today we also bring you a group of strong, young slaves who, we know, will serve the needs of Egyptians well," Abu's father said as he gestured with open hand to the line of slaves.

Joseph, Benipe, and the others stood in a row, hands at their sides, still shackled together. Abu's father and the overseer walked up and down the line of men, looking them over carefully. The rough trader jabbed Benipe in the back with his stick, saying "Stand up straight, boy."

"Do as he says," Joseph muttered under his breath.

Benipe pulled himself up as best he could. The droop in his shoulders was more the result of his despair than his exhaustion. But he followed Joseph's lead and lifted his head.

"Yes, yes, these are solid specimens. I'm sure they will sell also," the Egyptian remarked.

Abu whispered in his father's ear. "Oh, yes, and we also have some animals for sale today. Two cats, a dog, and a very exotic . . . camel," the father said doubtfully, gesturing over to Osahar. He looked at Abu as if to say, "Here goes nothing."

The men walked over to Osahar, who saw them coming. *Now's my chance*, the camel thought to himself. He shook his head side to side to try to remove any clumps of hair that still clung to him. Unfortunately he was still not finished molting, and hair went flying everywhere, including onto the overseer's striped headpiece.

Liz saw what was happening, but before she could stop him Osahar let out a loud, "HEY! PICK ME! PICK ME!" Liz shook her head. This would only make Osahar's quest for an owner all the more difficult.

Abu's father cringed, and quickly reached over to pull the clumps of camel hair off the Egyptian as he tried to come up with some positive things to say about the gross, noisy camel. "Uh, this is what camels do! They have strong lungs, yes, strong lungs and can be used as . . . sound beacons out in the desert to ward off wild beasts."

The overseer placed his hand firmly over Abu's father's arm and stopped him. "If this beast is best used in the desert, then let him *stay* in the desert. We have no need of him here," he said as he looked Osahar up and down with disgust. He was clearly not interested in even attempting to sell the obnoxious camel.

Osahar looked at Liz with panic in his eyes. "THEY DON'T WANT ME, LIZ! THEY DON'T WANT ME!"

Liz leaned over and put her dainty paw on Osahar's cheek. "We will think of something, *mon ami*. Do not worry."

"The cats, however, we will definitely want to sell. They are always prized by Egyptians. Show me the dog."

Abu ran over to find Max, who was still keeping an eye on Al. Abu slipped a rope around Max's neck and pulled him over to the Egyptian. Max at first resisted the rope but caught Liz's eye from where she sat on the crates. She nodded her head, indicating for Max to cooperate.

"Aye," Max growled to himself. "I don't like this a bit, lass!" he said as he walked by Liz.

"You must allow yourself to go with these humans, Max. I am looking at our options. For now, cooperate," Liz instructed, her tail whipping back and forth as she made mental notes of everything happening.

Abu put Max at the feet of the Egyptian overseer, who knelt down and petted the small dog. "What a sturdy little one you are," he said as he felt Max's muscles and opened the dog's jaws to inspect his teeth.

Max almost let out a growl but held his tongue, willing himself to cooperate. *This is degrading*, Max thought. He then looked over and observed a man doing the same thing to Joseph and the other slaves. They were being inspected for their health, their strength, and their usability. Max gained an understanding of how Joseph must be feeling at this moment, and stopped resisting the Egyptian.

The overseer stood and rubbed his chin. "I don't know about the dog. We will see if someone wants him. The cats serve a useful purpose in homes—rounding up pests—but I can't see this dog being of service except for maybe hunting. We will see if any hunters come to market today. Scribe, make a note he is available for sale."

Max was so mad he could hardly contain himself. "I be the best pest r-r-rounder-upper in all of Scotland! Jest let me show ye how I kin r-r-round up any beastie anywher-r-re!"

The Egyptian looked down and smiled at the dog barking at him with such enthusiasm. "Still, I do like his spunk." With that, the overseer shook the trader's hand and indicated he could go ahead and sell his goods. His scribe would send the buyers over to look at their resin, slaves, and cats. And maybe his dog. But definitely not the camel!

Liz was sitting above the scribe, leaning over his shoulder. She wrinkled her brow, frustrated she couldn't make out a word he was writing. This Egyptian language was so strange. Since she would be in Egypt for a long while, Liz was determined to figure out a way to understand the people's writing and ways.

Liz knew that, like the Egyptian writing, the situation here in the market was challenging. Osahar wasn't deemed worthy of sale, and was emotionally crumbling next to her. Max's sale would be dependent on hunters coming to market. Joseph was viewed as highly salable, but Liz had to make sure the right buyer selected him.

Gillamon did not tell her specifically where Joseph was supposed to go, but that he needed to get to the right place. Liz was given specific instructions that her assignment was Potiphar. Did that mean Joseph was supposed to go to Potiphar as well? She deduced that since this mission was about Joseph and where he would go, not where Liz would dwell, that the house of Potiphar must be the intended destination for Joseph. "Oh, Maker, I will search for Potiphar if that is where Joseph is to go, but please help me find him," Liz prayed.

Out of the corner of her eye Liz noticed something strange on the architects' table below. A roll of papyrus was moving by itself, as if something were slowly unrolling it from inside. It was erratically shaking, a motion that would drive any cat crazy with excitement and curiosity.

The scroll opened little by little until Liz saw something white fluttering on the edge of the unrolled parchment. She kept her eyes on the scroll to see what would come into view. Slowly some long, white whiskers emerged, followed by two pinkish-white, round ears. It was a tiny mouse. At first Liz thought it was nibbling its way through the scroll, but as she watched, she observed that this mouse was actually *reading.*

The little mouse finally poked his head out, evidently so engrossed in the subject matter he didn't notice he was clearly visible. Liz noticed that his little brown eyes were squinting, as if he was having a hard time reading. Perhaps this script was gibberish to him as well. Then she saw the mouse nod his head as he read the mysterious Egyptian script. He was not just reading the script—he understood what he was reading!

"Magnifique!" Liz said out loud, amazed at this little creature. He was obviously highly intelligent. Perhaps he could help her decipher the Egyptian language. And given how comfortable he appeared with his surroundings, perhaps he had a good understanding of the market and possibly who the buyers were. He could be her key to finding Potiphar. Liz was excited to have a potential new source of information.

But then she saw Al and her heart dropped.

Al was creeping up behind the mouse, pointy teeth showing with his mouth wide open, ready to pounce. His bushy tail was up and twitching and his shoulders were moving back and forth. Suddenly he lurched forward, landing directly on his intended target and scooping the mouse right into his mouth.

CHAPTER 11

Of Mouse and Men

ALBERT! STOP!" Liz yelled as she jumped down from the crates, landing on the table in front of Al. "DROP THAT MOUSE!"

Al's eyes widened as Liz startled him with her sudden appearance. His cheeks were stuffed full and the mouse's long, white tail sticking out flicked back and forth. He held up his paws in a questioning gesture and attempted to answer Liz, but all that came out were grunts.

"That is no ordinary mouse!" Liz said as she put her paw up to Al's cheek and spoke to the mouse inside. "*Monsieur*, please remain calm. I will get you out."

Al didn't want to give up his prize. He whined and mumbled some more. "*Oui*, Albert, you have to let him go. Do it now before he suffocates in there," Liz said, pointing her paw at the table.

Al finally showed his best "Yes, dear" look and lowered his head to the table. He gave one more glance at Liz before he let go of the mouse. Liz furrowed her brow and tapped the table once more with her dainty paw. "*Now,* Albert."

With that, Al opened wide his mouth, and out fell the mouse onto the table. He landed on his back and proceeded to shake himself off from head to tail.

"I do say, that was the finest Opening of the Mouth ceremony I have ever attended," the mouse remarked with the most impeccable British accent Liz had ever heard.

Liz and Al looked at each other, stunned.

"Monsieur? Pardon, but you are . . . British? And your accent I believe is from . . . Wales?" Liz asked, still taken aback by this unusual encounter.

Not only was this mouse obviously intelligent, but he appeared totally unshaken by the fact he had nearly been eaten alive by Al. And he hailed from their part of the world. The small white mouse wiped his face with his hands before stroking back the whiskers on each side. He was obviously concerned about his appearance and didn't wish his fur to remain ruffled.

"Right you are, my dear," the mouse replied. "And *your* accent—French, I believe? Normandy to be exact."

Liz could not believe her ears. What a delightful mouse! He even knew the region in France she was from. She was beaming with the delight of this chance meeting.

"Forgive me, but we have not yet been properly introduced. The name is Monaco. Nigel P. Monaco, at your service," the mouse said, bowing low with his small arm draped humbly across his chest.

"*Enchantée, Monsieur* Monaco. I am Lizette. Lizette Brilliante Aloysius. Please call me Liz. And this," she said, looking perturbed at Al, whose mouth still hung open, "is my husband, Albert. I do apologize for Albert's mistaking you for his *petite dejeuner.*"

"No harm done. He was just behaving normally for a hungry cat," the mouse replied, drawing a relieved smile from Al, who by this point was so embarrassed his fur looked as if it were turning from orange to red.

"I don't know what a pea-teet day-junay is, but I was just starvin' for some breakfast. Sorry to have nearly eaten ye, lad," Al replied.

Liz and the mouse shared a grin. *Petite dejeuner* is the French word for "breakfast."

"*Monsieur* Monaco, I was hoping you could help us. But I am curious. What did you mean, 'It was the finest "Opening of the Mouth ceremony" you have ever attended'?" Liz asked the mouse.

"Do call me Nigel, my dear. Right. The Opening of the Mouth ceremony is part of the Egyptian funerary customs for a mummy's journey to the underworld. They believe this fascinating ritual restores the mummy's senses for the afterlife—sight, hearing, breathing, receiving nourishment, etcetera," Nigel explained. "Of course, I was being metaphorical with the opening of Al's mouth to let me out. A bit of British humor, you know," Nigel explained with a jolly chuckle.

Liz chuckled as well, but Al didn't quite get the joke. "And you've attended such a ceremony?" Liz inquired. She was enthralled.

"Oh, my dear me, yes! I've attended hundreds of such rituals as I've studied the Egyptian ways of life and death. I never miss a mummification, and of course the rituals involved for large ceremonies in the pyramids are utterly fascinating," Nigel eagerly shared.

"Nigel, I wish to learn all you know, including your knowledge of Egyptian scripts and hieroglyphics, but we have an urgent matter at hand," Liz said as she saw a group of buyers walking over to inspect Joseph. "I will soon explain, but we are looking for a man by the name of Potiphar. Do you know him?"

Nigel smiled. "Indeed I do! He is quite the important fellow. See here, let me determine if he is present in the market," he said as he stood on his small back legs.

"Perhaps the view from the crates would help?" Liz suggested.

"By Jove, you're right!" Nigel said as he jumped from the table to climb the wooden pole that supported the striped canopy. He quickly made his way to the crates, with Liz and Al following along behind.

Nigel, Liz, and Al sat overlooking the busy market. A group

of buyers surrounded the slaves. They could see the traders lifting the arms of the slaves to examine their muscular development. Liz frowned as she noticed the rough trader holding Joseph's jaw while he forcibly turned his head for a side view.

"Looks as if that man likes our Joseph," Al remarked.

"Is that Potiphar, Nigel? The man looking at the slaves?" Liz asked, getting nervous. It appeared the man was seriously interested in buying Joseph.

"I'm afraid not. Potiphar is much taller, and I don't see him at the moment," Nigel replied, continuing to scan the crowds.

Liz couldn't allow this man to buy Joseph. How could she stop this? Suddenly an idea came to her.

"Osahar, I need you to do something for me, *s'il vous plaît,*" Liz said as she leaned over to the camel's ear. "I need for you to launch one of your large, green, smelly spit wads at that man who is inspecting Joseph. Do you think you can reach him?"

Osahar grinned. "WITH PLEASURE."

The camel made a terrible hacking sound and held his head back as he let loose a spit wad that sailed through the air and landed right in the man's ear, almost knocking him over. Abu's father's eyes were wide with shock as he frantically tried to clean off the man's ear. The spit was running from his ear down the side of his head and into his jeweled collar. The man screamed in anger, knocking Abu's father away.

"I'm sorry! I'm sorry! Please allow me to help you! Forgive our camel, but he is a pest!" Abu's father cried, looking angrily at Osahar and shaking his fist in the air.

"Your beast did this?!" the angry man exclaimed, shaking his head to remove the camel spit from his ear. "If this is how you allow your beasts to treat buyers, I want nothing from you!" The man signaled for his servants to follow him as they walked away from Abu's father and Joseph.

"Well done, *mon ami!"* Liz said, gently patting Osahar.

"I FIGURED I DIDN'T HAVE ANYTHING TO LOSE. THESE TRADERS ARE GOING TO RELEASE ME INTO THE DESERT ANYWAY. I'M GLAD I COULD HELP JOSEPH," the camel shouted in reply.

"I say! What an amazing beast you are!" Nigel remarked as he jumped over to Osahar's back. Nigel ran up and down Osahar's humps, causing the camel to giggle.

"THAT TICKLES!"

"You are certainly well adapted to desert life with not one but two humps. I've heard about your breed from the east. But I had no idea camels were so loud," Nigel said.

"Osahar suffers from klazomania, Nigel," Liz offered.

"Oh, I see. Compulsive shouting. Well, that explains that," Nigel remarked, once again astounding Liz with his knowledge. Nigel suddenly stood on his back legs. "I believe our dear Potiphar has arrived." The mouse pointed to a group of servants surrounding a well-dressed, tall Egyptian man.

Liz followed Nigel's direction and spotted Potiphar. He wore a long, white linen loincloth and around his neck was a wide collar of gold and lapis lazuli, a blue precious stone from the exotic east. On his head was a military headdress signifying his high station in the court of Pharaoh. He towered above his servants, and was a clearly formidable man. As the chief of executioners, Potiphar oversaw the royal bodyguards in Pharaoh's court. He was responsible for the jail and ordered the swift execution of anyone who crossed Pharaoh. This man held in his hands the power of life and death.

Accompanying Potiphar was a line of servants carrying baskets of goods purchased in the market, scribes, and other advisors. Among the men in his entourage was a rough-looking, plump man, also with a military insignia on the gold bangle around his forearm. He was the chief jailer for Potiphar. Liz noticed the market overseer greeting Potiphar with a respectful bow. The men spoke for a moment before the overseer nodded and motioned for

Potiphar's group to follow him over to the slaves.

"Merci beaucoup, Nigel. You have been invaluable to us! Please remain here with Osahar while Albert and I go intercept Potiphar," Liz said. "Come, Al dear. This is our cue."

"Glad to be of assistance, my dear," Nigel said with a slight nod of his head. "Osahar and I will become acquainted and wait for you here."

Al and Liz made their way down to the line of slaves, where Max also sat. "Did ye make that beastie spit on the Egyptian lad then, Liz?" Max asked with a mischievous grin on his face.

"Desperate times call for desperate measures, no?" Liz replied with a coy smile. "Max! Albert and I met a brilliant mouse named Nigel who has identified Potiphar as the man who now approaches. Everyone look lively. I believe things will happen quickly."

"Aye, and ye won't believe where the mousie is from," Al said to Max. "Wales!"

"Ye don't say? That's where Cr-r-raddock were from!" Max replied excitedly. Craddock was their dear whale friend who had helped the animals across the English Channel on their way to the Ark, and had saved Max's life as well.

"I kin't wait ta meet the wee beast. Jest tell me ye didn't try ta eat him then!" Max said with a chuckle, thinking he was making a joke. His smile left when he saw the look of guilt written all over Al's face. Max frowned. "Daft kitty!"

"Hush, you two," Liz scolded. "Here they come."

CHAPTER 12

Potiphar and Bastet

Abu's father wiped the sweat from his brow as he saw Potiphar approach. He nervously whispered in his son's ear and shooed him away, turning to grin and repeatedly bow low before Potiphar. Abu ran over to Osahar and held on to the camel's reins. He would make sure no spit flew all over Potiphar. That would mean certain imprisonment—or worse.

"I need five slaves. Show me," Potiphar said with his deep voice, arms folded over his chest, challenging the trader to impress him. His shoulders and biceps were huge. Potiphar radiated power. Abu's father gulped.

"Of course! Of course! Please, Your Excellency, I have only the best slaves available for your service. I know you will be pleased." Abu's father bowed and directed Potiphar down the line of his ten slaves, starting at the end opposite from where Joseph and Benipe stood. Joseph was ninth in line.

Joseph leaned forward and glanced at Potiphar. Surely this would be a man who would properly provide for his slaves. He was wealthy and powerful, and slaves belonging to such men were always treated well. "Benipe, look sharp," Joseph whispered.

The young boy straightened up and took a deep breath. He trusted Joseph and did as he instructed. Liz watched Potiphar reviewing the slaves. She frowned as she saw him pull two slaves from the line, his scribes making the proper notations. This wasn't good. Potiphar could choose his five slaves before even reaching Joseph.

"Stay here," Liz instructed as she left Al and Max to walk down the line of slaves. She darted in and out of the shadows of the legs of the men who stood in line, waiting for their fates to be determined by this powerful buyer. Potiphar chose a third slave. Liz knew she had to act quickly.

Liz boldly walked right up to Potiphar, wrapped herself around his legs and meowed. Potiphar felt the soft touch of this cat encircling him and looked down, smiling. "It appears this one has chosen me," he said, causing all his servants and Abu's father to join his amusement with chuckles.

Liz narrowed her eyes with a sign of affection as Potiphar gazed at her. *Ah, oui, but you have no idea, Monsieur,* she meowed.

Potiphar reached down and gently picked Liz up. "What a beauty you are, for you look like Bastet. Are you Bastet, come to give me guidance?" Potiphar asked as he gazed into the deep golden eyes of this cat.

Abu's father smiled, "She must be Bastet to choose such a worthy owner!"

"Yes, I will buy this cat. Her name will be Bastet. Come, Bastet, tell me which slaves I must choose," Potiphar said as he stroked Liz.

This was all too easy, Liz said to herself as she smiled back at Potiphar. She was amazed at the awe this Egyptian showed a cat. She understood that this man viewed her as a messenger from the cat god Bastet, which bothered her, but if she could wield her power to help Joseph, so be it.

Potiphar put Liz back on the ground to see what she would do. She encircled him once more before taking a few steps forward and looking back up to him, indicating he should follow. Potiphar held his hand out to Liz. "Please, Bastet. After you."

Liz walked down the row of slaves and gave Al and Max a wink as she approached them. Al gave Liz a goofy grin and winked back, while Max smiled and shook his head in astonishment as he watched this brilliant cat at work. This petite black cat had one of the most powerful, dangerous men in Egypt wrapped around her little paw.

Liz stopped in front of Joseph and looked back at Potiphar before curling around Joseph's legs and sitting at his feet. She meowed up at Potiphar, *Allow me to introduce Joseph.*

Potiphar was delighted and chuckled as he heard the cat meow. He stopped in front of Joseph. "It is as if our Bastet here actually heard my request. I must take heed of her recommendation." He then turned to Abu's father. "Show me this slave."

The rough trader jabbed his stick into Joseph's back, indicating he needed to step forward. Joseph stepped out so Potiphar could walk completely around him. Potiphar looked Joseph up and down and appreciated his strong build. He then came and stood face to face with Joseph with his hands on his hips, staring him squarely in the eye. Joseph didn't flinch, but wisely responded with a look of self-confidence and gave a solid nod of respect. Potiphar immediately liked Joseph. He stood back and once again looked him up and down.

"Bastet, you are very wise," he said, smiling down at the cat. "I'll take this slave."

Abu's father bowed. "An excellent choice! That leaves one more."

Joseph looked over at Benipe and saw the panic rising in his eyes. He looked down at Liz, willing her to understand she must help the frightened young boy. Liz stared back at Joseph and quickly wrapped her legs around Benipe. *But of course he is the one*

I was going to pick. I am not blind to how you have watched out for him, Joseph, she meowed.

Joseph smiled at Liz and nodded as he heard the cat meowing and choosing his frightened friend. Liz nodded her head in reply and Joseph did a double take, thinking, *Did that cat just nod at me?*

Potiphar looked Benipe over well and with a wave of his hand said, "Bastet has chosen this young one. So be it."

With that, the rough trader pushed Benipe over with Joseph and the other three slaves, and a smile grew over Benipe's face as he and Joseph shared a moment of relief.

Abu's father asked, "Is there anything else you desire, your Excellency? Another cat, perhaps?" The man reached down and lifted Al, who looked at Liz with concern. He didn't know if this was okay.

"No, nothing else. I already have Bastet," Potiphar replied, waving Abu's father away.

Al's eyes filled with anguish as he was put back down on the ground. Liz acted quickly. She wrapped herself around Al and meowed once again. Potiphar smiled. "You are quite the insistent one, Bastet. Very well, but this is the last of my purchases. I will give this orange cat to Pharaoh as a gift when I go to see him."

"That's me girl, lass!" Al whispered as he kissed Liz on the cheek. One of Potiphar's servants lifted Al and placed him in a basket.

Potiphar then picked up Liz so he could carry her with him as they left the marketplace. He instructed his scribes to make note of his transactions, and another of his servants to pay the traders. When they had finished, all turned to follow Potiphar to his chariot. Liz positioned herself on Potiphar's shoulder as he carried her away. All was well with Joseph, Benipe, Al, and herself. But what about Max?

Max sat alone on the sandy ground, restrained by the rope around his neck. He was tied to a pole. Liz's mind raced as she considered how she could help Max. If they were separated here, how could they ever find each other again? What if a buyer purchased

Max and took him far away to the hunting grounds downstream on the Nile?

Max barked several times and got the attention of one of the humans. Liz saw the jailer turn around and observe the dog. Then an idea came to her. She looked over at Osahar and saw the camel and Nigel paying close attention to what was happening.

"Nigel! You must allow Max to chase and catch you while the jailer is watching!" Liz called.

"Right!" Nigel said as he immediately scurried down the camel, causing Osahar to giggle. He ran right in front of Max, who took off running after the mouse, pulling himself free from the pole where the rope had not been securely tied.

Max gave great chase as Nigel led him all around the market courtyard, weaving in and out of booths, wending their way over to the jailer. Nigel turned to Max with a wink and allowed Max to scoop him up in his mouth. Max gently held Nigel in his teeth and went up to the jailer's feet. He held the mouse in his mouth and gazed up at the man, who smiled in return.

"Potiphar, I think I will buy this dog," the jailer said. "He will be of great use to me."

Potiphar stroked Liz and nodded, "Do as you wish."

The jailer called over to Abu's father, indicating he would buy the dog. While the men conducted their business, Max placed Nigel on the ground, spitting the mouse hair out of his mouth.

"Thanks, Mousie. I owe ye one! Sorry aboot the chase. I heard ye already had ta be in another big mouth today," Max said.

Nigel once again stroked back his whiskers and his fur. "You are most welcome. Osahar told me about your mission, so I am delighted to render assistance."

"I hear ye're from Wales," Max said. "Aye, I know it well an' had a good fr-r-riend from there."

"Splendid! You don't say? What is your friend's name? Perhaps I know the chap," Nigel replied, continuing to groom his ruffled fur.

Max chuckled, "No, I don't think ye would." If Nigel only knew that Craddock had swum the waters off the coastline of Wales almost two thousand years ago.

The jailer shook the trader's hand and was ready to leave.

"Well, I look forward to hearing more of your mission as it progresses. Do tell Liz I will be in touch. I know where you live," Nigel said with a hearty laugh. "Oh, and don't worry about Osahar. I have an idea that will work out for both of us."

"Aye! I'll tell her. Thanks again, Mousie," Max replied. He turned and fell in line behind the jailer as he picked up Max's rope and led him away.

Nigel nodded and scurried off back to Osahar. There was one more captive to free from the traders.

CHAPTER 13

In the House of Potiphar

The water was gently lapping against the riverbank as the hot Egyptian winds blew along the Nile, causing small waves to dance and ripple across the surface of the mighty river. The reflection of the sun joined the dancing waves, making the water in front of Potiphar's house sparkle like diamonds.

A servant girl squinted in the sunlight as she stooped to fill her jar with water. Fish darted in and out around her tiny feet, making her smile. The bottom of her white tunic always got wet as she waded in the water. She pulled a few crumbs from the fold in her tunic to sprinkle over the fish. They came and schooled around her, making her feel like a towering giant bestowing gifts on the hungry, less fortunate ones in her dominion.

Mandisa was a petite young girl with cropped black hair and adorable dimples. She wasn't supposed to go near the banks of the Nile, as hippos and crocodiles were always present, and could snatch her before she realized it. Such caution was warranted but today was ignored by this servant girl who loved the water. Mandisa enjoyed being outside and away from her household responsibilities. She was grateful to be a servant in such a fine house as that of Potiphar.

But she sometimes grew weary of her mistress, Zuleika, wife of Potiphar. Her mistress was frequently bored, and Mandisa had to daily endure her complaints. If only Zuleika could appreciate the beauty of the home in which she lived. Mandisa looked around at the incredible landscape, the gardens, and the grand villa belonging to one of the most powerful men in Egypt. It was a sight to behold.

The grand house was built up on a high slope above the banks of the Nile to allow protection from the river's annual flooding. A high wall completely surrounded the complex, with an intricately carved and decorated gate allowing access at the front of the house, two smaller entrances on the sides, and one lesser gate at the back leading to the river. At the north end of the complex stood the three-story house. Other buildings lined the south end of the complex, where servants worked and lived and where supplies were stored.

The house and buildings were built with mud bricks covered with limestone plaster to serve as a barrier against the hot sun. Several small windows were set high in the house to allow for minimal sunlight, and vents captured the cool north wind to funnel it into the rooms below.

The high walls were lined with giant sycomore fig, date palm, and acacia trees. Two long ponds flanked the courtyard, and were surrounded with greenery and papyrus plants. Ducks honked and splashed around the blue lotus plants growing in the ponds. The very center of the courtyard had been cleared in preparation for the planting of a new vineyard. Workers busied themselves throughout the intricate garden, carrying water back and forth with yokes on their shoulders for the many plants in the courtyard. Mandisa heard the shouts of the gardener as he instructed the servants. Things were not going well with this new garden project, and Potiphar was not pleased.

Potiphar appreciated the beauty of the natural world, and made sure everything surrounding him was perfect. From the flowering plants positioned so he could smell their sweet fragrance in the front portico, to the detail of the brightly painted walls and columns in the house and surrounding buildings, every aspect of the house of Potiphar had to be extravagant. A man of his wealth spared no expense for such a grand display. He hoped to please the gods with the way he built his home and treated his servants, for he wanted to ensure that what he created here on earth would be re-created in his afterlife.

The gardener told Potiphar he needed more slaves and tools to begin the vineyard project, which was massive in scope. So Potiphar went to the market in search of the needed slaves and supplies. He wanted this garden project to commence immediately, for he understood that it would take time to cultivate this vineyard.

The house of Potiphar hosted an annual harvest celebration at the end of June—before the flood season began. They celebrated the harvest of Potiphar's vast estate, and invited elite guests and officials to see the bounty of Potiphar's wealth. The party was held in the courtyard gardens, so this vineyard must look impressive, although it would still be young.

Potiphar had a secondary intent with this vineyard, and that was to provide Pharaoh with the finest wine possible for the Sed festival to be held in seven years. It would be the most important celebration ever observed for this Pharaoh, marking the thirtieth year of his reign. Known also as the royal jubilee, the Heb Sed would regenerate and renew Pharaoh's power. If it took years to accomplish what Potiphar desired with this vineyard, so be it. Potiphar was a very patient man. But by the time of the Sed festival, this vineyard had better be producing the finest wine in all of Avaris. Nothing was more important than securing the favor of Pharaoh, son of Ra.

Mandisa heard the ram's horn blowing at the northern gate. Potiphar must be returning. She quickly ran up to the house with her water jar splashing. Her mistress would want to be present in the portico when her husband returned to see if he had brought her any gifts from the market. Mandisa certainly hoped Potiphar brought something home to occupy his wife. Some new fabric or jewels, perhaps. Maybe a new cosmetic holder or a fine comb. Anything new would be welcomed by this bored, wealthy wife.

"This must be the place," Al called from behind as he bounced along in the basket on top of the servant's head. He rested his paws on the edge of the basket. "Look! There's even a bunch o' them kitty gods lined up to greet us!"

Liz gazed straight ahead at the impressive entrance to Potiphar's house. A long row of small sphinx statues lined either side of the avenue leading to a massive gate where servants stood at attention awaiting the return of their master. The gate was covered in colorful hieroglyphs. Liz furrowed her brow. She wished she could understand what those symbols meant. *"Oui,* we are at the house of Potiphar."

Potiphar's servants walked swiftly along the sphinx-lined avenue as they carried the heavy wicker litter that held their master. Potiphar stroked Liz and smiled as she meowed out the window of the litter. "Yes, Bastet, we are home. I hope you will be happy here. I look forward to showing you my garden."

Liz's ears perked up immediately. He had a garden? Oh, how long it had been since she dwelled in a place with a beautifully manicured garden! And by the looks of the entrance to this splendid house, it would be magnificent. Liz would have to make sure Al didn't come near it if catnip was present. She wondered how long Al would remain with her here before Potiphar took him as a gift to Pharaoh. Max would be moving on once they arrived. The jailer was accompanying Potiphar home, but would then take Max on to his own home.

Liz peeked out of the litter to see Max trotting along next to them on the road. "Max, it appears our time is short. You will be heading on with the jailer from here," she said, saddened to know they would be apart for a time. Her thoughts turned to Kate and how she must feel right now.

"Aye, lass. I figured that were the case. How will we know wha's goin' on with each other then?" Max asked.

How indeed? Liz thought a moment and then gave a grin. "Nigel! Since he will come here to Potiphar's house, I will send word with him to you at the jail. I am certain Potiphar visits the jail, but I do not know if he would allow me to accompany him. But we will see, *mon ami.*"

"That's a gr-r-rand idea! That mousie kin be our go-between then. Good thing Al didn't finish him off in the market," Max replied. "I have a feelin' that wee beastie will help us in more ways than one."

"I agree. Do take care, Maximillian. And remember what Gillamon told you. You may not like this assignment at first, but be patient. It will be worth it," Liz encouraged.

"Aye, if Joseph is here with Potiphar, I dunnot know why I must be at the jail. Ah, well enough, time will tell," Max replied.

The servants stopped in front of the gate and set the litter on the ground. Potiphar stepped out, holding Liz in his arms, and turned to the jailer.

"Sadiki, I will come by the jail soon. Make sure all is well and report back to me of any new prisoners who arrive this week," Potiphar said.

The jailer bowed low before his master as he held on to Max's rope. "Yes, my master. We will await your inspection. I will ensure everything is in perfect order." Liz and Max shared a silent look of farewell.

"See that it is so," Potiphar replied as he turned to enter the massive gate. He was greeted by his chief house steward.

"My lord, it is good to have you home," the chief steward said, bowing respectfully before Potiphar. "Was your trip to the market successful?"

"Yes, yes, we found all we needed. I trust all is well here, Ako?" Potiphar inquired as he walked ahead of his servant into the sumptuous anteroom at the entrance of the house. He took a seat in the wicker chair just inside the room.

Ako clapped his hands and servants came scurrying over with a basin of water and towels to clean Potiphar's feet.

"Ako, this is Bastet. She will be an important member of my house. See that she is well attended," Potiphar said as he carefully stroked Liz's soft fur.

Liz's eyes were darting everywhere, admiring the incredible architecture of this home. But she turned her attention to Ako and stared intently into his face. She always liked to know whom she was dealing with.

Ako smiled and bent over to gaze at Liz. "Welcome, Bastet. I am your humble servant."

Liz blinked her eyes slowly in return, indicating she was pleased. "My lord, this is a special cat. I will see to her every need," Ako said, taking Liz into his arms as Potiphar handed her over.

The servant carrying Al in the basket entered the room, and bowed before Potiphar with arms raised to present Al to the master. "Ah, yes, this cat will be a gift for Pharaoh. Take care of him also. Prepare them both for the splendor of royalty," Potiphar said as he nodded to the servant.

Ako once again clapped his hands and a group of servants surrounded them. Mandisa was among them, and Ako called her over. "Mandisa, I charge you to prepare these cats for the glory of the houses of Pharaoh and Potiphar. Watch over them carefully."

Mandisa bowed and took Liz from Ako. "It will be as you say, my master." The servant holding Al joined Mandisa and together they left the room.

Potiphar leaned back in his chair as the servants gently cleaned and applied perfumed oil to his feet. "I purchased five slaves for the gardener. Get them clean, fed, and let them rest today. Their work will begin tomorrow at dawn. Tell the gardener I wish to see him after my dinner."

"As you say, my lord," Ako said. "Allow me to see to that task," he continued as he bowed low before Potiphar before returning to the front gate, where the slaves waited.

Potiphar waved Ako away, closed his eyes, and breathed in the fragrance of the oils.

"Did you bring anything back for me?" Zuleika said, walking up to Potiphar and rubbing his shoulders.

Potiphar smiled. "Don't I always, my dear?" He opened his eyes to see the beautiful woman before him. She was dressed in a white, crimped linen cloth with a strap off her right shoulder. Her eyes were almost black and adorned with makeup. Her long black hair was beautifully braided, and she wore a gold band across her forehead along with gold earrings, a thick gold necklace, and gold bracelets. "You look like a goddess."

Zuleika smiled and kissed Potiphar on the top of his head. "So you must treat me like one."

"Very well," Potiphar replied, clapping his hands for his servant to bring in the basket of gifts for his wife.

His servant quickly came and bowed low with the basket of goods. Potiphar leaned over and took out a linen-covered package. Zuleika bit her lip in anticipation. Potiphar leaned his head to the side, teasing her as he hesitated. He laughed and then handed it to her.

Zuleika eagerly took the gift from his hands and smiled while she unwrapped the cloth. Inside she found a beautiful, ornately carved comb in the shape of a kneeling ibex, and a mirror disk of highly polished copper, with a carved papyrus plant for the handle. "Oh, they are beautiful!" she shrieked.

Potiphar smiled. "You like, my dear?"

"I shall be even more beautiful with these gifts to help me,"

Zuleika said as she held the mirror to her face and studied her reflection.

Potiphar watched his wife as she looked into the mirror. He wondered what she saw. He saw her as beautiful, but his smile turned to a frown. She was spoiled, and he knew it. She was never satisfied for long with anything he brought her. He instructed the servant to slip on his sandals for him.

"Enjoy, Zuleika," Potiphar said as he stood and walked away from her into the vast entrance hall lined with carved, colorfully painted columns.

His wife barely paid Potiphar any mind as he walked away. She was too engrossed with her image in the mirror.

Ako walked down the line of slaves who stood outside the gate of Potiphar's house. He inspected each one, not saying a word as he looked them over carefully.

"Listen well, slaves. You now belong to Potiphar. Nothing but excellence is expected of you. You will be treated well, but you will work hard," Ako said as he studied the faces of these slaves to see if they understood him.

Joseph frowned, as he didn't know a word this man was saying. He looked over at Benipe, who understood him clearly, as he was an Egyptian. "Help me," Joseph muttered under his breath.

"What's that, slave?" Ako said as he walked up to Joseph.

Benipe looked at Ako and then at Joseph and realized he would have to help. "Master, please. This Semite does not know our tongue. Please allow me to translate."

"Very well," Ako said to Benipe, pleased that this young boy could be of use immediately.

Benipe nodded and turned to Joseph. "I will interpret for you, Joseph. He says we are to work hard but will be treated well."

Joseph looked at Ako and nodded respectfully. Ako replied with a nod.

"You will first be cleaned and fed, and then be allowed to rest, for tomorrow your work begins," Ako instructed, clapping his hands again for servants to take the slaves away.

Joseph and Benipe turned and followed the others as they walked under the massive gate. Joseph looked up to see the etchings in the gate. "Benipe, what is that symbol, the one with the hawk-headed figure and the round disk above his head?"

"That is our most beloved god, Ra. He is the sun god, the god of light, heat, and vitality. He is the god above all gods. He creates and destroys," Benipe replied.

Joseph stared at Ra as he passed under the etching. *The sun*, he thought, his mind drifting once again to his father. Joseph knew this was a pagan god, but as he entered the house of Potiphar and gazed up at the figures with outstretched wings surrounding Ra, he rested in the memory of his dreams, enveloping his mind with the embrace of his father, who he knew loved him still.

"My God, help me," Joseph prayed as he entered this strange new house. He was grateful to have Benipe as his friend and interpreter, and felt that the one, true God was watching over him. It was a relief to know he would be able to understand the instructions given to him as he slowly learned the language and ways of these Egyptians. He knew he would have to deal with their gods as well as their language. He thought again of what Benipe had said about Ra.

Time would tell if Joseph would be created or destroyed in the house of Potiphar.

CHAPTER 14

A Cat Fit for a King

"Watch the eyes, will ye lass!" Al fussed as the servant washed him in a deep stone bowl on the beautifully tiled floor.

Al looked utterly pitiful as he submitted to this human bath. He didn't think he looked so bad, but evidently the Egyptians thought differently. The servant proceeded to lift Al's arms and scrub him with a sweet-smelling oil, causing him to giggle uncontrollably. He never knew he was so ticklish. But he had never been touched much by humans, so this was a new experience in many ways.

Liz came walking across the cool tile floor and jumped onto a ledge above the bowl to watch this humorous scene. When the servant finally finished rinsing Al, she left him sitting in the water bowl while she went to retrieve more supplies. Al sat with one eye closed, water dripping from his whiskers, and appearing half his normal size now that he was soaked to the skin.

Al heard Liz chuckle and opened his eyes wide when he saw her sitting there above him. Never before had he seen her looking so beautiful.

"Liz, me black beauty! What have they done to ye? Ye look like a goddess," Al exclaimed.

"Merci, mon cher. I do believe that is the idea, no?" Liz said as she jumped down onto the floor next to him.

Her fur was shiny and soft from the special oils Mandisa had used in her bath. And she now had golden earrings, a golden collar, and tiny anklets also made of gold around her front paws. Al's jaw hung open as he looked at Liz, now just as adorned as the mistress of the household.

Al jumped as he saw the servant return with yet another bowl, but this one was filled with milk. "Look, me lass! They know how to treat a kitty right!" He thought this bowl of milk was for him to drink, but the servant picked Al up and put him in the bowl. "What kind o' daft idea is this, puttin' a kitty in milk?"

"Albert, the Egyptians know milk has excellent properties, good for the body on the outside as well as the inside," Liz explained, grinning. "But I'm sure you can drink some."

The servant started laughing as Al began to eagerly lap up the milk. He looked up, grinning ear to ear and sporting a milk mustache and goatee. "Liz, I'm beginnin' to think we got the easy part o' this assignment, bein' treated as gods an' all. I do like the way these Egyptians clean a kitty."

"Well, cleanliness is next to godliness, no?" Liz replied, smiling at Al. Liz couldn't get over the Egyptian obsession with cleanliness. Everything was clean—the rooms, the people, the clothes, and the animals. She was grateful her assignment was here, but frowned as she considered the filth of the prison that certainly awaited Max.

While Al enjoyed his milk bath, Liz looked around to study this lovely room. The floor was actually a tiled mural of the magnificent Nile River. Beautiful birds were shown hiding in the thickets of reeds and papyrus, with blue waters surrounding the lush vegetation. Schools of colorful fish swam in the deep waters, and hippos and crocodiles floated on the surface, peeking at the birds with mischievous eyes. The walls were painted with intricate geometric patterns in various shades of green, yellow, and blue. Miniature palms were placed around the beautiful tiled room, creating a luxurious paradise.

"Time to rinse and dry off," the servant girl said as she lifted Al from the milk. His claws grabbed the side of the bowl. He wasn't ready to get out. He tried to take a few more sips of milk as another servant poured water over him, rinsing off the milk before wrapping Al in soft linen cloth. The servant quickly dried the orange cat's fur, making Al wriggle and squirm. Finally she released the damp cat onto the floor. Al shook from head to tail, his orange, fluffy fur spread out in all directions.

"Albert, you too are a sight to behold," Liz laughed as the servant picked Al up to carry him into another room.

"Aye, I think it's me turn to get all decorated then," Al said, his ears flat and eyes looking a bit concerned as the servant walked away. He wasn't used to all this attention.

Mandisa came into the room and smiled when she saw Liz. "There you are, Bastet. I'm sure I will find you all over my master's house, as you have free rein here."

Liz stood with her tail in the air and meowed a *"bonjour"* as she walked over to Mandisa. She liked this servant girl, who squatted down to give her a good rub under her chin. Liz's jewelry clinked as Mandisa petted her. She would have to get used to this adornment.

"When your cat friend is finished we will give you both something to eat," Mandisa smiled and said, her dimples showing.

Perhaps you should have fed Albert before his bath, Liz thought to herself. She knew how much her husband relished dinnertime, sometimes wearing what he ate.

"Here we are. A cat fit for Pharaoh," the servant girl said, following Al into the room. It was all Liz could do to keep from bursting out laughing.

Al strutted into the room with his head held high and his tail stuck in the air. Across his chest hung a golden breastplate, carved with various hieroglyphs, and in his nose was a golden ring. He walked over to Liz and stopped, striking an Egyptian sideways pose so she could appreciate his splendor.

"Oh, Albert, you look very royal, no? You even look like a noble, famous warrior with that breastplate," Liz said as she nudged Al with her nose.

"Ah, thanks, me love. I have to say I feel pretty special," Al said wriggling his nose and looking cross-eyed at the gold ring. "But how in Pete's name am I supposed to eat with this thing?"

"I believe we will find that out right now," Liz replied.

Al's ears perked up. "Ye mean we get to eat now?"

"Oui, my servant said we would do so when you were ready," Liz replied.

"If the Egyptian food is anythin' like the Egyptian bath, I know I'll be one happy kitty!" Al exclaimed.

Mandisa clapped her hands. "Oh, he looks wonderful! My master will be so pleased."

Al continued to strut as he and Liz followed Mandisa and the other servant down the corridor to the room where bountiful food was laid out for the cats. There before them was a low table full of more bowls of milk, fresh fish from the Nile, figs, and soft-cooked vegetables.

"I could get used to this," Al said, his mouth drooling.

Liz stopped Al with her paw before he pounced onto the table. "Albert, if you are going to dine in palaces, you must use manners pleasing to kings."

Al frowned. "Aye, I guess ye're right, lass." He walked over to the fish and gently picked it up to nibble in his mouth. He wasn't used to being so prim and proper but figured he'd better learn. He wriggled his nose as he chewed the fish. This nose ring would take some getting used to.

Potiphar entered the room and smiled as he saw Bastet and the orange cat all clean, adorned, and enjoying their food. "Well done," Potiphar said to Mandisa and the other servant, both of whom stood at attention behind the table. Liz looked up and smiled at Potiphar.

"Bastet, you are even more beautiful now," Potiphar said, reaching down to softly pet Liz. "And your friend here will certainly please Pharaoh when I take him tomorrow." He turned to his servant. "Mandisa, please make sure Bastet has a nice place to sleep and be prepared to bring me the orange cat in the morning. I will go to Pharaoh once my slaves begin their work in the garden."

With that, Potiphar left the room as the servants bowed in respect. Liz and Al looked at each other with heavy hearts. This would be the last night for them to be together under one roof for years to come. Gillamon had said they would see each other from time to time, but both realized they would still be apart more than they had ever been.

Al stopped eating. Liz knew he wasn't full since he had only taken a few bites of fish. "Albert, are you well?" Liz asked.

"Aye, lass, I'm well in me belly, jest not in me heart at the thought o' tellin' ye good-bye," Al said with his lip quivering. "I lost me appetite."

Tears filled Liz's eyes as she put her dainty paw up to Al's cheek. "How will I ever live without my precious Albert?"

If Liz had ever had any doubts of Al's love for her, there certainly was no room for such doubt now. When it came to Liz, Al's heart trumped his stomach.

CHAPTER 15

Potiphar's Vineyard

Benipe woke as he heard the slavemaster clapping his hands to wake the group of slaves in their quarters on the south end of Potiphar's complex. He rubbed his eyes and yawned. He didn't remember the last time he had gotten so much sleep.

Their first night in the house of Potiphar had been a quiet one for the new slaves. They were all bathed, given clean loincloths, and fed a decent meal before being told to go to sleep early. Benipe had to admit Joseph was right about the way a man such as Potiphar treated his slaves. If he had to be a slave, better here than in the harsh existence of the copper mines east of the Nile in the desert of Sinai.

Benipe looked over at Joseph's mat, but he wasn't there. Alarmed, the young boy sat up quickly and called out to his friend, "Joseph?" When he didn't hear a reply, he got up and walked around the dimly lit room until he found Joseph kneeling in a darkened corner.

"Joseph? Are you okay?" Benipe asked.

Joseph's head was bowed. Slowly he raised his head and turned to see Benipe. "I'm fine," he said with a smile.

"What were you doing?" the young boy asked.

"Praying," Joseph answered. "I'm grateful to be off the caravan and in a place where I can pray in quiet."

"Did your God tell you why you're here? Did he say how long you would be a slave?" Benipe asked sarcastically.

Joseph placed his hands on the shoulders of his doubting friend. "My God doesn't need to give me answers to all my questions. He has assured me He is here with me in this place. That is enough."

Benipe looked down and nodded. "If you say so, Joseph. But if you ever get around to it, can you ask your God to get us out of here?"

Joseph chuckled, "Well, I'd start getting used to the idea of being here awhile if I were you."

The slavemaster clapped his hands and all the slaves quickly lined up in a row. Ako came into the room and stood in front of them. "I am expecting much from you new slaves today. In his wisdom, Potiphar granted you rest and renewal before you begin his work. Do not expect such ease of living unearned in the future. Work hard and you will earn moments of leisure. Work lazily, and you will earn the hard rod of my master on your back. Come, it is time to begin."

Potiphar watched Zuleika as she combed her silky black hair with the comb he had brought her from the market. "You look beautiful, wife."

Zuleika turned and smiled at Potiphar. "And I hope to share my beauty with you all day, my love."

"I have to be in Pharaoh's court all day, you know that," Potiphar replied, standing still as his servant tied the wide jeweled collar around his neck, and handed him his headdress.

Zuleika frowned and picked up her mirror to gaze at herself. "Fine."

"My absence is the price you pay for the privilege of being married to a powerful man of Pharaoh," Potiphar replied as he leaned over to kiss his wife on the head. "I will see you this evening. I'm sure Mandisa can find something fun for you to do."

Potiphar walked away from their bedchamber and out to the breezeway where Mandisa waited, holding Al. She bowed and said, "Pharaoh's cat is ready for you, my master."

Liz was curled around Mandisa's feet and meowed at Potiphar. "Good morning, Bastet," he said as he picked Liz up and scratched her under the chin. "Come with me as I inspect our new slaves. I will show you the garden where they will be working."

"C'est bon!" Liz meowed. "Albert, did you hear this? Joseph will be working in the garden. If there was ever a place I could most assist Joseph, it is a garden!"

"I'm happy for ye, lass," Al said. "I know it makes yer heart glad to be back in a garden."

Liz peered at Al over Potiphar's shoulder as they walked down the breezeway. Al looked so sad sitting in Mandisa's arms. She knew he had never fully forgiven himself for destroying her garden so long ago, even though that act had enabled Liz to willingly leave her garden behind to travel to the Ark. But she also realized that, while she was excited about her assignment, Al had no idea what awaited him at Pharaoh's palace other than being apart from his love.

"Albert, I know the Maker will have something just as rewarding for you to do for Pharaoh. And somehow I know we will see each other soon," Liz said softly.

Al looked up and smiled his goofy grin. "I know ye're right, me love."

Mandisa stopped at the doorway while Potiphar proceeded outside. She would wait here until he was ready to depart. Liz and Al shared a final glance as Liz blew him a kiss and called with her paw up to her mouth, *"Adieu,* my dear Albert. *Je t'aime!"*

"Farewell, me love," Al said, returning the blown kiss.

The heat hit Liz's face as they stepped outside into the hot Egyptian sunshine. Potiphar saw the slavemaster, the gardener, Ako, and the slaves lined up in the center of the courtyard, awaiting his orders. He strode up to them, putting Liz down as he reached the group. He walked up and down the slaves, inspecting them once more as he had done in the market.

"Today you begin a project that will be the centerpiece of my estate, and will someday serve Pharaoh from its bounty. I expect my vineyard to not only produce the finest grapes, but to be the most beautiful display of any garden in Avaris," Potiphar explained. "In three months I will host the harvest celebration in this garden, and I expect the dignitaries and officials who attend to be astounded by what they see here."

Potiphar motioned for the gardener to pick up one of the hundreds of clay pots holding a grapevine. The gardener quickly obliged, holding the pot for his master. Potiphar placed his fingers on the vine and said, "From this plant you will grow my vineyard. See that it is so."

"It will be done as you say, my master," the gardener said with a low bow. Joseph followed suit and bowed as well, followed by the other slaves.

Potiphar noticed how quickly Joseph showed him respect without being told to do so, and nodded his approval before turning to leave. Ako quickly followed Potiphar out of the courtyard to see him off, clapping his hands for the servants to make ready his master's litter.

"You have heard the charge by our master, Potiphar," the gardener said to the slaves. "The fruit of your labor will be proof of your worth here. I have drawn up plans for this vineyard. Once the soil is prepared, you will build a network of trellises across the garden for the grapevines according to my design. This vineyard will require extensive watering each day, as well as daily training of the vines to grow along the trellis system."

Liz sat listening to the gardener, eager to learn his master plan for this vineyard. So far it sounded reasonable, but she was curious as to how he would construct the trellises. She took her paw and scraped the soil to inspect it for proper conditioning. *Good,* she thought, *it appears there is a good mix of dirt, clay, and sand.* Liz dug around a little deeper. *Of course, the addition of peat would greatly improve this soil. Oh, a rock,* she thought as she flipped over a stone. *All rocks must be removed.* She then snapped out her paw to shake off the soil before licking it clean. Liz then noticed Joseph staring at her.

Joseph had been watching Liz for a moment as she gazed up at the gardener. He smiled. *It looks like this cat is actually listening. How curious!* Joseph thought. But then he saw her digging in the soil. *Hmmmm, we need to make sure the soil is a good mix of dirt, clay, and sand,* he thought to himself. *Better remove all the rocks as well.* Although he had limited knowledge of gardening, having lived in the rugged, rocky land of Canaan, he knew nothing could grow without healthy soil.

"The creation of this vineyard begins with breaking the earth," the gardener said, taking a plow and slamming it into the ground. He then handed the plow to Joseph.

Liz watched Joseph as he took the plow and began the process of repeatedly striking the earth. His first task in the house of Potiphar had begun. She breathed a silent prayer of protection over Al as he departed for Pharaoh's palace, and also gratitude to the Maker for allowing her to remain here to help Joseph in the garden. Somehow from this hard place in Egypt, Joseph's path would lead to the birth of a new nation. She thought of the hardships he had endured so far, and wondered what was to come.

Ah, oui, the gardener is right, Liz thought to herself. *Growth of living things first comes from that which is broken.*

CHAPTER 16

Hapy in the Palace

Potiphar looked across the seat at Al, who was attempting to sit upright but was continually jostled about with the movement of the servants carrying the litter. Al kept sliding down the silky fabric. He finally allowed himself to sit in a slouched position with his back legs turned out and his belly exposed while his front paws propped his back up against the seat. This truly was a humorous animal and Potiphar couldn't help but chuckle at him.

"Don't worry . . . well, I don't have a name to call you . . . but Pharaoh will soon give you a name. We will be at the palace soon," Potiphar said.

Al meowed back, *Well that's a good thing, laddie, for I dunnot know how long I can keep from slidin' off this seat.*

Potiphar smiled. Between Bastet and this orange cat, he was amazed at how "talkative" they were with their meowing. *If only they could understand what I was saying,* he thought to himself.

Al gazed out of the window of the litter as they traveled down the dusty road from Potiphar's house to Pharaoh's palace and saw rows of big sycomore fig trees laden with fruit. His mouth watered. They turned right onto a long pathway lined on either side with enormous twenty-foot statues of Pharaoh sitting on thrones. Each statue sat with a regal pose, one hand resting on the thigh while the other hand held a folded cloth of some kind. The feet of each statue were barefoot and rested on a pedestal. Pharaoh was shown with a false, long rectangular beard and wearing a nemes headcloth squared off behind the ears and draped over the shoulders. Al looked at the face of each statue, all of which were identical.

Looks like a nice enough laddie, Al thought. *A bit on the skinny side, though. I hope he eats enough then.*

"You see, we are here already. I live very close to Pharaoh," Potiphar said as the servants stopped in front of the gate at the palace. Al grinned his goofy grin at the happy thought that he would not be living far from Liz.

The servants carefully placed the litter on the ground as the gate opened. Potiphar lifted Al and stepped out into the hot sun as they walked through the massive gate adorned with carvings of Pharaoh shown as a master hunter in his chariot. The colors painted all over the gate and the supporting columns were incredible. Deep blues and reds, golds, and greens made the images seem to come to life as Al looked up at them. Soon he and Potiphar stood at the base of an enormous stone staircase leading up into the palace. Guards lined the staircase, holding spears and looking straight ahead, clearly not distracted by anything. Yet as Potiphar walked by, the guards snapped to attention, holding their spears out in front of them as a sign of respect.

Potiphar strode confidently up the stone block steps while a servant and a scribe walked respectfully behind. Clearly, he was not intimidated by the entrance to the palace. Two palace guards slowly opened the tall, hammered gold doors covered with images of the gods Ra and Horus. This place felt powerful and pagan. Al gulped. Potiphar might not be intimidated—but Al was scared to death.

They soon observed servants who lined the granite columns along the corridor. Al studied the painted images covering the walls. They were all hunting scenes. One was of a group of servants in a papyrus boat throwing their spears into the water at a large hippopotamus while Pharaoh pointed to their prey. Another scene showed Pharaoh with a bow and arrow, pointing at a fleeing herd of gazelles. On and on it went, and Al soon realized the man he would be given to enjoyed the hunt.

But Al then saw scenes from sporting events. There were scenes of rowing, wrestling, fishing, boxing, and floor exercises. *No wonder the lad is so skinny,* Al thought. *He hunts an' exercises. I wonder if there be flamingo beasties here.* Al always enjoyed 'flamingorobics' on the Ark, but his justification for eating more for breakfast after his workout kept him pleasingly plump.

One of Pharaoh's court servants bowed and greeted Potiphar, "Good morning, my master."

"Assemble the court," Potiphar directed.

"It will be done as you say. Pharaoh has just returned from the hunt and is bathing. He will be here shortly," the servant said as he followed Potiphar into a majestic room covered with more scenes of chariots, gods, and hunting.

Light poured into the room from the high windows down to the luxuriant indoor plants surrounding the throne. Miniature palms and broad-leafed greenery made it feel like an oasis. Columns were painted with papyrus and lotus plants. The beauty and coolness of this room was astounding. And in the center of the room were steps leading to a golden throne.

Al smiled with his first glance at the base of the throne, which was carved with lion claws for feet and lion heads on the armrests. The sides of the golden throne were draped with carvings of the winged goddess Ma'at and images of the sun disk lined the back of the headrest. Rows of precious jewels bordered the frame of the throne. Carved cartouches—oval outlines containing hieroglyphs—spelled out the birth name and throne name of this Pharaoh. Al's smile faded as his gaze drifted to the top of the throne, where he saw two upright spitting cobra figures, or uraei. The uraeus was the symbol of the Egyptian goddess Wadjet, patron of the Nile and protector of the land of Lower Egypt. This cobra figure was the emblem of Pharaoh for his divinely appointed power to protect Egypt. Al shuddered to see cobras towering over the throne. It made him think of Charlatan, the snake who had struck Liz and Max. Al looked away and started shaking.

Potiphar felt Al shivering and held him close to his large chest, stroking his fur. Al crawled up onto Potiphar's shoulder and snuggled there. "Nothing to be afraid of. You will be treated well here," the royal official reassured the frightened feline.

Potiphar nodded to the servant, who then clapped his hands. In walked a stream of servants carrying trays laden with delicious food and pitchers of wine. Al's ears perked up and he stopped shaking. Following the food-bearing servants came the court musicians, carrying harps, small drums, and flutes. They sat on the side of the room and began to play soothing music. Next entered Pharaoh's officials and advisors.

Potiphar stood at the grand hall entrance and loudly announced, "Enter Pharaoh, powerful ruler of Egypt, son of Ra and the embodiment of Horus."

Everyone assembled there lowered his gaze and bowed as Pharaoh entered the room. Al was the only one who dared look at him.

Pharaoh strode in with arms crossed over his chest. He was carrying two scepters: the crook, a small cane with a hooked handle, gold-plated with blue copper bands and the flail, a rod with three strands of blue and golden beads. On his head he wore a blue-and-gold-striped nemes headdress with two large flaps that hung behind his ears and in front of his shoulders. On the top of the headdress was the uraeus, found only on the headdress of Pharaoh. He wore an ornately decorated loincloth with a golden lion's tail attached. Al chuckled as he watched Pharaoh's decorative tail swish from side to side as he walked. *Will ye look at that? This king wishes he were part kitty then!* Al thought to himself. He was feeling a little better. *Pharaoh may have a snake on his head, but he wears the tail of a lion. So he can't be all bad.*

Pharaoh walked up the steps leading to his throne, turned and sat down, placing his muscular arms on the rests. His sun-kissed skin was glowing from oils and his eyes were outlined with black kohl. He wore golden cuffs on his upper arms, an ornate necklace around his neck, and rings on his fingers. For a man in his mid-forties, he was in excellent shape. "Potiphar, what have you there? Come."

Potiphar rose and lifted his gaze as he slowly walked to stand before Pharaoh. "A gift for you, my master. I purchased a cat who would not allow me to leave the market unless I also bought this orange feline. He is larger than my cat and quite humorous. I know he will amuse Pharaoh," Potiphar replied, holding Al out for Pharaoh to see.

Al nervously waited to see what this powerful man would do. Pharaoh held his scepters out to the side and two servants hurriedly came to his throne with golden trays to hold the crook and the flail for him. Pharaoh stood to take Al from Potiphar's hands.

"He is a stocky feline, good and healthy," Pharaoh said as he lifted Al to inspect his girth. "He must enjoy the bounty of Egypt that springs from the Nile."

"If I may, my master, the black cat I purchased appeared to me as perhaps Bastet come to guide me. And she did lead me to select some excellent slaves. As this orange cat clearly enjoys the bounty of the Nile, perhaps he is the form of the god Hapy come to give your kingdom success in its crops from the flooding Nile?" Potiphar suggested.

Pharaoh smiled and looked Al in the eye. "Is this so? Are you Hapy?"

Al didn't quite know what to say. *Aye, I guess I could be happy,* he meowed. *That is, if ye feed me some o' that fish I see on the tray.*

Al was clueless that Pharaoh wasn't asking about his emotional state, but if he were the form of the Egyptian god Hapy, always portrayed with a plump belly and carrying offerings of food. Each year the Nile flood brought vital water and nutrient-rich soil for the crops the people depended on for food. The Egyptians did not know how the Nile flooded each year, but they did believe that Hapy was in charge of the process. If the Nile was too high, the excess flood could wash away homes. If the Nile was too low, Egypt could face a drought without sufficient water for the fields and cattle. So Hapy could be a destructive power, but also one that worked for Pharaoh. Little did Pharaoh know that at that very moment, he held in his hands a destructive power—Al in hunger mode.

Pharaoh laughed at this meowing cat. "What a remarkable beast! It's as if he answered me! Very well! Hapy you will be." He sat down holding Al in his lap. "You have my favor, Potiphar."

Potiphar gratefully bowed and smiled. *Bastet's insistence on buying the orange cat has given me favor with Pharaoh,* he thought. *I'll be sure to ever heed the direction of that black cat.*

"Tell me the progress of my new chariot," Pharaoh instructed. "The ibex outran me today, and next time I chase them I wish to *catch* them."

Pharaoh had given the command for an improved wheel system in his chariot. He used his chariot in war, but as things were quiet now and Egypt was at peace, he used his chariot primarily for hunting. He wanted the design to be fast and lightweight.

Potiphar nodded for the weaponry chief to answer Pharaoh. "My master, the wheelwrights have worked on a two-spoked wheeled chariot with leather tires. The craftsmen have also made a stronger draft pole for the chassis to link with the yoke on your horses. It will be ready to test within the week. Please allow my specialist craftsmen time to decorate and paint my master's chariot to match the glory of his name."

Pharaoh was pleased. "Very well, I will use it on the hunt next week. Potiphar, bring that jailer of yours and come on the hunt. I'm told he has an eye for ibex."

"It will be as you say, Pharaoh," Potiphar said, bowing in agreement.

"Now, what is the prediction of the harvest?" Pharaoh asked as he stroked Al, who sat on his lap.

I'm not very happy yet, Al thought, looking longingly over at the food while swishing his tail.

Potiphar looked to the line of advisors and nodded for the granary scribe to make his report. The scribe quickly walked to the throne and unrolled a papyrus scroll. "My master, last year the flood brought ample amounts of silt for fertile farming. Although the harvest will not start until next month, crop reports show a healthy supply throughout the land. It will be a good year, my master."

Pharaoh nodded and stroked Al. "With Hapy's entrance into my palace comes a good report from the fields. The favor of the gods is upon me and Egypt. Bring my cup."

The cupbearer filled Pharaoh's cup with wine, sampled it, and brought it over to his throne, bowing and holding up his hands to offer the ornate cup to his master. Pharaoh took the cup and lifted it, saying, "And now we will pay tribute to Hapy for blessing our crops. May the land of Egypt never cease to have plenty."

Potiphar nodded to the chief baker, who clapped his hands for the servants bearing food to surround the throne. Al was drooling as the smell of fish came wafting through the air. He couldn't stand it anymore. He sat up and lifted his paw out toward the tray of fish, almost knocking it over as he swiped at it.

Pharaoh laughed and placed Al on the floor. "See to it Hapy eats his fill."

A servant placed a golden plate of fish on the floor and Al proceeded to eagerly devour it. He was careful to mind his manners as Liz had instructed. He looked around at everyone gazing at him. Yes, this was a strange place, and some parts of it were scary. Al felt uncomfortable in his spirit with all the false gods on the walls, on the throne, and constantly mentioned by everyone in Pharaoh's court. And he didn't know what he was supposed to be doing here as part of the mission to help Joseph. But he figured the Maker would make that clear with time.

Al swallowed the fish and grinned from ear to ear. *I'm feeling happier,* he thought. He had food and was relieved to know the palace of Pharaoh was less than a mile from Potiphar's house. Yes, this assignment seemed pretty simple so far. He was clean, adorned, fed, and already adored. *I could get used to this,* Al thought as he took another bite of fish. For now anyway, he would just play along in his role as Pharaoh's happy cat as instructed.

He was, after all, supposed to be happy in the palace.

CHAPTER 17

The Prison

The air was so stale Max could hardly breathe. Being short and low to the ground, he was close to the dank, musty smell that oozed from the floors of the prison. This dungeon was little more than a hole where undesirable humans were tossed. There was no sunlight, no fresh air, and from the deplorable state of things, no hope for anything good to come out of this place.

Max sat in a corner with his head resting on his paws, listening to the sounds of groaning prisoners. Some were coughing and some were moaning and curled up on the floor. All of them were shackled, hungry, and filthy. The jailer, Sadiki, had brought Max here for the first time this morning. They had spent last night at Sadiki's home, which was a modest little place consisting of a roof, two rooms, a bed, and a rough wooden table and two chairs. But it was a palace compared with the prison.

Sadiki was gruff, but so far had treated Max well, naming him "Jabari." He obviously was a hunter, as wild game skins covered his floors and his bed. He lived alone and seemed to welcome Max as a companion. From what Max could tell, Sadiki expected him to hunt for rats that crept around the prison. While Max relished the chance to chase pests, the thought of doing so in this place and not in the wide-open fields left him feeling depressed. Max gave a slow, heavy sigh.

"Why the long face, old boy?" Max heard a familiar voice say from behind.

"Mousie!" Max jumped up and smiled to see Nigel standing there on his hind legs, holding a tiny papyrus scroll. "'Tis gr-r-rand ta see ye, laddie. Do ye r-r-really need ta ask aboot the long face? Just *look* where I am."

"Yes, it's quite dreadful, isn't it? Dregs of humanity cast aside in the bowels of the earth and all that," Nigel said as he looked around at the prison. "See here, I've come to offer my assistance, so chin up!"

"An' jest how is a mouse supposed ta help me then?" Max asked skeptically.

Nigel chuckled and unrolled the papyrus. "By giving you the lay of the land." Max cocked his head to the side, not following where Nigel was going. "I've been all over Avaris and know the ins and outs of every building here. I've mapped out the city and have it drawn to scale," Nigel said, squinting as he pointed to the map. He looked up to see if there was a better source of light than the dim torch on the wall above them. "Blast these eyes and this dim light."

"Kin ye not see well, Mousie?" Max asked, gazing over Nigel's shoulder at the little map.

"From my years of studying hieroglyphs in the pyramids and temples, drawing intricate architectural designs, and enduring the sand constantly blowing in my eyes, I'm afraid my sight is not what it used to be," Nigel said, rubbing his eyes before leaning down again to squint at the map.

"Sorry aboot that, Mousie. Is there anythin' ye kin do aboot yer eyes?" Max wondered.

"I'm afraid not. Just keep using them until they give out, I suppose," Nigel replied. He waved his hand to dismiss the matter. "See here, allow me to show you the map of Avaris. You are here, in the prison. Pharaoh's palace is here, and Potiphar's house there." Nigel pointed to each building.

"Ye don't say! Well, I'll be! Liz, Al, an' me aren't far apart at all then. That's a r-r-relief," Max said.

"Not only that, but there is an underground tunnel running between the prison and Pharaoh's palace," Nigel said excitedly. "Evidently it was used to secretly move prisoners from the palace to the jail but has long been abandoned and blocked off as the palace was expanded."

"Ye mean I kin travel through the tunnel ta reach the palace?" Max asked.

"Well, the barrier hasn't been a problem for me, but I am rather small. It may take a bit of moving some debris, but I believe you could make your way through," Nigel suggested.

"That's gr-r-rand news, laddie!" Max exclaimed, wagging his tail. "I kin see Al." Just the thought of not being isolated in this place was a relief. And to know he could keep a watch out for Al's movements was a good thing.

"Right. So you see, old chap, things aren't always as bad as they may seem," Nigel said with a smile. "Have you learned anything about your mission here and how this will assist the Joseph fellow?"

Max shook his head. "No, it doesn't make much sense. All I know is the jailer named me 'Jabari' an' I'm supposed ta keep the beasties in order here in the prison. Why I'm here an' Al is with Pharaoh I jest dunnot understand. At least the kitty lass is with Joseph at Potiphar's house."

"Splendid! Well, I must say the jailer named you appropriately, although being of little mind I'm sure he just gave you a name in keeping with his hunting mentality," Nigel quipped.

"Wha' does Jabari mean?" Max wanted to know.

"Brave," Nigel replied. "And from what I understand, you wear that title well."

"Aye! It's me middle name. But I don't think I'll need ta be very br-r-rave here in this prison with jest r-r-rats ta r-r-round up then," Max replied.

"But my dear boy, rats are not the only vermin to dwell in the prison. Snakes slither in here occasionally, too. The asp is such a nasty beast, and quite deadly, I assure you," Nigel said with a tone of seriousness. "And if you wish to pass through the tunnel leading to Pharaoh's palace, you most certainly will find them there."

A frown grew on Max's face. "Then I will need ta be on me guard. I know wha' it's like ta tangle with snakes."

"Right. Well, I know a fine canine such as yourself is up to the challenge," Nigel said. "Now see here, I will serve as communicator between you, Liz, and Al, as I can easily move about."

"Aye, Liz already said she'd be usin' ye ta be a messenger then," Max replied.

"Did she now? I must say I'm quite impressed with our French lady. Quite the smart one, and I'm thrilled with her interest in Egyptian culture and writing," Nigel said.

Max grinned. "If ye only knew how that lass has got us out of scrapes. She's a brainy kitty, but it's nice ta see she's met her match in a wee beastie like you. She'll have ta be the student instead of the teacher for a change."

"Right! I shall do my best. Hold down the fort here and I shall return posthaste with a report from your colleagues," Nigel said as he bowed low in respect.

"Thanks, Mousie. Before ye leave, where's that loud camel? Were ye able ta get him out of the market?" Max asked.

Nigel gave a jolly chuckle. "I wish you could have been there to see it, dear boy! I nibbled off the rope the traders used to tie Osahar. I sat atop his ears and with a grand blast of that beast's spit wad onto the traders, I yelled for him to charge through the market. He took off running, shouting 'I'M FREE! I'M FREE! I'M FREE!' and knocked over the traders' tables as we blazed by. They chased us, shaking their fists in the air, but we escaped into the desert. 'Twas quite the invigorating experience, I must say!" Nigel exclaimed. "Osahar dropped me off on the outskirts of the city and will hide by day near the tall brush of the Nile."

"I'm sure it were a funny scene, an' it's grand that ye an' the beast kin help each other then," Max said, looking over at a prisoner who groaned. He frowned. "I'm sure these prisoners wish they could shout the same words Osahar did as ye escaped."

"For the prisoners of Pharaoh, that is a doubtful outcome, I'm afraid. Once a prisoner is brought here, they usually end up dead either from prison life or by order of the chief executioner, Potiphar," Nigel somberly explained. "Freedom from this place is rare indeed. But remember, if a prisoner is in this place, it is by his own doing. He either broke the law or threatened Pharaoh's power structure, which in the end would lead to chaos in Egypt. So while it is sad for these humans, their choices led them here."

"Then why in the world am *I* here, Mousie? Wha' could possibly be me purpose in the prison?" Max asked with a frown.

Nigel placed his small hand on Max's shoulder. "I don't know, Max, but I believe the Maker does. Chin up then. Stay the course until I return," Nigel said before turning to leave. He then stopped and said, "Sometimes bravery is needed most for simply waiting in dark places."

With that, Nigel scurried off into the darkness, leaving Max alone once more in the prison. Max sighed again and placed his head on his paws as before. Nigel had given him much to think about. There were positive things, such as communicating with and being able to see Al and Liz, but there were also threats Max had not considered.

Snakes. Max shuddered as he remembered the words Charlatan the snake had screamed as he was thrown into the abyss after fatally striking Max and Liz after the Ark had landed: "You'll never defeat me. I'll . . . never ssssstop."

Max felt it deep in his bones—just as deep as the despair hanging in the air of this prison, and as deep as the false gods were enmeshed in the palace of Pharaoh himself.

Charlatan was here in Egypt.

CHAPTER 18

Rock, Papyrus, Scissors

Give me a hand with this basket of rocks, Benipe," Joseph called. He wiped the sweat from his eyes as he waited for his friend to come over to help. The sun was high and beating down on them.

Benipe and Joseph grabbed the sides of the basket and together they heaved and carried the heavy load over to the pathway of the vineyard. "These rocks are a pain," Benipe complained.

"Actually, I have an idea to use them," Joseph replied.

"For what? To stone our slavemaster when he isn't looking?" Benipe asked with a diabolical laugh.

Joseph frowned. "I'm just going to pretend you didn't say that. Do you know how quickly you'd be thrown into prison if you so much as held a single rock and glared at the slavemaster?"

Benipe nodded. "Okay, okay, I get it."

"Look, work with me here. Let's make the best of this. Maybe you can learn some new skills to use for yourself someday," Joseph said. "All right, I figure we can use these rocks to line the pathways of the garden. Not only will it make the garden look sharp, it will act as a barrier to hold the dirt."

"Whatever you say," Benipe said. "Sounds like a good idea."

"But *of course* it's a good idea," Liz said as she sat on a bench next to where Joseph and Benipe worked, curling her tail up and down. She had stayed close by Joseph all morning, observing his every move.

Just then the gardener walked over and saw Joseph and Benipe lining the path with the rocks. "You there, what are you doing?" he asked.

Benipe answered for them. "Joseph had an idea to use the rocks discarded from the soil to line the pathways. It's a way to dispose of them while improving the look of the garden."

The gardener raised his eyebrows and nodded in approval. "Very well, but do it quickly. I want at least half the vines planted today. Carry on."

"What did he say?" Joseph asked.

"He said to do it quickly, and that he wanted half the vines planted today," Benipe answered and then jabbed Joseph, smiling. "Okay, your turn to learn some skills to use for yourself someday." As he and Joseph worked, Benipe proceeded to teach Joseph the basics of the Egyptian language. Liz listened to every word, as she, too, wanted to better understand the language.

"Learning anything, my dear?" Nigel said as he jumped up onto the bench with Liz.

"Bonjour, Nigel!" exclaimed Liz. "I am so pleased to see you."

"Likewise, my lady," Nigel said as he kissed Liz's outstretched paw. "I have just come from the prison, where Max is to assist the jailer. He is quite dejected as to his post, but I assured him I will act as messenger to keep him apprised of things."

"Ah, *oui,* I am sorry he is in such a bad place, but I know the Maker has a purpose for this," Liz replied.

"I also shared with him that the palace and the prison are connected by an underground tunnel. And you will be happy to learn your beloved is living less than a mile from here," Nigel explained, showing Liz the same map he had shown Max.

"C'est bon! What good news!" Liz cried as she studied the tiny map, her paw gently feeling the papyrus. "Nigel, this map is extraordinary. I saw you reading the scrolls in the market made of this . . . this . . ."

"*Papyrus,* my dear. It is a magnificent Egyptian invention and is woven from the beaten reeds of the papyrus plant that grows along the Nile. The reedy plant is also the symbol for Lower Egypt, and you will find it painted and carved in houses, temples, and pyramids," Nigel explained.

"Ah! I have seen this on the columns in Potiphar's house. Tell me, how did papyrus get its name?" Liz asked.

"Splendid question! The very name of the plant indicates its importance, as it derives from 'pa-en-per-aa' meaning 'belonging to the pharaoh.' You see, the king has the sole right to make and sell papyrus for writing materials, and he sells it to neighboring countries far and wide—at a great profit, I assure you. The scribes of Egypt always carry their papyrus, reeds, and ink, and are among the most important workers in the land. These Egyptians write and record *everything* that happens, from the harvest reports to religious texts to Pharaoh's list of prisoners," Nigel detailed.

"So from the Nile comes a reed that brings wealth to Pharaoh and status to the scribes. But how did you make such a small piece of papyrus for your map?" Liz asked as she studied Nigel's map.

"With another splendid Egyptian invention called *scissors*. As I understand it, this cutting instrument has been in Egypt for the past one hundred years or so, and is perfect for cutting papyrus into mouse-sized documents," Nigel said with a grin. "Humans should be very appreciative of all the Egyptians have invented. And I find the development of their written word to be among their greatest achievements."

Liz sat and just studied Nigel for a moment, appreciating his vast knowledge of this incredible culture. "Nigel, what made you leave Wales to come study in Egypt for all these years? Don't you have a family back home?"

"I've always been a bit of an adventurer, my dear. The mysteries of Egypt drew me here as a young mouse and I never returned home. I'm sure my family has grown while I've been away," Nigel said with a sigh. "But I'm afraid my research here became my first love and my family. I suppose I'll always be the archaeologist bachelor mouse that I am. I hope to return to Wales someday. I do miss the greenery, you know."

"Well I am glad we met, and I am glad you are here now," Liz replied with her shy smile. "Nigel, allow me to be your student, *s'il vous plaît.* Will you teach me this language and all things Egyptian?"

"It will be my honor, *Madame,*" Nigel said with a low bow. "And perhaps you can teach me about all this gardening rot. I'm afraid gardening was never my strong suit. Never had the green thumb and all that, you know," Nigel said as he watched Joseph lift a clay jar to remove a vine. "I see that Joseph has begun his work here. How goes it?"

"Quite well. But I do wish peat existed in Egypt to help with the soil. It could make a great difference in the quality of the nutrients for the vines," Liz remarked.

"Peat?"

"Very well, Nigel, here is your first gardening lesson," Liz said with her coy smile. "You see, peat forms when plants located in marshy areas do not fully decay due to acids and lack of air circulation. Peat is made mostly of marshland vegetation such as trees, grasses, fungi, and other organic remains, such as insects and the like. I would think with the richness of the Nile we could find a close substitute along its banks," Liz said, always excited to discuss the intricate details of gardening.

"Care to take a walk by the Nile to continue both our lessons?" Nigel suggested. "I will show you the papyrus, and you can show me something on the order of peat."

"Allons-y! Let's go! The more I know about Egypt, the more I can help Joseph," Liz replied, jumping to the ground as Nigel followed.

As Joseph dug a hole to plant the vine, he threw dirt behind him. It landed all over Nigel.

"Alas, but gardening is such dirty business," Nigel said as he wiped the dirt off his long whiskers.

It was late in the evening when Potiphar returned home, and he asked to be left alone as he walked in the haven of his garden. He needed to unwind from his busy day at the palace, and he enjoyed the beauty his garden offered. He also wanted to see the progress of his vineyard.

A gentle breeze blew as Potiphar walked the garden path. Everyone had left for the day, including the gardener. The slave-master and all the slaves were back in their quarters, exhausted from their work. All except Joseph.

Potiphar stopped to study the rocks lining the pathway next to where Joseph worked. "You, slave. What are you doing out here so late?"

Joseph wiped the dirt off his hands as he stood to bow before Potiphar. He understood a few of Potiphar's words, as Benipe had given him quite a lesson in the Egyptian tongue. "My master, you say the . . . the vines . . . to plant today. I . . . wove—no, I wish—be sure it done as you say."

Potiphar raised his eyebrows as he listened to Joseph. "You are a quick learner. You do not know our tongue yet you speak it to me after only a day in my house. What is your name?"

"Joseph."

Potiphar looked down the row of freshly planted vines. Also after only one day, this young vineyard looked spectacular. "Why do you care what I say, Joseph? I have purchased you to be my slave and here you are working beyond what is required of you. Why?"

"I believe my God wants . . . best I do. For job I do . . . for my master," Joseph replied.

"Which god, Joseph? Tell me which god will bring favor to my vineyard with you here. Is it Hapy? Is it Bastet perhaps?" Potiphar wanted to know, looking around for his little black cat.

"My God is . . . of my father. I believe just one," Joseph replied.

Potiphar laughed. "Well, if your one god opens your mouth and multiplies my vineyard like this in a single day, I look forward to what else he will do for you on my behalf."

Liz was sitting in the shadows listening to this exchange between Joseph and Potiphar. She got up and came meowing up to Potiphar, wrapping her tail around his legs. "Ah, Bastet, there you are," Potiphar said as he picked Liz up, bringing her close to his cheek. "You see, Joseph, I believe you are blessed by the favor of Bastet. And she is from a god that I know is real."

You have no idea how real, Liz thought as she looked at Joseph and winked.

Joseph again did a double take at Liz's wink and smiled at her. "She is . . . beautiful and by me all day."

Potiphar stroked Liz and studied Joseph. There was something special about this boy. And clearly he was favored by the gods, or somehow gifted. "Good work today, Joseph. I shall look forward to what you will accomplish on your second day. I imagine by the third day, you will accomplish the impossible," Potiphar said with a grin.

"Think—no, thank—you, my master," Joseph replied with a bow.

Potiphar turned and walked down the path, calling back to Joseph, "I like the rocks."

Joseph smiled. He felt good about his hard work today, which obviously had pleased Potiphar. He was determined to prove to Potiphar that his God was the one, true God who indeed would grant His favor in this place. Little did Joseph or Potiphar know that Liz *did* come from God. His God.

"Oh, Father, please help me do the impossible by the third day," Joseph prayed.

A cool breeze blew the hem of Joseph's dirty loincloth, which was the only garment he now owned. Nevertheless he felt wrapped in a cloak of the presence of God as he looked up at the night sky, now filling up with the moon and the stars. He thought about his dream and wondered how he could possibly ever go from a garden to the heavens. He didn't know *how*, but he did know *who*. And that was enough for Joseph.

CHAPTER 19

Egyptology 101

"Where are we, Nigel?" Liz asked as they walked up the steps leading into a column-lined portico. The sun was just beginning to rise, and the soft pink hue of the sky slowly brought light to the horizon. Liz and Nigel left Potiphar's house early to travel down the road to this building.

"We are at school, my dear. If you wish to learn Egyptian writing, I feel you should start by seeing how and where it is taught. I've been coming here to learn for years, and consider myself the beloved school mouse," Nigel said with a chuckle. "We have arrived before the students, and will need to hide soon. I have the perfect spot."

Nigel led Liz into a simple room where stacks of wooden tablets covered with white plaster sat in the middle of the floor. Next to the wooden tablets were several wooden ink palettes and a basket full of rolled papyrus sheets. They climbed up to a ledge that overlooked the room so they could observe yet not be seen, and not a moment too soon. Several young boys aged five to nine entered the room, one jumping over the other as they played leapfrog all the way down the hall. Their heads were completely shaved except for the braided sidelock of black hair that trailed down one side of their heads. Barefoot and wearing only short white loincloths, the boys were totally carefree in this environment.

"Settle down, boys. We have much to accomplish today," said a tall Egyptian man who followed the boys into the room. The boys immediately obeyed and sat down in a circle on the brown floor mats in front of the teacher, who sat in a simple wooden chair. Leaning on the chair was a long, thin stick. On his lap the teacher held a scroll, and he slowly unrolled it while telling the students, "Today we will start by reciting from *The Book of Instruction.* Who would like to start today's lesson by reciting from 'The Teaching of Ptahhotep'?"

The boys were squirming and looked at one another to see who would go first. One of the older boys raised his hand and the teacher nodded his approval. "Very well, Chibale, begin."

The boy stood and put his hands by his side. "The moral ideal for Egyptians: Respect for parents and superiors is fundamental to our beliefs. But those who are inferior must always be treated well and should not be humiliated by those of a higher rank. Respect is gained by knowledge and polite words. One must resist envy and jealousy. Always be generous and treat friends well, and choose silence if you have nothing interesting to say."

"Very well recited, Chibale. Now, may I have someone recite from 'The Instruction of Amenemope'? How about you, Rashidi?" the teacher asked as he unrolled another scroll of the Egyptian hieratic text.

The young boy nodded and stood, clearing his throat. "It is better to be praised for neighborly love than to have riches in your storeroom. Never let a powerful man bribe you to oppress a weak one for his own benefit. Mock not the blind. Behave justly toward your god, your king, your superiors, and your inferiors, too; in return you will enjoy health, long life, and respect."

The teacher nodded in approval. "Excellent, Rashidi. And can you conclude by summarizing the aim of the Egyptian moral system?"

Rashidi looked to the ceiling as he thought for a moment, trying to remember the exact phrasing. "When judging the dead, god will deal with you in accordance with your past conduct. Those you leave behind, too, will be glad to acknowledge your good deeds by reciting life-giving words and by bringing gifts to ensure you life eternal."

"I am most pleased, Rashidi. You may sit down," the teacher said as he rolled up the scroll. "Now, take your wooden palates and let us begin our writing exercises."

Liz leaned over and whispered to Nigel, "I am quite impressed! The Egyptians appear to raise their children with the highest standards of behavior. Do you have a copy of *The Book of Instruction?* I would very much like to learn to read with this text."

"Yes," Nigel replied in a hushed voice. "Children are taught well and the texts have much wisdom. I do have these texts here, and will give them to you." Nigel directed Liz to the teacher and the boys.

"You will notice that the teacher does not hesitate to discipline the children with the stick by his chair, and is even encouraged to do so by the parents in order to prevent laziness and disrespect. But formal education is reserved for only a privileged few—sons of rich and powerful civil servants and dignitaries. The children of farmers or craftsmen are taught those same skills of their fathers. Daughters of all social classes stay home with their mothers and learn to run a household, cook, do chores, and develop skills such as spinning and weaving. But royal princesses are not only taught how to read and write, but are expected to have a love for literature."

"So the ability to read and write separates the elite in Egyptian society," Liz observed.

"Sadly so. Literacy is not available to everyone, so children who are given the privilege of reading and writing appreciate and take their training seriously," Nigel told her. "But the Egyptians do believe in healthy play time for children, and encourage sports and games after their schooling or chores are done."

"I see. So when do these boys learn about hieroglyphs?" Liz asked. She was eager to get started.

"Some may learn them, but not all. You see, there are two forms of Egyptian writing. One is hieroglyphs—the picture symbols you have seen. The other is hieratic script, which is used for everyday reading and writing, and the one these boys are practicing now by copying *The Book of Instruction.* Only those destined to be priests or artists practice hieroglyphs, or sacred writing, as they are known," Nigel explained.

"So even the elite are separated from the elite by what they learn," Liz exclaimed. "Well, I wish to learn it all, Nigel. I want to understand everything I see drawn on walls or written in scrolls. And I promise you will not need to use a stick on me, for I am an eager student."

"I am most certain you will not be lazy or disrespectful, Liz," Nigel chuckled. "Fancy that. A mouse with a cat as the teacher's pet."

Liz giggled, *"Oui, mon professeur.* Let us begin, no?"

"Right. Observe the boys. They learn by memorizing or copying text, or by taking dictation of letters from reports and the like. I shall begin by having you do the same. And I shall also take you on field trips to the pyramids where the hieroglyphs and pyramid texts are quite extraordinary," Nigel said.

"But let me caution you to be patient, Liz. It has taken me years to learn both the hieroglyphs and the hieratic script, as I had to translate from Egyptian to English. It will most likely take you a long time as well. There are more than seven hundred hieroglyphs to master, and then comes learning how to put them together to form words and phrases. So above all, learning this language will require practice, practice, practice!"

"Je comprends, Nigel. I will be patient and I promise to practice. I have all the time in the world," Liz said, smiling.

"Jolly good! Very well then, here we go," Nigel said as he scurried over to a cubbyhole in the corner where he had hidden some papyrus and ink. He unrolled the papyrus, took a tiny, mouse-sized reed, and began to draw.

"We will begin with hieroglyphs, which fall into three basic categories: sound signs, labeling signs, which are clues to the meaning of words they follow, and finally word signs, which stand for entire words. Do you follow, my dear?" Nigel asked as he drew a series of pictures.

"Oui, I follow, Nigel," Liz replied, gazing at the papyrus.

"Splendid. Sound signs are also called *phonograms*, and form the basis of the language. *Unilaterals* are the most common and stand for one sound, like letters of the alphabet. See here," Nigel said as he drew a picture of an owl. "This owl is the sign for 'm'." Next he drew a rectangle with an open side. "Then we have *bilaterals,* which stand for a combination of two sounds. This open rectangle is the symbol meaning 'house' and stands for the combination 'pr.'"

Nigel looked to see if Liz understood. She clearly did. "Go on," she said.

"Now labeling signs are silent but give clues to the meaning of words they follow." Nigel drew a pair of walking legs. "So you see, if I put this labeling sign after the house symbol, that would mean . . ."

"Go forth?" Liz suggested.

"Brilliant!" Nigel exclaimed. "Liz, I must say you are quite the fast learner."

"Merci, mon professeur," Liz replied with a shy smile.

"Now word signs can be recognized by a single vertical stroke, telling the reader that the sign is to be read as an entire word," Nigel continued.

"There are twenty-four distinct sounds the Egyptian signs represent in the hieroglyphic alphabet. Let us practice some now," the mouse told Liz as he drew a series of symbols.

Nigel drew an Egyptian vulture, a reed leaf, an outstretched arm and hand, a quail chick, a human foot and lower leg, a horned viper, and a wave. "These hieroglyphs stand for *a* as in 'asp'; *i; e; w,o,* or *u; b; f;* and *n* as in Nile. Now you try," Nigel said, giving the reed to Liz.

Liz curled her paw around the reed and began to copy Nigel's symbols. He squinted as he looked over her shoulder. Liz was very deliberate as she drew, taking great care to make the symbols exactly like Nigel's. When she finished, Liz stood back and noticed Nigel rubbing his eyes.

"Are you all right, *mon ami?"* Liz asked worriedly.

"Blast these eyes! My eyesight seems to get worse all the time," Nigel said as he stopped rubbing his eyes to look at Liz. "I pray I will be able to teach you what you need to learn before my sight leaves me completely."

Liz furrowed her brow. "I am very sorry, Nigel. I do not wish to tire your eyes. Should we stop the lesson?"

Nigel waved his hand to dismiss the idea. "No, my dear. I will muddle through, for I am determined that my pet learn the full alphabet today. Let us continue."

Nigel picked up the reed and drew a few more symbols while Liz looked on at the diligent little mouse. She was concerned for Nigel's eyes and breathed a silent prayer for his sight.

"Now, you must understand that hieroglyphs are not just symbols but works of art. The Egyptians take their inspiration from the world around them by using animals, plants, household objects, and even buildings for hieroglyphs. But to the Egyptians, these symbols are not just "words on a page," if you will. They believe these designs have actually been given magical powers. They believe words have the power to create, and just pronouncing the name of an object or being can bring it to life," Nigel explained. Then he stopped, taking a serious tone.

"I have been in a temple where I felt almost an overwhelming evil presence as I read the hieroglyphs on the walls. The Egyptians believe that reading carved words in such a sacred place can be dangerous, especially if the name spoken is that of a harmful god such as the serpent Apophis, who from a distance threatens the sun each morning," Nigel went on, obviously very serious. "To prevent such divine creatures from entering the world, the hieroglyphs representing them are often scraped over or stabbed by daggers."

"Surely you don't believe such a thing, Nigel. There is only one true God," stated Liz to her little tutor.

"Of course, of course there is only one true God," Nigel said, glancing back over the symbols drawn on the papyrus. "But isn't there one true Evil One as well?"

Liz watched as Nigel pointed to a symbol drawn on the papyrus. It was the sign of a cobra. "Just as God is represented in many ways by the good things He created, so, too, couldn't the Evil One be represented in many ways by bad things?" Nigel asked her.

Liz shuddered as she looked at the symbol of the cobra. Certainly what Nigel said was true. She had only encountered Charlatan in one form—the form of a snake. But he had changed from a chameleon snake to a cobra in a matter of seconds. What if he appeared again in a different form altogether? Would she be able to recognize him?

"Nigel, you said you felt an evil presence in a temple? What temple was that?" Liz asked.

"The temple of Anubis," Nigel replied. "Why?"

"Just curious," Liz answered as she practiced drawing the hieroglyph of the cobra.

"It seems our lesson has grown from hieroglyphs to Egyptology 101," Nigel said. "Very well, my pet, we shall go to the temple of Anubis and you will learn about mummification and *The Book of the Dead.*"

Liz took the reed and in a symbolic gesture scrawled the ink across the hieroglyph of the cobra. She wondered if daggers would be necessary as well. But then she noticed the reed in her paw. It was a reed that had delivered the devastating blows to Charlatan before.

Perhaps, Liz thought, *the reed is mightier than the sword.*

CHAPTER 20

The Third Day

Joseph and Benipe stood with the other slaves as the gardener came to give them today's instructions for the vineyard.

"The vines are planted. Now we need to erect a trellis system with pillars for the vines in order for them to grow above the ground," the gardener explained. "We will use wooden pillars with wooden poles laid on top. Today you will go through the supply yard to get the wooden pillars and then plant them in the ground."

"We should have dug holes for the pillars before we planted the vines," Joseph muttered under his breath. "We're doing this completely backward. I hope we can do this without damaging the vines."

Benipe looked at Joseph with surprise. "Wait a minute. Did you understand what the gardener just said about the trellis system?"

Joseph looked at Benipe with an equally surprised look. "Yes, I guess I did! How is that possible? Quick, say something in Egyptian."

"The gods have opened your mouth," Benipe replied in his native Egyptian tongue.

Joseph laughed, "No, Benipe. THE God has opened my mouth! I understood every word you said, as well as every word the gardener said."

"But how? You only started learning Egyptian two days ago," Benipe observed.

"I asked God to help me do the impossible by the third day in the house of Potiphar. It appears He has answered my prayer," Joseph said with a smile and a hand on Benipe's shoulder. "He took the little bit of understanding I had and made it grow overnight." Joseph looked around the vineyard. "And I believe He will do the same for this vineyard."

Benipe couldn't believe it. He had listened to Joseph speak of his God, and witnessed how faithful Joseph was to spend time in prayer each day. A small glimmer of hope entered Benipe's heart. *Could there be something to Joseph's God?* he wondered.

"Some trick, Joseph! Well, your God answered your prayer this time. Let's see if He does it with the vines," Benipe said with a bit of skepticism in his voice. "At least I don't have to translate for you anymore."

"Thank you, Benipe, for helping me. I pray God will bless you for giving me the first words of Egyptian and teaching me how to begin," Joseph said.

"You're welcome. How would you have your God bless me?" Benipe asked.

"By revealing Himself fully to you, however He can," Joseph replied with a smile.

"You slaves, Joseph and Benipe. What are you discussing?" the gardener asked.

"We were discussing how the pillars could be planted without damaging the already-planted vines, my master," Joseph replied, drawing a surprised look from the gardener.

"What kind of trick is this that you speak our tongue? Were you fooling us before when you said you did not understand?" the gardener asked.

"No, my master. My God has given me the knowledge of your tongue so I can serve you well," Joseph replied with a respectful bow.

"Indeed? Well, perhaps your god will give you knowledge of the trellis system we need for the vineyard," the gardener replied. "What do you think of my plan, Joseph?"

Joseph thought a moment before replying. He didn't want to offend the gardener, but he had another idea that might work far better, at least for the centerpiece of the vineyard. "While the wooden pillars and wooden poles will surely suffice for the trellis system, I think we need something grand for the center of the vineyard. Potiphar desires an impressive display, and I think columns with rafters could provide the far richer detail Potiphar seeks. I noticed a group of unused columns stacked over in the supply yard. We could carve and paint designs on the columns to honor Potiphar and his vineyard."

The gardener listened and stood still, staring at Joseph. He realized Joseph was right. He didn't want to admit the fact that in his hurry to impress Potiphar he had planted the vines before erecting the trellis system. He should have built the trellises first. Perhaps this columned centerpiece would make up for his mistake.

The gardener walked around Joseph and slapped his measuring rod in his hand. "I give you today to build this centerpiece for the vineyard. Erect four columns with rafters by the time Potiphar returns. And make sure it looks nothing short of impressive." He then turned and addressed the five garden slaves: "Pay heed to Joseph."

Joseph nodded and bowed low in respect as the gardener walked away. The other slaves quickly gathered around Joseph for instruction. Joseph picked up a stick and drew a circular outline in the dirt. "Very well, the five of us are capable of carrying one column at a time. We will need to make eight trips to the supply yard to carry the eight columns to place here, here, and here. There are then plenty of wooden poles we can use as rafters."

Benipe looked up at Joseph and shook his head with a laugh. "Uh, Joseph, I think you haven't quite learned Egyptian math yet. The gardener said four columns—that's only four trips to the supply yard."

"Who said we'd stop at four columns?" Joseph said with a smile. "We're going to make it eight."

"This goes against the grain of my cleanliness routine, but I suppose it must be done," Liz said as she and Nigel stood on the bank of the Nile below Potiphar's house.

"Terribly dirty job, but you must do it if you feel the Nile peat substitute will help Joseph," Nigel said. "I equally dislike the thought of this, being a white mouse as well as a proper Brit. At least you are black, my dear. It won't look as dreadful on you as it would me."

Liz glanced at Nigel rubbing his small hands together. "We must sometimes be willing to get dirty to help others, no? And I am convinced that the nutrients in this silt, if added directly to the soil around the vines, will yield a far richer grape," Liz assured Nigel as she dug around the silt with her paw.

"Best of luck and all that," Nigel said as Liz stepped forward into the muck.

Liz proceeded to sink herself into the black silt of the Nile, then rolled around in the muck until she was completely covered. Her gold collar and earrings were caked with the black silt until all that could be seen were her golden eyes peeking out from her black form. *Max would love this,* Liz thought to herself. He never seemed to mind getting his paws in muddy banks.

"Simply dreadful," Nigel muttered under his breath as he watched Liz get caked with the wet soil.

Liz then walked onto the bank and stood by Nigel. "Let's hurry up and get this over with so I can get clean. I know Mandisa will give me a bath when it's done."

Joseph's shoulder was rubbed raw from carrying the stone columns. As the leader for this group, he took on the burden of being the man in front to bear the load. The slaves struggled to carry the heavy columns from the supply yard to the center of the vineyard. "Father, just as you multiplied my words, please multiply our strength and our time," Joseph prayed silently.

"Almost there, stay with me," Joseph said to encourage the others behind him.

They finally reached the center of the vineyard and set the eighth column in place. All the slaves collapsed on the ground in exhaustion. Just then Mandisa came to the men carrying a water jar. She held it out to Joseph.

"Thank you, but let the others drink first," Joseph said, resting his hands on his knees as he caught his breath.

Mandisa walked over to Benipe, who eagerly took the water jar and gulped down the cool water. She smiled with her dimples showing as Benipe drank. He wiped his mouth with the back of his arm and smiled at Mandisa, giving a slight bow and saying, "Thank you."

"You're welcome," she said as she moved to the other slaves.

Joseph looked around at the eight columns equally spaced in a perfect circle. Now they needed to get the wooden rafters to install on top of the columns. He could just envision how magnificent this would look when complete. He looked up at the sky to judge the time of day. He felt the sun should be higher.

"Mandisa, how soon until Potiphar returns?" Joseph asked.

"Not for a long while. It is not even noon yet, Joseph," Mandisa replied as she brought the water jar over for Joseph to have a drink.

"How can that be? We've already moved the columns and it isn't even noon?" Benipe asked from where he sat on the ground.

Joseph took a swig of water and poured some over his upturned face as well. "You see, Benipe? Anything is possible with God." He threw some water on Benipe with a laugh.

"If you say so," Benipe said, enjoying the refreshing splash.

"Now we only need to retrieve the wooden rafters, which will be *easy* to carry after lifting those columns," Joseph said, handing the jar back to Mandisa.

Just then, Liz came strolling right up to Joseph and rubbed her muddy fur all over his legs, smearing him with the silt from the Nile.

"Bastet! Look at you!" Mandisa said. "You're a mess!"

Joseph laughed and wiped the silt off his legs. He then rubbed it between his fingers and looked at it closely. "It appears Bastet has been swimming in the silt of the Nile," Joseph said as he continued to study the mud. He then wiped off a handful of silt from Liz's fur. "I think she has a very good idea. If we add this silt to the soil around the vines, I'm sure it will provide added nutrients and yield larger grapes."

Joseph went over to a freshly planted vine and mixed the silt with the newly tilled soil. Then he stood and wiped off his hands. "After we get the trellis system set up, we will work on conditioning the soil for the vines."

"I think I liked it better when the cat had your tongue instead of your attention," Benipe laughed. "You're wearing me out—first rocks, then columns, now silt. How many more ideas do you have for Potiphar's vineyard?"

"If my Egyptian math is correct, I'd say I have a million of them," Joseph said with a sly grin. "Potiphar demanded that this be the finest vineyard in all of Avaris. I intend to make it so."

With that, Joseph took off to the supply yard to gather the wooden rafters. The other slaves slowly got up and followed him. Liz sat there looking quite the mess but smiling a broad grin. Nigel hid behind one of the columns and caught Liz's attention with a "psst."

"Jolly good show, my dear! Your dirty plan worked," Nigel hoarsely whispered.

"Oui, that it did. I just know that Joseph's beautiful design for the vineyard will now be matched by grapes that far surpass those anywhere. But I am quite ready to get clean," Liz said with a snap of her paw to flick off some of the muddy silt. "Did you hear Joseph? It sounds like he is already speaking Egyptian."

"Yes, yes, that he is. I can only assume he is a fast learner like you, my pet. Carry on then and enjoy your bath. I will now head to the palace to check on your Albert. Cheerio," Nigel said with a wave of his paw as he scurried off.

Mandisa walked up to Liz. "We'd better get you clean before my master returns home. What would he think if he found his beloved Bastet in such a state?"

Liz looked over Mandisa's shoulder as the young girl carried her back to the house. She smiled. Joseph had already surpassed what the gardener had instructed him to do, and it wasn't even noon. Plus he was speaking Egyptian. This day had the marks of the impossible written all over it. And Liz knew exactly which God was behind it all.

Potiphar walked briskly through the front portico, eager to inspect what had happened in the vineyard today. He had been thinking about his conversation with Joseph two days earlier when he almost challenged Joseph's God with what he could accomplish by the third day.

Ako greeted Potiphar and clapped his hands for the servants to clean his feet. "Not yet, Ako. I wish to inspect the vineyard first."

"Very well, my lord. I think you will be pleased," Ako said with a grin and a low bow.

"Then let us see," Potiphar said as he walked along the breezeway to reach the outer garden. Ako followed after him.

The gardener had remained behind this evening, along with Joseph and the other slaves. He wanted to see Potiphar's reaction to what had happened today. "Welcome, my master," the gardener said with a low bow. "If you will follow me."

He led Potiphar along the pathways lined with the rocks Joseph had set in place. Potiphar gazed at the young vines and frowned. "Why are not the supporting trellises in place? This is a vineyard, and I don't expect my vines to trail along the ground."

The gardener gulped. "Yes, the trellises are coming, but the slave Joseph had an idea that I felt was worth trying, my master. Come see what he has done."

"I intend to," Potiphar said as he passed the gardener with his long, swift gait.

Joseph stood in front of the circle of columns with his hands clasped behind his back. He bowed low as Potiphar neared, and welcomed him: "My master, I hope you will be pleased with the centerpiece of your vineyard."

Potiphar stopped and gazed up at the circle of eight columns. On top of them was a woven canopy of wooden rafters, perfectly set in position for the vines to grow and cover. In the center of the circle was a stone bench; oil lamps on tall stands placed in front of each column lit up the centerpiece. Although unfinished, it was exquisitely beautiful and held tremendous potential. Potiphar walked around the columns and studied the canopy of rafters before sitting on the bench.

"Joseph, come here," Potiphar instructed. Joseph walked over to join Potiphar under the canopy. "This was your idea?"

"Yes, my master. I hope you are pleased. We plan to carve and paint the columns, but first we must put the other wooden pillar trellis system in place," Joseph replied. "And I think adding silt from the Nile will greatly improve the condition of the soil for a greater yield."

Potiphar's eyebrows rose in surprise. "It appears your God has opened your mouth even wider. How is it that you can speak our tongue so well on just the third day?"

"I asked my God to give His favor to me, to multiply my words, our strength, and our time. He has faithfully done so," Joseph replied.

Potiphar studied Joseph, completely stunned by what he heard. "And he certainly has multiplied your ideas for my vineyard as well."

Potiphar stood and stepped in front of Joseph, towering over him, but looking down to stare him in the eye. Gradually a big grin grew on his face and he said, "Joseph, I don't know how your God has done all this, but there is no doubt in my mind His favor is upon you. I am very pleased with what you have accomplished here. You captured the vision for what I wanted in my vineyard—to not only produce fine grapes, but to be equally as fine in beauty to the eye. I greatly approve of your work. You have my favor," Potiphar said with a hand to Joseph's shoulder.

Joseph winced as Potiphar touched him where his shoulder was raw from carrying the columns. Potiphar lifted his hand and looked at the scrapes and bruises. He looked intently into Joseph's eyes and saw that he uttered not a word of complaint for his wounds. "Ako, see to Joseph's wounds and to those of the other slaves. Make sure they are well taken care of this evening."

Joseph bowed his head, saying, "Thank you, my master. I am glad I have won your favor. I have many more ideas for your vineyard that I hope will please you as well."

"Gardener, come here," Potiphar called to his servant. "Joseph is to have complete oversight of the vineyard while you tend to the rest of the garden. See to it he has everything he needs or wants."

"It will be as you say," the gardener replied with a low bow.

Liz sat in the shadows, now clean and smelling lovely again. She walked up to Potiphar, meowing as he picked her up. "Bastet, do you approve of what Joseph has done today? He says his God allowed him to do the impossible on this third day." He held Liz up to his cheek and stroked her silky fur. "My, how clean you are."

Joseph caught Liz's eye and he winked at her. She smiled in return.

Did he just wink at me? Liz wondered.

Potiphar looked at Joseph and the other slaves. "Very well. You have worked hard today. Ako, see to it that the slavemaster gives these slaves additional food for dinner and fresh loincloths after they bathe. They have earned it." He nodded in approval to Joseph and walked away.

Joseph stood there silently thanking God for all He had done this day. Benipe came over and nudged Joseph. "Hey, now you're not so talkative. What's the matter? Cat got your tongue?"

Joseph watched as Liz bobbed along on Potiphar's shoulders gazing back at him. "Yes, Benipe, I believe she has."

CHAPTER 21

The Hunt

Max heard Sadiki coughing in the other room. He yawned, stretched out long, and shook all over before going to check on the jailer. Sadiki sat on the side of his bed, hands on his knees, leaning over. He had coughed so hard he was short of breath.

He sounds as bad as the pr-r-risoners, Max thought. *Must be that terrible jail air.*

When he saw Max enter the room, Sadiki held his hand out to pet Max on the head. "Jabari, I will need your bravery today. I have been called by Pharaoh to go on the hunt, and will take you with me," Sadiki said, clearing his throat.

Max stood by while the jailer packed a sack of supplies. He was going on the hunt with Pharaoh! Max was glad to be able to spend time away from the dank prison and go on an exciting adventure. Perhaps the fresh air would also help Sadiki.

Before long they were walking to the palace. As they entered the gate, Max looked up at the enormous carvings of Pharaoh on the hunt and wondered what they would chase today. Soon they walked down the corridor lined with hunting scenes and Max eyed the picture of the hippopotamus hunt in the small papyrus boat on the Nile. *Aye, please let it not be a hunt on the r-r-river then.* Max had heard the prisoners talking about the dangers of crocodiles and hippos. One of the prisoners was in jail because his clumsiness had led to a dignitary falling into the Nile when they were surrounded by crocodiles on such a hunt. They never saw the man again, and the prisoner was charged with his death.

"Good, you are here," Potiphar said as Sadiki entered the foyer where the hunting party was assembled. "I see you brought your dog. How is he serving you in the prison?"

"Jabari is a fine dog. He has already cleaned out the rats in the jail," Sadiki answered.

Max sat by Sadiki, grinning. *Told ye I were the best pest r-r-rounder-upper anywhere.*

"Very well. We'll see how he does in chasing big game," Potiphar said as he leaned down to muss Max's head with his large hand. "What do you say, Jabari? Are you ready to hunt the wild ibex?"

Max's stomach dropped. Now he wished they were hunting crocs. Ibex were wild goat antelopes, and just the thought of hunting something that looked like a member of Gillamon's family made him sick.

Suddenly Potiphar stood as he heard the court slave enter the room to let him know Pharaoh was about to enter. He clapped his hands and everyone stood at attention. "Enter, Pharaoh, powerful ruler of Egypt, son of Ra and the embodiment of Horus."

Max looked up to see Pharaoh stride into the room carrying none other than Al in his arms. It was all he could do to keep from bursting out laughing as he observed Al dressed up in his royal attire with the golden breastplate and nose ring. Suddenly Al caught Max's eye and a goofy grin poured over his face. He waved and said, "Max! Ye're here! Top o' the mornin' to ye!"

Max shook his head and chuckled. Al was still Al, so that was good.

"It is a good day for the hunt!" Pharaoh exclaimed, stroking Al as he meowed in his arms. "Good, jailer, you are here. And who is with you?" He had spotted Max.

Sadiki bowed low before Pharaoh. "My master, this is my faithful dog Jabari. He is a fine hunter—I know he will bring us success on the hunt."

"Very well, I look forward to seeing how he performs," Pharaoh said. He looked at Al. "Perhaps I shall bring Hapy on the hunt. Since he supposedly brings plenty, perhaps he will bring us success as well."

Max and Al shared a grin. They would get to spend the day together.

"Is my new chariot ready?" Pharaoh asked, putting Al on the floor. "I am eager to test it."

"It is indeed ready, my master," Potiphar replied. "We are ready to depart."

"Let us be off," Pharaoh commanded as he turned to lead the hunting party down the corridor.

Al sauntered over to Max and head-butted him. "It's great to see ye, laddie!"

"Aye, 'tis gr-r-rand ta see ye all dolled up like that, Big Al. I were worried ye might let the r-r-royal tr-r-reatment go ta yer head," Max said with a grin. "But it looks like ye're the same Al." Max patted Al on the belly. "But I have ta say, the r-r-royal tr-r-reatment may be gettin' ta yer stomach."

Al looked down at his large belly. "I can't help it, Max. All they do is feed me here. All day." He patted his belly. "I think they want me to look jest like the god Hapy in the pictures on the walls. I'm tryin' to play me part."

"Good job, laddie. Well, enjoy havin' plenty at yer post while ye kin anyway," Max replied.

"Nigel came by the palace a few nights ago and told me all aboot Liz and how well Joseph is doin' in Potiphar's house. I miss me love, but I'm glad she is well," Al said.

"Aye, an' Nigel visited me in the jail. Did he tell ye there is a secret tunnel between the palace an' the prison?" Max asked.

"Ye don't say! Maybe we can meet in the middle then," Al said excitedly.

"Nigel warned of snake beasties in the tunnel. Would ye be up for that challenge?" Max asked.

Al gulped. "On second thought, maybe ye can jest come meet me here in the palace."

"I figured as much," Max said with a laugh.

"Make ready our chariots," Potiphar said to the steward as the hunting party followed Pharaoh to the stables.

Max and Al trotted along behind Sadiki. There were more than five hundred magnificent horses lined up in stalls filled with fresh hay. A row of twenty chariots coupled with two horses each sat waiting for Pharaoh's hunting party. A series of carts carrying supplies for Pharaoh were at the back of the line.

"Don't ye know Giorgio would have loved this then," Max said to Al, remembering their Italian stallion friend from the Ark. "Although, he would want ta be asleep ta r-r-run fastest in the hunt!"

"Sure, that he would. But Don Pedro would be the best hunter o' them all if he got to go on the chase," Al replied, thinking of the bull who charged after fast-moving objects, namely Al. Al rubbed his backside at the thought of it.

Pharaoh and Potiphar joined the weaponry chief to inspect the new chariot, taking time to inspect the new wheels, draft pole, and superb paint job. The large wooden wheels were covered in leather and painted gold with red trim and blue stripes evenly spaced around the circumference. The body of the chariot was shaped like a horseshoe, painted with blue and gold leaf, and was open in the rear. A guardrail ran around the top of the cockpit for Pharaoh to hold on to. The side walls were ornately decorated with animal designs, including a leaping lion and a coiled snake. The decorative quiver for arrows was positioned on the side of the chariot. The horses that would pull the chariot were covered in richly decorated saddlecloths.

"I'll take it," Pharaoh quipped, much to the relief of the weaponry chief, who was nervous about Pharaoh's approval. "Now let us see how she handles."

Pharaoh stepped into his chariot and motioned for the others to get into theirs, which were far less ornate but well constructed nonetheless. "Jailer, I want you to ride lead chariot with me. Today we hunt ibex."

"As you say, my master," Sadiki replied, lifting Al into Pharaoh's chariot. He then jumped into his chariot and whistled for Max to join him.

Potiphar was positioned directly behind Pharaoh and Sadiki, and the rest of the servants, including a scribe, rode along behind. With a snap of the lead and a "HYA!" Pharaoh charged his horses to take off. Dust kicked up behind the chariot and the tall gates in the stable courtyard opened wide to allow the hunting party to depart. Soon they were flying down the road at top speed as the horses ran with all their might. Pharaoh wanted to see how fast his new chariot could go.

Max propped himself up on the ledge at the front of Sadiki's chariot with his paws on the guardrail so he could peer out. The wind blew back the fur around his face and his tongue was hanging out the side. "'Tis a gr-r-rand r-r-ride!" Max barked, unable to contain the thrill of the speed of his first chariot ride. Sadiki smiled as he looked down at his canine sidekick, whose tail was wagging excitedly.

Max looked over and saw Al on the floor of Pharaoh's chariot, bouncing around like a pebble in a rockslide. He was sliding back and forth as the chariot moved, getting airborne as the chariot hit objects on the rocky desert road. Max saw Al dig his front claws into the side of Pharaoh's chariot to hold on while his back legs flew up in the air. "MAX! HELP ME! AHHHHHHHHH!! I'M A GONER!"

"Al, jest get yer feet under ye, lad! Crawl up ta the ledge in front of where Pharaoh is standin' an' put yer paws on the guardrail. Ye have ta get off the floor," Max shouted.

Sadiki noticed his dog barking wildly at Pharaoh and saw Hapy was about to fly out the back of the chariot. He pulled alongside Pharaoh. "My master, Hapy is not secure."

"YE CAN SAY THAT AGAIN! I'M NOT HAPPY *OR* SECURE," Al screamed.

Pharaoh, without missing a beat, leaned down to pick Al up and place him on the ledge. Al held on for dear life, his teeth rattling and his face turning pale from fright. He looked over and saw Max laughing his head off.

"Maybe ye kin tie a harness ta yer nose r-r-ring ta hang on," Max teased.

"Very funny!" Al said, wrapping his arms around the guardrail and shutting his eyes tight.

Soon the hunting party reached the desert and Sadiki scanned the jagged, rocky cliffs for their prey. He saw nothing for a while but suddenly saw movement in the distance. There was a herd of gazelle grazing in the fields. It wasn't ibex, but perhaps Pharaoh would want to pursue a gazelle. "My master, a herd of gazelle in the fields! Looks like twenty head. Do you wish to pursue?"

"Yes! Sadiki, you take the left flank and Potiphar, you take the right. I'll run through the middle of them," Pharaoh instructed.

Sadiki and Potiphar came on either side of Pharaoh as he snapped the reins on the horses to pursue the gazelles, whose tails were now up in alarm at the approach of the chariots. The gazelles were brown and white with a black stripe on the side. Several males had long, curved horns. Suddenly they began jumping high into the air, lifting all four feet off the ground at once as they took off running.

Pharaoh tightly secured the harness while he reached back to ready his bow and arrow. "On my mark!" Pharaoh yelled.

He waited until he was almost on top of the gazelles and held the arrow close up to his chin. Suddenly he released the arrow and it missed its mark. Pharaoh quickly pulled another arrow from the quiver and shot again, but missed his target a second time. Frustrated, Pharaoh roughly pulled another arrow from the quiver and took careful aim at a male gazelle. He released the arrow, this time hitting the animal in the hindquarters. Max barked as the beast took a tumbling fall and rolled in the dust while the others in the herd kept running. *Poor laddie,* Max thought to himself.

"SUCCESS!" Pharaoh shouted as he took the reins and brought his chariot to a full stop. Al still held on with his eyes shut. Pharaoh jumped out of the chariot and went over to see his kill. He squatted down next to the fallen gazelle as the other chariots stopped and surrounded Pharaoh.

"Congratulations, my master," Potiphar exclaimed. "It is a fine beast!"

"Sadiki, you had a good eye to spot the gazelle. I will give you a portion of the meat," Pharaoh said, waving over his servants, who gathered around him. He held on to the horns of the beast while a scribe hurriedly sketched a picture of Pharaoh's victory. "Bring me Hapy. I wish to have him with me in this sketch."

Potiphar put his hands around Al but found the cat's paws tightly clenched around the guardrail. He grinned and assured Al, "It's okay, Hapy. You have brought your master success. He wishes to have you captured in a picture of his victorious kill."

Al opened his eyes and climbed up on Potiphar's shoulder. "Did ye hear that, Max? I'm to have me picture made with Pharaoh. Maybe I'll be up on the wall soon!"

Max grinned as he trotted along with Potiphar. "Aye, Al, yer image will be captured for all time. Don't forget ta smile then."

Potiphar handed Al to Pharaoh, who placed him on top of the dead gazelle.

"Aye, but I don't think I'd like to be remembered sittin' on top o' a dead beastie," Al said, holding his paw up to his mouth, looking squeamish.

"'Tis the price of royalty, Big Al, so str-r-rike yer best pose," Max joked.

Al put his paw on the gazelle's back and held his head up tall and proud. "How's this?"

"Lookin' like a tr-r-rue warrior ta me, lad," Max replied.

"Sadiki, why do the gazelles jump like that? It seems their movement actually slows them down," Pharaoh said.

"This behavior is called 'stotting,' my lord. Predators tend to hunt old or unhealthy animals, so the gazelle jumps up excitedly to let the predator know it is very healthy and strong, hoping the predator will choose another animal in the herd," Sadiki explained.

"So although stotting slows it down, the gazelle is willing to lose time with its grand show of health, hoping to fool the predator into going after another unlucky beast," Potiphar remarked.

"Interesting. Sounds like a few dignitaries I know," Pharaoh said, causing forced laughter to erupt among the hunting party.

"So where have you found the best hunting grounds for ibex, Sadiki?" Pharaoh asked.

"About five miles south of Avaris, my master," Sadiki answered.

"Pharaoh, if I may," Potiphar interjected, "I have received word the outer construction of your pyramid is nearly complete. If you wish to head south for ibex, perhaps we could also go inspect the progress of your pyramid as it is in that direction."

Pharaoh smiled and answered, "Ah, yes, my masterpiece. I am eager to see it. Very well, it is done. We shall go to my pyramid. Scribe, hurry and finish your sketch. My pyramid and ibex await," Pharaoh instructed.

Potiphar clapped his hands and two servants ran over for instruction. "Take this kill back to the palace as we travel south."

As the hunting party regrouped to mount their chariots, Al called over to Max, "We get to go inside the laddie's triangle, Max!"

"Aye, Big Al. I know Liz would love ta be there ta see it," Max replied.

"Maybe we can bring her with us next time," Al suggested.

"I don't think Potiphar will be allowin' 'Bastet' ta leave his house," Max said. "But maybe she could leave without his knowin' . . . with a mouse."

Al had a very deadpan expression on his face. "Max, ye're rhymin'."

"Aye! I be a poet an' didn't know it," Max said with a grin. "Maybe I should try bein' a scr-r-ribe."

"Won't Liz be surprised to see how cultured we got out on the hunt? Art, poetry, and tourin' triangles. Sure, and she'll wish she were here," Al said, letting his mind wander to Liz.

Max noticed Pharaoh picking up the reins of his horses while Al sat on the floor of his chariot in a dreamy state thinking of Liz. "Ah, laddie, ye best hold on. Ye don't want ta arrive at the pyramid only ta check in as a permanent guest."

Pharaoh yelled "HYA!" and his horses charged again down the rough desert road. Al hung on to the chariot for dear life, his back legs flying in the air, screaming his Hapy head off all the way to the pyramid.

CHAPTER 22

Pyramid Progress and Passages

The smell of fresh-baked bread wafted through the air as the group of chariots arrived at Pharaoh's pyramid complex. Immediately they were surrounded by servants who took the reins of the horses and opened a path through workers lined up to greet Pharaoh. Al's fur was spread out in all directions, but he had managed not to fly out of the chariot. He lifted his nose in the air to sniff the delicious bread and immediately snapped out of any traumatic aftereffects from their bumpy ride through the desert.

Pharaoh lifted Al and stroked his fur, saying, "Come, Hapy, let us see where we will spend eternity."

Al ignored his comment and continued to sniff the air. "I smell somethin' wonderful," Al said, wiping the drool from his mouth.

"Aye, an' I *see* somethin' wonderful, Big Al. Would ye look at that?" Max exclaimed with his jaw open as the men stepped out of their chariots and gazed at the scene before them.

An enormous pyramid rose four hundred feet in the air with more than a million stone blocks carefully set in place from bottom to top. In front of the pyramid was a large mortuary temple with two pairs of sphinxes guarding the entrance. A tall obelisk carved with hundreds of hieroglyphs stood among the sphinxes. From the temple a long, sloping causeway ran down to another valley temple located by a canal. The canal flowed from the Nile and was filled with barges laden with supplies.

Next to the pyramid was an entire city buzzing with activity. The smell of bread came from the bakery, where women sat stirring giant mixing bowls of dough. Next to the bakery was a butcher shop, a granary, a clinic, and houses built flush against one another as far as the eye could see. A cemetery was located on the outskirts of the city. Thousands of workers scurried about, barefoot and dressed in simple white undergarments. But they were all efficiently organized by task.

A group of carpenters with wooden mallets hammered large round pegs into several wooden sleds, inspecting each one carefully. Nearby a group of stonecutters used copper chisels at evenly spaced intervals along an enormous block of stone, hammering the chisels to loosen the stone blocks that had been squared off. A man used a set square and plumb line tool to make sure the blocks were perfectly smooth and straight before a team of men loaded the blocks onto waiting sleds.

Max and Al sat in amazement as they watched a group of twenty men slowly climb a ramp surrounding the pyramid, pulling an enormous block of stone tied on to a sled with strong ropes. While two men pushed behind the block, two men poured water in front of the sled to allow it to more easily slide across the sand. As their gaze followed the ramp, Max and Al saw at least twenty such teams at regular intervals climbing the ramp that wound around the great pyramid.

Pharaoh, Potiphar, and Sadiki stood by admiring the beehive of activity. A scribe began sketching the construction scene, portraying Pharaoh in the foreground with arms crossed, carefully inspecting his masterpiece. They were soon greeted by the overseer and the architect, who rushed up to them, each carrying scrolls.

"Welcome, my master! Your pyramid has risen from the sands of Avaris!" the overseer said as the men bowed low before Pharaoh.

Pharaoh raised his hand over the men, saying, "Yes, the gods are bringing my pyramid to the heavens with each stone block put into place. You have done well."

"Thank you, my master. Yes, the gods have been good to us as we've labored these past twenty years," the architect said. "Please allow me to show you the latest plans for finishing the top of the pyramid with the pyramidion stone."

Potiphar clapped his hands, and two servants brought over a table to place before Pharaoh, who put Al on the ground next to him. The architect quickly unrolled the scroll on the table and the men bent over to see the incredible plan for this massive project. The drawing revealed the outline of the pyramid and an intricate web of passages inside the structure leading to various chambers. On the uppermost tip of the pyramid was the pyramidion stone: a slender, pointed stone painted in gold and covered with hieroglyphs.

The architect pointed to the top of the pyramid. "We have just received from Aswan the hard granite stone from which we will cut the pyramidion for the top, as well as the sarcophagus to hold Pharaoh's coffin. The workers are unloading the granite now at the canal."

Pharaoh directed his gaze along the extensive causeway that ran from the pyramid down to the water, where several boats lined the man-made harbor. Hundreds of workers were assembled to transport the special stone from the boats to sleds headed for the pyramid.

"And here is the design for the pyramidion," the architect said as he unrolled yet another scroll. On it was drawn a narrow pointed capstone with a picture of the god Anubis taking Pharaoh by the hand to be received by the god Osiris. Written below the image were the hieroglyphs reading 'May Pharaoh live forever in the presence and favor of Osiris.'

"Excellent. May Anubis and Osiris be pleased with their likenesses," Pharaoh said with a nod. "It appears the outside of the pyramid is in good form. I wish to see the inner chambers."

"Very well, as you say, my master," the overseer said as he led the men down the path to the entrance of the pyramid.

Al nudged Max. "They're goin' inside the triangle!"

"Aye, come on then, laddie. Let's go see it," Max replied.

Max and Al followed closely behind the men. As they entered the pyramid, they had to stop and allow their eyes to adjust from the intense sunlight to the dim glow of the torches lining the corridor. The air inside was cool, and once their eyes adjusted, they couldn't believe what greeted them.

They stood in a vestibule with four massive statues of Pharaoh, two standing on either side of an ornately carved entryway to a long corridor. On the entryway were carved two images of Pharaoh facing each other, with smaller images of his sons carved by his feet. Above the mantel of the entryway was a series of hieroglyphs carved with a message to Anubis and Osiris. Up ahead workers in the corridor were painting various scenes on the walls—the gods welcoming Pharaoh to his new existence in the afterlife. Other workers carried buckets of supplies back and forth along the corridor.

Al sat staring at the hieroglyphs above the entryway, a puzzled look on his face.

"Wha' are ye thinkin' aboot, Al?" Max asked.

"I'm wonderin' what those symbols mean. How do these humans know what they're even sayin'? It's all Egyptian to me," Al said, throwing his paws up in the air.

"Beats me. I'm sure that kitty lass of yers is tryin' ta learn wha' the pictures mean, so she kin tell us sometime," Max said.

"I think the Egyptians could use our help with drawin'. Our picture o' Henriette and Don Pedro were better than any o' these!" Al said with a goofy grin.

Max looked down the passageway and couldn't see Pharaoh, Potiphar, or Sadiki. "We'd better catch up with the laddies."

As Max and Al entered the corridor they looked up at the ceiling soaring twenty feet above them, supported by wide beams. Max couldn't help but feel small as they walked down the long passageway deep into the pyramid. Al stayed close behind, always wanting Max to lead the way when they were in new territory. Soon they came to a room where stood statues in the likeness of Pharaoh's family. At the end of the line was a small statue of a round cat.

Al went up to the statue and stood next to it. "It looks jest like me!"

"Aye, looks like ye're part of the family now," Max said.

"I look good in stone," Al said, standing back to admire his statue.

"Don't be gettin' a big head, laddie, even though ye been in sketches an' sculptures today. R-r-remember why we're here. It's not for ye ta become God's gift ta art then," Max said. "Let's keep goin'."

Leading off the statue room were two new corridors, one leading up and one leading down.

"Which way do we go?" Al asked.

Max frowned and tried to listen for footsteps but heard only muffled noise coming from either direction. "Well, seein' how there's no fire cloud ta tell us which path ta take, I guess we should jest choose one. We kin always come back ta this point an' go the other direction if we don't see the laddies."

Just then Max heard something coming from the corridor leading upward into the pyramid. It sounded like voices. "Did ye hear that, Big Al? I think they went this way," Max said as he began to trot to the upper corridor.

Max and Al proceeded through the upper corridor and saw mural after mural depicting Pharaoh in various scenes of the afterlife, surrounded by gods. They came to another ornately painted room of hunting scenes and the corridor split again, with one passage going up and one passage going down. Max perked his ears up and listened for the voices he had heard earlier. "This way," he said as they took the downward passage toward the voices. They walked on for quite a while, following the passageway that seemed to never end. Finally they came to a dead end. The corridor just stopped.

"Gr-r-reat. A dead end," Max grunted.

"Why in the world would the Egyptians make a passage that leads nowhere?" Al asked, scratching his head.

"I dunnot have a clue, laddie. It makes no sense ta me," Max said, turning around and trotting back in the direction they had come. Al was close on his heels.

"Sure, and I'd hate to get stuck in this big triangle," Al said, looking nervously up at the eyes of the gods staring out at them as they walked past.

"Never fear, Al. I'll get us out," Max said, boldly trotting ahead of Al.

Al started thinking about his statue. "Did ye hear what Pharaoh said when we were gettin' out o' his chariot?" Al asked.

"No, wha' did he say?" Max replied.

"He said, 'Come, Hapy, let us see where we will spend eternity.' Ye don't think he meant 'we' as in he and me make 'we,' do ye?" Al asked, a worried look on his face. "I don't think I'd be happy spendin' eternity in here."

"That's exactly what he meant," came a voice from the shadows.

CHAPTER 23

A Triangle of Secrets

"Who said that?" Max asked with a growl.

A scrawny four-legged animal stepped out into the dim light and looked nervously around. He was a jackal and appeared very timid and unsure of himself. He was so skinny his ribs poked out under his dull, shaggy salt-and-pepper fur. He had a slender nose and slightly pointed ears. His legs were long and slender with a black stripe along the back of his forelegs.

"Who ar-r-re ye, an' how do ye know wha' Phar-r-raoh meant anyway?" Max asked in a defensive tone.

"I'm Wep," said the jackal. "I've been dodging humans around pyramids for a long time, and I've seen the horrible things they do."

"Why are ye dodgin' the humans?" Max asked, scanning the pitiful-looking creature.

"And what kind o' horrible things do ye mean?" followed Al, putting his paws up to his mouth in fear.

"The humans are always chasing me away from the pyramid and the city, throwing rocks and sometimes hitting me," Wep replied. "I'm just trying to get something to eat. Out here in the desert there's not a lot of food, and the smell of their bread makes my mouth water. I try to sneak a loaf here and there."

"Oh, ye poor laddie!" Al said, walking up to Wep. "Ye're right, that is the most horrible thing I could ever imagine, deprivin' a beast o' food."

"Thanks, but for a jackal I'm treated well—especially compared with what I've seen them do to cats," Wep said.

"Are ye daft, jackal?" Max asked, a frown on his face. "Egyptians *love* cats. They tr-r-reat them as gods. Kin't ye see how they dressed this kitty here in gold an' obviously make sure he doesn't miss any meals?"

Wep looked around, scanning the corridor for any sign of humans, then told them, "Well, that may be, but I've seen cat mummies in the pyramids south of here."

"Cat mum-mum-mummies?" Al asked, his lip quivering.

"Yep, it seems the nobles like to have their pets join them in the afterlife," Wep said looking mournfully at Al. "They put cats in coffins just like their masters. So when Pharaoh said 'where we'll spend eternity,' sorry to tell you this, but he did mean *you.*"

"Well, wha's wrong with that? Seems like a gr-r-rand thing ta do for the kitties when they die, honoring them with the same care they give their masters," Max said.

Wep looked around at the walls and said, "See how they're getting this pyramid ready for Pharaoh when he dies? It could be a long time from now, but when he dies, he and all his possessions for the afterlife are put in here, and the pyramid is sealed to keep robbers out. So that means when Pharaoh dies, so does his cat. The kitty mummies I've seen must have met with an unfortunate accident to be buried with Pharaoh."

Al put his hand over his heart and gasped, "Don't let them take me, Max! I'm too young to die!"

Max shook his head. "Calm down, Al. Ye're not goin' anywhere. Pharaoh's in good health an' it will be a long time before he is laid ta r-r-rest in this pyramid."

"Unless he has an accident in that wild chariot o' his!" Al whined. "Did ye see how reckless he were drivin'? I jest knew we were goin' to crash or tip over."

"Al, remember also *why* ye wouldn't pass on," Max said, looking Al right in the eye as Gillamon always did to make a point.

Al stared at Max and a blinked a few times as he thought about what Max said. It took a while to register, but he finally remembered why he wouldn't die. He was immortal. He *couldn't* die. He could get hurt or sick, but he couldn't die. He wiped his brow with relief. "Oh, thank goodness. I forgot aboot that."

"Forgot about what? You cats have nine lives or something?" Wep asked.

"Somethin' like that," Max said with a grin. "So how did ye see the kitty mummies if the pyramids were sealed up?"

"There are secret passages in and out of pyramids," Wep explained. "I've found out lots of hidden things about these places. Secret chambers, false doors, coded messages."

"Well, kin ye help us find the r-r-right passage out of this pyramid? We came down this way but it were a dead end," Max said.

"Sure, I can get us out of here. I know every square inch of this pyramid," Wep replied. "Come on, I'll show you the way out."

"Wha' were ye doin' down here anyway?" Max asked as he and Al followed Wep down the corridor.

"I came in here to hide from the humans who chased me after I nabbed some bread," Wep replied. "It's easy to lose humans in here."

The threesome went about fifty yards down the passageway and were making a turn when Max heard voices once more. "There they go again. Do ye hear that?" Max asked. He started worrying he was hearing things.

"You'll hear voices throughout the pyramid. The passages wind around and around, up and down, and sometimes come close together, where you can hear voices through the walls," Wep explained. "It's probably just the humans inspecting Pharaoh's burial chamber."

Al gulped. He envisioned his tiny coffin lying next to Pharaoh. Up and around, down and back they walked through the corridors, until soon they arrived at the main corridor of the pyramid where they had started. Max and Al were relieved.

"'Tis gr-r-rand that ye helped us find the way back, Wep. Thanks!" Max exclaimed.

"Glad to help. I'll leave you here so I can stay out of sight until dusk, but you can find your way to the entrance right down that passage," Wep directed.

Al looked at how skinny Wep was and felt sorry for him. He thought of how much food he had back at the palace. "Wep, why don't ye come by the palace and I'll be happy to share some food with ye. I've got more than I can eat, as ye can tell," Al said with a grin and a pat to his belly.

"Do you mean it? You'd give me food?" Wep asked excitedly.

"Aye, laddie! Any kind o' food ye can imagine is there, from fish to fruit to veggies to nuts. Sure, and I'll set ye up anytime ye like. Jest come after dark to the north wall o' the palace and give a good yelp to let me know ye're there. I'll let ye in the kitchen," Al said with a big grin.

"Thanks, Al. I'll definitely see you soon," Wep said with a grin. "Hey, and good luck riding in Pharaoh's chariot."

"Great! I'll be seein' ye, Wep. Sure, and I'll have a chat with Pharaoh's horses aboot the reckless drivin'," Al replied with a laugh.

Max and Al made their way back to the entrance and were innocently sitting there when Potiphar, Pharaoh, and Sadiki joined them from the other corridor. Pharaoh smiled and picked Al up, saying, "Hapy, I'm sorry you weren't with me to see my burial chamber. No one will ever be able to find us—except the gods, that is."

Al looked at Max, anguish written on his face. "Max, make him stop talkin' aboot lockin' me up in his triangle!"

Max shook his head. Al should have realized he was safe under the Maker's care, but the threat of the moment caused Al to forget the reality of who his true Master was. "How aboot a little distraction then?"

Max proceeded to bark at Sadiki and run toward the exit, looking back for Sadiki to follow.

"What is it, boy? Do you smell something?" Sadiki asked, following Max to the door.

"Perhaps he smells ibex," Pharaoh said with a chuckle. "It's time to continue the hunt. I'm pleased with the progress of my pyramid, Potiphar. Now let's be off. And Sadiki, let's see if your dog can drive the ibex off the cliffs into the path of my arrow."

"As you say, my master," Sadiki said with a bow as Pharaoh, carrying Al, strode out of the pyramid.

"I'll assemble the chariots," Potiphar said, following behind Pharaoh.

Max gulped as he sat by the door. He hated the thought of being the one to lead Gillamon's relatives toward certain death. He got up to leave when he heard a "Psst!" from behind.

Max turned to see Nigel sitting on Pharaoh's statue. "Mousie! Wha' in the name of Pete are ye doin' here?"

"I brought Liz out to tour the pyramid, old boy. She's back in one of the chambers studying the hieroglyphs," Nigel replied. "Had to dodge Potiphar in the corridor, you know. I say, it would have been dreadful if he'd seen her here."

"Aye! Al will be sad he missed seein' his lass," Max replied. "Nigel, I have a pr-r-r-oblem. Pharaoh wants me ta flush out the ibex so he kin kill them, but I jest kin't br-r-ring meself ta do it."

"I see," Nigel said, tapping his fingers on his chin in thought.

Max heard Sadiki calling him from outside.

"Right. Go with Sadiki and do as Pharaoh asks. Tell the ibex to play the part and allow you to chase them. Leave the rest to me," Nigel instructed.

"How in the world are ye supposed ta help me in the hunt for ibex?!" Max questioned with his head cocked to the side.

"With my secret weapon," Nigel said with a sly grin as he scurried off into the dark corridor.

"Wha' is it aboot this pyramid an' secrets that makes all the beasties think such daft thoughts?" Max said out loud to himself. "An' wha' makes a wee mouse think he kin beat Pharaoh an' his arrow?"

Max looked at the carved images of false gods on the walls around him and felt an eerie presence. This was a consuming place, both in ideas and in scope. Thousands of workers had built a city and labored on this pyramid for two decades, all so Pharaoh could live forever with the gods of their own making. This place was Pharaoh's dream for eternity. But Max knew what was on the other side of death. He and Liz were the only ones in this pyramid who knew the true secret of eternity.

"Maker, please help me keep me mind aboot me in this str-r-range place," Max prayed. "An' help me with the ibex beasties. I've had aboot all the death I kin take today."

He trotted out of the pyramid, glad to get out of there despite the challenge ahead.

CHAPTER 24

Nigel's Secret Weapon

Pharaoh led the charge of chariots once again as they headed south. This time Al didn't let him take off until he was securely wrapped around the guardrail at the front of the chariot. Not only did Al want to be secure from flying out, he needed to have a word with the horses.

"Can ye hear me, horsies?" Al asked as they galloped down the road.

"It's kind of hard not to, cat," one of the stallions called back. "We've heard you screaming all day."

"Oh, well, good, I guess," Al replied. "I'm jest a wee bit worried aboot Pharaoh's drivin'. Has he ever wrecked his chariot?"

"He's come close but always seems to maintain control," the other stallion replied. "But there's always a first time for everything."

Al gulped and held on tight.

Sadiki scanned the rugged terrain and suddenly saw them. A group of ibex was grazing in the tall grass up ahead. He pulled up next to Pharaoh and called, "My master, ibex on the right! Allow me to go ahead of you, and I'll set Jabari to flush them out in your path."

"Excellent! Be off!" Pharaoh ordered, pulling back slightly so Sadiki could advance.

Sadiki snapped the reins of his horses, his chariot kicking up dust behind him. Max frowned as he looked ahead and spotted the ibex. There was a cluster of about ten of the wild mountain goats. They stood only three feet tall at the shoulder and were a light tan color with a white underbelly. All were female except for one male with a dark brown stripe down his back and three-foot ridged horns curved back behind him. He looked like he had the wheels of a chariot mounted on his head. Max wondered if this was why Pharaoh wanted to hunt such a beast—for a trophy.

"Jabari, on my mark, go flush them out," Sadiki said as he came to a screeching halt. He jumped out of the chariot and slapped Max on the back. "NOW GO!"

Max took off running toward the group of grazing ibex as fast as his short legs would carry him. As he neared the herd, they raised their heads in alarm. Max called out to them, "Listen up, beasties! Pharaoh is after ye so r-r-run for yer lives! Get out of here! R-R-RUN!"

Okay, Nigel, wher-r-re ar-r-re ye? Ye an' yer secr-r-ret weapon? Max frantically thought.

All of a sudden he heard an unmistakable voice. "HEY! YOU GUYS! FOLLOW ME!"

It was Osahar the camel, galloping toward the ibex from an outcropping of rocks on the left, shouting at the top of his lungs. Nigel sat on top of the camel's head, pulling his ears like reins to steer the beast. Liz was crouched down between Osahar's humps, hanging on tight.

Gr-r-reat! That camel beastie is Nigel's secr-r-ret weapon?! Max grunted to himself. *Jest as I thought. Now the mousie is daft, too!*

"HYA!" Nigel shouted as he steered Osahar in front of the ibex, which took off running away from Pharaoh's fast-approaching chariot.

"MAX! KEEP CHASING THE IBEX! DON'T STOP RUNNING AFTER THEM!" Osahar shouted.

Max didn't know what else to do, so he picked up speed and continued to chase after the ibex, which kicked up dust in his face.

Suddenly Nigel pulled on Osahar's right ear and made him turn around to charge directly at Pharaoh's chariot. They were aimed for a head-on collision and Osahar was shouting at the horses in his path. "CHIC-KEN! CHIC-KEN! CHIC-KEN! I BET YOU'RE CHIC-KEN! BAWK, BAWK, BAWK!"

Al's eyes were as big as saucers, and he joined his own screams with Osahar's: "We're all doomed!"

"That beast is mad!" Pharaoh's horses screamed.

"He's going to kill us!" yelled Potiphar's horses, terror filling their eyes.

"What is this beast?!" Pharaoh shouted as the deranged camel charged dead ahead toward his chariot. "I'll let my arrow take him out!"

While Pharaoh put his arrow in place on his bow, Al suddenly noticed Nigel on Osahar's head and Liz riding between the humps. "LIZ!" he screamed, looking at Pharaoh pointing his arrow directly at the camel. He had to do something.

Al let go of the handrail and popped out his claws, sinking them directly into the buttocks of the horses, causing them to neigh loudly and rear up. Pharaoh fell backwards and tumbled out the back of his chariot. All the horses followed suit, rearing up and dumping all the charioteers. It was complete pandemonium!

"What a jolly good sporting event!" Nigel shouted with a laugh. "Chariot tipping!"

"Hurry, Nigel, now let's get out of here!" Liz said as she held on tight to Osahar's hide.

"Right! Our work here is finished. Osahar, retreat!" Nigel said as he pulled the camel's ears to direct him in the opposite direction.

"HORSES ARE CHIC-KEN! HORSES ARE CHIC-KEN!" Osahar shouted as he turned and ran in the direction of Max and the fleeing ibex.

Liz peered out from between Osahar's humps to see if Al was all right. He was flat on his back in the now-still chariot, shaken but okay. "Well done, Albert, my noble, famous warrior!" she called with a blown kiss.

Al looked up and saw Liz's outstretched paw and was relieved she was okay. He couldn't believe he had assisted in causing the very thing he dreaded—a chariot wreck. He laughed at himself, stood on his hind paws, and waved back at Liz. "Me lass, I'd wreck a chariot for ye anytime!"

Potiphar rose and ran over to Pharaoh, who was sitting up now, holding his head. "My master! Are you all right?"

"Yes, yes, I'm fine. What *was* that strange beast?" Pharaoh asked, looking at the camel running off in the distance. "It made the horses rear up like mad."

"I've only seen one other beast like that in my life, at the market," Potiphar said staring at the fleeing Osahar. "I think it is called a 'Bactrian camel.'" Suddenly Potiphar thought he saw a black cat sitting on top of the beast and rubbed his eyes again. "I must have hit my head harder than I thought."

Max had chased the ibex way out of range and stopped to see the chaos behind him. The hunting party was clearly a mess, with chariots and horses tipped over on the road. He saw Osahar now heading his way. He cocked his head in disbelief. "Time ta get ta the bottom of this."

"Good show, old boy!" Nigel called as they met Max on the road. "We saved the ibex!"

"How in the name of Pete did ye manage ta stop Pharaoh?" Max asked.

"Didn't I tell you I had a secret weapon?" Nigel asked with his jolly chuckle as he patted Osahar on the head.

Osahar grinned a mile wide. "HEY! DID YOU SEE ME, MAX? I DID GOOD!"

"Now you'd better get back to Sadiki and Al to help them ride back to the palace," Nigel said. He patted Osahar. "I've got to get Liz to Potiphar's house before he returns home. Onward ho, camel!"

"It is good to see you, *mon ami,* but please hurry and check on Albert. I know this was a frightening experience for him," Liz's voice trailed off as Osahar started trotting away.

Max sat in the road with a furrowed brow, stumped. None of this made sense. "But how, Nigel? How were Osahar a secret weapon against Pharaoh?" Max called after the departing group.

"Why, didn't you know, old boy?" Nigel called back with a hand to his mouth. "Horses are afraid of camels."

CHAPTER 25

The Favor of Potiphar

Mandisa stood behind Zuleika, braiding her hair while her mistress looked at the ornate headpiece she would wear for the harvest celebration party. It was a gold band, one inch thick, with clusters of rosettes inlaid with blue, green, and red semiprecious stones. Zuleika's fingers touched each rosette, admiring the beauty of this jewelry that Potiphar had commissioned for her to wear on this special occasion. She would also wear the matching collar necklace, with its seven rows of colorful beads surrounded by gold.

"Your new jewelry is beautiful, my mistress. I'm sure you will be the most lovely lady at the party," Mandisa said with a smile.

Zuleika set down the headpiece and held up the mirror to admire her necklace. "Yes, Mandisa, I believe you are right. Do hurry with my hair; I need to make sure everything is . . . ready."

"Yes, my mistress. As you say," Mandisa said, tying the final braid and lifting the headpiece to place it on Zuleika's head.

"Now go see to Bastet. You know how Potiphar loves his cat and wants her looking perfect for this evening," Zuleika instructed.

As Mandisa bowed and left the room, Liz remained hidden for a moment longer behind the sheer curtains in the bed chamber, studying Zuleika as she looked at herself in the mirror.

"Just as you will be seen in a new light tonight, so may you see me," Zuleika said to herself, a sly smile on her face as she twirled a braid in her fingers.

Liz frowned and turned to leave the room. Potiphar's wife was truly beautiful, and she knew it. With her new jewelry and a new white linen gown, she would be the center of attention. *But whose attention does Potiphar's wife desire most of all?* Liz wondered. She would have to keep a close eye on her tonight.

Mandisa quickly finished Liz's bath so she could get on to other chores for the party. She had used special oils, so even Liz was looking her best for the big event. Liz's jewelry was polished to a high sheen. She was extremely curious as to the events of the evening, so she slinked around from room to room on the property to see what was going on. Liz decided to check on the kitchen, the busiest spot in the house of Potiphar.

Ako clapped his hands to direct the group of slaves in the kitchen to ready the food for the party. "Quickly, quickly! The guests will arrive shortly, and Potiphar wishes everyone to be served immediately," Ako directed.

Potiphar's house was jumping with activity as everyone prepared for the long-awaited harvest celebration. It had been an extremely good year, and Potiphar's garden had never looked better. Especially his new central masterpiece—the vineyard.

"I want everyone looking their best and waiting on Potiphar's guests hand and foot. Make sure the plates are full and the glasses overflowing," Ako continued, wiping his brow. He was exhausted and had to sit down. He didn't know how much longer he could keep up this pace. The daily running of Potiphar's house was a formidable task, let alone a party for the highest dignitaries in all of Avaris.

Ako is getting old and needs to retire soon, Liz thought. *I hope Potiphar has realized this.*

Liz left the kitchen and went outside into the garden where Potiphar walked with Joseph for one last inspection before the party began. She meowed up at Potiphar as she wrapped her tail around his legs. "My, don't you look beautiful, Bastet! You may be the fairest of them all tonight." She purred as he stroked her shiny fur.

Under the grand arbor the musicians were setting up their instruments to prepare the entertainment for the party. A harpist was joined by two flutists, two percussionists with small drums, four reed pipe players, two bell players, three vocalists, and several dancers who held carved wooden clappers.

"Joseph, you have outdone yourself. When you said the columns would be painted, I never dreamed they would look so exquisite. And the tile floor you installed under the grand arbor is magnificent!" Potiphar exclaimed.

Liz was beaming. The columns were beautiful because of the plan she left lying out for Joseph to find. Three months ago, after visiting Pharaoh's pyramid and studying the ornamentation on the walls, she had formulated an idea for Joseph's columns. She had Nigel prepare a tribute message in hieroglyphs to Potiphar, calling on God to grant him success. Nigel made sure no false gods were mentioned. The design for the base of the columns was carved papyrus reeds sprouting out of the Nile. Then painted on the columns were bountiful grapevine clusters curving around to the very top.

Liz and Nigel left the design plan for the columns sitting on the stone bench under the grand arbor. The cat and the mouse then hid behind one of the columns to see what Joseph would do when he found the plan. Liz and Nigel quietly cheered when they saw Joseph nod his head and smile as he looked at the plan. Joseph assumed Potiphar had left it there, so he started immediately on applying the design to the columns.

"Thank you, my master. I am glad you are so pleased," Joseph said, bowing in respect. "The vines are young, but by this time next year I predict a huge harvest of grapes. The Nile silt seems to have been the key to enriching the soil."

Liz beamed even more.

Potiphar stood face to face with Joseph and put his hand on his shoulder. "I see the favor of your God upon you. *Everything* you do prospers. I've never seen anything like it."

"I give credit to my God, for He is the one who brings me success," Joseph said.

"Joseph, I want you to go clean up and be here for the party. I instructed Ako to leave fresh loincloths for you, Benipe, and the other workers. I want my friends to meet the man responsible for this masterpiece," Potiphar said as he waved his hand out across the vineyard.

"As you say. I will be honored," Joseph said. With that he bowed and left Potiphar in the vineyard.

Potiphar stroked Liz as he watched Joseph walk away. "Bastet, some changes are coming tonight, all thanks to you, as it started with you that day at the market. I hope you will be pleased," he said. He smiled as he considered how Joseph would respond when he made the announcement tonight. "But first, I have to tell Ako," he said as he put Liz down on the pathway. Liz followed along behind him. The events of this evening were growing more curious, and she wasn't about to leave his side.

"Ako, I need to have a word with you," Potiphar said when he found Ako busily directing the servants to receive the chariots and litters that would be arriving shortly. Potiphar held a package wrapped with golden cords behind his back. Liz wanted to know what was in the package.

"As you wish, my lord," Ako said, following Potiphar into the colonnade. "Is everything as you wish for the party?"

"Yes, yes, you have done a tremendous job, as usual. You look tired. Here, come sit," Potiphar instructed as he sat and pointed to the adjacent chair.

Ako did as Potiphar directed, but was a bit nervous. Something seemed wrong. Potiphar smiled and said, "Ako, you have served me well for many, many years. I could not have asked for a more trustworthy steward. But it does not escape me that you are tired. A man of your years now deserves a time to rest and enjoy life."

Good! I am glad he realized this, Liz thought as she hid behind a green plant, eyeing the package in Potiphar's lap.

Potiphar leaned over and put his hand on Ako's shoulder. "Today I release you to enjoy life free from the work of my household. From now on you can pursue whatever life interests you wish while remaining welcome to live under my roof."

A look of relief came over Ako's wrinkled face and Potiphar smiled. "My lord, I am grateful to you for the opportunity to serve you these many years. Indeed I am tired. Thank you for releasing me to enjoy my older years. I will be happy to stay with you as I do so. But who will manage your affairs?"

"I have someone in mind," Potiphar replied, handing the wrapped package to Ako. "And when I give the word tonight, you are to bring this to me."

Liz wrinkled her brow as Potiphar and Ako stood. Ako took the package, bowed, and walked off. Potiphar went in the other direction. *What's going on?* Liz wondered. *I'll find out soon, but I'm beyond ready for this party to get started.*

An endless line of chariots and litters arrived at the front gate of Potiphar's house. Mandisa and the other household servants lined the entry hall to welcome the guests. Potiphar and Zuleika stood together as the dignitaries and their wives arrived, and everyone seemed to be gushing over how beautiful Zuleika looked.

"My wife is fairer than the Nile, is she not?" Potiphar said as he proudly introduced her to the wealthy and powerful men in attendance.

"Indeed she is," they would reply, bowing low in honor of meeting her.

Zuleika loved the attention, and as the men gathered to discuss matters of state, she invited their wives to stroll with her through the beautiful gardens, listening to the lovely music and admiring the grounds. Servants busily hovered around the guests, providing them with food and drink. Everyone was having a marvelous time.

Joseph and Benipe stood behind the grand arbor, clean and well-dressed for the party. Benipe was mesmerized by the music. The harpist held a beautifully carved and painted arched harp with ten strings. He sat with it on the tile floor, legs crossed and leaning into the harp as he adjusted the pegs to tighten the strings. Benipe observed closely how the harpist adjusted the strings until he finally heard the perfect pitch as he plucked the strings hard, smiling when the right tone was reached.

"Joseph, I've never heard such beautiful sounds before. I can't explain it, but my heart is stirred by that harp," Benipe said.

Joseph looked at Benipe and smiled. "Perhaps God is stirring your heart with a desire to play."

"How could I ever hope to achieve a position like that, Joseph? I know nothing about music," Benipe replied.

"Since when should a lack of experience be a reason not to pursue something that interests you? If you are drawn to try something you've never done, that is a perfect reason to *get* experience," Joseph replied. "I don't think that harpist was born knowing how to play, do you?"

Benipe laughed. "No, I'm sure he had to learn music and how to play. But Joseph, remember, I'm a slave. I'm not in the right part of the social structure to be able to learn how to play, even if I wanted to."

"Well, I wasn't a vinedresser until Potiphar assigned me the task. My interest in learning about vines and landscaping, coupled with my passion to honor God and my master with my work, led to what we've accomplished here," Joseph said, looking out over the vineyard. "I'm learning that if you have a driving desire to do something honorable, and that desire seems to come from nowhere, it has been placed there by God. And if that desire is *truly* placed there by God, He will make it a reality," Joseph said thoughtfully. "So I tell you, if you desire to learn to play the harp, a way will come."

"You're a dreamer, Joseph," Benipe replied.

"So I've heard," Joseph answered with a sad smile, thinking of his brothers taunting him over his dreams.

"Look, I'm a slave assigned to work in the garden, and that's all I'll ever be. You are, too, so you'd better get used to it," Benipe replied. "If the gods wanted me to play the harp, I would have been born into a family of means to be trained."

"I didn't say 'gods,' I said *God*. There is a difference—although you don't see it yet, Benipe. I hope one day you will," Joseph told him.

They stood a moment and just listened to the melodious sounds of the harp. Benipe closed his eyes. "I can almost 'see' the music in my mind."

Joseph smiled and looked at Benipe, who was clearly swept away by the music. *Oh, how I wish you would open your eyes to see the real God, my friend.*

"Oh, good, you're here, *mon ami!*" Liz said as Nigel joined her in the garden.

"But of course I am, my dear. I wouldn't miss it," Nigel said with a gracious bow. He took Liz's paw and kissed it, saying, "And might I say how lovely you look."

"*Merci,* Nigel," Liz replied. "Everyone in the house of Potiphar is looking their best this evening. Potiphar bought special clothes and jewelry for the occasion. And you look quite, how do you British say, 'dapper,' no?"

"Al asked me to join him for one of his milk baths, and it was quite an enriching experience, I must say," Nigel chuckled, wiping back his long whiskers on either side of his face. His coat was shiny white and clean.

"Ah, how is my precious Albert?" Liz asked. "I wish he could have been here."

"He is pining for you, my dear, and sends his love. I hope we can arrange another meeting for you two soon," Nigel said with a smile.

Liz appreciated how Nigel helped her sneak out of Potiphar's house to meet Al in the palace. They had to be extremely careful not to be seen. But Nigel was a master at hiding on their outings, such as when they visited the pyramid. They continued to hide in the loft of the school for their weekly lessons. But Nigel insisted Liz learn a bit more of the language before they returned to Pharaoh's pyramid or visited the temple of Anubis. He wanted her to be well versed in the language to appreciate and understand what was written on the walls.

"Nigel, Potiphar said some changes are coming tonight, and it is all 'thanks to me.' It must have something to do with Joseph, but I'm not certain what it means," Liz explained.

"Well, keep a sharp eye. Looks like we're getting ready to find out," Nigel replied.

Just then they heard Ako assembling the servants, who walked ahead of Potiphar, Zuleika, and their guests, carrying oil lamps to illuminate the garden. They were heading to the grand arbor in the center of the vineyard. The musicians continued to play softly as Potiphar stood in front of the beautiful columns.

"My friends, thank you for coming tonight as we celebrate the harvest. The gods have been good this year!" he said with a glass raised as a toast. The guests lifted their glasses and echoed their approval.

"Zuleika and I have been blessed with plenty and we invite you to enjoy the bounty of our table this evening. But I am most pleased to share with you the crowning achievement of my garden this year," Potiphar said with arms outstretched, "my vineyard."

The guests clapped and murmured in approval. Benipe jabbed Joseph in the ribs and Joseph lowered his head with a grin. Liz and Nigel looked at each other and shared a nod of congratulations for their part in Joseph's success.

"I was fortunate to have a very unique individual come to my house and make this vineyard possible. He was a very unlikely candidate to bring something so grand into being, as he is a slave—but an unusual slave, mind you. He always talks about his God and how his God gave him the ability to make this the finest vineyard in all of Avaris. Well, whoever this God of his is, I have to believe He has indeed put His favor on this slave," Potiphar said. After a pause, he added, "Joseph, come here."

Liz's ears perked up as she wondered what was happening. Joseph's heart jumped when he heard Potiphar call his name in front of all these important people. They were the most powerful people in Egypt aside from Pharaoh, and yet Potiphar was recognizing him in their presence. Joseph humbly walked over to Potiphar and bowed in respect, standing before him.

"I wish to make an announcement. Ako, bring me the package," Potiphar directed.

Ako walked up to Potiphar and with both arms held out the wrapped bundle. He looked at Joseph and smiled before stepping back with the other servants. Liz jumped up on a garden pedestal to get a better view. Nigel scurried up onto the pedestal and crouched down to stay out of sight behind Liz as they watched the scene.

Potiphar held the package in one hand and loosened the gold cord tied around it as he spoke. "Never before have I seen anything like the favor that is clearly on Joseph. Everything he does prospers, and so I believe it is a sign for me to elevate this slave to a new position." Potiphar unrolled the garment that was wrapped in the package and held out a beautiful robe to Joseph. "I hereby appoint Joseph as my chief steward and personal assistant. With this robe he is no longer a lowly slave but is the top servant in the house of Potiphar. Joseph will have complete charge over all my affairs and my estate. May the favor of his God be upon everything I own."

Joseph was stunned. He couldn't believe what was happening. As he held out his arms for Potiphar to put the new robe on his back, Joseph's gaze met Liz. They shared a smile and a wink.

Joseph turned to face Potiphar in his new robe, bowed low, and said, "Thank you, my lord. I will serve you with all I am so you will worry for nothing."

Potiphar put his hand on Joseph's shoulder and assured him, "Of that I have no doubt. Joseph, you have the favor of Potiphar." He then turned to the crowd and lifted Joseph's hand, shouting, "Welcome Joseph, chief steward of Potiphar!"

The crowd erupted in cheers and immediately came over to surround and congratulate Joseph and Potiphar. It was a surreal moment for Joseph. He caught Benipe's eye and smiled. Benipe nodded with a returned smile and shook his head in amazed but joyful disbelief. What was happening to Joseph just didn't happen. This was not the way it was done in the social structure of Egypt. A Hebrew slave made chief steward to Pharaoh's chief of the guard? How was it possible? Benipe looked over at the harpist and a surge of hope entered his spirit. Perhaps what Joseph had said about his God was true.

Liz grabbed Nigel with a consuming hug and twirled him around, exclaiming, "Do you realize what this means?"

"That Joseph has done well?" Nigel replied, uncertain as to the full import of the moment.

"*Oui, oui,* of course Joseph has done well and earned the favor of Potiphar. But the robe, Nigel, the robe! This is the second robe in our mission, as foretold by Gillamon! He said to look for the sign of four robes. The first was the one given to Joseph by his father, and this is the second, given by Potiphar!" Liz said excitedly.

"How utterly splendid, my dear! I say, how thrilling to be here for the occasion," Nigel said beaming. "I will be sure to pass on this information to Max and Al."

"Oh, please do, *mon ami.* This is good news!" Liz said, continuing to look at Joseph.

"I wonder what his next two robes will be like," Nigel pondered.

"And when they will come," Liz added, thinking out loud. "But still we have other signs to observe as well: eight dreams and three schemes. Of the dreams I know nothing specific other than that Joseph must have dreamed something for his brothers to call him 'Dreamer.' And of the schemes, so far only one has transpired, that of Joseph's brothers selling him into slavery."

Liz continued to observe the celebration surrounding Joseph and noticed one person in particular whose eyes were solidly fixed on the handsome young man. She had a mischievous grin on her face. Liz's heart caught in her chest.

"Nigel, I have a feeling many changes are coming in the house of Potiphar with Joseph's promotion," she said.

"Whatever do you mean, dear girl?" Nigel said. When she didn't answer, he followed Liz's gaze over to the person in question.

It was none other than Zuleika.

PART THREE

THE LORD

CHAPTER 26

Kate and Benjamin

SIX YEARS LATER

"Did you finish your breakfast?" Leah called after Benjamin as he hurriedly ran out of the tent, Kate trailing along behind.

"Yes, Aunt Leah! Every bite," Benjamin replied as he grabbed his knapsack and wrapped some pistachios in a cloth to put in his pack. "You ready, Amisa?" Benjamin petted Kate on the head and grabbed his walking stick.

Kate wagged her tail as she followed Benjamin out of the tent to the field behind Jacob's camp. It was a beautiful spring day and she enjoyed going with Benjamin on his outings. He was now eleven years old, and was growing into an independent young man.

"Benjamin, be careful," Jacob called from his tent. "Keep Amisa with you at all times."

"I will, Father," Benjamin said as he waved and smiled. "We won't be gone long."

Jacob closed his eyes and said a prayer of protection over Benjamin as he felt the warmth of the sun on his face. He was grateful Benjamin had a little dog to be a friend and companion as well as a protector. The loss of Joseph was hard on all of them, but Benjamin was especially grieved. Joseph was his full brother and his hero. They had shared a special bond, and it was difficult for Benjamin to lose his brother after never even knowing his mother. Jacob watched and smiled at the little dog they had named 'Amisa,' meaning 'comfort.' He thanked God for bringing her to their camp, for she had brought nothing but comfort to him and Benjamin during these hard years.

Benjamin's curly locks fell over his forehead as he walked through the fields, now bursting with wildflowers. He picked a dandelion and blew off the seeds, which scattered across the field in the breeze. As his gaze followed the blowing seeds, he saw his brothers in the distant fields with the sheep and waved. He was glad they were home for a while. It seemed everyone wanted to stay close to their father these days. Everyone, that is, except Judah. He had packed up and left, not really giving a good reason as far as Benjamin could see. Maybe he missed Joseph so much he just couldn't be reminded he was gone.

"I still miss him, Amisa," Benjamin said as he and Kate walked through the fields. Benjamin tapped his stick on the rocks they passed. "I wish you could have known Joseph," he said with his lip quivering. "He was my best friend."

Kate looked up at Benjamin with a look of compassion. *I know, young one. I wish I could tell you he is not gone—he's just not here.*

Benjamin smiled at Kate. "Now *you're* my best friend." He wiped his eyes with the back of his arm. "Come on, I'll race you to my fort!"

Kate barked and hopped with joy as Benjamin took off running ahead of her. Together they ran through the fields down to a creek where Benjamin had made a hideout fort with tree limbs, branches, and rocks. He jumped down the boulders and landed with his feet in the gooey mud of the creek bank. "Beat ya!" he exclaimed as he pulled his knapsack off his shoulder and knelt down to cup some water from the creek.

Kate lapped up some water next to Benjamin and noticed the creek was higher today. The recent storm had brought heavy rains that now ran off into the swollen creek. Benjamin turned to inspect his fort. "Oh great, some of the big sticks must have gotten loose with the wind and the rain," he said as he walked inside and saw a gap in the covering. "We'll just have to get more sticks. Come on, girl."

He put his knapsack down and went walking along the banks of the creek. Kate stayed close behind, watching the water rush over the rocks and boulders. They soon reached the old oak tree that snaked over the creek. Evidently it had fallen on its side decades ago, yet it continued to grow on a horizontal plane out over the creek. Its green, leafy branches extended in all directions and the rough bark was gnarled where it had fought gravity to grow at odd angles.

This was one of Benjamin's favorite places to climb. But it made Kate nervous as he walked out over the water, balancing with his arms out as he stepped bit by bit along the broad trunk of the tree. A kingfisher went flying by, and Benjamin had to dodge the low-flying bird as it swooped down, eyeing fish in the fast-moving creek. His foot slipped but he managed to keep his balance. Kate sighed with relief. She felt responsible for this boy.

Benjamin jumped from the overhanging tree to the other bank of the creek, landing with a thud. Kate barked at him and he called back, "Come on, Amisa! You can do it, girl."

Kate looked at the rushing water and remembered walking across a slippery rock jetty back in England when they were trying to cross the Channel. From the jetty she had to cross over Craddock the whale's large flippers to reach his back while the waves lapped under her. If she could do that, certainly she could do this.

Kate slowly stepped out onto the tree trunk and carefully made her way across, trying not to look at the rapidly flowing water under her. She made it to the other side, joining Benjamin as she jumped off the trunk onto the muddy bank.

"That's a good girl. I knew you could do it," Benjamin said with his sweet smile and a pat on Kate's back. "Look, I see some branches that would be great for my fort," he said as he walked over to a cluster of fallen limbs.

Benjamin proceeded to pull out some of the limbs, casting some on the bank and tossing others he deemed too small into the rushing creek. Kate noticed an old stump of a tree hanging off the bank directly above where Benjamin worked. He spied a good-size branch right under the stump and began to pull, digging his feet into the mud below. He yanked and pulled, but the branch was stuck. Benjamin put a foot on the side of the bank to get a better hold and leaned back with all his might.

Suddenly the branch broke free, and because of the softened mud around it, the stump also came tumbling down. The heavy stump landed right on Benjamin's right leg, pinning him on the bank. He screamed as the impact of the stump broke the bones in his leg. It all happened quickly, but Kate felt as if she watched it unfold in slow motion.

Quickly Kate rushed all around Benjamin to see how she could free him of the stump. She put her teeth on one of the branches growing out of the stump and pulled with all her might, but it was no use. The stump was much bigger than it had appeared when it was embedded in the muddy bank. There was no way she could pull it off Benjamin.

"Oh, please, Maker! Help me know what to do!" Kate prayed as she feverishly tried to dig the mud around Benjamin so he could get out from underneath the stump. He cried out in pain as he tried to push the stump off his leg. But there was no moving it, either by digging or pushing. Tears streamed out of his eyes as Kate stood over him, feeling helpless. What could she do? Even if she managed to pull him out from under the stump, with his broken leg he could not make it back to camp. Kate had no choice but to leave him and run for help.

"Go . . . get help," Benjamin cried, throwing his head back in excruciating pain.

Kate barked, *I'll be back! Don't worry, Benjamin, I'll get help!*

She turned and hopped back onto the tree trunk to cross the creek, running over it at top speed. But as she landed on the other side, she heard the unmistakable scream of a cougar. Her head snapped back, and she saw the large cat standing on the bank above where Benjamin lay. It pulled its ears back and hissed, crouching down on its front paws as it spied its helpless prey.

"No!" Kate barked wildly at the cougar. "Don't touch the boy!"

She ran back across the tree trunk as the cougar made its way down the side of the bank to where Benjamin lay screaming, now from fear as much as pain. Kate jumped in between Benjamin and the cougar, growling and showing her teeth in a defensive display. She was not about to let this cougar get to Benjamin.

The cougar was a juvenile male, as its tawny coat was pale with black spots on its flanks. It was most likely newly out on its own and looking for new territory. The cat, pacing back and forth, growled and hissed at Kate, unsure if it wanted to tangle with her. Never before had Kate put up such a ferocious front. She barked wildly and the fur on her back stood on end. When it appeared the cougar would test Kate's strength and moved closer, Kate lunged at the cougar, barking wildly and nipping at its legs. It held up its large front paws as if to strike but merely hissed at Kate.

Benjamin yelled, "Amisa, keep barking!"

Kate barked and barked, growling and showing her teeth. She edged closer to the cougar, which turned its head to the side and gradually backed off, deciding it would rather not tangle with her. The cat growled and turned away, jumping ten feet up to the top of the bank and disappearing from sight. Kate didn't budge until she knew the threat was gone.

Benjamin closed his eyes in relief as he saw the cougar run off. "You did it, girl! I thought I was going to die!"

Just then Kate looked over to see Kerra, Benjamin's cousin, on the other side of the creek. She barked at the girl, who looked across, trying to figure out what had happened. She ran over the tree trunk and crouched down next to the boy.

"Benjamin! What happened?" she cried, trying to lift the stump.

"It fell on me. Go get help. It's too heavy for you," Benjamin said, now about to pass out from the pain.

"Stay with him, girl," Kerra said as she looked at Kate. "I'll get the men."

With that the young girl crossed the creek again and ran back to the fields where the brothers were grazing the sheep. She cried out to them for help.

Kate was shaking all over as she was flooded with relief. The cougar was gone and help was on the way. She sat next to Benjamin and licked his face. "Hang on, dear boy," she whimpered.

Benjamin moaned and winced from the pain and closed his eyes. He reached his hand up to touch Kate. "Good girl. You . . . saved me. Good girl."

Soon Kerra led five of Benjamin's brothers running to the creek carrying a makeshift litter. Reuben was the first to reach him. "Hang on, little brother, we're here and we'll get you out."

Reuben looked at Simeon and Levi and said, "We three will lift the stump. Issachar, help pull Benjamin out while Zebulun slides the litter under him. Ready? HEAVE!"

The three men each grabbed a branch from the stump and strained with all their might, slipping in the mud as they struggled to lift the massive stump enough to be able to pry Benjamin out. Carefully Issachar wrapped his arms around Benjamin's chest and pulled while Zebulun helped position the litter under him. Benjamin screamed from the pain as his broken bones shifted while they moved him.

When Issachar and Zebulun had moved Benjamin out of the way, they yelled, "He's clear!"

Reuben, Simeon, and Levi let the stump drop and fell back, breathing heavily from the exertion of lifting the huge weight.

"His leg is broken, looks like in multiple places," Issachar said as he examined Benjamin's wounds. "We will need to bind his leg tightly with splints, but at least the bones didn't break the skin. This leg will heal with time."

The brothers gathered around Benjamin, their faces filled with grief at seeing their little brother in such pain. "Okay, carefully, let's lift him," Reuben instructed. The other four brothers each took an end of the long sticks to which they had strapped a leather hide for Benjamin to lie on.

Kate stepped back to get out of their way as they slowly walked down the creek bank. They realized they would have to somehow get across carrying Benjamin. Reuben walked into the creek, and the water level was almost up to his chest. With the rushing water and the rocks on the creek bed floor, it would be too risky for the brothers to walk through the water. They would have to cross over the tree trunk carrying Benjamin.

"Simeon and Levi, you two will need to carry Benjamin alone over the tree. Issachar, Zebulun, and I will walk through the creek next to you to steady you in case you fall. Let's go," Reuben said as the brothers took their positions.

Very slowly and deliberately Simeon and Levi lifted the litter. Simeon was in front, facing backward, while Levi held the other end facing forward. Reuben, Issachar, and Zebulun walked beside them in the creek on either side of the tree. It was a tense few minutes, but they gradually made it across. Zebulun and Issachar quickly grabbed two corners of the litter and the four men walked as fast as they could to get Benjamin back to camp.

Benjamin winced as the brothers carried him along. "Reuben, Amisa saved my life. She . . . she stood in between me and a cougar until it finally ran off. It was going to kill me."

"God be praised! Well done, little one!" Reuben said as he looked down at Kate trotting along next to them.

"All I could think about was Joseph and how a wild beast got him," Benjamin said, his lip quivering. "I just knew the same fate awaited me."

The brothers looked at one another with shame. The burden of guilt they carried over their lie about Joseph's death was far greater than the weight of Benjamin. It crushed each of their hearts just as heavily as the stump had crushed Benjamin's leg. Watching their father's grief had become so unbearable for Judah that he had left all he knew and loved, fleeing from seeing the effects of their actions.

Reuben's eyes welled up with tears as he considered Benjamin's emotional pain as well as his physical pain. "Thank God Amisa was there. She protected you. On my life, I will never let anything happen to you again."

Benjamin closed his eyes and fought back the tears. "Thank you, brothers. Thank you for bringing Amisa home with you that horrible day we lost Joseph. If you had not brought her home . . . I surely would have died today."

Kate looked at the brothers and saw the remorse they felt. The grief was heavy in their eyes and in their expressions. Her heart was filled with hope that perhaps they were truly sorry for what they had done. Maybe with time they would even repent of their horrible sin against Joseph, Jacob, Benjamin, and God.

Kate was glad she was here, not only to save Benjamin, but also to bring comfort to the jealous, scheming brothers as they realized that by bringing her to live with them, they had in fact saved Jacob's youngest son.

CHAPTER 27

The Dream Book

"Are you sure?" Nigel asked Liz as he sorted through his collection of papyrus scrolls at the school. He squinted as he tried to read the titles on the scrolls.

"Oui, I am positive. Zuleika told Mandisa to pack her things, and that they would not be home until tomorrow morning. She mentioned going to the temple and something about an incubation," Liz explained, her tail curling up and down. "She's been fasting and bathing continually for three days now. What does this all mean?"

Nigel frowned as he continued to fumble with his scrolls, pulling one out and then tossing it aside and taking another. "It means, my dear, Potiphar's wife is seeking assistance with dreams. She plans to spend the night in the sanatorium at the temple where a lector priest will assist in her ability to have helpful dreams."

"Helpful dreams? Are you telling me she actually believes she can affect what is in her dreams?" Liz asked.

"The Egyptians believe that what they dream has a bearing on their daily lives. They believe that dreams are messages from the gods, foretelling disaster or good fortune," Nigel explained. "Some people believe they can 'encourage the help of a god' to solve a problem or make a decision. So they perform these incubations at the temple of the god they wish to influence."

"Why, this is absurd, no?! Not that the one, true God doesn't send dreams that mean things; of course this is true. But to think she could enlist a false god to affect a dream? Pfft! *C'est ridicule*—this is nonsense," Liz said. "I grow weary of these false gods, Nigel. The Egyptians are obsessed with them."

Nigel didn't reply for a moment as he was squinting to read a scroll. "Ah, yes, here we are," he said as he motioned for Liz to come read. "Tell me if you can make out this script, my dear."

Liz leaned over Nigel's shoulder and read out loud, "*The Dream Book.* Nigel, what is this? I see a table with columns entitled 'Dream' and 'Interpretation.' I also see two categories: 'good' and 'bad.' "

"Excellent, my pet!" Nigel exclaimed. "I do say, your ability to read hieratic script is coming along splendidly!"

"Merci, Nigel, but please, what is this book about?" Liz asked, eager to understand.

"Very well. *The Dream Book* lists 108 dreams and their meanings, either good or bad. The word 'bad' is always written in red ink. A third of the interpretations deal with the dreamer's gains or losses. Other dreams predict physical events that will happen to the dreamer, such as starving or being cured of a dreadful sickness. Others still deal with situations where the gods will make judgments or a change in the dreamer's position in the village. Utterly fascinating," Nigel said as he scanned the scroll.

"So they believe they can accurately interpret dreams based on a formula written in a book?" Liz asked. "Nigel, do some of the dreams deal with feelings, like love?"

"Yes, dreams about influencing feelings like love and anger are most certainly in *The Dream Book.* But what the Egyptians *believe* and what is *reality* are two separate issues for dream interpretation," Nigel quipped. "I'm afraid this book is not very precise, and similar dreams are often given different interpretations."

"Which would leave a lot of room for the personal interpretation of whoever was assisting the dreamer, no?" Liz observed.

"Precisely, my dear. So this practice of interpreting dreams is rather unreliable at best. I dare say the Egyptians do not have a uniform way of interpreting dreams. I've heard tell of one priest who believes that a dream actually means the exact *opposite* of its symbols."

Nigel's small hand drifted down the columns as he muttered under his breath. "Ah, see here. I shall read some of the interpretations:

If a man sees himself in a dream . . .

. . . as dead: good—this means a long life

. . . eating crocodile: good—he will become a village official

. . . with his face in a mirror: bad—he will have another wife

. . . wearing sandals: bad—he will roam the earth."

"If interpreting dreams is unreliable, why then do the Egyptians continue to pursue priests and consult *The Dream Book?*" Liz asked, her tail swishing back and forth.

"Hope, I suppose. These Egyptians are extremely superstitious and not only wish to know about dreams but are terrified of nightmares. They actually believe harm can come to them through dreams! This is why they paint protective symbols on those dreadfully uncomfortable head rests, to keep away demons or even spells sent by others. I've heard tell of a belief that one can send the anger of the god Seth against his enemies, causing nightmares or death!" Nigel explained, now rubbing his eyes.

"I just do not understand how anyone could believe this. Back to what you said about influencing the gods for helpful dreams.

What could Potiphar's wife be trying to accomplish by her incubation at the temple?" Liz asked.

"Well, which temple did she say they would attend?" Nigel asked.

"The temple of Hathor," Liz replied.

"Hmmm, Hathor, you say? Well, then, more than likely, I would say she wishes to affect love of some kind," Nigel replied. "Why don't we go find out?"

"You mean go to the temple of Hathor for Zuleika's incubation?" Liz asked, her eyes wide at the idea.

"Why not? Potiphar is gone on a trip with Pharaoh, and Mandisa will be away from the house as well, so no one will look for you as usual. Of course, we need to make sure Mandisa does not see you there," Nigel pointed out.

"What if Joseph seeks for me? Since Potiphar is away, I'm sure he will take extra care to ensure my well-being," Liz said.

"I see. Well, Joseph may lose some sleep, but perhaps what we learn will be of benefit to him," Nigel said with a determined look. "You've told me how Zuleika keeps throwing herself at Joseph behind Potiphar's back."

"Oui, it is terrible. Ever since Potiphar made Joseph his chief steward and Zuleika saw him in a new light, she has been pursuing him. I've watched Joseph try to keep away from her, continually telling her to stop her advances. He does everything he can to not be in the same room with her. His integrity is solid and he has not told any of this to Potiphar, as he does not wish to bring shame upon his house," Liz said, her brow wrinkled. "You are right, Nigel. Let us attend this incubation and see what she is up to. If she is scheming to hurt Joseph, I intend to find out."

"Very well, let us depart the school and continue our lesson at the temple of Hathor," Nigel replied.

Nigel and Liz waited outside the temple until late in the evening, but saw no sign of Potiphar's wife. Liz studied the carvings all over the temple and noticed Hathor portrayed in multiple forms. "Nigel, why so many forms for one god?" Liz asked.

"Oh, my dear, the Egyptian gods take on many forms and change with time as the stories about them grow. Hathor is a cow deity, the daughter of Ra and Nut," Nigel explained.

"Ra being the sun god and Nut being the goddess of the sky or night?" Liz asked. "And their daughter is a cow?"

Nigel gave a jolly smirk. "It is quite strange, isn't it? I see you've been studying your mythical gods, so 'well done,' my pet. Understanding the origin and meaning of the gods of Egypt will help you understand why these people believe and act as they do."

"It seems the Egyptians would want a god that would not change with time or circumstances, but would be the same yesterday, today, and forever. How can you rely on a god that changes form or has fickle behavior?" Liz asked, clearly frustrated. "How could anyone place his faith in such inconsistent beings?"

"Yes, I know, I know, Liz. It is odd, but so it goes in Egypt. Here we have Hathor, who is shown sometimes as a human with cow ears, or as a full cow, or as a human with a cow head," Nigel explained. "Sometimes the gods even blend together with other gods to take on entirely new forms. Or they team up with certain gods to accomplish whatever they will. Look at the carving there on the side of the temple, the one with the snakes on either side of Hathor. She is closely associated with the cobra goddess Mertseger."

A shiver went down Liz's spine. There it was again. The cobra—the form Charlatan took in his full fury as the Evil One. His influence was everywhere among the gods of Egypt.

Suddenly they heard the footsteps of men coming down the street and looked to see the litter carrying Zuleika and Mandisa stop in front of the temple. Nigel and Liz stayed well hidden as the two women walked up the steps leading inside.

"Quickly, and stay out of sight," Nigel said as he scurried up the steps, Liz close behind.

They ran into the shadows, darting from one pedestal to the next, each pedestal supporting a statue of one of the various forms of Hathor. The low, flickering light from the oil lamps cast an eerie glow on the faces of the statues.

The women were led into a dream chamber by the lector priest. Inside the chamber was a black bed with a golden *u*-shaped headrest. Above the bed on the wall was painted a huge mural of the cobra goddess and a woman lifting her arms in adoration before it. On opposite sides of the bed were black chairs with gold trim and arms carved with the image of the cobra goddess Mertseger. The priest instructed Zuleika to lie on the bed under the mural and Mandisa to sit in one of the chairs while he lit an oil lamp next to the bed. He then sat down in the other chair.

"You have come to beckon Hathor for a dream of bringing lovers together. First, you must recite the poem of *The Golden One*. Did you memorize this as I instructed?" the priest asked.

"Yes, I am ready," Zuleika responded.

"Then proceed," the priest directed as he and Mandisa sat by silently.

Zuleika lifted her hands to the cobra goddess and recited the poem:

O Golden One,
I worship her majesty,
I extol the Lady of Heaven;
I give adoration to Hathor,
Praise to my Mistress!
I called to her, she heard my plea
She sent my mistress to me:
She came by herself to see me,
O great wonder that happened to me!
I was joyful, exulting, elated
When they said, "See, she is here!"
As she came the young men bowed,

Out of great love for her.
I make my devotions to my goddess,
That she grant me (the girl he loves) as a gift
Three days now that I pray to her name
Five days since she went from me.

"Well done. Now I will give you a drink that has been offered to Hathor. This is a potion to induce sleep. When you wake you will tell me your dream, and I will interpret its meaning," the priest said as he lowered a golden goblet to Zuleika's lips.

"I believe you were right, Nigel. It appears Zuleika is trying to induce a dream about a young man bowing low out of love for her. Who could this be, other than Joseph?" Liz said in a whisper.

"It does appear so," Nigel responded quietly.

Liz studied Mandisa as this was going on, and observed her cringing as she watched her mistress take the cup. Mandisa remained silent and obedient as instructed. But Liz knew this servant girl would rather be anywhere than this dream chamber.

After Zuleika drank the potion she laid her head back onto the rest, which was painted with various incantations. She closed her eyes and slowly drifted off to sleep.

"I've seen this potion used in such heavy doses it leaves the one drinking it in a hypnotic state, unable to move or speak," Nigel said.

"Why would anyone drink this?" Liz asked, horrified.

"Evidently at the right dose it can induce the perfect dream state," Nigel explained.

Liz watched Zuleika as she drifted off to sleep. "Is there an antidote for drinking too much of the sleeping potion?"

"Yes, but the ingredients are hard to come by, and the formula is given in an obscure passage in *The Book of the Dead* in case a deceased mummy tries this trick alone to dream in the afterlife," Nigel responded. He shuddered as he considered what could happen to someone ingesting too much of the potion. "If the antidote is not given in time, the person drinking the potion is doomed to sleep forever."

"Nigel, I believe we are witnessing one of the eight dreams as foretold by Gillamon," Liz said seriously. "And possibly the second scheme."

"Do you think Joseph would ever fall in love with Zuleika as she so desires?" Nigel asked.

Liz looked Nigel squarely in the eye, and with a voice of solid conviction said, "Only in her dreams."

Mandisa was resting her head on the chairback, dozing. The priest had left the room during the night, obviously to go sleep in his chamber. He now walked into the room, tapping a bell with a metal tong. Liz woke and yawned. Then she gently shook Nigel as she saw the first rays of sunlight pour into the hallway. "Wake up, Nigel."

Mandisa stirred and sat up straight as the priest came over to stand by the bed. He tapped the bell several times over Zuleika, who was still asleep. Nigel awoke and brushed back his whiskers. He and Liz sat in silence to wait for the verdict concerning the dream.

Zuleika slowly stirred and gradually sat up. Rubbing her eyes, she looked at Mandisa and the priest. She then put her hands over her face and leaned forward in the bed.

"What did you dream?" the priest asked, putting down the bell and picking up a copy of *The Dream Book.*

Zuleika took her hands from her face and plopped them in her lap, shaking her head.

"Clearly she isn't pleased with her dream," Liz observed.

Zuleika drew her knees into her chest and wrapped her arms around them. "I dreamed of strange things, things I can't quite remember. It's all muddled in my mind," she began. After a moment she said, "I saw Joseph, and I saw the slave Benipe."

Mandisa's head snapped to attention and her expression was one of surprise and concern.

"What were Joseph and the slave Benipe doing?" the priest asked.

"I can't really remember what Joseph was doing—running, I think. Benipe was playing a harp," Zuleika answered.

The priest thumbed through *The Dream Book* and his finger rested on a certain passage. He looked down at Zuleika and said, "Listen as I interpret your dream:

If a man sees himself in a dream with a harp:
Bad—something evil will happen to the person in question.

Because you dreamed of seeing someone else—the slave Benipe—playing the harp, something evil will happen to him. And since Joseph was there as well, the evil will also pour over him."

"But this is not what I asked Hathor for in my dream! Joseph is not to be harmed, he is supposed to . . . " Zuleika exclaimed but then stopped herself. She didn't want to reveal her true desire to the priest or Mandisa.

"As it is written, what I've told you is what will happen from your dream, regardless of what you desire," the priest said, closing his book and bowing. "You may leave now."

He turned and left the room, leaving Zuleika and Mandisa alone in the dream chamber. Zuleika jumped off the bed in a huff, glaring at the mural of the cobra goddess. "Come, Mandisa. We're leaving."

Mandisa stood with a hand on her stomach and said, "Y-y-yes, my mistress." She didn't sound well.

"Are you ill?" Zuleika said with her head cocked to the side.

"No, my mistress. I am fine," Mandisa answered softly.

"Get my things," Zuleika said as she stormed out of the room.

Liz and Nigel remained hidden in the shadow of a pedestal and watched Mandisa. She looked up, her face in anguish, and put her hands up to her cheeks in fear. While Zuleika was unmoved by her dream (other than feeling disgust because it wasn't what she asked for), Mandisa looked as if she'd just experienced a nightmare.

"It appears the dream of true love in this room actually is that of Mandisa for Benipe," Nigel observed.

Liz watched Mandisa walk slowly out of the room. She then furrowed her brow as she sat in deep thought, staring at the mural. "Nigel, do you suppose the Evil One could make dreams come true?"

"I suppose so, if he is the one to give the dream in the first place," Nigel responded somberly.

"Then I have two young men to watch over now," Liz said, looking at Nigel with a grave expression. "Joseph arranged for Benipe to learn to play the harp."

CHAPTER 28

A Woman Scorned

That's what she instructed, my master," the slave said to Joseph as he stopped the group of men getting into the papyrus boats by the Nile. "She said she wanted tilapia fish for dinner, and that all of us were to go find her a big catch. She said not to return until we had caught at least a hundred fish to feed all of Potiphar's household tonight."

"But you are starting to fish well after dawn! Everyone knows this is the worst time of day to catch fish. You'll be gone for hours trying to catch that much tilapia," Joseph said with a frown.

"Well, you know how Potiphar's wife is when she's made up her mind about something. I thought she would have cleared it with you first," the slave replied.

"Yes, I know her persistence far too well," Joseph said. "And no, she didn't clear this with me. I had other projects for you men to do today. Very well, I suppose she must have her fish. There's nothing more miserable than seeing that woman disappointed."

The men all laughed as they continued loading the boats with spears and nets. "Benipe, I want you to stay behind at least. I have something you can help me with today. I promised Potiphar I would have a project completed, and so it shall be," Joseph instructed.

"Sure, I'll stay behind, Joseph," Benipe said as he carefully made his way out of the small papyrus boat, trying not to tip it over. "Good luck!" he called to the rest of the men.

As the men shoved off, Joseph and Benipe stood by the bank. "Thanks for getting me out of that day of fishing, Joseph. I'd rather do anything than fish."

"You're welcome, my friend. I also know you'd rather be anywhere than away from Mandisa," Joseph replied with a knowing grin.

Benipe smiled and looked down at the ground as they walked. "Ah, Joseph, it's true. When I see her, my heart just pounds out of my chest! I hope I can learn to play the harp well enough to play her a love song soon."

"How are your lessons coming along?" Joseph asked.

"Not so great. I have such a desire to play, but something is missing. I just can't get the feel of it. But I'm determined to keep trying," Benipe said. "Thank you, Joseph, for making it possible for me to learn. I won't let you down."

"That's the right spirit, Benipe. Never give up. And you're welcome. I pray you can become the greatest harpist in all of Avaris," Joseph said with a hand on Benipe's shoulder. "Perhaps if you finish the project for Potiphar early, you'll have time to sneak in some practice later this afternoon," Joseph said. As the men walked from the river up to the house, Joseph gave Benipe his assignment to finish tiling around a new fountain outside the courtyard of Potiphar's bedchamber.

The men saw Mandisa walking toward them, carrying a large jar. "Good day, my master," she said with a bow to Joseph. Then turning to Benipe, "Hello, Benipe." Her dimples were like exclamation marks for her big smile.

"Good day, Mandisa. Is all well in the house?" Joseph asked.

"Yes, my master. We are all very busy. My mistress has given the lady servants chores to do outside today. She said it was such a beautiful day we deserved to enjoy the fresh air," Mandisa answered. She and Benipe shared a quick look and a smile.

Joseph looked at Mandisa with doubt. "That's very *thoughtful* of her, thinking of the enjoyment of her servants," he said sarcastically. "Benipe, you go ahead and get started in the courtyard." *I'm going to get to the bottom of this*, Joseph thought to himself as he walked away. *What is that woman up to now?*

"I'll see you later, Mandisa," Benipe said and smiled, taking her hand for a quick squeeze. "Maybe we can take a walk."

"I'd love to," she replied.

Joseph walked briskly down the breezeway of the house, noticing how quiet everything was. Not a soul was around. He frowned. Zuleika had totally usurped his authority over the house servants with all her special assignments today. Normally he tried to avoid her at all costs, but he had to know what she was up to.

Liz and Nigel were studying the hieroglyphs on a huge mural in the breezeway when Joseph came walking by. He was in such deep thought he didn't notice them.

"Something is wrong, Nigel," Liz said as her gaze followed Joseph down the hall. "Did you see the look on Joseph's face?"

"I'm afraid not, my pet," Nigel replied as he squinted at the wall.

"None of the servants are around. Doesn't this seem odd to you?" Liz asked, her tail slapping the cool tile floor over and over as she thought about things.

"Now that you mention it, I haven't had to scurry behind pedestals and plants at all this morning. Indeed, something *is* different today," Nigel said. Then he quickly added, "Oh, my!"

"What is it, *mon ami?*" Liz asked in alarm.

"It has been five days since Zuleika went to the temple to influence Hathor," Nigel explained.

"*Oui,* go on. What does that mean?" Liz asked.

"In the poem she quoted to the cobra goddess, it said:

I make my devotions to my goddess,
That she grant me (the girl he loves) as a gift
Three days now that I pray to her name
Five days since she went from me.

She spent three days preparing for her incubation. And according to the poem, she would expect her 'gift' to be granted five days afterward," Nigel explained.

"But the dream she had was not about Joseph falling in love with her. In fact, he was running away. How could she expect something to happen five days after that?" Liz asked.

"Perhaps she is taking the fulfillment of dreams into her own hands to force an outcome she desires," Nigel said, a grave look on his face.

Suddenly it all made sense to Liz. The missing servants. Joseph angrily walking toward her chamber. "Nigel, she has schemed to get Joseph alone. Hurry, we may not have much time!"

Liz and Nigel took off running down the hall behind Joseph.

"Come in," Zuleika said with a lilt in her voice as she heard Joseph knocking on her door.

Joseph stepped inside but didn't see her anywhere. He remained by the door, not wanting to get close to Zuleika. "My mistress, I had work plans for the servants today yet I find them scattered in every direction. I wish to know why," Joseph called.

"Come here and I'll show you," Zuleika called from the other room.

Joseph hesitated but slowly walked toward the pool room beyond the bedchamber area where he heard her voice. There was a small indoor pool Joseph had installed for Potiphar so he could relax after his long days at the palace. As Joseph peeked around the corner, he saw Zuleika sitting on the side of the pool with her feet dangling in the water.

He remained by the doorway as he talked with her. Liz and Nigel crept up behind Joseph and peered through the crack in the door.

"What is this all about, my mistress?" Joseph asked.

"I like the sound of that when you call me 'my mistress.' Am I truly yours, Joseph?" she said with a mischievous grin.

Joseph didn't answer but held his defensive stance, not looking at her.

"Why don't you join me for a swim, Joseph? You've been working so hard I thought you deserved a relaxing time today. No one is here, so you can enjoy being with me. Come on in, the water feels fine," Zuleika said as she stirred the waters with her hand, playfully splashing Joseph.

Joseph didn't flinch. "I've told you time and again, I will not be alone with you. With me here, my master doesn't worry about anything in his house because he has put everything under my care. There is no one greater in this house than me now. He hasn't withheld *anything* from me except you. You are his *wife!* How could I possibly do this great evil and sin against God?"

The smile left Zuleika's face at the mention of God. "You and your God. I'm sick of your God! He's the real One who has kept you from me, isn't he? For no one has ever rejected me!" She quickly got up from the side of the pool and came over to Joseph, grabbing the side of his robe. "I am the most beautiful woman in all of Avaris and I get what I want! And I want you, Joseph! Kiss me!"

"NO!" Joseph yelled, pushing her back.

Zuleika held tight to Joseph's robe as she fell back slightly. He pulled away from her, coming out of his robe as he turned to run away. Joseph didn't care about the robe. He was not about to spend one more moment there with her. He fled down the hall to get outside as fast as he could.

Liz and Nigel looked helplessly on. There was nothing they could do. As Zuleika screamed in anger, throwing a temper tantrum, they heard another voice from the other doorway, leading out to the courtyard. Liz's heart dropped when she looked to see Benipe standing in the doorway.

"Is everything okay in here?" Benipe said with a frown as he looked and saw Zuleika standing there holding Joseph's robe.

Zuleika turned with fury and screamed at him, "What are you doing here?! You're supposed to be with the other men!"

"Joseph had me working on a project for him here outside your door," Benipe replied. "I couldn't help but overhear you and Joseph . . . and see how he ran away." Benipe was angry. He didn't care how boldly he spoke to this scheming woman.

"Wipe that judgmental look off your face, slave," Zuleika said as she walked over to the door where Benipe stood. "You heard nothing. You *saw* nothing. I will make sure of that. Now turn around and get out of here."

Benipe slowly turned around and walked out the door. Zuleika grabbed a small stone idol sitting by the pool and ran up behind Benipe, hitting him on the head with all her might. Benipe fell to the tile floor outside, knocked out cold. Zuleika then took some water from the fountain and splashed it around Benipe's feet to make it look like he had slipped.

Zuleika slowly backed up into the pool room and clenched Joseph's robe in her fists. She looked down at the floor as her mind raced with what to do next. Liz stood there, glaring at her, a low cat growl in her throat. "There, there, Bastet, I'm okay. I'll fix this," she said, and she immediately began to scream and run down the breezeway into the main part of the house.

Nigel appeared around the corner of the door and he and Liz stared at each other in disbelief. "Hurry, let's check on the boy," Nigel said as he and Liz scurried outside to help Benipe.

CHAPTER 29

Potiphar's Decision

Mandisa and some of the other household servants heard Zuleika screaming all the way from where they stood by the Nile below the house. She called over to the men in one of the boats to come quickly while she ran back to the house. Soon the men reached the shore and they all ran to the house toward the screams of Potiphar's wife.

"Help me! Help me!" Zuleika wailed as the servants reached the house, finding her crumpled on one of the long reclining couches in the breezeway.

"My mistress! What happened? Are you hurt?" Mandisa said as she knelt down by Zuleika, placing her hand on her arm. She noticed Joseph's robe in her hand.

"It was Joseph! That Hebrew slave my husband brought into the house has come to make sport of us!" she wailed, crying hysterically. The black kohl makeup around her eyes started smearing down her cheeks, stealing away her beauty. "He entered my room and tried to attack me, but I screamed. It must have startled him enough so he left his robe and ran outside," she cried. "Someone find him and catch him. Lock him up until my husband returns. And send a servant to the palace to get my husband—NOW!"

Mandisa looked at her mistress and knew this couldn't possibly be true. She took her hand away from Zuleika's arm and stood up, nodding in obedience. Zuleika got up from the couch clutching the robe and ran back to her room. The servants looked at one another in dismay before scattering to do as their mistress had instructed.

Liz came up to Mandisa and meowed, beckoning her to follow. "What is it, Bastet?" Liz meowed again and went a few steps, turning her head for Mandisa to come along. Mandisa immediately went with Liz as she led her out to the back courtyard where Benipe lay unconscious. As soon as Mandisa saw him, her heart started beating wildly and she ran over to his side. "Benipe!" she screamed as she looked him over to see if he was dead. She was relieved to see him breathing. She gently lifted his head and placed it in her lap, feeling the large knot on the back of his head. Tears streamed from her eyes as she stroked the side of his face. "Wake up, Benipe, wake up! Please wake up." She rocked him back and forth as she wept, willing him to be okay.

Zuleika peered out the window from behind a sheer, gauzy curtain, staying hidden as she watched what was going on outside. In the distance she saw several servants roughly pushing Joseph down the garden path. His hands were tied behind him and they were taking him down to the slave quarters to lock him up. She grinned wickedly and left the window.

Liz stood there next to Mandisa and Benipe, feeling helpless. Nigel stayed hidden and looked on, a long frown on his face as he shook his head from side to side. Chaos was tearing through the house of Potiphar, and there was nothing they could possibly do.

The men carrying Potiphar's litter ran with urgency up the road to his house. As they arrived at the main gate, Potiphar jumped out and ran inside, calling for his wife. He hurriedly ran down the breezeway to their bedchamber and crashed open the door. Zuleika was curled up on the bed and next to her was Joseph's robe.

"Husband!" Zuleika cried, holding her arms out to Potiphar.

He rushed over to her side and held her close. "What happened, wife? I came as soon as I could."

"It was horrible! That . . . that *slave!* That Hebrew slave you brought home to us . . . he . . . he came after me into my room. I screamed and screamed and he finally ran out of here. But he left this," Zuleika cried as she held out Joseph's robe.

Potiphar took the robe from her hand and anger welled up inside him. He looked at the makeup-stained face of his wife and began to burn with fury. "WHERE IS HE?" Potiphar boomed with a voice that made her shiver.

"They locked him up in the slave quarters," Zuleika said, sniffing.

Potiphar immediately ran out of the room and down to the slave quarters. He barged into the building and yelled to the slavemaster, "Open the door!" The slavemaster quickly unlocked the door and stepped aside. Potiphar entered the room where Joseph sat on the floor and yelled back at the slavemaster, "Leave us!" He slammed the door behind him.

Joseph got up on his knees from the floor and struggled to stand, as his hands were bound behind him. Potiphar went up to him, and with fury in his eyes, towered over Joseph and demanded, "What have you done?! How dare you touch my wife?!"

Joseph looked down at the ground but said nothing. Potiphar threw Joseph's robe in his face. "You left your robe in our bedchamber!"

Still Joseph remained silent while Potiphar hurled his accusations at him. "Don't you realize I have the power to execute you or to release you? What do you have to say for yourself? Speak!"

As Potiphar glared at him, Joseph lifted his gaze and stared him directly in the eye. He was completely calm as he answered his accuser. "My master, you know me. You know me well. Does this sound like something I would do?"

"Are you saying my wife is a liar?" Potiphar yelled. "She said you came into her room and attacked her!"

Joseph looked with penetrating eyes at Potiphar and again said, "You know me."

Potiphar turned his back on Joseph and put both his hands on the stone wall of the cell, hanging his head. After a few moments he turned around and stood in front of Joseph. "Yes, Joseph, I know you." He paused before he said, "And I know my wife." Potiphar shook his head and threw his hands up in the air.

"I know you would not do something like this. If not for my sake, for the sake of your God," he said as he paced around the cell. Potiphar looked up at the ceiling and shook his head. "And I know you have too much integrity to accuse my wife and bring shame upon me. But just as your hands are tied, Joseph, so are mine."

Joseph stood in silence and lowered his head.

"There is evidence from your robe, from her screams and accusations before everyone in the household, and from how you ran away, Joseph," Potiphar explained. "Normally for such an offense I should have you executed immediately. But how can I?" he said as he walked to the door, ". . . when I know the truth?"

As he lifted the latch on the door, Potiphar turned and said, "Pray to your God, Joseph. And pray for me to know how to handle this." He left Joseph in the cell, slamming the door behind him.

Mandisa hid in the shadows as Potiphar walked back up the garden path to the house. "My master," she said with a whimper.

Potiphar stopped and tried to see who called him. "Mandisa?"

"Yes, it is I. Please. Benipe . . . Benipe is badly hurt," she said, crying softly.

"What happened?" Potiphar said, alarmed.

"He had a blow to the back of his head that knocked him out. He finally awakened, but . . ." she said, unable to control her quivering lips.

"What is it, Mandisa? Tell me," Potiphar said with his hand on her shoulder to steady her.

Mandisa wiped the tears from her cheeks and turned her eyes to meet Potiphar's. "My master—Benipe is . . . blind."

Potiphar wrapped his arm around the young girl, who sobbed and shook. His fury once more was kindled as he looked up at the house. "Where was he when this happened?"

"He was working on the tile outside your pool room. Joseph had him stay behind to work on the project while your wife sent all the other men fishing," Mandisa explained. "He was the only one around when . . . when the incident happened with Joseph."

Potiphar understood immediately what Mandisa was trying to tell him. He knew she dared not reveal what had really happened, for fear that she and Benipe might be put into prison for so boldly approaching a powerful man as Potiphar with such damaging news against his wife. He closed his eyes and clenched his jaw. "I'm sorry, Mandisa. Go, take care of Benipe. I will be by to see him later."

Mandisa pulled away and bowed. "Thank you, my master." She then ran off down the path back to Benipe's room.

Potiphar stormed up to the house and stood next to the fountain where Benipe had been working. He looked down and saw the broken stone idol on the tile. He clenched his fists and entered the door into the pool room. As he walked around the corner from the pool room to their bedchamber, Potiphar saw Zuleika looking at herself in her mirror. She was smiling.

"Pleased with yourself?" Potiphar said, startling Zuleika as he entered the room.

She quickly put down the mirror and the smile left her face. Zuleika started to cry again, and to say something. "You can stop with all the drama, wife," Potiphar said as he held up his hand for her not to speak a word.

Zuleika's face turned angry and she put her hands in her lap. "What do you mean?"

"You've cost me two slaves today with your scheme," Potiphar said as he sat down on the bed. "And you've cost me the best chief steward I've ever had."

Zuleika was furious and defiantly held her head in the air. "I don't know what you're talking about."

"Of course you do. It hasn't escaped me how you've thrown yourself at Joseph these past few years. But he is too fine a man and would never betray me. I know that *you* were the true attacker today. You attacked Joseph, but he would not bow to your will. Then you attacked Benipe—the only witness to the truth," Potiphar said, amazed at how calm he was. He realized he must keep his head about him to salvage all he could from this impossible situation.

"You'd believe the word of a slave over your wife?!" Zuleika rebuked him.

Potiphar shook his head. "No. No words were spoken about you. None were necessary," he said as he finally stood, his jaw clenched. "Your actions have spoken much louder than the words of a slave could ever speak." He turned and walked toward the door.

"What are you going to do? Joseph should die for the accusations I made against him! If you don't have Joseph executed, I will be shamed!" Zuleika screamed.

"Exactly," Potiphar said as he left his wife sitting there to think about the full import of all she had done.

Zuleika threw her mirror across the room, narrowly missing Liz and Nigel, who were hiding behind a tall palm plant. They had heard everything Potiphar had said, and looked at one another in anguish but also with relief. Joseph would not be executed. And that could only mean one thing.

Joseph was heading to prison.

CHAPTER 30

The Secret Passage

"AHHRROO! AHHRROO!" Wep yelped loudly outside the northern wall of Pharaoh's palace.

"There they go again, my lord," Potiphar said to Pharaoh as they enjoyed a meal in the royal dining chamber. "I will send a servant down to chase the jackals away."

Pharaoh wiped his mouth with a napkin as he swallowed a bite of food. He waved his hand to dismiss the idea. "Never mind them, Potiphar. It's strange, but I like hearing their call. It makes me feel like I am out in the desert on a hunt."

"As you wish, my lord," Potiphar replied. "Perhaps they follow the scent of the wild game you bring back to the palace after the hunt."

"Indeed. Those desert jackals go for easy prey," Pharaoh said with a laugh, patting his stomach in satisfaction from the meal. "I am pleased with your report today, Potiphar. It appears matters of my court have improved greatly over the past few months—for that matter, over the past few years."

"Thank you, my lord. As I've had no concerns over my personal estate, it freed me to have greater time to focus on the affairs of Pharaoh, thereby increasing the efficiency of your court," Potiphar explained, wiping the crumbs off the table.

"How is it possible for you to have no concerns over your house and your fields, Potiphar? Do you no longer own anything?" Pharaoh said sarcastically.

Potiphar nodded and smiled sadly. "I had an excellent chief steward. Everything he touched turned to gold. Everything he did was successful. His vision and ideas for farming improvements increased the yield of my crops and my vineyard tenfold. And his management skills made my house run as smoothly as the cheetah. The only concern I had was what I chose to eat for dinner."

Pharaoh raised his eyebrow in surprise. "Yes, I heard you had lost your chief steward, Potiphar. What a pity. But it seems with such an accusation against him you would have killed him immediately."

Potiphar nodded silently before turning his gaze to Pharaoh. "My lord, things aren't always what they seem."

"Well, at least one thing seems clear. Despite what happened the gods have been good to you, Potiphar," Pharaoh observed. "Now, let's see what the baker has prepared for dessert."

"Certainly, my lord," Potiphar said as he clapped his hands to call in the servants to remove the leftover food to the royal kitchen and bring in trays of sweet delicacies.

Al waited for the servants to bring the leftovers back to the kitchen while he hid behind a row of tall clay storage jars. His mouth watered as he saw the servants set down the platters of uneaten food from Pharaoh's table and rush out again with the final course of desserts. He knew he had only a few minutes before they returned to discard the food.

Al jumped onto a ledge next to the wooden door leading from the kitchen to the outside garden. Carefully he leaned over and swiped his hand repeatedly to reach the iron latch to open the door. "Aye, I must be as daft as Max says I am! It's only a matter o' time before I get caught doin' this."

Finally his paw hit the latch and he swung down with his full weight to open the door. Waiting outside were two jackals, Wep and his friend Tef. They grinned widely as Al peered around the door to let them in.

"Hey, Al! What's on the menu tonight?" Tef asked as he and Wep hurried into the kitchen.

"Evenin' to ye both. Looks like they cooked up some o' Pharaoh's game from yesterday's hunt," Al said, looking worried as he eyed the kitchen door leading to the hallway. "Make it fast. Ye barely made it out last time before the servants came back. If they ever catch ye jackals in here, Pharaoh will have yer heads mounted on a wall before ye know it!"

Tef put his paws up on the counter to reach a platter of food. "Don't worry, Al. We'll grab a bite and get out of here. Thanks for letting us in like this."

Tef couldn't quite reach the platter that had several hunks of meat and vegetables on it. He placed his paw as far over as he could and pulled the platter to the edge. As he leaned over to grab a hunk of meat, his muzzle brought the platter crashing to the floor.

"Now ye've done it! Hurry and get out before they catch ye!" Al yelled.

"Sorry about that, Al. I hope we don't get you in trouble," Tef said, talking with his mouth full.

Wep quickly jumped in, "Let us make it up to you. We found a new stash of food at one of the temples. Why don't you come with us and get some?"

Al kept eyeing the kitchen door. "I . . . I don't know. What kind o' food?"

"A delicacy we've never seen before, even from Pharaoh's table. Some traders from the south came through the market and brought some sort of exotic yellow fruit shaped like a crescent moon. The priests bought bunches of them for the temple offerings," Wep replied.

"Bananas?!" Al said, now taking his eye off the door. His attention was drawn away at the hint that his favorite fruit might be here in Avaris. He hadn't had a good banana in years.

"Yeah, yeah, bananas. I think that's what we heard them call it. Want to come with us?" Tef said, grabbing another hunk of meat as he headed to the door.

Al's mouth watered. "Sure, and it's temptin'," Al said, wiping his mouth. He didn't take very long to make up his mind. "Okay, I'll sneak out later tonight. Wait for me outside then," he said. Suddenly he heard footsteps running down the hall. "Hurry, get out o' here!"

"Okay, we'll be outside," Wep said, grabbing a hunk of meat and following Tef out the door.

The servants came into the kitchen and found Al sitting in the middle of the floor surrounded by the broken platter and food scattered everywhere. He looked up at them with sorrowful eyes and his big goofy grin. "Uh, sorry aboot that," he meowed pitifully.

"Oh, Hapy! Look at the mess you've made!" a servant scolded as she shooed Al away from the mess. "Go on, get out. Scoot!"

"Looks like that door latch came open again," another servant said, walking over to the door and closing it tightly.

Al sheepishly ran out of the room and snuck down the hallway to the open corridor. *Aye, I don't know if I can keep feedin' the jackal beasties like this. When I invited Wep I didn't know he'd bring a friend,* Al thought to himself. *Tef seems to have an even bigger appetite than me. But bananas!* He allowed his mind to drift back to his carefree days on the Ark when he'd go on his morning banana runs. His mouth watered at the thought of eating his favorite fruit again. *On the other paw, if the jackals can lead me to bananas, I think I can let them into Pharaoh's kitchen anytime.*

"How much farther?" Al whined.

"We're almost there," Wep said. "I know you're used to traveling by chariot, Al. Sorry you have to travel on foot like us lowly jackals."

"Sure, and I've gotten spoiled ridin' in Pharaoh's chariot. I used to walk a lot in me travels," Al replied with a huff and a puff. "Liz would be pleased I'm gettin' me exercise."

"How do you think we stay so skinny? We're always running around out here in the desert," Tef explained. "But it will be worth it when you see the food we've found."

The sky was dark above the threesome as they traveled into the desert. Al didn't realize the "banana" temple wasn't near the palace in town but was out by Pharaoh's pyramid. Somehow the massive, dark pyramid looked larger at night.

"I didn't know the temple were even open yet," Al said as they reached the funerary complex. Torches lit up the outside of the temple walls, casting long shadows on the walkway leading into the temple.

"The priests have been using this mortuary temple for a while now. It wasn't built just for Pharaoh's use when he dies. He allows high-ranking officials and people in society to be mummified here," Wep explained.

"Mum-mum-mummified?" Al said, fear gripping him as he envisioned himself as a cat mummy.

"Sure. It's an honor to be mummified in the temple of Anubis," Tef answered.

Wep laughed. "Don't worry, Al. I haven't seen them mummify any cats here. Just people."

"That's a relief," Al said, his paw to his head. "Why is there food here, anyway? Seems ye wouldn't eat in a place where ye have . . . mummies," Al said with another gulp.

"Well, the temple workers have to eat. But so do the gods," Wep explained. "The priests offer new food to Anubis every morning before his bath."

"Ye mean to tell me there's a REAL, livin' god in there who eats and takes baths?!" Al asked. He couldn't believe what he was hearing. "Does he take milk baths?"

"Well, it's a statue of Anubis in the innermost part of the temple. Whether he is living or not . . . well, that's up to you to decide. No one is allowed in there but the priests," Wep replied.

"But the priests offer Anubis food that he magically 'eats,' and then they bathe and dress the statue for the day," Tef added.

Al had a completely blank look on his face. He didn't get this at all. "So if Anubis really eats the bananas, why did I come all the way out here?"

"Anubis 'eats' the essence of the food, soaking up the nutrients but not really eating it. The priests take the food out every day so they and the workers here around the temple can eat it," Wep explained.

"Aye, these Egyptians get stranger by the day," Al said. "So take me to the bananas."

As they walked down the path leading to the temple, suddenly Wep veered off toward the pyramid, heading to the main entrance.

"I thought we were goin' to the temple then. Why are ye headin' to the pyramid?" Al stopped and asked.

Wep turned around. "There is a secret passage leading underground from the pyramid into the inner chamber of the temple. It is well hidden but leads directly to the statue of Anubis . . . and to the food."

"But why can't we jest go in the main entrance o' the temple to get in?" Al asked, looking nervously up at the massive pyramid. He suddenly felt very creepy about all this.

"The temple is well guarded. We'd never make it past the guards posted outside the doors of the inner chamber. They place a seal on the door every night to protect the privacy of Anubis," Wep explained.

"So the only way to the bananas is through the secret passage," Tef added.

"I don't know aboot this," Al nervously told the jackals. "I don't like the idea o' goin' through that big triangle, especially at night."

"What, are you chicken?" Tef said with a smirk.

Al had images of Henriette run through his mind and looked back at Tef with a puzzled look on his face. He didn't understand what the jackal meant, but for once he wished Henriette were here. She was never afraid to speak her mind. "I'm jest . . . not sure o' things."

"Well, I'm going in. You two stay out here if you want," Tef said. "I'm having bananas tonight."

As Tef took off into the pyramid, Wep looked at Al, who stayed put. "So are you coming, Al?"

Al looked up at the dark pyramid and then at Wep, who had kindly guided him out of this pyramid once before. Wouldn't he be okay with Wep? Al's whiskers trembled. *Sure, and I shouldn't have come. I be a daft kitty to have followed these jackals way out here,* Al thought, shaking his head at himself. *Always thinkin' with me stomach.*

"Well?" Wep asked.

"Ye go ahead," Al said with a weak grin. "I'll be right behind ye."

CHAPTER 31

Blind Faith

Liz frowned, watching Nigel as they sat on Potiphar's desk. He was squinting harder than she'd ever seen him do before. He kept rubbing his little eyes and trying repeatedly to get the hieratic script to come into focus. Finally, he threw his hands up in frustration.

"I'm sorry, my dear. It would appear my farsightedness has gotten so bad I am unable to read. I'm not the young mouse I used to be," Nigel said. "Blast these eyes!"

Liz put her dainty paw on Nigel's shoulder. "I am so very sorry, *mon ami.* I wish there were something I could do for you."

Nigel smiled. "Well, I'm sorry I haven't completed teaching you so many things. We haven't even made it to *The Book of the Dead* text, which I was so eager to share with you. Such fascinating passages and insights into the beliefs of the Egyptians, but alas, now I can only read large print on the walls, I'm afraid."

"S'il vous plaît, Nigel, do not feel badly about this. You have taught me so much, perhaps I can figure out the text, no?"

"Perhaps you can, my bright pet. But I cannot complain, not when I consider how it must be for Benipe," Nigel said, shaking his head sadly.

"Oui, it is so very sad. He lost his sight *and* Joseph on the same day at the hands of that scheming woman, Zuleika. I get so angry whenever I see her!" Liz said, her tail slapping the ground. "It appears the Evil One made her dream become reality."

"Yes, and she was the instrument of evil that was used against Joseph and Benipe. Evil scheming always rebounds on the schemer," Nigel said thoughtfully. "Whatever will become of the blind slave now?"

"Right now he is resting and adjusting to his sightless world, as ordered by Potiphar. He told Zuleika that since Benipe's blindness was her fault, that she would lose Mandisa as her servant. Potiphar assigned Mandisa to care for Benipe at all times until they figure something out," Liz explained.

"Well, I know that is a bittersweet thing for both Mandisa and Benipe. But I am glad Potiphar has been so gracious to the young boy. I understand he was learning to play the harp," Nigel noted. "Ah, it is my favorite instrument to play. Nothing stirs the soul like the harp."

Liz nodded and said, *"Oui.* He has such a desire to play, but has not been able to get the feel for the instrument. I don't see how he can continue now."

"But my dear girl! There was never a better time for him to get the feel for the harp! See here, to play such a melodious instrument *well* requires it to be played not just with hands and eyes, but primarily with the heart," Nigel said, tapping his chest with his small paw.

"So perhaps the very thing Benipe has longed for is coming about, but in an unexpected way," Liz said, suddenly smiling. "Nigel, I have an idea. Now that Benipe is blind and cannot see you, you can talk to him and he will not know you are a mouse. You can give him the type of lessons he really needs—lessons to play from the heart."

Nigel chuckled and nodded, "My dear, I think you are on to something here. I would love to impart my musical skill to the lad. But what do you think he will make of my British accent?"

Liz smiled and said, "Just tell him you are from way up north, *mon ami.*" She thought a moment and added, "Although you were not called by name for this mission, it is obvious the Maker appointed you to join us at the market. Perhaps meeting you was not just for our sakes, but for Benipe's sake as well. So I would say you are a messenger, Nigel P. Monaco. A messenger from God himself to help this lost, blind soul find his way in the darkness."

"I am grateful the Maker would honor me with a role in such a vital mission to help Joseph, and now to help Benipe," Nigel said, bowing low with his paw draped across his chest. He stood and wiped back his whiskers. "I'll do it, my pet. I say, it appears you have come up with a way for two blind mice to do something wonderful together."

"C'est bon! I look forward to seeing how the Maker will use you on the mission with the blind harpist," Liz said with a soft smile. "But for now, all in Potiphar's house are asleep. Shall we depart for the palace? I've been waiting to see Albert all day."

Nigel and Liz made their way down to the palace unseen. They had to dodge a human here and there, but finally crept into the palace grounds. As they silently walked down the corridor toward the kitchen, Liz looked up to see that a new mural had been added since she'd been in this hallway. "Albert has been painted in a hunting scene with Pharaoh!"

They stopped to study the mural of Pharaoh beside his kill of gazelle. Al stood majestically next to him, as if he had something to do with the success of the hunt. "I do believe they captured Al's best side," Nigel quipped.

Liz grinned at her funny Albert. Only he could be memorialized for all time like this in the palace of Pharaoh. They continued on to the kitchen—which was where they usually found Al.

"If the palace painter wishes to paint the real likeness of Albert, he should paint a mural of him in the kitchen. This is Albert's *true* hunting ground, no?"

But when they reached the kitchen, Al was nowhere to be found.

"Do you suppose he is in the garden, my dear?" Nigel suggested.

"It is worth a look," Liz said, jumping up on the counter to reach the door latch. "He does indeed love to eat fresh vegetables from the garden."

"Albert? Albert? Are you out here?" Liz called softly in the garden.

There was no reply. "Perhaps Pharaoh took him into his room for the evening," Nigel said.

Suddenly they heard a low hiss and turned to see an Egyptian asp behind them. Liz and Nigel jumped at the sight of the snake. He raised his head off the ground and was staring hungrily at Nigel. Nigel stepped behind Liz, whose fur bristled.

"Good evening. Are you looking for the orange cat?" the snake asked, keeping his eye on Nigel.

Liz wrinkled her brow. If this snake had information about Al, good or bad, she needed to know. But her impulse was not to trust a word he said. She would keep this conversation short and to the point.

"*Oui,* do you know where he is?" Liz asked with suspicion.

"Yesssss. He left about an hour ago to go with the jackals," the snake replied, drawing closer.

Liz's fur puffed up in response. "Jackals? What jackals?"

"The ones who come by for food all the time. Al gives them ssssscraps from Pharaoh's table," the snake explained.

"Oh dear, I'm afraid your Al has been taken in by the jackals. They are never to be trusted," Nigel whispered in Liz's ear.

"And just where did they go?" Liz asked, not wanting to be taken in by this snake.

The snake spat out his tongue a few times as if tasting the air. "I heard them sssssay sssssomething about food at the temple."

Liz's guard was up. She wasn't about to believe this snake. "Why would they need to go to the temple for food when the finest food in all of Avaris is here at Pharaoh's palace?"

"I don't know—sssssomething about bananas," the snake replied.

Liz's heart dropped. "Bananas? Oh, no. Nigel, would temple priests buy exotic foods to present as offerings to the gods?"

"Why, yes they would. Sometimes they offer delicacies not even Pharaoh himself has at his table. They seek out anything exotic they can find to bring the favor of the gods," Nigel explained, staying behind her.

Liz didn't take her eyes off the snake for a second. "Bananas are Albert's favorite food, and I know he has missed eating them. If the temple priests have bananas as a special offering, the temptation would be too much for Albert to resist. I do not believe I am saying this," Liz said, shaking her head. "But I think this snake is telling the truth."

The snake got a puzzled look on his face. "Of courssssse I'm telling the truth. Why would I lie?"

Liz rolled her eyes. "Did they mention which temple they were going to?"

"I'm sure their favorite one, of courssssse. The one that looksssss like them," the snake replied. "The temple of Anubisssss."

"Oh, dear," Nigel said with a worried expression.

"*Merci,*" Liz said to the snake, motioning for Nigel to retreat. "We must go now."

"You're welcome," the snake replied, looking disappointed as Nigel backed away. "Anytime. I'm always here."

Of that I have no doubt, Liz thought. She and Nigel took off running to find Osahar to ride to the temple of Anubis. No telling what could be happening on such a dark night, and in such a dark place.

CHAPTER 32

The Book of the Dead

HEY! WE'RE HERE!" Osahar yelled as he came over the ridge of a large sand dune. In the distance stood Pharaoh's pyramid, looking large and dark under the moonless sky. "LOOKS PRETTY DEAD AROUND HERE."

Nigel patted Osahar on the head, laughing, "What a choice of words! Well done, old boy. Just head straight for the workers' cemetery. You can hide there out of sight while we go to the temple."

"OKAY, NIGEL. WHATEVER YOU SAY," the loud camel replied.

"Where are the thousands of workers, Nigel?" Liz asked. It was like a ghost town without the bustle of activity of workers running about everywhere. "Have they finished building the pyramid?"

"It's harvest season, my dear. Workers are in the fields. Why do you think it takes so long to build a pyramid?" Nigel said. "There's only a short 'pyramid-building season' each year. But to answer your question, the outside of the pyramid is complete. A small number of workers remain to complete the inside, including murals, statues, furniture, carvings, and the like."

"Oui, this makes sense," Liz said as they approached the cemetery. This was where the lower-class workers were buried in tombs cut out of the rock. A wall surrounded the cemetery to mark it as sacred ground. Outside the workers' houses nearby they saw a few fires lit here and there, evidence some workers still remained. "Nigel, why the fires?"

"Some fires the workers use for cooking. Others are to burn scraps from various building projects," Nigel said as he pulled on Osahar's ears to stop. "We shall get off here and make our way to the temple. Osahar, please stay hidden. We shall return soon."

"I'M NOT GOING ANYWHERE," Osahar replied as he lowered himself down to sit on his folded legs. "UNLESS SOME HORSES COME AROUND." The camel grinned as he remembered his triumph in the desert. "I BET HORSES ARE AFRAID OF THE DARK, TOO."

Liz followed Nigel along the wall built around the cemetery and noticed paintings of all sorts of scenes. "Nigel, what do these paintings mean?"

"Here we have the common worker's version of *The Book of the Dead* painted on the walls of their cemetery complex. I may not be able to read the scroll, but I can give you a crude explanation of some of the book from these paintings," Nigel said.

Liz furrowed her brow. "Is this book as strange as *The Dream Book?"*

"My dear girl, it is even *stranger!* The purpose of this book is to guide the deceased in the afterlife, and it is placed alongside the mummy so it will be close at hand for quick reference," Nigel explained.

Liz rolled her eyes. "Nigel, I just do not understand how the Egyptians can possibly believe that their mummies can read, or eat, or go on boat rides, or use all the objects we have seen in their tombs. It is nonsense!"

Nigel stopped in front of the wall. "Of course it's nonsense! But to the Egyptians, it makes a world of sense. Perhaps when you understand what they believe about life and death, you will better understand this world God has brought you into. If the Maker is to birth a new nation within such a culture, it is worthwhile to understand all they believe," Nigel explained. "If only to be amazed at how the Maker could birth a nation of His people in the middle of a culture so far away from Him."

"The Maker does things in very strange, unexpected ways, no?" Liz replied.

Suddenly they heard some animals running by and crouched low next to a stone pillar. "Jackals," Nigel whispered.

"Are those the jackals Al followed?" Liz asked anxiously.

"Perhaps, but more than likely they are not the ones. You see, here jackals are always present in the cemeteries and around the pyramids. We will see many of them here, but it is wise to stay out of their way at night," Nigel explained. "Al is not with these jackals. If he went with the others to the temple of Anubis, that's where we must look."

"I see," Liz said, her heart falling.

"Chin up, dear girl. We'll find your Albert, never fear. Come, let's keep going," Nigel said as they pressed on to the temple. They passed a fire that was lit but abandoned by humans for the moment. A threesome of jackals sat by the fire, digging out scraps of food left behind. They growled at Liz and Nigel as they hurriedly passed by.

"I had planned to teach you about these things later, but as we work our way to the temple of Anubis, let me review the basics of the Egyptian religion," Nigel said, darting in and out of the stones in the path. "The first thing to understand is there is no unity in their beliefs. There is no one set book of truth. Many things independently make up their belief system: the way they prepare mummies and send them into the afterlife, their many gods, their moral and ethical thoughts, and their belief in magic."

"Magic?" Liz asked.

"Yes, my dear. Magic plays a big part in their belief system, and they wear all sorts of amulets and jewelry to protect themselves from harm. Their jewelry isn't just meant to look beautiful; it has secret messages written all over it," Nigel explained, looking back at the jewelry Liz wore.

"Even this gold *I'm* wearing?" Liz asked, suddenly uncomfortable wearing her earrings and bangles carved with hieroglyphs.

"I'm afraid so, my pet. I'm sure Potiphar desires even his 'Bastet' to be protected," Nigel said. "And their beliefs change over time to meet whatever truth is relevant to them in that day and age. For instance, it used to be only Pharaoh who could hope to join Osiris in the afterlife as a god. Now, of course, that is open to anyone," Nigel explained as he led Liz through a series of passages in the cemetery.

"So the Egyptians change up what they believe about death to meet whatever outcome they desire? There is not one consistent truth?" Liz asked, amazed once again.

"I'm afraid that's how it works," Nigel said. He suddenly stopped and pulled Liz behind a tomb entryway while another group of jackals ran past. Above them was another mural. Nigel softly whispered, "Tell me, what do you see in the mural for this deceased chap?"

Liz looked up at the wall painting. "I see various scenes of the afterlife. He is eating at a banquet surrounded by friends. He is fishing and hunting the hippo on the Nile. He appears to be enjoying 'life.'"

Nigel held his finger high in the air. "Precisely! Life! The Egyptians believe death doesn't really happen. In fact, they deny it as much as possible. They believe they simply transition from one phase of life to another, just like a dream state." Nigel pointed up to the pyramid. "Many scenes like this are painted in Pharaoh's chamber. When Pharaoh dies they will fill his room with all sorts of items he'll need in the afterlife. Everything you see on the walls and everything that will be placed in his tomb will magically become real parts of the mummy's life. Whatever surrounds him in the tomb, that is what he will enjoy," Nigel explained.

"Oui, I know some of this, Nigel. They put *shabti* figurines of workers to do 'work' for the Pharaoh, food for him to eat, and even a boat for him to ride in," Liz added.

"Excellent! Yes, and all sorts of gold and treasure to enjoy. The Egyptians truly believe you *can* take it with you when you die," Nigel chuckled. "His tomb is a place where Pharaoh can come back to visit from time to time – a 'home away from home' if you will. The better the stuff in your tomb, the better your afterlife will be."

The jackals passed and the coast was clear. "Where did they dream all this up, Nigel?" Liz asked with a frown as they scurried into the darkness once more.

"Well, the afterlife for them is like a dream state. And like a dream, the afterlife is *irrational.*"

"So far that makes the most sense of anything you've said, Nigel! This is *all* irrational to me," Liz said.

"Allow me to try to make sense of this for you, my dear. At the center of the universe is the earth, or the land of the living. This is where the deceased hope to return after they enter the afterworld. Since their tombs are on earth, ties with this world are never really broken. But to make things run smoothly, they must do important things like be mummified, have a proper burial ceremony, have an Opening of the Mouth ceremony, and have their spirits maintained by offerings by family members and priests."

Liz stopped. "Nigel, didn't you tell me Anubis performs the Opening of the Mouth ceremony?"

"Yes, my dear. Anubis is the jackal god of the dead. A priest dressed as Anubis prepares the body with mummification. Anubis or the other jackal god Wepawet then acts as the 'opener of the ways' to lead the deceased by the hand to the afterlife. Anubis oversees the Weighing of the Heart ceremony as well," Nigel explained.

"I told you I felt the presence of great evil at the temple of Anubis. Anubis takes part in every aspect of death."

Liz shuddered at the thought. "Do the Egyptians believe Anubis is ever responsible for the actual death of someone? It sounds like he is a dangerous god."

"No, but he enters the scene at the moment of death. As soon as an Egyptian dies, a dangerous journey begins, even more dangerous than what caused death itself. So, he needs to carry with him *The Book of the Dead*," Nigel said with a sigh. "I have so much to show you in the book, if only I could see it to read it to you."

"Well, for now, tell me what you know about the book," Liz encouraged.

"Very well," Nigel said as they continued to make their way to the temple. "The book is full of many, many pictures, hieroglyphs, and instructions. No two copies of *The Book of the Dead* are the same. Egyptians can actually purchase a 'template' and then pay to have a scribe write in certain scenes they want. The order of chapters can also change from individual book to book."

"Well, they are certainly consistent about being inconsistent, no?" Liz quipped. Suddenly she heard something and pulled Nigel from behind into the shadows. "Nigel! I hear another jackal coming. Hide!"

CHAPTER 33

Through a Glass, Brightly

Nigel and Liz heard an animal stumbling down the pathway, moaning. "It sounds like it could be rabid. These jackals are mean enough as they are. But if they turn rabid, watch out," Nigel hoarsely whispered.

Liz and Nigel stayed hidden behind a block of stone. In front of where they hid was a large fire loaded with debris. It smelled rather strange, and no humans or jackals were around it. They heard the moaning animal draw closer, then stop by the fire.

"OHHHHHHHHHHHH. AHHHHHHHHHHHH. OWWWWWWWWWWW," the beast moaned.

"Pitiful. Must be a bad case of rabies," Nigel said shaking his head.

"Oh, me achin' head!" the beast continued.

"Albert?!" Liz said, popping up to look out from behind the stone. "That's not a rabid beast, Nigel! It's a wailing Albert!" She ran over to the fire, where Al sat holding his head.

"Mon cher!" Liz exclaimed, putting her paw up to Al's face. "What happened to you?"

"LIZ! Oh, am I glad to see ye, me love," Al said. "I were runnin' away from the pyramid and I didn't see the obelisk standin' right in me way. Sure, and who puts an obelisk in the middle o' the dark like that? I ran right into it and fell back. I hit me head pretty hard."

"Let me see," Liz said as she pulled Al's paw away. "Oh, Albert, it is only a small scratch. But you do have a rather large knot on your head. I am glad this is all that happened to you out here."

"Your bride is right, old chap. Did you not realize that jackals are not to be trusted?" Nigel said as he joined them by the fire.

Al looked at Liz and Nigel with a guilty expression. "So ye heard I ran off with the jackals?"

"Oui, Albert, of all things—a snake in the garden told us," Liz said with a frown. "Bananas? You followed them out here for *bananas?"*

Al hung his head. "Aye. I jest couldn't stand the thought o' not havin' a banana when I knew they were so close. But if it makes ye feel better, I didn't have one."

"Did you not go into the temple of Anubis? I say, wise decision!" Nigel said with a clap of his paws.

"The jackals get into the temple through a secret passage in the pyramid. I were jest too afraid to go into that big triangle at night," Al said sheepishly.

Liz kissed Al's "boo-boo" and said, "Oh, Albert, I am so relieved you didn't follow the jackals all the way inside! Don't ever follow them anywhere again."

"Aye, I learned me lesson, lass," Al said, touching his knot with a wince. "I think I got some sense knocked into me."

"I say, a secret passage in the pyramid leading to the temple?" Nigel asked excitedly. "Liz, this I must investigate. In all my years of roaming this pyramid, I've never seen such a passage. I thought I had seen them all."

"But please, Nigel, not tonight. I think we need to get Albert home after he rests a moment," Liz said, continuing to study Al's head.

"As you say, my pet," Nigel said as he picked up a stick to dig around the fire. He glanced up to see the light from the fire illuminating the wall behind Al. "While we wait, look here," Nigel said as he pointed to the wall with his stick. "This mural shows a scene from the first of four sections of *The Book of the Dead.*"

"Some dead laddie wrote a book?" Al asked.

"No, Albert," Liz chuckled. "Nigel was explaining to me the book the Egyptians write for mummies to place in their coffins for the afterworld. There are several scenes from the book painted around the walls of this cemetery."

Al put his paws up to his mouth. "Ye mean we're in a cemetery? And ye're readin' from some dead laddie's book?" Al gulped. "Maybe it would be safer in the triangle with the jackals."

"No fear, old boy! See here, Liz, there are usually four main sections of the book. First, the deceased enters the tomb and descends to the underworld," Nigel explained. "The mummy must regain the physical abilities it enjoyed on earth: senses, breathing, eating, speaking, moving, etc. This mural shows the jackal god Anubis preparing the mummy, leading it through this reviving exercise, and then on to judgment."

"Anubis? The jackals told me all aboot him! Said he eats and takes milk baths and everything!" Al said. Liz and Nigel looked at Al as if he had hit his head harder than they had first thought.

"Second, the deceased are made to live again to arise as the reborn morning sun. Third, the deceased travels across the sky, eventually appearing before the god Osiris as one already judged worthy. And last, the deceased assumes his power in the universe as one of the gods," Nigel explained.

"Sounds like the dead laddie who wrote the book hit *his* noggin," Al mumbled, touching his knot.

Liz shook her head. "Nigel, none of this is real. It's all one elaborate scheme."

"You are absolutely right, my dear. But unfortunately, how the Egyptians spend their lives preparing for this fictional end is quite real. I will take you to a mummification soon," Nigel said as he poked the fire repeatedly with a long stick. "What you will witness is very real, my dear. I want you to be prepared, especially when we visit the temple of Anubis."

At the mention of 'Anubis' the fire flickered with a gust of wind, making the images appear to move on the wall behind Al.

"Well I never want to go near the temple o' Anubis again after all I've heard tonight. Bananas or no bananas," Al said with a wince as Liz tended to the scratch above his eye.

"If the Egyptians believe there really isn't death, but just a transition like a dream, why do they call their instructions for the afterlife *The Book of the Dead?*" Liz questioned. "It seems to me they would want to call it *The Book of the Living.*"

"Perhaps the only thing they have right and true about the book . . . is its title," Nigel said as he stoked the hot embers with the stick.

Suddenly Nigel felt something gooey on the stick and leaned in to study the fire. He lifted the stick and out came a molten glob of something strange. Liz came over to study the glowing goo. Nigel twirled it in the air and the goo began to harden into a solid, clear mass. As they looked at the mass from either side, Liz and Nigel jumped back when they caught one another's gaze. They couldn't believe what they were seeing.

"I say, did you see that, Liz?!" Nigel exclaimed.

"Oui! You appeared much larger through this object. Nigel, put your face on the other side again," Liz instructed.

Nigel and Liz put their faces up to the object and marveled at what they saw. Liz grinned as she saw Nigel's eyes appear five times larger than they really were. She then looked around the fire to see what objects were thrown into it, digging around with a stick.

"Nigel, there must be some combination of objects in the fire that has produced this substance. I see some crushed limestone, sand, and some other substance here. What is this?" Liz asked.

"Ah, that would be natron, my dear. The Egyptians use this mineral for multiple purposes around the pyramid. When added to castor oil it produces a fuel they use to give light as they paint the murals because it does not leave smoky residue on the walls. It is also a prime ingredient for making the splendid *Egyptian blue* paint color," Nigel explained. "And natron is used as a drying agent for mummification at the temple of Anubis. I say, since this fire was lit to burn trash from the pyramid site, it must be that the lime, sand, and natron have melted into this . . . clear . . . whatever you call it."

Suddenly Liz had an idea. "Nigel, don't move. Stay right here," Liz said as she went over to a nearby basket of scrolls belonging to the pyramid workers. She pulled one out and took it back over to Nigel. She unrolled the scroll and held it up for Nigel to see through the clear substance.

"Now, Nigel, can you read this?" Liz asked.

"By Jove, yes, I can! Utterly splendid! I can read every word!" Nigel exclaimed.

Liz threw her head back with joy. "Nigel, do you realize that we've found something to help you see? This substance magnifies things. *C'est magnifique!*"

"My dear, you have made an *incredible* discovery!" Nigel exclaimed.

"What incredible discovery?" Al asked as he bent over to gaze through the object next to Nigel. It was then that Liz noticed Al's nose ring glowing by the light of the fire.

"Albert, you and Nigel stay still for a minute while I study this," Liz said.

Nigel and Al obliged and remained still while Liz looked from one to the other, sometimes muttering under her breath as if she were making calculations. The cat and the mouse glanced sideways at each other and shrugged their shoulders, not knowing what Liz was doing.

"It appears this substance is causing some sort of optical effect with approximate axial symmetry to focus light. Hmmmm . . . That's it! Nigel, I have an idea to give you a tool to use as you read," Liz exclaimed. She carefully removed her gold earrings. "If we take my two earrings and melt my bangles to form wire, and then mold this clear substance inside the rings, you could set them on your nose. This object would magnify the words so you could read again!"

Nigel's whiskers quivered with excitement. "Astounding, my dear! Utterly astounding! I do say, I think it will work! Imagine that—'reading . . .' um-m-m, 'reading somethings.' What could we call such a tool?"

Al was making silly faces now at Liz through the clear object, causing her to giggle. "Albert, you just love to make a spectacle of yourself, don't you?"

"By Jove, that's what we'll call them—spectacles!" Nigel exclaimed.

Liz laughed and shook her head at her "daft" husband as Max would call him. "Very well, Nigel, we will call them 'spectacles.' But we should also name the clear substance. It is a rather lustrous *mass*, is it not?" Liz asked as the three of them studied it.

"Indeed. I'm so *glad* we discovered it," Nigel said.

Al looked at the substance and said, "Glad. Mass. *Glass.*"

"What did you say, *mon cher?*" Liz asked.

"Jest puttin' together yer words. How aboot *glass?*"

"I say, I think you've hit on a splendid word, old boy! *Glass.* I like it," Nigel said with a chuckle.

"C'est bon, Albert!" Liz said with a head-butt to her mate. "*Oui,* and I am delighted to use my jewelry for something good. Nigel, do you suppose the pyramid artisans have tools around here we can use to assemble your spectacles?" Liz asked as she removed the bangles from her front paws.

"Most certainly, my dear. And the fire is just right for smelting gold. I've spent some time in the Egyptian jewelers' workshop, so I know how it's done," Nigel said, stoking the fire with the stick.

Liz nuzzled Al. "I'm glad we came looking for you, *mon cher*. You are safe, and hopefully have learned your lesson with the jackals. And we've found a way for Nigel to see out here in this dark place."

"Right! Good show, old boy! I will now be able to see through a glass, brightly," Nigel added as he held up the glass to the fire.

"Aye," Al said with a goofy grin. "I always knew bananas were good for ye."

CHAPTER 34

Joseph, the Jailer, and Jabari

Max followed Nigel over to the dark corner of the prison cell. "Psst! Mousie, where did ye go?"

"Over here, old boy," Nigel whispered from the shadows. "I thought I'd better get out of sight while the prisoners are up and about for their daily food rations. But as I was saying, Liz sends word for you to be patient," Nigel whispered. "She said to remember there will be eight dreams in all for this mission. All we know of so far are the two recurring dreams Joseph has told you about here in prison, and the one Potiphar's wife had before she betrayed him."

"Aye, that leaves five more dr-r-reams. Wha' if it takes five more *years* for that ta happen? I jest kin't stand the thought of it," Max said with a frown.

"Chin up. Joseph has only been in here a few days. I'm sure God is still with him here just as He was in Potiphar's house," Nigel said. "I think that's why Joseph keeps having the same dreams each night about the celestial bodies and the grain bundles bowing before him."

"Ye r-r-really think those dr-r-reams mean somethin'?" Max asked.

"See here—why else would Gillamon have foretold them to you as part of this mission if they meant nothing?" Nigel replied.

"Aye, I guess ye're r-r-right, Mousie," Max said as he looked over at Joseph sitting with his back up against the wall, eating a stale crust of bread. "I guess if ye're stuck in a place like this, all ye'd have ta hold onta would be dr-r-reams. I kin see why the Maker would send them."

"And why the Maker would send *you* as well, Max. When we spoke upon your arrival in Egypt six years ago, you didn't know why you were sent to live with the jailer and work in the prison. Now it has become rather clear, hasn't it?" Nigel asked cheerily.

Max raised his head. "Aye, 'tis true, Mousie. Sometimes we kin't see things very well at first, but they become clear with time then. Kind of like yer spectacles. I r-r-really like those on ye, Mousie. Makes ye look even smarter than ye did before."

Nigel bowed low in humble gratitude. "Why thank you, old boy. Yes, these spectacles are utterly splendid and I'm thrilled I can read again." Then with a wave of his hand he said, "Enough of me. Let's talk about Joseph. Is there any way we could help him here in prison?"

"I've been thinkin' aboot that. Since Potiphar is the jailer's boss, I'm sure they've talked aboot Joseph over the years, an' how he were such a gr-r-rand chief steward," Max replied. "This prison is a r-r-royal mess. I'm sure if Joseph were given the chance, he could whip this place inta shape jest like he did Potiphar's house."

Nigel put his hand up to his chin as he thought about what Max had said. "How could we convince Sadiki the jailer to give Joseph such a chance?"

Max and Nigel sat a moment, thinking and listening to the moans and coughs of the prisoners. The sounds of iron shackles scraping across stone added to the sounds of despair.

"By Jove, I think I have it!" Nigel exclaimed. "How about a note from Potiphar himself?"

Max looked at Nigel with a suspicious grin. "Ye don't mean it would be Potiphar *himself* ta write the note. Don't ye mean a note from a wee mouse instead?"

Nigel chuckled, "My dear boy, if it comes from the desk of Potiphar, does it matter really *who* writes it, as long as he signs it?"

"Jest be careful, Mousie—ye an' that kitty lass—as ye both wr-r-rite it then. Bring the note ta me an' I'll make sure it gets in Sadiki's hands," Max said with a wink.

"Right! I'm off. Cheerio," Nigel said with a hand wave as he disappeared into the dark cell.

Max grinned and walked back over to sit next to Joseph. He looked up at the discouraged young man with his soulful eyes, thinking, *Jest hold on, lad. Help is on the way.*

"I'm glad you're here, boy," Joseph said as Max snuggled close. Joseph drew comfort from the little dog by his side in this dark prison.

Nigel and Liz sat on Potiphar's desk, searching through a stack of papers waiting for Potiphar's signature.

"Potiphar signs papers like this each week. The management of the prison as well as his estate requires paperwork to approve the purchase of supplies and the like. Now that Joseph is gone, Ako is once again handling this task, and prepares the papers for him. Potiphar is so busy that many times, Joseph would just make addendums to his letters for Potiphar's approval," Liz explained as she glanced through the stack. "There must be one to Sadiki in this stack, no?"

"I hope you're right, my dear," Nigel said. "See if you can find one with a blank space at the bottom for a P.S."

Liz flipped over a few more pages. *"Voila!* Here is a letter to Sadiki approving the purchase of food rations for the prisoners," Liz said as she slowly read the note with a growing look of disgust on her face. "Pfft! This is hardly enough to feed five men, much less a hundred!"

Nigel adjusted his spectacles on his nose as he looked over Liz's shoulder. "Tsk, tsk, what a pity. I'm sure Joseph would agree this is a poor amount of food for the prisoners."

"Oui! And this is exactly what he will see. Nigel, I know what Potiphar's 'P.S.' should be," Liz said with a coy smile.

Over the next few minutes, Liz carefully wrote a note on the bottom of the existing letter that would go to Sadiki, the jailer. Nigel guided Liz here and there so she wouldn't make a mistake.

"Yes, yes, that's right, dear girl. Now put a cross mark on that figure there," Nigel instructed Liz as he read her note.

"Like this?" Liz asked.

"Perfect! Well done. I think this will give Joseph the chance he needs with the jailer," Nigel said.

Liz and Nigel heard Potiphar calling as he headed into the room, "Ako, get my litter ready. I'll sign the papers so I can get to the palace."

Nigel quickly jumped off Potiphar's desk and hid behind a plant while Liz stayed put. She wanted to make sure he signed that letter.

Potiphar smiled as he sat down at his desk, "Good morning, Bastet. You have reviewed my letters to make sure they are in good order, I hope?" He chuckled and stroked Liz as she sat next to the letters, purring. *If you only knew, Monsieur.*

Potiphar took a seal to affix his mark to the letters before him. He picked up the one to Sadiki and noticed the P.S. Liz had added, thinking perhaps Ako had written the note. He nodded his head and mumbled, "Good idea, Ako," and signed the letter with his seal. Liz affectionately head-butted Potiphar with her thanks and approval. "I hope this helps Joseph, Bastet. He doesn't deserve to be in that pit."

Liz appreciated how Potiphar felt about Joseph. He had done what he had to do after Zuleika's accusations against Joseph, even though he knew it wasn't justice. Potiphar wished he could find a way to release Joseph from prison, but there just wasn't a way out for him or Joseph. Perhaps that opportunity would come later. For now, he could at least relieve Joseph's suffering. Potiphar hurriedly finished signing the other letters and gave Liz one final caress before he got up and left for the palace.

"Good show, my pet! It worked!" Nigel said as he jumped back up on the desk with Liz. "When will this letter be delivered?"

"It could take a few days, as there are more pressing letters to be delivered in this pile. Ako sends his messenger out weekly with Potiphar's letters, and the prison is always last on the delivery list," Liz said.

Nigel took the letter and proceeded to roll it into a nice, tight scroll. "Not this one, my dear! This letter shall arrive today, courtesy of Mousie Express."

Sadiki let out a long burp as he pushed back from the rough pine table. He took another swig and set his cup down, wiping his mouth with the back of his hand. He brushed the crumbs off his soiled tunic, yawned and rubbed the stubble on his face. It had been a long day at the prison and things weren't going well. New inmates, more fights, one death. Sadiki was tired.

Max sat next to Sadiki's chair, eyeing the rough linen sack the jailer had tossed in the corner when they returned home. Sadiki used the sack for papers, cell keys, and carrying supplies to and from the prison. When Nigel had delivered the scroll of Potiphar's letter to the prison, Max had stuck it in Sadiki's sack. Now he had to get the tired jailer to open it.

Sadiki put his head on the table to rest. *He's goin' ta fall asleep,* Max thought with a frown. *Sorry, laddie, but there's a letter ye need ta read first.* He walked over to the sack and started pawing at it, barking wildly.

Sadiki sat up and looked at Max as he nudged the sack repeatedly with his nose, like some creature was hiding underneath. Max managed to open the sack enough so that the scroll was poking out of the top. "What is it, Jabari? Did a rat get in the house?" He got up quickly and picked up the sack, but didn't see any creature underneath. Max ran barking into the other room, like he was chasing something.

"Get it, boy," Sadiki said as he noticed the scroll and immediately recognized the mark of Potiphar. He took the scroll from the sack while he let Max round up the phantom pest. He sat back down at the table and unrolled the scroll. Max came quietly back into the room and watched him intently to gauge his reaction. Sadiki mumbled as he read the letter half-out-loud.

"Supplies . . . 20 at such and such . . ." Sadiki read. Suddenly he stopped and sat up as he read the note at the bottom of the letter. "As you know, Joseph was my chief steward for six years and served me well. It is a waste not to use his skills, as I know he could make the prison run smoothly. Since he is now under your watch, put him to work and see what he can do for you there. Begin with this supply list for food rations."

Sadiki scratched his head. "Huh, allow Joseph to work for me in the prison? What do you think about that, Jabari?"

Max wagged his tail and barked, *Wha' a gr-r-rand idea, laddie! Why didn't I think of that? Wait, I did!*

Sadiki yawned and petted Max on the head, too tired to remember that Max had been chasing something. "Maybe he'll make my job easier. I'm tired and could sure use the help." He yawned again. "Very well, Joseph starts tomorrow."

Max grinned from ear to ear. *Mission accomplished,* he thought.

"Joseph!" Sadiki called through the hole in the prison door early the next morning. "Come!" Max stood outside the door with the jailer. He couldn't wait to see this.

Joseph quickly rose, his chains clanking as he walked to the door. "Yes, sir?"

"Guard, open the door," Sadiki instructed. "Come with me, Joseph."

Joseph gave a curious look, but followed Sadiki down the stone corridor to his office. The jailer took a set of keys and unlocked the irons around Joseph's hands, neck, and feet. He took the shackles and tossed them onto the floor. Joseph rubbed the back of his sore neck, stunned by what was happening. "Sir? Am I to be released?"

"No, Joseph. Not released from prison, but at least released from your shackles. On the condition you will work for me here at the prison," Sadiki said, assembling a pile of papers for Joseph to look through.

"Of course. What would you like me to do?" Joseph asked, wondering how this had come about.

Sadiki tossed the papers in front of Joseph. "Start by looking over this list of supplies for the prison. I hear you're quite good at managing things, so tell me where we can improve," Sadiki said as he got up to leave. "Joseph, do well on this for both our sakes."

"It will be done as you say, my master," Joseph said as he stood and bowed. "May I ask what made you decide to ask me to work for you?"

Sadiki called back in reply as he walked out the door, "Potiphar recommended you."

Joseph smiled and looked down at Max. "Did you hear that, Jabari? Potiphar sent word in order to help me!"

Max grinned and wagged his tail. *Aye, laddie. I know all aboot it.*

Joseph closed his eyes, reached his hands up in praise, and whispered, "Thank you, Father! I know this is truly from You. Please grant me favor here in the prison as You did in the house of Potiphar."

He then turned his attention to the stack of papers and gave Max a quick pet on the head. "Okay, Jabari, let's get to work."

CHAPTER 35

Heart Strings

Benipe sat outside and listened to the wind blowing through the reeds along the Nile. He spent a lot of time alone thinking these days. Mandisa was ever available to be with him and to help him, but he needed time alone each day to ponder what had happened to his world. He preferred to sit out here on the cool grass where he could hear the sounds of the water and the birds singing. It helped him to hear good sounds, the sounds of life. He was amazed at how his sense of hearing was more acute now after losing his sight.

"Good morning, Benipe," came a voice next to him.

"Who's there?" Benipe answered.

"My name is Nigel," the mouse replied.

"What a strange name. And what an even stranger accent. Where are you from?" Benipe asked, looking blindly around.

"Let's just say I'm from up north, dear boy," Nigel chuckled. "I've come to assist you."

"Assist me how? I've already got Mandisa to help me. Did Potiphar send you?" Benipe asked.

"No, Potiphar didn't send me. But I'm pleased with how he has allowed Mandisa to be by your side to help you. I daresay she is a wonderful girl," Nigel replied.

Benipe sat there with a puzzled look on his face. "So if Potiphar didn't send you, who did? And how do you know about Mandisa?"

Nigel decided to take a chance and just speak plainly with this poor, lost boy. What could it hurt for him to know the truth?

"I know all about Mandisa, you, Joseph, and everyone here," Nigel started. "I've been here since the day you were bought at the market by Potiphar. And as for who sent me . . ."—Nigel hesitated—". . . God sent me."

Benipe wrinkled his brow in apparent disbelief. "Which god?" he asked.

"The one, true God. Joseph's God," Nigel explained.

Benipe gave a laugh. "Well, this God doesn't seem to care very much about Joseph or me. Look at what's happened! Joseph has been falsely accused and thrown in prison by that lying woman, and she made me go blind!"

Nigel paused before answering. "Yes, I know. I saw it all happen, and I'm sorry for the injustice you both received at the hands of such a schemer," Nigel sympathized. "But you're very wrong, dear boy. God cares for both of you a great deal. I know it is difficult to understand why God could allow such dreadful things to happen to you, but you haven't seen the whole story unfold yet. Many amazing things are still to come."

"You're right, I haven't *seen* the whole story, nor will I ever *see* it. I'm blind. And how do you know what is to come?" Benipe asked.

Nigel smiled. He liked this boy. He had a quick-wittedness about him Nigel admired. "I don't know specific things, just general things about Joseph. But as for you, I see you becoming the finest harpist in all of Egypt."

"Well, you must be even more blind than me! How is that supposed to happen?! I couldn't get the hang of playing the harp before. Now how am I supposed to learn? I'm *blind.* I'm worthless," Benipe said, his face drifting toward the ground.

Nigel took off his spectacles and rubbed them on his soft fur to clean them, chuckling. "You are right in one regard. I was blind, but with a little intervention I can see quite well now," he said as he placed the golden spectacles on his nose. "And so it shall be for you, dear boy. I'm here to help you *see* how to play the harp—not from sight but from your heart."

Benipe was confused and didn't know how to respond. But he felt a small surge of hope in his spirit. He still longed to play the harp but had all but given up on that dream.

"And as for you being worthless, that is rubbish! See here, do you know what your name means?" Nigel asked.

"No. No one ever told me," Benipe said softly.

"Benipe means 'iron.' Tell me, before you went blind, did you ever work with the blacksmith down by the slave quarters?" Nigel asked.

"Just once or twice," Benipe replied.

"Splendid! Then you must understand that in order for the blacksmith to know if the iron is good or worthless, he must temper it. Do you recall how the blacksmith tempers the iron?" Nigel asked.

"He puts the iron in the fire, and while it is hot, he strikes it repeatedly with the hammer. Finally he plunges it into cold water," Benipe replied, not understanding where this was headed.

"Precisely! And if the iron begins to crumble after one or two of these tempering tests?" Nigel continued.

Benipe threw his hand up in the air and let it fall to his lap, not getting the point. "If the iron crumbles, it is because it is weak, and it is then thrown onto the trash heap. It is worthless."

Nigel waited a minute to respond. He wanted Benipe to think about what he had just said. Slowly he smiled and said, "And from what I've heard, you've been tempered multiple times in your life and are still here. That means the iron in you is strong and valuable, dear boy. It just needs to be molded for the purpose it was meant for all along."

Benipe looked in the direction of Nigel's voice. "But I don't know what my purpose is."

"Ah, but it is not so very hard to see. Your purpose is to be loved by your Maker and to allow Him to fill your heart with His presence," Nigel explained. "Then He can give you your heart's desire, which I know is to play the harp. When God is allowed into your heart, that's when the beautiful music comes out."

Benipe nodded. "You sound like Joseph," he said with a smile. "He always said God waits for people to come to Him of their own free will. Unlike the gods of Egypt where there is no free will at all."

Benipe felt around on the ground for his walking stick and used it to help him stand. He tapped it on the ground in front of him and walked a few steps closer to the reeds. He put his head back to feel the wind on his face as he closed his eyes. "Nigel, it seems so hard to believe that such a God as yours and Joseph's could exist, much less care about me. Even before I lost my sight, there was no way to even see this God, unlike the gods of Egypt. Their images are everywhere you look. How can you believe in something you can't see?"

"I say, do you believe in wind?" Nigel asked as he followed Benipe closer to the bank.

Benipe laughed, "Uh, yeah, Nigel, who doesn't?"

"Ah, but you can't *see* it, can you?" Nigel asked pointedly.

"Well, no, but I can . . . I can feel it," Benipe replied.

"Right. And do you think I'm here standing beside you, dear boy?" Nigel asked.

"Well, obviously you're here," Benipe answered. "I can hear you."

"Indeed. But can you *see* me?" Nigel questioned.

Benipe thought a moment and smiled. "I know where you're going with this. I'm supposed to believe in something I can't see, right? Joseph called it 'faith.'"

"Brilliantly stated! You can't see the wind or me, but you know we are both here because you can feel and hear us," Nigel exclaimed. "My, my, I believe you are a fast learner indeed, but we must 'strike while the iron is hot,' so to speak," Nigel said with a hearty laugh. "Do you really wish to learn to play the harp, Benipe?"

"Yes, Nigel, with all my heart. I'm willing to learn." Benipe held out his hand to shake Nigel's.

Nigel, who stood only a few inches tall, looked up at Benipe. "Ah, I'm afraid I can't shake hands. I have a . . . condition. I'm rather, ah, short. Trust me, dear boy, you don't want to know!"

Benipe lowered his hand with a puzzled look on his face. "Okay, whatever you say."

Nigel went over to a reed and nibbled at its base until it broke off. He carried it to Benipe and held it up as high as he could reach. "But just so you know I am real and that you're not hearing things, please take this reed to remember that I was indeed here."

Benipe leaned over and waved his hand but didn't feel anything. "Lower," Nigel instructed. Benipe leaned over to his knees and finally felt the reed Nigel held out for him. "You weren't kidding about being short!"

Nigel laughed. "You see, we all have our flaws. Now, shall we begin with your first harp lesson?"

"Sure, except I don't have my harp out here. It's inside," Benipe explained.

"No matter," Nigel said with a wave of his hand. "Today we shall begin with theory. You've been taught the mechanics of how to play the harp, dear boy. What you haven't learned is how to make it truly sing. Have a seat and just hold the reed in your hand. I want you to feel the vibration of the wind."

Benipe did as he was instructed. He sat down and firmly gripped the reed, holding it in the air. The gentle breeze vibrated in the reed. "Okay, I feel it."

"Good. The key to playing the harp is *feeling* it. What is so grand about this instrument is that it is the only one you 'hug.' You actually can feel it tingle through every fiber of your body. As you pluck the harp strings, you get an immediate response not only through sound but through the vibrations," Nigel explained.

"So the goal, dear boy, is to become so close to the harp that you *feel* as well as hear every note. But before your fingers ever pluck the strings of the harp, the true notes begin by the plucking of the strings in your *heart,* and a fine harpist allows those vibrations to then flow into his fingers."

Benipe thought a moment as he tried to absorb all Nigel was saying. "Before I lost my sight, I watched the harpist tune his harp. As he held it close he would strike a chord with a sharp, quick blow. While the harp quivered almost like it was in pain, the harpist would lean in close to catch the first note that came out of it. If the note was harsh or not right, he would frown and then tighten the strings, striking it again and again."

"Until he heard the beautiful sound of the perfect note," Nigel added with a smile. "If the harpist doesn't strike the strings and turn the torturing thumbscrew to tighten them, the harp will be forever doomed to sound harsh, never experiencing what it was meant to do—create beautiful music."

Nigel allowed a moment for all this to sink in for Benipe as they simply listened to the sound of the wind in the reeds. Finally, Nigel brought the lesson to a conclusion.

"What I wish for you to realize is that the string sounds truest just below its breaking point. Only when it is at its tightest point does it vibrate with the fullest, purest, strongest sound. So you see, dear boy, the harp must trust the harpist even through the blows and the tightening of its strings to their breaking point," Nigel said. "The harp knows only then how much it is loved by the one who plays it."

"I see, Nigel. I see exactly what you mean," Benipe said, his mind illuminated with understanding. "It's just like the tempering of the iron to prepare it for a valuable purpose."

"And you thought you were blind!" Nigel said, drawing a big grin from Benipe. "The harp and the harpist are tempered by tuning—the harp by physical stretching and the harpist by spiritual stretching."

"I've been feeling like I'm at my breaking point lately," Benipe said.

Nigel smiled. He was getting somewhere with this boy. "Then you are in the most perfect position to allow the all-powerful Harpist to make beautiful music with you."

"I see how it is. So I'm an iron harp?" Benipe said.

"Utterly splendid insight!" Nigel exclaimed. "Well, Benipe, I believe that is enough for today. Tomorrow I will come to you here at the same time. Bring your harp with you and we will put what we learned today into practice. Agreed?" Nigel asked.

"Okay, I'll be here," Benipe said. "And thank you, Nigel. You've given me some hope today."

Nigel closed his eyes with gratitude and bowed low with his paw draped across his chest, even though he knew Benipe couldn't see him. "You are most welcome, dear boy. It is my honor indeed. I shall see you tomorrow then."

With that Nigel scurried out of sight before he was seen by Mandisa, who was walking toward Benipe. She walked up behind him and touched him softly on the shoulder. Benipe placed his hand on hers. "Hi, Mandisa. Did you get a look at the man who was just here?"

She looked all around them. "No one is here, Benipe. I didn't see anyone as I walked down from the house."

Benipe smiled, holding the reed. "I thought I heard someone."

"I've come to tell you lunch is ready. I need to get some water and then I will take you inside, okay?" she said, and then kissed him on the head.

"Sounds good," Benipe said with a smile.

As Mandisa walked down to the river with her jar, Benipe heard a soft murmur from the wind blowing through the reed in his hand. He couldn't be sure, but the murmur almost sounded like words. He put the reed up to his ear and listened carefully as the wind swirled around him.

The reed softly whispered, "COME . . . COME . . . COME."

Benipe felt a warmth and a stirring in his heart he had never known. Questions entered his spirit. *Could Joseph's God be real? Could He possibly care about me, a blind slave? Is it possible there is only one true God, and that He . . . loves me?*

The wind picked up, and the reed vibrated in Benipe's hand. "COME TO ME," it hummed.

Benipe clutched the reed to his chest. Tears welled up in his eyes as he felt enveloped in the loving embrace of the one, true God. His heart began to pound from the embrace. What Nigel was trying to teach him suddenly made sense.

"I am the strings on Your harp, tuned to their breaking point," Benipe prayed for the first time. "Please, God . . . play."

CHAPTER 36

A Hair-Raising Morning

Pharaoh was half asleep as he shook his head from side to side. The jackals had been howling loudly for hours. Al pulled the silky pillow off his head with a *harrumph.* He'd been trying to ignore the jackals. He looked over and watched Pharaoh squirming in the uncomfortable headrest adorned with hieroglyphs designed to keep away the evil spirits.

If I don't go down there, they'll never leave, Al thought with a frown. *Sure, and I wouldn't want Pharaoh to lose sleep. But how this superstitious laddie can sleep with his head in that contraption, I'll never know!*

Al got up and snuck down the corridor to make his way through the palace to the kitchen. The sun's rays were just peering in through the hallway, and he knew the kitchen workers would be preparing Pharaoh's breakfast. Al carefully poked his head in the door to see who was in there. Even though he was Pharaoh's cat, the baker and the cupbearer had scolded him more than once for getting in their way, so Al tried to steer clear of them.

Al smelled the wonderful smells of breakfast, and his mouth started watering. A spread of Pharaoh's favorite foods and beverages was already placed on two trays ready for delivery. Al heard the baker yelling at the other kitchen servants.

"NO! That's not how you do it! If you had just listened to me and prepared the food the right way, I would not have to do this," the baker ranted as he tossed an entire bowl full of batter across the room, splattering it all over the poor kitchen servants. "This is no good! Start over! And hurry, because this dish takes all day to prepare. If you don't get started now it won't be ready for Pharaoh's dinner tonight. Now MOVE!"

"AHHRROO! AHHRROO!" Tef wailed outside the door.

The baker put his hands up to his ears. "I can't stand the sound of those jackals! How Pharaoh can possibly 'enjoy' it I will never know. I'm leaving for a few minutes to get my head clear. I expect everything to be RIGHT when I return. The cupbearer will call soon for Pharaoh's breakfast," he said as he stormed out of the kitchen.

"AHHRROO! AHHRROO!" Tef continued.

"Those jackals are relentless!" a kitchen servant said, wiping the batter off her clothes.

"Yes, and so is the baker. Look at us," the other kitchen servant answered. "Before I do anything else I've got to clean up from this food he threw all over us. The gods forbid we get any of it in the next batch."

"I'm with you. If we hurry we can get cleaned up before the cupbearer calls us," the first servant replied.

Al stayed hidden until the servants were out of the kitchen. "AHHRROO! AHHRROO!" Tef wailed outside the door.

"Okay, okay, I'm comin'," Al said as he jumped on the counter to reach the door latch.

As soon as he opened the door, Tef barreled his way into the kitchen. "I thought you'd never answer the door. We're starving."

Tef helped himself to the food that had fallen on the floor during the baker's tantrum.

"And I thought ye'd never shut up! Listen, ye can't come here anymore. This is the last time I'll let ye in," Al said determinedly.

"Come on, Al, after all the times we've done this you're kicking us out now? I thought we were friends," Wep said as he looked around the kitchen for something to eat. "Remember how I showed you the way out of the pyramid that time?"

"Aye, Wep, and I were grateful. But ye also led me right back to the pyramid at night when I shouldn't have gone. Friends don't put friends in bad places," Al replied. "So take one last bit o' food and be gone."

"Sorry to hear that," Tef said as he talked with his mouth full. Suddenly he spotted Pharaoh's trays.

"Yeah, but that was to lead you to the bananas, remember? You said they were your favorite food," Wep countered, keeping Al distracted while Tef jumped up to Pharaoh's trays. "We only tried to help you enjoy what you said you wanted anyway."

Al frowned. He was a bit confused, but he remembered what Liz and Nigel had told him about jackals. They were not to be trusted. "Bananas or no bananas, I'm not followin' ye anywhere else, and I don't want to see you around Pharaoh's palace anymore."

"Suit yourself," Tef said, jumping down from the counter. "Consider us out of your hair." He looked at Al with a wicked grin as he walked past.

"Sorry we can't be friends anymore, Al. I guess we'll be seeing you around," Wep said as he turned to follow Tef out of the kitchen to the garden.

"Aye. I'll be . . . seein' ye," Al said, slamming the door behind them. "There! I finally did it. Those jackals won't be botherin' me ever again." Al felt proud of himself and grabbed a piece of honey cake that had fallen on the floor, munching it with delight as he left the kitchen.

"NO! That's not the headdress I want to wear today," Pharaoh complained to the servant helping him dress. "Get the other one!"

The servant bowed and went to retrieve the other headdress while Pharaoh rubbed his sore neck. He was snapping at everyone from having slept so badly.

"Good morning, my lord. Did you rest well?" the cupbearer asked with a cheery manner and an irritatingly bright smile.

Pharaoh glared at the cupbearer, who was already getting on his nerves. "Do I *look* like I rested well? Enough of your questions. Is my breakfast ready?"

The cupbearer swallowed hard and bowed low. "Y-y-yes, my lord. I will have it brought to your table now." He slowly backed up and then quickly ran down the hall, clapping his hands for the kitchen servants to bring Pharaoh's breakfast.

The two kitchen servants returned to the kitchen and were startled to find the baker standing with arms folded, already waiting for them. "WELL?! You heard the cupbearer! Get Pharaoh's breakfast out immediately while I decide if you are worthy to continue working in the kitchen when you return. GO!"

The servants quickly picked up the trays and left the kitchen. As they walked down the hall, one servant noticed the food was out of place. "Hey, looks like someone was messing with this food."

"Did you see Hapy in the kitchen this morning?" the servant replied.

"No, I didn't see him, but that doesn't mean he wasn't there. If Hapy did this, Pharaoh shouldn't be mad. It is *his* cat after all," the servant said.

They quickly entered the dining room where Pharaoh sat, drumming his fingers on the table. Potiphar had arrived and joined Pharaoh at his table to discuss the court's business for the day ahead.

"My lord, the prison is running extremely well. Sadiki is managing food and supplies with peak efficiency. The sanitary conditions of the prison are greatly improved, and this has helped the health of the prisoners. The violence has all but ceased, and the prisoners are being used for projects inside the prison that we previously used paid labor for," Potiphar explained. He knew that Joseph was the one actually running the prison under Sadiki's authority, but he had to give the credit to Sadiki.

"Well done, Potiphar," Pharaoh said, smiling for the first time all morning.

The cupbearer motioned for the servants to place the trays on the table in front of Pharaoh. He took Pharaoh's golden cup and took a small sip to prove to Pharaoh it was safe to drink. He cleaned the rim of the cup and placed it in front of Pharaoh.

"Very well," Pharaoh said as he picked up the cup. He took a long drink and set it down on the table next to his plate. Just as he lifted a fig cake from the plate, he started pushing something around in his mouth, a severe frown on his face. Then he noticed something on the fig cake and threw it on the plate. He put his finger to his tongue and pulled something out.

"My lord? Is something wrong?" Potiphar asked, leaning in to the table.

"CUPBEARER! BAKER!" Pharaoh yelled so the entire palace heard him. "THERE IS HAIR IN MY DRINK AND ON MY PLATE!"

The cupbearer's face turned white and his knees began to knock immediately. The baker came running into the room and over to Pharaoh. "M-m-my lord, I don't know how this happened," the baker said, glaring at Al sitting on the floor next to Pharaoh. "Perhaps Hapy jumped up to inspect my lord's food?"

"I did not taste any hair in the c-c-cup, my lord," the cupbearer groveled.

Pharaoh stood and threw the plate of food all over the baker and tossed the drink all over the cupbearer. "Well, you must have missed it!" Pharaoh spat out at the cupbearer. "And you, baker! How dare you blame Hapy for this! Even if he did jump up on the counter, it is your job to make sure whatever touches my plate is perfect!"

The cupbearer and the baker stood there, covered with food and drink, not saying a word, but dreading what Pharaoh would do.

"Potiphar, get this worthless rabble out of my sight! You have two new prisoners as of this moment! Take them away now!" Pharaoh screamed as he stormed out of the room. "And have another tray of *hairless* food brought to my chamber!"

The baker and the cupbearer looked at one another with sheer terror written all over their faces. Potiphar stood and clapped his hands for the palace guards to come bind the hands of the two men. "How could you be so careless? Consider this the mercy of Pharaoh that he is only casting you into prison! Guards, take them away."

As Potiphar followed the guards to escort the men to the prison, Al sat with his jaw on the floor, grief in his eyes. *This is all me fault! Those poor laddies are goin' to prison because I let those jackals in the kitchen. That TEF! He got hair all over Pharaoh's food! What have I done?* Al thought to himself. He put his paw up to his head and knocked himself on the brow. *Daft kitty!*

Al got up and went out into the corridor, watching Potiphar and the guards walking away. *I got ta tell Max what happened.*

CHAPTER 37

The Baker and the Cupbearer

Joseph heard men shouting as they neared the entrance to the prison. He looked up from his desk where he was writing and laid down his reed. He would have to finish his report later. First he had to see what this commotion was all about.

"It's your fault! You're the one who had full charge of the kitchen staff!" the cupbearer yelled.

"Well, as Pharaoh's cupbearer, you are to inspect everything that Pharaoh puts in his mouth, including the food. But seeing how you couldn't even get the cup right, it's no wonder you missed seeing the hair in the food!" the baker blasted back.

The guards shoved the two men, yelling, "Keep moving!"

Joseph walked to the entrance gate of the prison and calmly stood with his hands behind his back as the men drew near. He then saw Potiphar behind them, commanding the guards to open the gate. Joseph stepped aside so the men could enter. The cupbearer and the baker looked angrily around them and at each other. Joseph knew from their high quality dress, eye makeup, and jewelry that these were officials of Pharaoh's court.

"What is this about, my lord?" Joseph asked Potiphar.

"Wait here," Potiphar instructed the guards as he motioned for Joseph to follow him out of earshot of the men.

Potiphar spoke quietly to Joseph as they stood in the hallway of the prison. "These are two of Pharaoh's servants, the baker and the cupbearer. This morning Pharaoh flew into a rage when he found hair in his cup and on his plate," Potiphar explained, staring back at the two men. "So Pharaoh told me to throw them into prison."

"How is it possible for such men to be so careless?" Joseph asked.

"Yes, I know. The baker accused Pharaoh's cat, which made Pharaoh even angrier. He loves that cat," Potiphar said with a laugh.

Joseph chuckled. "Yes, I hear he takes the cat on hunts and even has murals and statues made in his likeness. 'Hapy' is his name, right? Was it actually cat hair in the food?"

"I didn't think it looked like cat or human hair. It was long, coarse, and wiry. I don't know what it was," Potiphar told Joseph. He rubbed the side of his face, sighed, and threw his hands in the air. "So I had to bring them here. Joseph, I am placing them directly under your care. Watch out for these men."

"Certainly, my lord. You have my word they will be well cared for," Joseph said. "Do you think Pharaoh will release them when he has calmed down?"

"Perhaps. But in the mean time I have to make arrangements for another baker and cupbearer by noon," Potiphar replied, clearly frustrated with this situation. He looked Joseph in the eye and smiled. "It's good to see you, Joseph. I gave a report to Pharaoh this morning about how smoothly the prison is running. And I know it's all because of you. Sadiki tells me he doesn't even have to check on your work. He leaves everything up to you. It seems as if your God's favor has followed you even into the prison."

Joseph bowed his head in gratitude. "Thank you, my lord. Indeed, God's favor has allowed me to improve the conditions here. My God has not left me."

Potiphar placed his hand on Joseph's shoulder. "Joseph . . . I'm . . . well, you know. I wish things were different. I wish I could release you from this place."

Joseph looked into Potiphar's eyes with compassion and grace. "I understand, my lord. When God says I am to be released from this place, it will happen."

"Do you really believe that? Is your God more powerful than these prison walls or the circumstances that keep you here?" Potiphar asked.

"My God is more powerful than any walls that would keep me in or out of His perfect will. So do not fret, my lord. I bear you no ill will for what happened," Joseph said.

Potiphar smiled sadly and shook his head in amazement at how Joseph spoke. He had never known anyone who exhibited such grace. How he wished Joseph were back with him at the house. He would give anything to release Joseph, but he had no grounds to do so. He hoped something would happen to change the circumstances.

"Very well. Thank you, Joseph. I knew I could count on you," Potiphar said with a pat on Joseph's shoulder.

"You are welcome, my lord," Joseph replied as he followed Potiphar back to the men.

"Joseph will be your personal guard while you are in prison. Do as he says and things will go well for you here," Potiphar instructed the men. "Guard, open the door."

"Please, petition Pharaoh for us!" the cupbearer cried. "Please don't let him leave us in this terrible place."

Potiphar walked away and answered back over his shoulder, "I'll see what I can do."

The cupbearer and the baker stood before Joseph and glared at him. They looked him up and down, disgusted with the fact that they had to do what this dirty slave in the prison said. It was beneath them.

"Guards, release their shackles. These certainly aren't dangerous criminals," Joseph instructed. "Men, if you'll follow me."

The two men looked up at the walls of the prison and scanned the faces of the prisoners as they walked by. Fear began to creep into their minds as the reality of their situation started to sink in. Pharaoh had sent them here, and it was rare for prisoners to ever get out, except by dying.

Joseph led the men down the corridor by a group of dark cells filled with prisoners. The prisoners looked at the two men walking by, smiling to see such powerful men brought down to their level. Joseph opened the door to a vacant cell that had two straw beds on the floor, two buckets, and two sets of tin plates and cups. He walked ahead of the men into the cell and spread out his arms. "This is where you will stay."

The baker brashly walked around with his hands on his hips. "I can't believe this. An hour ago I was giving orders to the kitchen staff on how to prepare Pharaoh's favorite dish for dinner, and now I'm confined to this . . . this pit!"

"Well, if you'd just done a better job with your kitchen staff, neither of us would be in this pit!" the cupbearer yelled.

The baker lunged at the cupbearer and the two of them fell to the floor fighting. Joseph stood back and let them have at each other. One of the guards was about to step in and break it up, but Joseph put up his hand and motioned for the guard to stop. "Let them get it out of their systems. They'll regret it soon enough," Joseph said as he and the guard stood back and watched the men fight.

Neither man was in very good shape, so they tired quickly, with no victor. They sat on the floor, covered in dirt, breathing heavily. The cupbearer had a bloody nose and the baker was holding his stomach where the cupbearer had punched him.

"Are you finished?" Joseph asked. "If not, please, continue. We'll wait."

The two men looked up at Joseph and shook their heads in disgust with themselves. Joseph squatted down to address the men.

"Now, I know you don't want to be here. Believe me, I know how that feels. But the fact remains you are now prisoners in the prison of Potiphar, chief of the guard of Pharaoh. So while you are here, I will provide for your needs, but I expect you to act like the men of high status you are," Joseph instructed them.

"Even in a place like this?" the cupbearer said, holding his linen shirt-cloth to his bloody nose.

"*Especially* in a place like this. Or are you going to act like animals, like the common prisoners in here? Because if that is your intent, I will gladly put you in their cell where you will feel much more at home," Joseph said.

The baker and the cupbearer looked at one another in alarm and quickly responded to Joseph. "No, this cell will be sufficient," the baker said, holding his stomach.

"Very well. I will send in water and food for you, and I will have chairs and a small table brought into the cell for your comfort," Joseph said, standing above the men.

"Thank you, Joseph," the cupbearer said demurely.

"Yes, thank you," the baker said. "What exactly will we be having to eat?"

Joseph smiled. "Well, it will be simple and not like the finery of the palace. But I can assure you it will be nutritious—and hair-free."

The baker gave a weak grin and nodded silently. Joseph bowed a nod of respect and turned to leave. He had the guard lock the door behind him, leaving the two men to ponder their new fate in prison.

Sadiki stood in the hallway with Max by his side. "Don't you think you were a little hard on them, Joseph?"

"How so, my master?" Joseph asked as he leaned down to pet Max on the head.

"Well, by scaring them into thinking they would be put into the other cell with the criminal prisoners," Sadiki answered, rubbing his neck. He felt a little nervous about these prisoners.

"On the contrary. I scared them into appreciating the cell they were placed in. In the course of two minutes they went from complaining about their cell to saying it would be fine," Joseph said, standing upright again. "It was actually a way to help them adjust to a very hard situation."

Sadiki smiled and shook his head. "I don't know why I even bothered to ask. Joseph, you just know how to manage every situation. And I'm glad you were here to handle these men. I've seen them a lot in Pharaoh's court, so I feel funny having them in my prison."

"Well, don't worry. Potiphar asked me to look out for them myself, so I will," Joseph said. "Now, excuse me while I go see about their food and water."

"Carry on," Sadiki said with an outstretched arm.

As Joseph walked away, Sadiki looked down at Max. "So, Jabari, it looks like Joseph has things under control with our royal prisoners. I think I'll go rest," he said, rubbing his chest. "I'm tired. See if you can round up any rats."

Max barked an affirmative, "Aye!" and trotted off to the dark cells.

That daft kitty has done it again! I bet he got inta Phar-r-raoh's food an' left his cat hair all over the place, Max thought with a low growl. He had to know exactly what had happened, and what was now taking place in the palace as a result. Nigel had been so busy lately at Potiphar's house teaching Benipe, and since there wasn't much news to report on Joseph, Nigel wasn't coming daily to the prison. But Max just had to know the truth, so he decided to do something he hadn't yet tried in all his years in the prison.

Max headed for the secret tunnel that led to Pharaoh's palace.

CHAPTER 38

The Tunnel

Max stood at the tunnel entrance, hidden deep inside one of the older cells no longer used to house prisoners. Nigel had shown Max the entrance, which was covered with debris and long forgotten by the humans. Nigel doubted that humans had been in this tunnel for more than a hundred years. There was a small opening behind a boulder where Max squeezed through to gain entrance.

I'm as daft as that kitty ta do this, but I got ta find out wha' happened at the palace, Max thought to himself. He took a deep breath as he peered into the dark tunnel. He thought of Nigel's warning about what was down here. Snakes. He would most likely encounter snakes. Max shook all over to get rid of the creepy feeling. *Here goes nothin'.*

The tunnel was narrow at the start but soon widened to about eight feet across. It sloped downward and Max felt the stale air get cooler as he followed the stone block pathway. His eyesight wasn't as good as Liz's in the dark, but he could at least see right in front of him. He could make out things no farther than five feet or so. Hopefully he would have enough time to respond if he came face to face with a snake.

Max's hearing was another matter entirely, since his ears could pick up the tiniest sounds. As he trotted along the path, his paws made a clicking noise where his nails hit the stone. The sound echoed in the tunnel, making it sound as if he were being followed. He looked behind him, just to be sure. Nothing was back there. He pressed on.

Nigel had told Max that the distance to the Palace was not that far, a half-mile at most. Max tried to remember all Nigel had instructed: "Just keep straight and follow the tunnel as it slopes down. You will come to a level place and then the tunnel will slope upward to the palace. It's not far, but I'm afraid it is wriggling with dreadful creatures. Be swift, old boy! Run straight ahead and don't stop until you reach the palace."

"Aye, I wonder wha' 'wrigglin' creatures the mousie meant besides snakes," Max muttered to himself.

Suddenly Max heard something making a clicking sound on the tunnel ceiling and looked up to see a mass of scorpions above him. "Never mind!" Max said out loud to himself as he took off running as fast as he could.

Max could tell no one had been in the tunnel in a very long time. He felt the tunnel sloping deeper and deeper until finally he reached the level place. Then he heard them.

Sssssssssssssssssssssssss. Sssssssssssssssssssssssss. Sssssssssssssssssssssssss. Sssssssssssssssssssssssss. Sssssssssssssssssssssssss. Sssssssssssssssssssssssss.

Snakes. Max could hear them slithering about. It sounded like a massive den of them down here. Their hissing echoed off the walls to an almost deafening pitch. But then he heard another voice in the middle of the snakes.

"Ple-e-e-e-e-e-e-e-e-e-ease! Let me go! I'm jest passin' through and I don't want any trouble!" Al cried.

"AL! Is that ye, lad?" Max called, trying to follow the sound of Al's voice.

"MAX! Help! I'm surrounded!" Al screamed.

Max growled and ran over to where Al stood with his back up to the wall. There were at least a hundred asps hissing all around him, slithering around and over each other, eyeing the frightened cat.

"Steady, Big Al. I'm here, lad," Max said.

Al grabbed Max and hid behind him as Max put up his defensive posture against the snakes.

"Listen up, snake beasties! There will be no tr-r-rouble in this tunnel today. The kitty an' me are passin' thr-r-rough an' ye are goin' ta let us pass without a fuss. Ye got that? An' if any of ye tr-r-ry ta make a move, I'll clamp me str-r-rong jaws on yer slimy backs an' hur-r-rl ye so hard against the wall ye'll wish ye'd never been born," Max threatened.

"Ooooh, good one, Max!" Al whispered in Max's ear.

"Ha-ha-ha-ha-ha," the lead snake chuckled. "Sssssssssssoooooooo ssssssssssscary, aren't you, little dog? Do you think you'll really get out of here, you and the ssssssssssscaredy cat? You are sssssssssssurrounded."

Sssssssssssssssssssssssss. Sssssssssssssssssssssssss. Sssssssssssssssssssssss. Sssssssssssssssssssssssss. Sssssssssssssssssssssssss. Sssssssssssssssssssssss.

The mass of snakes hissed and grew closer to Max and Al, cutting them off in both directions.

"I can't look! Max, what are we goin' to do?!" cried Al, covering his eyes with his paws.

"I'm thinkin', I'm thinkin'," Max replied as he looked all around, growling at the snakes. *Maker, kin ye please get us out of this?*

Al pushed his back as far up against the wall as he could. He felt some sort of stone block pressing into his backside. "OUCH!" he cried. He turned and looked at the wall.

"Al! Did one of them beasties strike ye?" Max asked, not taking his eyes off the snakes.

"No, but this piece o' stone is pressin' into me backside," Al complained.

Max rolled his eyes. "Like that is somethin' ta worry aboot at a time like this!"

"We've been waiting for sssssssssssome tasssssssssssty morsssssssssssels like you two. It'sssssssssss been a long time, and we have many mouths to feed," the lead snake threatened as the others writhed and came right up to Max and Al.

Max was prepared to grab the lead snake and hurl him across the tunnel, but he didn't know how he could hold off the others. There were just too many. Still, he knew they were all fearful to be the snake to make the first move. The snakes realized whoever struck first would be killed by Max's strong jaws. None of them wanted to be the victim, so they held back.

As Max stood his ground, he felt Al bumping him. Al pushed and pushed against the piece of stone with all his might. "Wha' in the name of Pete are ye doin'?!"

"I'm tryin' . . . to . . . get . . . this . . . stone . . . to . . . stop . . . pokin' . . . me!" Al grunted, pushing as he said each word.

"All of you sssssssssssnakes are cowards! I'm going in!" called a snake from the back of the mass. He was wriggling his way to the front of the group with rapid speed. Max growled and knew this would be it. He would have to tangle with this asp.

Suddenly Al's backside finally pushed in the stone, and a massive door started rising out of the floor, sending sand and dust flying everywhere. Max and Al braced themselves as the vibration of stone grinding against stone caused a loud rumble in the tunnel. The snakes all looked up in surprise, hissing and coiling around each other. Al covered his eyes with his paws and Max's jaw dropped to the floor. The door finally stopped when it hit the ceiling with a solid thump.

Max and Al sat there, breathing heavily. The snakes were cut off on the other side of the door. "Ha! Did ye see that, Big Al? Ye must have hit a lever ta open this door," Max exclaimed.

Al slowly removed his paw from one eye and peeked up to see the door now in their way, cutting off the corridor and the snakes. Relief poured over him and he grabbed Max with a huge hug, jumping up and down, saying, "The snakes be gone! The snakes be gone! The snakes be gone!"

Suddenly they heard another stone door opening from the tunnel wall, evidently triggered by the rising of the first door. Max and Al sat and watched a new opening appear before their eyes. They looked at one another and then peered into the new tunnel. Light was coming from inside.

"Laddie, ye not only saved us from the snake beasties, I think ye've discovered a whole new tunnel. An' someone's doon there," Max said, walking toward the entrance.

"Are ye sure we should go doon there?" Al asked fearfully.

"Well, yer path back ta the palace is blocked now, so unless ye want ta be seen r-r-runnin' thr-r-rough the pr-r-rison an' causin' even more tr-r-rouble for the humans, I suggest we see wha's down here," Max said, not waiting for a reply but trotting on into the new tunnel.

"Oh, did ye hear what happened this mornin'?" Al asked as he followed Max. "I were comin' to tell ye aboot it."

"Aye, an' that's why I were makin' me way ta the palace. So tell me, laddie, wha' exactly happened? Did ye decide ta take a bath in Pharaoh's punch bowl an' r-r-roll around on his plate then?" Max asked with a frown.

"It weren't me! It were those jackals! They were howlin' all night so I went to the kitchen to shush them. I let them in to tell them I wouldn't let them in any more . . ." Al started to explain.

"That makes gr-r-rand sense," Max said as he rolled his eyes.

"Tef jumped up on the counter and must have gotten his hair all in Pharaoh's food and drink. Wep and I were talkin' when he were up there so I didn't know until it were too late. But they're gone for good now," Al explained. "I told them never to come back."

"Well, at least that's somethin' good ta come from this. Wha' happened next?" Max asked as they followed along the dimly lit tunnel.

"The cupbearer and the baker were there, and when Pharaoh felt the jackal hair in his mouth, he screamed and told Potiphar to throw the men in prison. Sure, and I've never seen him so mad," Al explained. "It were not a pretty sight."

"Aye, an' I'm sure jackal hair in his food were not a pretty sight ta Pharaoh. Well, the two lads are under Joseph's care in the prison now. He put them in a special cell an' Potiphar told Joseph ta watch over them," Max said.

"Oh, that's a relief. I were worried aboot them, even though they've been nasty to me some. I never would want to hurt them back," Al said.

The light in the tunnel started getting brighter. Max and Al began seeing ornate paintings and drawings on the walls. Magnificent friezes of Egyptian gods and goddesses were carved into the stone.

"This be no ordinary tunnel," Max said as they neared the light source.

Max and Al saw an oddly shaped lamp hanging from the ceiling of the tunnel. It gave off a soft glow that lit up two seated statues of the gods Ra and Horus. The statues looked lifelike with the flickering light moving shadows around them. Max picked up his pace and ran past them, Al close behind.

They soon saw another lamp from the ceiling, then another. All along the corridor were lamps lighting the way. "I told ye someone were here. They'd have ta be here ta light these lamps," Max said, trotting straight ahead.

"But who is doon here," Al asked. "And why?"

"We'll hopefully know that at the end of this tunnel," Max answered.

Max and Al moved steadily through the tunnel, relieved to not see any snakes or other wriggling beasties. They finally came to a fork in the tunnel. "Gr-r-reat, jest like in the pyramid. The corridor splits off. Well, Al, which one do we choose?"

Al sat a moment with his paw pointing back and forth to each corridor, mumbling to himself. "It scares me, it scares me not, it scares me, it scares me not." Finally he pointed and said, "Sure and it dunnot matter, Max. They both scare me."

Max shook his head. "No fear, Big Al. I'll protect ye. Let's jest take the one ta the r-r-r-ight. It's worked before."

CHAPTER 39

The Banana Key

As Max and Al entered the right-hand corridor, they traveled on for what seemed an eternity before coming to yet another fork.

"We'll jest stay ta the right," Max said as he again trotted down the corridor on the right.

On and on it went, and Max realized they were in an impossible labyrinth of underground tunnels. He had no idea where they were, but he kept on running ahead like he did. No need to get Al upset down here. They turned a corner and finally started hearing voices.

"I hear people! I hear people! I never thought I'd be so happy to hear people!" Al piped up with glee.

"Aye, lad, but we don't know wha' kind of people," Max replied. They carefully crept behind the various statues lining the hall, and noticed the slope of the tunnel turning up.

"We must be reachin' an exit," Max whispered. "Stay close, Al."

The two turned a corner and saw an ornately decorated chamber. In the center was a white limestone block with a slab on top. On the slab were baskets filled with bread, fruit, meat, and jugs of drinks.

"Food!" Al said.

"Don't even think aboot it, Al. This looks like some sort of preparation chamber for offerin's. Leave it alone then," Max warned as they came up to the table, careful to look out for the humans.

"But Max, there be bananas here!" Al exclaimed, jumping up onto the table. He took a banana and clutched it to his chest. "Come to me, me little jewel!"

Max frowned. "Didn't ye tell me it were bananas the jackals tried ta take ye ta see at the temple of Anubis?"

Al's eyes were closed as he peeled a banana and took a big bite of the delicious fruit. He mumbled, "Uh-huh."

Max looked around the room, and there were murals and carvings of Anubis all over the walls. He peeked around the corner and saw two long hallways going in different directions. One was lined with statues of Anubis. The other was dimly lit but sloped upward. "It couldn't be!" Max said. "Come on, Al. Gr-r-rab yer banana an' follow me."

They walked very slowly and silently down the hall lined with Anubis statues. Max felt engulfed by a dark presence. Al didn't seem to notice, his attention engrossed in his banana. Max stopped and peered around the final statue in the hall, and beyond it was a massive chamber with ceilings thirty feet high. On the back wall was an enormous, black statue of Anubis holding the ankh cross symbol in one hand and the adze tool to open the mummy's mouth in the other. The statue was massive and ominous, and surrounding it were mounds of food and drink offerings, burning lamps, and incense. No humans were around.

"This must be the inner chamber in the temple of Anubis! But how kin we be out this far from the palace?" Max exclaimed.

Al wasn't listening as he sat and took another bite, tears of joy streaming from his eyes.

"We best try the other hallway," Max said as he turned and led them back to the offering chamber. Al grabbed another banana and Max shook his head, thinking to himself, *As long as it keeps the laddie's mind occupied. Bananas are a good thing at the moment.*

They followed the other hallway as it sloped up and after a while came to a dead end in a small chamber. A single lamp hung from the low ceiling. Al sat down on the floor, oblivious, while Max ran around the room. "There must be another secret exit here. There must be!" He proceeded to look carefully for another stone jutting out of the wall like the one they had found back in the other tunnel.

"What are ye doin'?" Al finally asked with his mouth full.

"I'm lookin' for another secr-r-ret lever ta open a secr-r-ret door," Max replied, slowly walking around the room.

"Oh, well, ye might want to look for a picture o' a jackal," Al said, taking another bite.

"Wha' do ye mean, Al?" Max asked.

"When I turned to look at the stone that were jabbin' me in me backside in the tunnel . . ." Al said, then took a big swallow, ". . . I saw a picture o' a jackal next to it."

"Aye! I didn't know ye were that astute then, laddie!" Max said excitedly, looking for a jackal on the wall.

"What's a *stoot*?" Al asked, finally tossing the banana peel on the floor.

"Never mind, jest help me find a jackal," Max directed.

The two went around looking at every block on the wall, but they didn't see either a jackal or a piece of stone jutting out from the wall. Max was frustrated. "I dunnot see a way out of this chamber. Maybe it's a dead end after all."

"I wish ye wouldn't say things like that," Al said, getting spooked by their surroundings.

Suddenly they heard voices coming from the hallway behind them. "Someone's back there," Max hoarsely whispered, running around the room again trying to find the secret lever. "We've got ta find a way out."

Al was so frightened he began running all over the room in a panic. "AAAHHHH!" he screamed as he ran around and around in circles. The voices grew louder and Al went running zigzag across the room, slipping on the banana peel. It took him sliding across the room on his backside until he landed squarely on a block at the bottom of the wall. Suddenly the stone block he was sitting on began to sink. As it did so, a door on the other side of the chamber began to open slightly.

"AL! That's it! Ye found the secret exit!" Max exclaimed. "Hurry, come on!"

Al jumped up and looked at the sunken stone in the floor. On top of it was etched a jackal. He ran over to the open door and followed Max as they barely squeezed through the opening. Just as Al passed through, the door closed, catching the very tip of Al's tail hair.

"AHHHHHHH! It's got me!" Al cried with his tail stuck in the door.

"Hang on!" Max said as he took Al's tail in his mouth and yanked it until it finally came loose. They took off running down a dark passage.

"Thanks, Max. Ye saved me tail!" Al joyfully exclaimed as they ran.

Max spat out cat hair and frowned. "Ye're welcome. But I sure didn't enjoy it," Max said, still spitting. "I see why Pharaoh were so mad."

Soon they reached a turn in the corridor and followed it up through a series of more turns. Finally they came to the room where the statues of Pharaoh's family stood, with the round statue of Al at the end. "Hey, there I am again! Another statue o' me!" Al exclaimed.

"That's not a new statue, Big Al. It's the *same* statue," Max said, trotting on ahead.

Al was admiring the image of himself when he turned to see Max gone. "MAX! I'm comin'! Wait for me!"

Soon they were at the entrance chamber of Pharaoh's pyramid and stepped out into the bright sunshine. They had to shield their eyes as they grew accustomed to the bright light.

"I kin't believe it. That tunnel between the prison an' the palace leads all the way out here," Max said.

Al looked up at the pyramid and put his paws up to his mouth. "Max! Do ye realize where we were? We were in the secret passage them jackal beasties took to reach the Temple of Anubis . . . and the bananas!"

Max shook his head, chuckling at how Al was just now realizing all this. "Aye, so it would seem. An' I see how Nigel missed this passage in the pyramid before. He's too small for his weight ta open the levers so he scurried on past without triggerin' them. Ye dun good, laddie. Ye an' yer banana saved the day again."

"Sure, and me banana were like a key," Al grinned. But then he realized something. "If we're all the way out here, and the palace is all the way over there, how do we get back?"

Max looked across the desert to Avaris in the distance. "We best get walkin'. We kin always go back through the tunnel if ye don't want ta walk across the desert," Max said with a grin.

"Sure, and the desert's fine! I never want to go back in that triangle and through that creepy tunnel," Al said with a gulp.

Max looked over and saw one of Pharaoh's carts. The men had emptied their load of goods for the pyramid and waved farewell to the workers. They were headed back to the palace.

"Hurry, Big Al. I think we kin hitch a ride," Max said. They ran over behind the cart, and when the men took the reins of the horses to leave, they jumped up in the back, hiding under a tarp.

Al sighed with relief. "Max, remind me to do somethin'."

"Wha's that, kitty?" Max asked.

"Remind me to never, ever, ever, leave the palace again," Al said.

Max chuckled. "Aye, I will. But while ye're at the palace, ye best behave. No more guests for dinner."

"Sure, and I'll be happy with whoever Pharaoh invites to the table," Al said. Then he looked up at the sun in the sky and saw it was directly overhead. "I hope we make it home in time for lunch."

Max grinned. It appeared the traumatic events of the morning hadn't left any lasting effects on Al, as his mind was once again on the next meal. Max began to think about their adventure in the tunnel, and questions entered his mind. Who knows that the secret tunnel from the palace to the pyramid even exists? Nigel said humans hadn't been in that tunnel between the prison and the palace in more than a hundred years. The debris at the entrance, the stale air, and the nest of snakes would confirm that.

But if the lanterns in the tunnel were lit, it would only make sense they were lit to guide someone either in or out of the tunnel to reach the temple of Anubis.

The question was, Who?

CHAPTER 40

What Dreams May Bring

FIVE MONTHS LATER

"See wha' I mean, Nigel? The prisoners are thr-r-rashin' aboot like they be havin' crazy dreams. Both of them," Max said, pointing to the baker and the cupbearer.

"I say, I believe you're right, old boy. Do they usually sleep like this?" Nigel asked.

"Not that I've seen in all the months they've been here," Max replied. "I'm glad ye came by tonight, Mousie. I were lonely in the prison since Sadiki left me here. He felt sick an' went home early yesterday, so I stayed behind."

"He's been quite ill a lot lately, hasn't he? I know he's relieved to have Joseph to watch over things, you know," Nigel said as they continued to watch the two men. "Do you suppose . . .?"

"Suppose wha'?" Max asked.

"Do you suppose we could be witnessing two more dreams in your mission as predicted by Gillamon?" Nigel asked.

Max thought a minute. "Could be, Mousie. We'll have ta stay close by an' see wha' happens in the mornin'." He and Nigel stretched out on the cool stone floor outside the cell to wait for the night. "So how are things with Liz at Potiphar's house?"

"Utterly splendid! Liz is well and continues her studies of writing and reading the various texts I've given her to learn. And the boy Benipe is becoming quite the harpist. Once he opened his heart to the Maker, he truly began to come alive in many ways," Nigel said, adjusting his golden spectacles on his nose. "He still has much to learn, but I have faith in the boy's talent."

"That's gr-r-rand news, Mousie. I know Joseph would be glad ta see how well the lad is doin'," Max replied. "Have ye been doon in the tunnel yet? I'm tellin' ye, someone here knows aboot it for those lamps ta be lit."

Nigel chuckled. "I hate to burst your suspicious bubble old boy, but those lamps in the tunnel have been lit for decades."

"Wha' in the name of Pete do ye mean? That's impossible!" Max exclaimed.

"Actually, it's not impossible. But it *is* completely fascinating. Egyptian priest-chemists long ago developed what I like to call 'ever-burning lamps.' I've studied them for years in the tunnels under the pyramids and the Sphinx at Giza," Nigel said excitedly. "As best I can tell, the Egyptians use some sort of braided asbestos or 'salamander's wool' that appears to remain lit without replenishment of fuel."

Max looked deflated. "An' I thought I were on ta some sort of conspiracy."

Nigel smiled. "Chin up, old boy. There are plenty of conspiracies and mysteries in Egypt to solve. But you can check the ever-burning lamps off your list. My guess is when the palace-prison tunnel was in active use, the branch-off tunnel leading to the pyramid was used by a previous Pharaoh who maybe had plans to put his complex out there."

"So ye're sayin' the current Pharaoh may not even know aboot that tunnel?" Max asked.

"Possibly not. See, these Egyptians are masters at creating massive networks of tunnels in the subterranean earth. They go on forever on the Giza plateau, and the Sphinx is the main entry gate if you will. Once I thought I'd never find my way out of there!" Nigel exclaimed with a shudder. "So it's only logical to assume that over time, they lose track of the tunnels they've made as one kingdom passes to another. But I must say what a *splendid* discovery you made!"

"Aye, well, that kitty actually found the tunnel by jest bein' his daft self. Here we were surrounded by a nest of asps an' the laddie's worried aboot somethin' pokin' his backside. Still, we did find the secret tunnel in the pyramid leadin' ta the chamber of Anubis," Max said, growing serious. "Nigel, I don't want ta go there again. I felt an evil presence in there."

Nigel nodded in agreement. "Yes, yes, yes, I know the feeling, old boy. But you've told me where to find the passage in the pyramid so I shall look for it. Alas, I cannot open the lever by myself, but perhaps I will have an assistant to help me one day."

"Get off! Get off!" the baker moaned in his sleep, swiping at his head.

Max and Nigel peered into the cell of the sleeping men, then looked at one another. "I wonder if nightmares count as dreams," Max said.

Joseph was up early as usual and retrieved a bowl of fruit, wheat cakes, and a jug of water for the prisoners. He reached the cell of the baker and the cupbearer, unlocked the door, and took the food to the table.

"Good morning," Joseph said as he poured the water into their cups.

They didn't say a word in reply. The cupbearer sat on his mat with his legs drawn up to his chest. The baker sat with his back against the wall looking very depressed. Max and Nigel stayed hidden outside but were listening carefully to what was being said.

"Why the long faces? Is something wrong?" Joseph asked.

"We both dreamed strange dreams last night," the cupbearer said.

"And there's no one to tell us what they mean. Back at the palace, Pharaoh's lector priests are always on hand to consult *The Dream Book.* Here we have no one to help us," the baker added.

"Doesn't the interpretation of dreams come from God?" Joseph asked, drawing curious looks from the men. "Tell me what you dreamed."

The cupbearer stood and went over to the table to sit down. He took the cluster of grapes from the fruit bowl and said, "I dreamed there was a vine with three branches. I watched as it budded and blossomed with bountiful clusters that soon ripened into grapes."

"Go on," Joseph encouraged.

"I took the grapes and squeezed them into Pharaoh's cup, giving it to him to drink. That's it," the cupbearer said.

Joseph smiled. "This is what your dream means. The three branches are three days. Within three days, Pharaoh will call you back to the palace and you will be restored to your old position as cupbearer. You will once again place Pharaoh's cup in his hand."

The cupbearer's face lit up with hope. "Could it be?" he wondered, as he smiled at the possibility of being released and restored to his former role in the palace.

Joseph studied the cupbearer and knew this might be his one shot at getting Pharaoh's ear. The cupbearer put his life on the line with every sip he took for Pharaoh. So it was the cupbearer who more often than not was closest to Pharaoh, because Pharaoh's very life depended on this man. Potiphar's hands were tied, but perhaps the cupbearer would be Joseph's way out of prison.

"When you are released and things go well for you again at the palace, please tell Pharaoh about me and help me get out of this prison. I was kidnapped from the land of the Hebrews and I've done nothing wrong to be thrown into this prison," Joseph said, hoping to have the favor returned.

"What about *my* dream?" the baker asked excitedly, pulling out the other chair and joining the men at the table. He had hope after hearing the good interpretation of the cupbearer's dream. "I dreamed there were three baskets of white bread placed on my head. In the top basket were all sorts of pastries for Pharaoh, but the birds were eating them. What does that mean, Joseph?" The baker took one of the wheat cakes from the basket on the table and started eating it.

Joseph stood at the table and tapped his knuckles on the rough pine, a frown on his face.

"Well, what does it mean?" the baker said, spitting out crumbs from his full mouth.

Joseph threw his head back, searching for the words. Finally, he put his hand in the air and laid out the reality of the poor man's dream. "This is what your dream means. The three baskets are also three days. But in three days, Pharaoh will order your execution, and you will lose your head. I'm sorry."

The baker swallowed hard and threw the wheat cake on the table, putting his hand to his throat.

Max and Nigel looked at each other with shock. "We were r-r-right, laddie. These two dreams are part of the mission, since Joseph interpreted them. The prisoners are goin' back ta the palace."

"Yes, but what dreadful news for the baker," Nigel lamented. "On the other hand, do you realize the cupbearer may be Joseph's way out of prison?"

"Aye, that's gr-r-rand news for Joseph. Go tell Liz wha's happenin'. This means five dreams have passed out of eight," Max said, his expression growing into a frown.

"I say, old boy, why the long face? This is a tremendous development for your mission!" Nigel exclaimed.

"I'm worried aboot Al. This is goin' ta be hard for him ta take when he sees wha' happens ta the baker. He felt bad enough that it were his fault the lad were thrown in prison," Max explained. "I dunnot know how he'll do when he hears the baker will be . . . executed."

CHAPTER 41

Pharaoh's Birthday

I'm going and that's final, *mon ami!* You can either take me there or I will go myself," Liz protested.

"But, my dear, it is the middle of the day! We've only gone to the palace at night. What if we're seen? Worse yet, what if Potiphar sees you?" Nigel asked.

"Oui, je comprends. I understand the risk, but Albert is going to need me as he has never needed me before, Nigel. I must be there," Liz argued. "He is so tenderhearted and I know he will crumble when the baker's sentence is announced."

Max, Liz, and Nigel had all agreed it would be better if Al wasn't told in advance about the events to come. No need to worry him before the time, and besides, there was nothing he could do.

"Very well, my pet. I advise against this, but I understand your concern. We must be quiet and unseen," Nigel instructed. "Now, let's get to Potiphar's litter before he does."

Nigel and Liz snuck outside, where the servants were assembled to transport Potiphar to the palace. They hid inside a wicker storage compartment in the litter and hoped Potiphar's servants would not be placing any items in there today. Soon Potiphar came out and stepped into the litter. He had several items in his hands.

"Shall I put those in the storage compartment for you, my master?" the servant asked.

Liz and Nigel held their breath.

"No, I will hold them. We're only going to the palace. Hurry, let's be off," Potiphar directed.

The two stowaways let their breath go and remained quiet as they rode to the palace. Once inside the gate they waited for Potiphar to leave and for the litter to be taken to the holding area. Once they were on the ground and the servants were gone, they quietly got out of the litter and snuck in and around columns, plants, statues, or whatever they could hide behind. They finally made it to the throne room and hid behind a cluster of plants in the corner.

Chariots were lined up as far as the eye could see. The guards at the palace gate wore specially ornamented loincloths and golden plates around their necks to greet the guests with a stunning display of pageantry. Special flags flew from the top of the palace today. It was Pharaoh's birthday, and the entire kingdom was to celebrate.

Potiphar assembled Pharaoh's court to give last-minute instructions. In the kitchen the workers scurried about, putting final touches on the outrageous amount of food and drink that would flow from Pharaoh's table. The new baker had a special surprise planned, and was handling it himself.

"Look lively. Here they come," Potiphar said as the first of the guests arrived in the hallway leading to the throne room, where a huge banquet table was spread for the guests.

"Ah, it is good to see you all. Welcome!" Potiphar bowed to greet the guests and directed them into the throne room.

When all the guests were seated, Potiphar made his customary announcement before Pharaoh entered the room. He stood at the grand hall entrance and loudly announced, "Enter Pharaoh, powerful ruler of Egypt, son of Ra and the embodiment of Horus."

The guests all stood and assumed a bowing position as Pharaoh entered the room. He was dressed in exquisite jewelry with a new necklace around his neck and a fine linen loincloth with semiprecious stones sewn into the fabric. He carried Al in his arms, and servants followed him holding massive fans of ostrich feathers over him. He took a seat at the head of the table and placed Al on a silky pillow next to him on the floor.

Potiphar clapped his hands and the court musicians played lively music while a group of dancers entered the room to entertain Pharaoh and the guests. A row of servants began pouring wine into the cups of the guests. The new cupbearer brought Pharaoh's gold cup and tasted it before humbly placing it before Pharaoh. He was clearly a fearful soul, and not one Pharaoh had been able to take into his confidence. He performed his job well, but Pharaoh thought to himself how much he missed his old cupbearer.

Al was thrilled when a servant brought over a bowl of milk for him. He lapped it up quickly and burped, a milk moustache covering his goofy grin.

"Well, the lad is enjoying himself for the time being anyway," Nigel whispered to Liz.

Liz smiled, watching Al in his element. He was the center of attention for Pharaoh and loved being in his court. "*Oui*, I wish it would only last, *mon ami.*"

When the dancers finished their performance Pharaoh clapped and held his hand up to the guests. "And now, let us feast!"

Potiphar motioned for the new cupbearer and baker to bring the meal. A long line of servants streamed into the room bringing tray after tray of beautifully prepared food. Finally the new baker himself entered the room carrying an elaborate food sculpture made from various fruits and vegetables. It was a scene of the Nile, with papyrus reeds and lotus flowers, birds, and even crocodiles and hippos. The new baker wore a big smile as he placed the tray in front of Pharaoh. "Happy birthday, my lord."

Pharaoh's face beamed with pleasure as he gazed at the food sculpture. "This is magnificent! How did you ever design such a thing?"

The new baker humbly bowed and answered, "Thank you, my lord. Pharaoh deserves something magnificent for his birthday, and if I may, let me show you an additional surprise." He turned the tray around and on the other side was a sculpture of Al made from carrots. He was crouched down in the reeds, ready to pounce on a fleeing bird.

"Hapy!" Pharaoh said as he picked Al up to show him the sculpture. "Look! Another sculpture of you."

Al looked at his likeness and meowed. *Me likeness in carrots! Me ears sure look tasty.* Al's ears were made from the ends of carrots with clusters of pine nut seeds in the middle. The guests all applauded.

Liz giggled, still amazed at Al's adoration. "Albert art. He's been portrayed in paint, stone, clay, and now carrots."

"I dare say, what will be next, gold?" Nigel chuckled.

Pharaoh clapped his hands in approval. "Baker, you have outdone yourself. I am very pleased. And Hapy is as well."

The baker bowed and made his way down the table to see to the needs of the guests. Pharaoh watched him and nodded. This new baker was far better than the old baker. His thoughts again turned to his old cupbearer. He wanted him back. He wanted him back now.

"Potiphar! Send for my old cupbearer and baker from the prison. I want them here now," Pharaoh instructed.

Potiphar stood and bowed. "As you wish, my lord." He called over the palace guards and instructed them to bring the men from the prison. They immediately left the throne room.

"Right on schedule," Nigel said with a frown. "Are you ready, my dear?"

Liz gazed at Al and sighed. *"Oui,* I am. Oh, but my poor Albert. Be strong, *mon cher."*

"What's this all about?" Joseph said as the palace guards entered the prison.

"Pharaoh has summoned the baker and the cupbearer. He wishes them brought to the palace now."

Joseph felt a jolt of mixed emotions go through him. The revelation God had given him about their dreams three days ago was coming to reality, just as he had foretold. He was elated on one hand, as the cupbearer could help him out of prison. He was also elated to see that finally his interpretation of a dream was coming true. What did that mean for his recurring dreams of the celestial bodies and the bundles bowing before him? But as Joseph walked down the prison corridor to get the men, his heart was heavy for the baker. He was about to face death. It was a sobering moment as Joseph gazed at the man when he opened the cell door.

"Pharaoh has summoned both of you," Joseph said to the men sitting at their table.

They looked at each other nervously. They knew what Joseph had told them about their dreams, but who knew if what Joseph had predicted was true? The cupbearer was worried that perhaps his dream meant his blood would be spilled for Pharaoh. The baker discounted Joseph's interpretation. He didn't want to think Pharaoh could possibly execute him for something so ridiculous.

The men stood and nodded at Joseph as they quietly exited the room. When they got to the entrance of the prison and the door was shut behind them, leaving Joseph inside, Joseph called to the cupbearer, "Remember me."

The men were quickly taken to be cleaned up before they faced Pharaoh. They were given new clothes and then ushered into the throne room.

"Ah, here they are. Good," Pharaoh said as he stood. "Come, come, the two of you."

The baker and the cupbearer humbly bowed before Pharaoh. "Please, have a seat," Pharaoh said as he directed them to the head of his table. The men looked at one another and did as Pharaoh instructed, smiles on their faces. So far this was going well. The baker breathed a sigh of relief.

"Now, as it is my birthday, I want to give a show of my compassion and my power as a gift to all of you," Pharaoh said as he spread his arms out in front of his guests.

Potiphar stood in the back of the room with his muscular arms crossed over his chest. He frowned, as he understood 'Pharaoh-speak.' He knew this would be bad for one of the two servants.

Pharaoh leaned over to the table and took his golden cup in hand. "I have been served well for many years by this man," he said as he placed his hand on the cupbearer's shoulder. "He has been my confidant and has faithfully taken the risk to sip my cup. Although he missed the mark one day, giving me the hair of an animal to drink, I compassionately forgive him this error. I now restore you to the position of my chief cupbearer," Pharaoh said as he handed the gold cup to the man.

The cupbearer got up and then knelt before Pharaoh, kissing his hand as he took the cup. Tears of joy filled his eyes. "My lord! Thank you for your mercy. I shall serve you faithfully and never again allow anything to bring you displeasure."

The guests all applauded in favor of the restoration of the cupbearer. Liz sighed as she looked at the baker. Nigel placed his hand on her back. "Hang on, dear girl."

Pharaoh then placed his hands behind his back and slapped one hand on top of the other. "But there is a limit to my compassion. And so no one in my kingdom thinks they can sloppily serve Pharaoh, I must render a sentence as a message to all. I am Pharaoh, all-powerful ruler of Egypt. Let no one forget this," he said as he hovered behind the baker, who now squirmed as he listened.

"Baker, your work was deplorable at best. How dare you serve me food covered with the hair of an animal! You failed Pharaoh, and you will now be an example of how I reward such poor performance," Pharaoh said angrily. "Potiphar, this man is to be executed immediately! Take him out of my sight now!"

"My lord, please show mercy!" the baker cried as he fell to his knees and groveled on the floor.

Potiphar motioned to the palace guards, who grabbed the baker by the arms and dragged him screaming out of the throne room. Potiphar turned and bowed before he left the room. "As you say, my lord."

A hush fell over the guests. It was an uncomfortable moment for everyone, as they didn't know what Pharaoh would do next.

"Please, cupbearer, we have guests to attend to. Bring more wine, and begin by filling my cup first!" Pharaoh instructed. "Musicians, play! Dancers, dance! This is a party, after all!"

The merriment started again as the cupbearer quickly took a jug of wine and filled Pharaoh's cup. He took a swig, wiped off the cup, and handed it to Pharaoh with a low bow. "Thank you, my lord."

Pharaoh took the cup and lifted it in approval to the cupbearer. "Welcome back."

Al sat there shaking on the pillow. He thought he would be sick from what had just happened. He had to get out of there. He slowly got up and left the throne room while Pharaoh was distracted by the dancers. Liz and Nigel snuck out from behind the plants and followed Al into the hall.

Al was sobbing, shaking his head. Liz softly came up to him. "I'm here, *cher* Albert." Nigel stood quietly behind.

Al looked up at Liz, tears rolling down his cheeks. "Gillamon told me that me part o' this mission would be the hardest o' all. I never knew what he meant . . . until now."

"Albert, I know this is very hard and you feel responsible for the baker's death, but remember—he did not do his job. He was supposed to inspect Pharaoh's food and failed to do so. The burden for his fate rests on his shoulders alone, *mon cher*, not yours," Liz said with her paw up to Al's cheek. "Besides, you do not know the full story of all that is happening here. I believe that the Maker can use your mistakes for good, even as bad as this is."

Nigel joined Liz to help ease Al's mind. "Your bride is right, Al. Do you realize there is a chance now for Joseph to get out of prison with the help of the cupbearer?"

Al sniffed. "How?"

"Joseph has asked the cupbearer to put in a word with Pharaoh on his behalf," Nigel explained. "And if Pharaoh listens, Joseph will be freed."

"And that will be all because of you, Albert," Liz said consolingly, softly wiping away Al's tears. "If the cupbearer and the baker had not gone to the prison, they never would have encountered Joseph. So please, *mon cher,* hold on to the hope of something good coming from something so bad."

"Well, how long will it take until the cupbearer helps Joseph?" Al asked, wiping his nose.

"Only time will tell, old boy," Nigel said. "You'll have to be patient."

"I dunnot know how I can stand it. My grief is heavy. Until I see somethin' good come from this . . . I dunnot know what I'll do," Al said, resting his head on Liz's shoulder.

Liz looked at Nigel and they shared a moment of grief with Al.

Little did they all realize that while the cupbearer was busily filling cups for the guests, he was so overcome with the joy of the moment that he put the horrible experience of the prison completely out of his mind. He didn't want to even think about what could have happened. He was incredibly relieved to be restored to his former high status.

And along with forgetting about the prison, the cupbearer completely forgot about Joseph.

CHAPTER 42

Very Superstitious

My corpse is permanent, it will not perish nor be destroyed in this land forever," Liz read aloud from *The Book of the Dead.*

"Splendid, my dear! I believe there is little more I can teach you of hieroglyphs or the hieratic script. You have mastered the text, and you are now ready," Nigel said, wiping off his spectacles before placing them back on his nose.

"Ready for what, Nigel?" Liz asked, rolling up the scroll.

"Why, for your first mummification, my dear! Now that you have learned from *The Book of the Dead* what the Egyptians believe about death and the afterlife, I can show you the process they undergo to achieve their afterlife status," Nigel explained. "I must warn you, it may make you feel a bit squeamish, but it is a fascinating process."

"Oui, Nigel, I am ready to see this. When will we go?" Liz asked.

"I've learned that two mummies are to be prepared tonight. One is a local high-ranking scribe named Ipuy who passed away yesterday, so he will undergo the initial phase of mummification to prepare the body for drying. The other mummy is a priestess named Henutmehit who has been partially wrapped and will be completed and placed in her coffin tonight," Nigel explained. "We will go to the local embalming house here in Avaris to observe the rituals."

Liz breathed a sigh of relief. "Thank goodness we don't have to go to the temple of Anubis. After all you've told me of the evil presence there, and how Max and Al felt when they were in the inner chamber, I am not in a hurry to visit that temple."

"My dear, dear girl! Do not be frightened. Although I would like to take you to the temple of Anubis, I certainly would never impose that on you," Nigel said with a reassuring pat of Liz's paw. "But remember that although there is an evil presence there, you have the protection of the Maker. As long as the one, true God is your protector, why should you be afraid anywhere you go?"

Liz smiled. "Nigel, you have an amazing faith, *mon ami.* I should act more like you sometimes. It's just that this Egyptian culture is so . . ."

"Superstitious? Yes, yes, yes, the Egyptians are very superstitious, so it is easy to get swept away by what they believe when you study it as closely as you've been doing. But never lose sight of the truth, Liz. All the superstitious writings on the wall and in the texts and even on the mummies themselves are not truth. You must keep this in mind, my pet," Nigel explained.

"Oui, Nigel, I will. You are right, of course. I must keep my focus on the Maker alone," Liz said.

"Right! Very well then, we shall go for your first mummification this evening," Nigel said, adjusting his spectacles. "You keep your focus and I'll keep us hidden, my dear."

The flicker of candlelight illuminated the entrance to the embalming house as Nigel and Liz crept up the steps. Two columns lined with hieroglyphs held up the portico at the top of the steps, and murals of scenes from *The Book of the Dead* were all over the walls inside. As they snuck down the hallway toward the embalming chamber, Liz shook her head as she read all the hieroglyphs on the wall. *Very superstitious*, she thought, but then reminded herself, *Keep your focus.*

Nigel scurried into the embalming room, Liz close behind. They jumped up onto a granite block and then up to a statue of Osiris where they could get a view from above the table where the body of Ipuy lay. Surrounding the table was a group of priests laying out various tools and ingredients to be used for the embalming. The scent of incense was heavy in the air. A lector priest walked around the room, chanting various prayers and spells.

Liz was suddenly startled to see a jackal-headed man walk into the room, carrying the ankh cross symbol in his hand. "Nigel! What am I seeing? This looks like Anubis, no? And he is alive and walking!"

Nigel chuckled softly. "No need to fret. The embalming priest wears the mask of Anubis during the procedure. Since Anubis is the god of mummification, they act it out as if Anubis himself were here."

"Nigel, that cross with the circle loop on top—that is the ankh symbol in the jackal's hand. It means 'life,' no?" Liz asked.

"Precisely. The Egyptians put the cross everywhere to signify life, which is what they long for, both in this world and the next," Nigel explained.

"Interesting," Liz noted. "So what happens first to make a mummy?"

"The first thing they must do is remove the internal organs and apply natron to dry the body," Nigel said. "I say, are you quite well as I discuss the medical part of mummification?"

Liz wrinkled her nose. *"Oui,* continue, Nigel. I am fine."

"Right. Well, you see them working on the chap's head there? They are removing his brain first. Unfortunately, the Egyptians believe the brain is useless, so they discard it," Nigel explained.

Liz looked at Nigel with shock. *"C'est impossible!* Where do they think intelligence comes from then?"

"They believe the *heart* is the center of intelligence, conscience, and emotion. It is the only organ left in the body, because they feel the mummy will need it close at hand when he or she judged in the next world," Nigel explained.

"I read about this judgment. It is the Weighing of the Heart ceremony, no?" Liz asked.

"Precisely, my pet. And tell me what you learned about that ceremony," Nigel said, pointing to the far wall.

Liz fixed her gaze where Nigel pointed. A mural depicted the scene of the deceased being led by the hand by Anubis into the court of justice, presided over by the god Osiris and a jury of forty-two other gods.

"Well, after the jackal god Wepawet guides the deceased to the underworld, the jackal god Anubis leads the deceased into a room where a set of scales stands in the center. On one scale is the deceased's heart and on the other a feather, which is the symbol of truth, and the goddess Ma'at. Anubis conducts the Weighing of the Heart to determine if the deceased has behaved well enough in earthly life to be worthy of eternal life," Liz explained. "Thoth the scribe god takes notes, and behind him sits the eagerly waiting monster Ammut who is part crocodile, part lion, and part hippo. If sins on earth make the heart too heavy, it is thrown to Ammut, who will devour the heart instantly. But if the heart balances with the feather of truth, the mummy passes the test and earns eternal life."

Nigel wiped back his whiskers and clapped his hands. He was clearly proud of his student. "Bravo! And do you recall the deceased's part in this judgment?"

"Ah, *oui,* in Chapter 125 of *The Book of the Dead* he makes a 'negative confession,' claiming all the terrible things he has *not* done in life," Liz replied.

"Well done! And as we will see later, a heart scarab is placed on the mummy with a special spell to keep his heart from blurting out sins or betraying the deceased by lying," Nigel added.

"This is madness! Why would someone's own heart betray him if it meant being eternally lost?" Liz asked.

"Because the Egyptians are paranoid and superstitious about everything—even their own hearts turning on them at the moment of truth," Nigel explained. "Oh, wait, now they are ready to remove the other organs. Look."

The jackal-headed priest took a black obsidian blade and made an incision on the body.

Liz winced and turned her gaze away.

"Now they remove the other organs, which they will preserve with natron before putting them into special canopic jars," Nigel explained. "Each jar has a lid made in the likeness of a god to protect specific organs."

"Nigel, one of the jars has a lid in the form of a jackal. Is that supposed to be Anubis?" Liz asked.

"No, that is the jackal god Duamutef, protector of the stomach," Nigel answered.

Liz had a passing thought about the two jackals who had tried to get Al into the temple of Anubis. *Duamutef. Tef. Wepawet. Wep. Hmmmm. I guess even real jackals have their heroes.*

"Now when the jars are sealed, they will be placed in a wooden chest next to the coffin in the burial chamber," Nigel said. "After all, the mummy will need these vital organs in the afterlife."

Liz rolled her eyes. "*Oui,* I also read they are terrified of dying a second, eternal death due to hunger or thirst in the afterlife. This is why a vast storage of food offerings is placed in the tomb."

"I must say, you have become quite the Egyptologist, my pet. Well done!" Nigel exclaimed.

The priests started washing the body with palm wine. "Now they are cleaning the body well inside and out and applying spices and natron to dry out the body. The mummy will be placed on a slanted bed and by the end of seventy days it will have shrunk and lost seventy-five percent of its body weight. Fascinating!" the mouse exclaimed.

Liz looked at Nigel with a coy smile. "So you say you never miss a mummification? I think once will be plenty for me."

Nigel grinned. "To each Egyptologist his or her own."

Another group of embalmers entered the room carrying a lion-footed bed holding the mummy of Henutmehit. Another pair of workers brought in an ornately painted mummy case and set it down next to the table.

"Splendid! I say, now we're getting somewhere. Next we get to see the final wrapping of the mummy," Nigel said excitedly. "This is my favorite part."

Liz looked at Nigel and shook her head with a grin. *"Oui,* I can see this."

"They have been wrapping this mummy for more than two weeks, as it takes a long time to do it right. The optimum linen for a mummy is that which has been used previously to dress a god statue. It just adds that extra punch of protection, you know," Nigel said with a smirk.

"But of course it does," Liz said, rolling her eyes.

"Ah, yes, and we're off! First they place a shroud on top, then they wrap each finger and toe separately. The hands and feet are wrapped, followed by the torso, and finally the entire body," Nigel described as they watched the embalmers wrapping the body.

"What are they putting all over the bandages?" Liz asked.

"Ah, but that is sticky, liquid resin to help glue the mummy together," Nigel explained. "Oh, look! There are some amulets. Do you see them, my dear?"

Liz gazed at the beautifully jeweled and painted charms and stones in the shapes of animals, gods, plants, and body parts. "Nigel, there are hundreds of them."

"I KNOW!" Nigel said, his whiskers quivering with excitement. "And they are placed on the body between the strips of linen according to the direction of *The Book of the Dead* so they can protect the mummy all over. Some magic charms have inscriptions to ward off evil spirits."

"Very superstitious," Liz mumbled.

"Splendid! Do you see the large heart scarab they are sewing above the mummy's heart? That little gem is to keep the mummy's heart in line during judgment," Nigel said.

"So it won't betray the mummy," Liz said, shaking her head.

"Oh, now comes the mummy mask!" Nigel whispered excitedly as the jackal-headed priest placed a beautifully painted golden mask resembling the priestess Henutmehit. "They take great care to make the mask's face look just like the deceased so the mummy's spirit can recognize it as it flies through the air looking for its bodily home."

"But of course. We wouldn't want the mummy's spirit to land on the wrong mummy," Liz said with a grin. "That would be quite unacceptable."

Several workers brought in two more wooden coffins. One was covered completely in gold. The other was larger and covered with gold and paintings of hieroglyphs and scenes from *The Book of the Dead.*

Nigel clapped his hands in anticipation. "I must say, this priestess has a splendid set of three nesting coffins!"

Liz remembered what Max and Al had said when they were first touring the pyramids so many years before. She heard Al's voice in her mind. "I may not be very bright, but it seems to me the old pharaoh couldn't get to his stuff if he's locked up, much less dead!" She giggled, as she couldn't help but agree with Al as she watched them place the completely wrapped mummy in one coffin, then another, then another, finally placing the top lid over the mummy. She noticed a strange eye painted on the outside of the coffin.

"Nigel, why the eye?" Liz asked.

"Oh, that is the Wedjat eye of Horus, my pet. You may recall that the god Horus magically had his eyesight restored after losing it in a fight with evil. The Egyptians believe the Wedjat eye has healing powers and offers protection," Nigel explained. "It's also placed on the coffin so the mummy can see what is going on outside."

"But this makes *perfect* sense, no?" Liz giggled again. "This has been very fascinating, Nigel—thank you. I am happy to finally attend my first—and hopefully my last—mummification."

"You are most welcome, my dear," Nigel said, rolling up and down on the soles of his feet with his hands behind his back. He then hesitated, looked down and back up with a huge grin.

"What is it?" Liz asked.

"Oh, just something I've always wanted to say after a good mummification," Nigel said with a sly grin.

Liz grinned back. "What, Nigel? Say it."

"Very well," Nigel said, clearing his throat. "That's a wrap!"

CHAPTER 43

Sleepless in the Palace

The sun was dancing on the water as the current of the Nile moved along at a brisk pace. The lushness of the green grass on the banks of the river felt good to Pharaoh's toes. He breathed in the fresh air and listened to the wonderful sounds of the birds, the crickets, and the frogs. The Nile was bursting with life and health. Pharaoh crossed his arms with great satisfaction, not minding that the hem of his robe was wet.

Suddenly Pharaoh noticed the water swirling and churning about. He leaned in to see what was causing the water to move, and jumped back when he saw a cow's head emerge from the water. A strong, healthy cow walked up onto the bank of the Nile, right next to Pharaoh, shaking the water off its silky hide. It walked over to the tall, lush grass and started grazing there. Pharaoh laughed with the curiosity of this event. This was indeed odd, but somehow it felt right.

But then he heard a "moo" coming from the Nile and turned to see another cow come up from the water. Pharaoh watched in awe as the cow came up on the bank and joined the other cow to eat the lush grass. When he looked back to the river there was still another cow. And another. Then three more cows came out of the water. All seven cows were hungrily eating the grass, looking back occasionally at Pharaoh as they chewed, their tails swishing back and forth.

Pharaoh didn't understand what was happening but was pleased to see the cows so healthy and strong. He walked among the cows, patting them and feeling their hides and strong, sinewy muscles. Suddenly one of the cows mooed with a fearful look on its face as it looked back to the river. The other cows lifted their heads and nervously gazed at the river.

Pharaoh stepped out from among the cows to see what was causing such alarm. Then he saw an ugly, skin-and-bones cow coming out of the Nile. Its eyes were sunken in its head and flies swarmed around it. Pharaoh was immediately repulsed by this beast and went to stand between it and the healthy cows. He didn't want the healthy cows to catch whatever disease this sickly cow had.

But to his dismay, six more ugly, skinny cows came up out of the Nile. They stood in a line on the bank of the Nile, staring eerily at the seven healthy cows. Suddenly they started walking toward the seven healthy cows.

Pharaoh looked on in horror as the seven skinny cows started eating the seven healthy cows.

"NO! NO! Don't eat them!" Pharaoh screamed, but they wouldn't listen. Soon the seven healthy cows were gone and just the seven skin-and-bones cows stood there, looking just as skinny as they had before. It was as if they hadn't eaten a thing. "This can't be!" Pharaoh screamed.

Suddenly Pharaoh awoke and sat up with a start. He looked around the room and tried to catch his breath. His pulse slowed down as he realized he was in his bed, not standing on the banks of the Nile. He put his head in his hands and rubbed his eyes, trying to quickly forget the dream. He lay down on his bed, and soon drifted back to sleep.

Pharaoh walked through the fields of grain, allowing his fingers to graze the top of the stalks. He watched the wind blow across the full, plentiful field and smiled. It was a good year for grain. He squatted down to inspect a single stalk, and suddenly saw seven plump ears of grain grow fat and robust on the stalk.

Pharaoh put his fingers up to touch the silkiness of the plump ears, but then he quickly withdrew his hand as seven more ears, thin and scorched by the east wind, sprouted all around them. Before he knew it, the seven dry, thin ears swallowed up the seven plump ears. As the east wind blew harder, the seven dry ears started blowing off the stalk.

Once again Pharaoh woke up in a sweat and with his heart racing. He looked around his palatial room and to the foot of his bed. He saw Al sitting there, looking at him. "Oh, Hapy, I had two nightmares. Come and lie next to me until morning. Keep me company."

Al walked over and snuggled next to Pharaoh, allowing the disturbed king to gain comfort by stroking him repeatedly. Al put his head on his paws and frowned.

This means somethin' but I don't know what. It's been two years since I seen Pharaoh dream like this. Two full years since he woke up so mad he sent the cupbearer and the baker away on the same mornin'. Two full years since he executed the baker, Al thought. Suddenly he realized something. *Two full years Joseph's been sittin' in the prison, waitin' for the cupbearer to help.*

Al looked at Pharaoh, who was drifting back to sleep. *He's goin' to want answers in the mornin' aboot these dreams and I know jest where he's goin' to get them. It's time that cupbearer remembered Joseph.*

The kitchen workers were busily preparing Pharaoh's breakfast. Al snuck into the room unnoticed and waited until they had finished preparing the trays. When the workers stepped out into the garden to pick vegetables for the noontime meal, Al realized now was his chance.

Well, here goes nothin', Al thought.

Pharaoh stood over the wash basin with his hands gripping the sides. He closed his eyes and let the water drip off his face for a moment as he just stood there, trying to wash away the night. A servant handed him a towel and he blotted his face slowly. The servant noticed that Pharaoh was shaking. Potiphar and the cupbearer stood by in his bedchamber, having been told by the servant something was wrong with Pharaoh. He was visibly upset.

"Call them all. The magicians and the wise men. I want them in my court immediately," Pharaoh directed.

"But what about your breakfast, my lord?" the cupbearer asked.

Pharaoh brushed the suggestion aside. "I will not eat until I've consulted the magicians and wise men. No one will eat until I have answers! Hurry! Get those men here now!"

"As you say, my lord," Potiphar said with a bow as he motioned for everyone to leave Pharaoh's room. The servants quickly left Pharaoh and went out to summon the men, who arrived within the hour.

Ten magicians and twelve wise men surrounded Pharaoh's throne as he recounted his two dreams. They clustered in small groups with hushed voices, consulting *The Dream Book*. They looked back at Pharaoh with terrified expressions. No one could find anything even resembling such dreams in their books.

A group of magicians mixed some oils and spices together in a cup and frantically searched the swirling liquid for some sort of sign to tell them what the dreams meant.

"Well?" Pharaoh said, his voice indicating he was impatient and growing frustrated.

One wise man stepped out in front, clutching *The Dream Book* to his chest. He looked at the others, who silently urged him on with looks of unity. "My lord, we have consulted *The Dream Book* and attempted divination in the cup, but we have no explanation for your dreams. Nothing like what you've described has been recorded before, so we have no way of interpreting them."

Pharaoh's fists tightened around the arms of his throne as he grew more and more anxious. "Not one of you?! The finest sages in all of Avaris? Not ONE of you has an answer for me?" Pharaoh yelled. "What good are you to me?!"

Al peeked his head around the throne and meowed up at Pharaoh. Pharaoh picked him up and placed him in his lap. "Hapy here has greater understanding than all of you put together!" Pharaoh's voice cracked as he spoke. His mouth was dry from the stress of the night.

The cupbearer looked to see that the baker had ordered the servants to bring Pharaoh's trays into the throne room, including Pharaoh's full cup. He went over to retrieve Pharaoh's cup and took a sip, knowing Pharaoh needed to drink something.

As Pharaoh stroked Al, he looked down at his tail. "Hapy, why is your tail wet?"

Al grinned and watched as the cupbearer wiped the rim of Pharaoh's cup. The cupbearer started rolling his tongue around with a frown. He stuck out his tongue and pulled off a piece of orange cat hair and looked up quickly at Pharaoh. His face was suddenly illuminated with an idea. He set Pharaoh's cup down and hurried to the throne to whisper in Pharaoh's ear.

"My lord! Forgive me for not telling you this sooner, but I have just been reminded of something that happened two years ago when you were so angry with me and the baker. You had us locked up in the prison for several months. One night both the baker and I had dreams and were very disturbed when we woke up. A Hebrew slave was serving us the next morning and asked why we were so upset. We told him our dreams and he interpreted them immediately for us, each one separately," the cupbearer spit out.

"And?" Pharaoh said as he wiped off Al's tail.

"Things turned out exactly as the slave had foretold. Within three days you restored me to my post, and you had the baker executed," the cupbearer explained.

"Get me the Hebrew slave now," Pharaoh demanded.

"As you wish, my lord," Potiphar said. "I will go myself to get him."

Pharaoh handed Al over to the cupbearer. "And get Hapy cleaned off. He got into something."

Al was grinning from ear to ear as the cupbearer carried him away to be cleaned.

Nothin' like a little hair o' the cat to set right the hair o' the jackal.

CHAPTER 44

Never in Your Wildest Dreams

Joseph noticed Sadiki sitting with his head down on his desk and went over to put his hand on his shoulder. "Are you all right, my master?"

Sadiki lifted his head and gave a grunting sigh. "Yes, I just keep having this tight feeling in my chest, and then I feel so tired."

"Have you asked the physician about this?" Joseph asked, a concerned look on his face.

The jailer shook his head. "No, I'm sure it's nothing," he said as he stood up and stretched. "Thank you, Joseph, for asking. How is it that you care about anyone else after all the time you've been here? If I were you I'd be so angry at the world no one would matter to me."

Joseph squeezed the rag in his hand tightly. "I'd be lying if I said I've never been angry in the past over the injustice I've experienced. But my only way out of that prison of anger was to let it go. I had a choice to either grow bitter or trust God with what happened to me. I guess I've chosen to trust in God and not man in all this. So that frees me to care about others," Joseph explained. "Even an old jailer like you."

Sadiki smiled. "Well, you're wise beyond your years, Joseph. Does that mean you'll keep trusting in your God even if you never get out of this prison?"

Joseph nodded. "He's all I have to hold onto, so, yes, I'll keep trusting. Besides," Joseph said as he saw the key ring dangling from Sadiki's side, "by my God's side swing keys that can unlock the most unlikely doors."

Sadiki raised a finger to Joseph and advised him, "You keep thinking that." He took the keys and opened the front gate, closing the door behind him with a turn of the lock that reverberated throughout the prison.

Joseph stood behind the prison bars and watched Sadiki walk away. He looked down and noticed Max sitting beside him. "Jabari," Joseph said as he knelt down to pet Max. "Sadiki must think I'm dreaming," he said with a laugh. "I guess he's right. My dreams about the sun, the moon, and the stars still come to me, even in this dark place."

Max nudged Joseph with his head. *Aye, laddie. I hope ye never stop dr-r-reamin'.*

Joseph looked up at the prison doors and added, "I guess night is the best time to see the stars." He gave Max one last pet and stood to go finish his morning chores. As he walked down the corridor, he suddenly heard a familiar voice calling his name.

"Joseph!" Potiphar called. "Guards, open up this door."

Joseph turned and went back to the gate. "My lord?"

Potiphar entered the prison and smiled. "Joseph, finally a way out has come. Pharaoh has had a dream and wants you to interpret it. Follow me."

A puzzled look appeared on Joseph's face as he threw the rag on the floor and followed Potiphar out of the prison. The prison guard shut the gate behind him and Max scurried up to the bars to watch the men walking away from the prison.

Aye! Looks like God's keys are shaped like dreams then!

Joseph was quickly ushered into a bathing area to clean himself up and shave so he would be presentable to Pharaoh. He was given a clean loincloth and hurriedly sent out to the room where Potiphar stood with his arms folded, smiling at the now-clean Joseph.

"I knew there was a Hebrew slave under that dirt," Potiphar said as he led Joseph to the throne room. "Now Joseph, this is your chance. The most powerful man in the world will be hanging on every word you say. Make it good and take advantage of every opportunity you can."

"I'll do as God directs, my lord," Joseph said as Potiphar swung wide the door to the throne room.

"My Pharaoh, I ask you to allow the Hebrew slave Joseph to approach your throne," Potiphar said.

"Come," Pharaoh said with a wave of his hand.

Potiphar stepped aside and nodded for Joseph to proceed. All eyes of the court of Pharaoh were on Joseph as he walked toward the throne. Joseph looked back at the magicians and wise men, who eyed him suspiciously. He then looked down by the feet of Pharaoh to see an orange cat beaming up at him. *You must be Hapy*, he thought to himself. If Joseph only knew how happy Al was at that moment.

Joseph stopped at the throne of Pharaoh and bowed, not making eye contact with him, as directed by Potiphar. "My lord, I am at your service."

Pharaoh leaned forward on his throne and looked Joseph up and down. "Joseph, is it? You may look at me as I talk to you. I want to see your eyes."

Joseph slowly lifted his gaze and met the eyes of Pharaoh, who stared back at him as if to convince himself he should consult this lowly slave.

"Very well, I've had a dream. And no one here seems to be able to interpret it," he said with a look of disdain aimed at his sages, who all looked to the ground to avoid Pharaoh's gaze. "But I hear that you can interpret dreams just by hearing them."

"I can't interpret them, but God can. God can tell you what your dreams mean and set you at ease," Joseph replied.

Pharaoh studied Joseph's face for a moment. Then he said, "In my dream I was standing on the bank of the Nile and up came seven healthy cows from the water. They proceeded to eat the lush grass. Then out of the river came seven gaunt, sickly cows that ate the seven healthy cows. Never have I seen such ugly beasts, and when they had eaten the healthy cows, they looked just as skinny as before. Then I woke up.

"Then I dreamed again. This time a healthy stalk of grain with seven plump ears was overtaken by seven shriveled, thin ears withered by the east wind. The seven blighted ears swallowed up the seven plump ears of grain," Pharaoh explained. "I've told all this to the magicians but no one can tell me what it means."

Joseph nodded as he prayed silently for wisdom. "Pharaoh's two dreams are actually the same dream, for they mean the same thing. God is telling you far in advance what He is going to do in the land of Egypt. The seven healthy cows are seven years and the seven plump ears of grain are seven years—they represent seven years of prosperity in the land. The seven skinny cows and the seven shriveled ears mean seven years of famine will follow."

Ye tell him, laddie! Al cheered silently.

The magicians and wise men looked at one another as if to say, *Of course, why couldn't we see that before? It's so obvious now!*

"God is clearly telling Pharaoh what is going to happen. This is good news for Pharaoh. Seven years of plenty are coming to Egypt, but right on their heels will come seven years of famine. And the famine will be so severe there will be no trace of the seven years of plenty. No one will even remember the good years," Joseph explained. "And because you dreamed this twice, it means God is determined to bring these seasons upon us soon."

Pharaoh sat with a frown on his face as he pondered all that Joseph was telling him.

"But there is plenty of time to prepare for the seven bad years. Pharaoh needs to look for a wise, experienced man and put him in charge of Egypt's affairs. Then Pharaoh should appoint managers over the land to collect one-fifth of all the crops during the seven good years. By stockpiling and guarding the grain in their home towns under Pharaoh's authority, Egypt will escape the devastation that is surely on its way," Joseph reasoned.

Potiphar stood in the back of the room, clenching his jaw as he thought to himself, *Now, Joseph! Seize the opportunity! Tell Pharaoh you should be the man in charge. Speak up for yourself!*

But Joseph humbly remained silent, not saying a word on his own behalf.

Potiphar couldn't stand it any longer. "My lord, this is a brilliant idea," he said as he approached the throne. The other court officials quickly agreed with Potiphar, echoing his remarks.

Pharaoh held up his hand to silence them and then looked directly at Joseph. "Isn't it obvious this is the man we need? Can we possibly find another man like this who has the spirit of God upon him?"

Potiphar looked at Joseph and nodded. *God's favor has followed him all the way to the court of Pharaoh.*

Then Pharaoh stood and walked down the steps of the throne to look Joseph right in the eye. "You're the man we need. Since God so clearly revealed to you the meaning of my dreams, your intelligence and wisdom is obvious. No one is as qualified as you for this role. From this day forward I appoint you, Joseph, to be in charge of all my affairs. All my people will take orders from you and report to you. Only I will be more powerful than you in the land of Egypt."

Pharaoh looked over at a servant who held two of his robes. In his distress he hadn't been able to decide what to wear, so he had just left wearing his loincloth and headdress. He clapped his hand and the servant came over to him and bowed low. Pharaoh took one of the fine linen robes and held it up for Joseph to put on. Joseph bowed his head in humility as he turned for Pharaoh to slip the new robe over his shoulders. "I hereby put you in charge of the land of Egypt."

It be the third robe! Al meowed.

Pharaoh looked down at Al and smiled. "I think Hapy approves."

Joseph wrapped his arms around himself to feel the soft linen robe, and smiled down at Al. Pharaoh removed his own signet ring and placed it on Joseph's finger, making it clear Joseph now had the authority and power of Pharaoh himself. Pharaoh then removed a gold chain from his own neck and put it over Joseph's head. He put his hand on Joseph's shoulder and smiled. "May God's favor be on Egypt as it is on you."

Pharaoh motioned for Potiphar. "Potiphar, Joseph is to ride in my second chariot, and the people of Egypt are to kneel as he passes."

"It will be as you say, my lord," Potiphar said, catching Joseph's eye. They shared a smile.

"I am Pharaoh, but no one will lift a hand or a foot in the entire land of Egypt unless you give the word. Joseph, you shall now be called 'Zaphenath-Paneah.' I also give to you for your wife Asenath, daughter of Potiphera, the priest of On. Pharaoh has spoken." Then he nodded that Joseph could now go.

Joseph bowed low before Pharaoh, "Thank you, my lord. I will fulfill my duties with the honor due the name of Pharaoh."

With that Joseph turned and went with Potiphar out of the throne room to be driven in the second chariot through the streets of Avaris.

When they reached the corridor, Potiphar stopped and turned to Joseph. He placed his hand on Joseph's shoulder by habit, then quickly withdrew it as he realized Joseph now outranked him. "My lord," he said with a smile and a bow. "May you find me to be a worthy servant."

Joseph put his hand on Potiphar's shoulder and smiled. "Rise, Potiphar. May the God who placed His favor on me under your roof and in your prison now grant His favor on me as your lord. May He honor your kindness to me. Thank you," Joseph said. He looked around to make sure no one was listening, then whispered, "my lord."

Potiphar rose and nodded as the two men shared a moment of surreal wonder as they realized their roles were now reversed. They both laughed with joy as they walked down the corridor.

"And I thought your God's miracle on the third *day* in my house was amazing," Potiphar said, shaking his head. "It seems I underestimated your God, Joseph. The true miracle now is your third *job* in the land of Egypt."

"Who could have ever dreamed that?" Joseph quipped.

"Not even you, Joseph," Potiphar laughed. "Never in your wildest dreams."

PART FOUR

THE REVEALER OF SECRETS

CHAPTER 45

Death of a Jailer

"My lord," Imenand said as he bowed before Joseph. "I have some distressing news, I'm afraid."

Joseph looked up with concern from his desk, which was covered in papyrus scrolls. He was working on the granary storage plan for all the provinces of Egypt. "What is it?"

"It's the jailer, Sadiki. He has suffered some sort of problem with his heart and is near death," Joseph's chief steward explained.

Joseph immediately pushed back his chair and put on his headdress, a grave look on his face. He didn't have to tell Imenand what to do. Imenand knew Joseph like a book after only three months of serving him in the palace.

"I'll make ready your chariot, my lord," Imenand said as he bowed and exited the room.

"Thank you," Joseph said as he knelt on the floor.

Max sat next to Sadiki's bed, his chin resting on the edge as he looked up at the dying man. He was saddened with the realization the jailer would soon be gone. The physicians had attempted to treat Sadiki as best they could, but the heart attack he apparently suffered left him too weak to live much longer. Max heard the chariot pull up outside Sadiki's humble home and turned to see Joseph enter the bedroom. There were two servants in the room attending to the jailer. They bowed before Joseph and he lifted his hand in acknowledgment as he entered.

Joseph petted Max on the head with one hand as he leaned over the jailer and softly called, "Sadiki. It's Joseph."

Sadiki's eyes fluttered open and he blinked a few times to focus. He turned his head slightly and looked over at Joseph. "My master, you've come?" His voice was very weak.

"Of course, Sadiki, as soon as I heard. I'm so sorry. Is there anything I can do for you?" Joseph asked.

Sadiki closed his eyes tight and a tear streamed from his right eye down his cheek as he slowly shook his head. "No. My time is short," he replied. He then opened his eyes and smiled at Joseph. "Can you pray to your God for me? When He opened the doors of the prison for you, I saw . . . the truth."

Joseph smiled and tears welled up in his eyes for this man he had served in the prison for seven long years. "I already have," he said as he squeezed Sadiki's hand.

Sadiki nodded. "Thank you, my master."

Max gently rose to put his paws on the side of the bed. He looked at Joseph with sad eyes. Joseph petted Max as they silently comforted each other.

"Please . . ." Sadiki whispered, now taking in a deep breath, ". . . take Jabari?"

Joseph looked at Max and nodded his head, a tear running down his cheek. "Of course, Sadiki. Jabari will be welcome in my home," he said, mussing Max's head. "He and I have been friends a long time. I will make sure he is well cared for."

Max reached up and licked Sadiki on the cheek. Sadiki smiled and closed his eyes. Joseph and Max clung to each other as they watched Sadiki's breath slowly become erratic. Before long he breathed his last and was gone. Joseph reached over and placed his hands over Sadiki's eyes. "May you enter the presence of the one, true God. Rest now, old jailer."

As Joseph gave instructions to the attending servants to have Sadiki's body well cared for and embalmed immediately, Max looked around Sadiki's home one last time. This had been his home for thirteen years. He was surprised to find himself so sad to lose Sadiki and to leave this humble home. *Aye, me mission here is complete,* Max told himself.

Joseph walked to the door calling for Max to follow. "Come on, boy. Let's go home."

Max trotted right behind Joseph out to the chariot. Like Joseph, he was leaving the prison and heading to the palace.

Because he was prime minister, Joseph's home was part of the palace complex connected by outdoor corridors covered with ornately decorated porticoes. Joseph informed Imenand that Jabari was to have freedom to go about the palace. He would be able to keep an eye out for a stray asp or rat that might try to make its way into the palace. Max was glad he didn't have to sneak around, and he couldn't wait to surprise Al.

Max waited until nighttime to go find Al, spending the day just being with Joseph. He was happy to be with him in this new setting. He quickly saw that Joseph's elevated status had not affected how he treated others. Joseph was the same as he had ever been, except perhaps deeper in character.

Max was amazed at how iron seemed to have entered Joseph's soul after his time in the prison. He wasn't bitter and jaded but strong and resolute. The dreaming boy they once knew was now a solid man of God, fully equipped to handle the incredible task placed before him. The weight of saving Egypt and the world had been placed squarely on his shoulders, and he accepted it with complete confidence.

All was quiet in the palace as Max made his way down to Pharaoh's wing. But he heard noises coming from the kitchen. Someone was in there.

Max peeked his head in the doorway and didn't see any humans. He walked as quietly as he could around the counters to the source of the noise. He had a good idea what was causing it but wanted to make visual contact to be sure. Max smiled when he saw Al sifting through some scraps the kitchen servants had left for him on his special tray on the floor. The new baker had finally realized that in order to keep the cat off the counter, they should leave food and milk out on the floor.

Max grinned and crept up behind Al. He reached out his front paw to touch Al on the shoulder. Al screamed, jumping five feet into the air. He landed on the counter, knocking over a jug that came crashing to the floor.

"Wha' in the name of Pete are they feedin' ye ta make ye jump so high?" Max asked, laughing at the big-eyed Al.

"Max?! Ye done scared me to death. What are ye doin' here?" Al wanted to know, jumping off the counter. "Did ye fight yer way through a hundred asps in the tunnel to reach me?"

"No, but I'm yer new neighbor, laddie. I'm livin' with Joseph now," Max explained. "Sadiki died this mornin'."

"Sure, and that's the best news I ever heard!" Al said with a big head-butt to Max. "Oh, but that's the saddest news I ever heard aboot the jailer."

"I understand, lad. I feel the same way," Max said.

Al sniffed and leaned in close to Max. His usual goofy grin grew wide on his face.

"Wha'?" Max asked with a frown.

"Ye had a milk bath," Al said.

"Aye, Joseph had his servants get me all cleaned up. I hadn't had a bath in years," Max explained. "But it sure were tasty."

"I always think so," Al said with a grin. "Sure, and I love bath day."

"Sorry aboot startlin' ye," Max said as he looked at the broken jug on the floor.

"That's all right, Max. But we best get out o' here before someone sees it were us," Al said. "I dunnot want to get in trouble in here again."

Too late. Footsteps were coming down the hall toward the kitchen.

"What'll we do?" Al cried.

"We take it like gr-r-rown laddies. We br-r-r-oke the jug so we best take r-r-responsibility for it then," Max said, not moving from where they sat.

Max and Al soon saw it was Imenand who followed the crashing noise into the kitchen. He came around the counter and saw the dog and the cat sitting there looking guilty over the broken jug. He chuckled to himself and started picking up the pieces. Max and Al looked at each other with surprise.

"I wondered where you went, Jabari. I had a feeling you would find your way here to the kitchen," he said with a grin. "I believe you and Hapy have met before." Imenand was tall and slim, and had deep brown eyes. He seemed to possess a very calm demeanor. Max and Al immediately liked this human.

"I know this was a hard day for you, Jabari, so I'm glad you found a friend," Imenand said as he discarded the broken pieces of the jug into a basket. "Don't stay out too late." He walked out of the room and left Max and Al sitting there in the kitchen.

"It's like he knew we understood wha' he were sayin'," Max said. "Joseph talks ta me like that all the time."

"Aye, he's a good human. He hasn't been here long, but he's kind to me every time I see him," Al replied.

"I'm glad he's Joseph's servant. When did he come ta work for him?" Max asked.

Al thought a moment, his paw on his chin. "Aboot three months ago."

"I cannot believe Joseph's been the prime minister of Egypt for three months already. I hear he's doin' a gr-r-rand job," Max said.

"But of course he is," Liz said as she sauntered into the kitchen, Nigel by her side.

"Liz, me beauty!" Al said as he ran to give Liz a big kiss on the cheek. "Max and me are neighbors now!"

"Oui, so I've heard," Liz said, walking over to Max. *"Bonsoir,* Max. It is good to see you, *mon ami."*

"Aye! 'Tis gr-r-rand ta see ye, lass. How did ye know I were here?" Max asked.

"I heard the news this morning, old boy, and immediately went to inform Liz of the latest developments," Nigel explained. "I'm terribly sorry about Sadiki."

"It were sad, but I'm glad ta be here now," Max replied.

"I do say, I believe this is the first time we've all been together since the market," Nigel observed.

"And so very much has happened, no? I never would have imagined that our Joseph could go from being a slave in the market to the second-highest ruler in Egypt. *C'est impossible!"* Liz exclaimed.

"Not only that, it's impossible!" Al added, drawing a grin from Liz, who head-butted her beloved Albert.

"Obviously it's not impossible or we wouldn't all be standing about discussing it," Nigel observed.

"Aye, so we're down ta one dream, one scheme, an' one robe for our mission then," Max said. "I hope it all comes soon. I miss me Kate."

Liz put her dainty paw on Max's chin. "Be patient, *mon ami.* Remember that Gillamon said this mission would take us about twenty years."

"I say, since thirteen years have passed, what do you suppose happens in seven years to bring Kate and Max back together?" Nigel asked. The four animals sat and pondered this a moment.

"I heard Joseph say there were comin' seven years o' plenty and then seven years o' famine in Egypt," Al said. "What's a famine, anyway?"

"This means there will be no food in the land," Liz explained.

The blood drained from Al's face as he finally understood what all this was about. "Ye mean I'll go hungry for seven years?! Sure, and I'll never make it!"

"Chin up, old boy," Nigel said, adjusting the spectacles on his nose. "Joseph is on the case to make sure there is food saved in these seven years of plenty to tide us over for the seven hard years. I've read his plans and they are absolutely brilliant."

"So that must mean Joseph's brothers are goin' ta get hungry enough ta come lookin' for food. Then I'll get ta see Kate!" Max said. "I kin't wait for the famine!"

Al's eyes got as big as saucers. He leaned over and whispered to Liz and Nigel, "I'm worried aboot Max. He must be daft to wish for such a thing."

"Aye, but while we wait we best be on our guard for the last scheme," Max warned. "Now that Joseph's so powerful, we best be expectin' a mighty blow from the enemy ta br-r-ring him down."

"Or something quite small, but unexpected," Nigel said.

"Oui, and it might just take all of us to defeat such a scheme," Liz added.

The four friends were grateful to be together again. But they realized that in order to meet the final challenge facing them, they just might need Kate as well.

CHAPTER 46

The Blind Harpist

"I believe there is nothing more for you to learn from me," Nigel said as Benipe finished rehearsing another song. "Your playing is utterly splendid, dear boy."

"Thanks, Nigel. Are you sure I'm ready? I'm really nervous about tonight," Benipe said.

"Why, there's nothing to be nervous about. You've mastered not only the mechanics of playing the harp, but you truly play it from the heart," Nigel said.

"Thanks for all you've done for me, Nigel. I hope I make you proud. Will you be there tonight?" Benipe asked.

"You're most welcome, dear boy. I can't be there as you would wish, but know that my heart will be cheering you on," Nigel said. "And you've already made me proud."

Benipe and Nigel heard Mandisa calling. "Benipe, it's time to get ready."

"I have to go," Nigel said, snapping his fingers. "Remember your proper finger position, and a good thumbs up with that balled fist."

Benipe snapped his fingers to practice good form and smiled. "I will, Nigel."

"Play your heart out, dear boy!" Nigel said with a chuckle.

Potiphar's house was buzzing with activity as the servants made ready for the annual harvest celebration. This was to be their largest, grandest celebration ever. Joseph himself would be the guest of honor.

Potiphar couldn't wait to welcome Joseph back to his home, and spared no expense to make this a perfect evening. He even sent Zuleika away on a trip, for he didn't want her to spoil the party. Potiphar also had a special event planned as the highlight of the evening. He hoped Joseph would be pleased.

The chariots started arriving and the servants lined up to welcome the guests. Potiphar anxiously waited in the foyer for Joseph to arrive. He finally heard the people giving praise to Zaphenath-Paneah. Potiphar walked out to personally greet Joseph at the gate and smiled as he saw people bowing before the young man's chariot. He raised his hand in greeting as the chariot arrived. Joseph smiled and raised his hand in reply.

"Welcome back to the house of Potiphar, only this time as *my* lord," Potiphar said as he bowed low before Joseph.

"It is good to be back, Potiphar," Joseph said, smiling as he stepped out of his chariot. Joseph looked up at the same gate where he had arrived that day so long ago as a slave. It was surreal to think of all that had happened since he was last here.

Together Joseph and Potiphar entered the house. After making the obligatory greetings to other officials, Potiphar took Joseph out to the vineyard. Joseph couldn't believe what he saw. It was magnificent. Rich, lush vines grew thick across the arbors throughout the vineyard. The grape clusters were so plentiful they weighed down the branches. Joseph reached down and pulled off a grape. He smiled as it burst in his mouth with rich flavor.

"I told you Nile silt would do the trick," he said as both he and Potiphar shared a good laugh at the amazing turn of events.

"You've been right about many things, Joseph. I'm grateful for how life has turned out for you. And I'm grateful your God's favor remained on my house and on my vineyard even after you left," Potiphar said as they walked along the path through the beautiful vineyard. "I wasn't expecting that, especially after what happened here."

"I'm glad God has continued to bless your house," Joseph told Potiphar. "But I know now God used that bad experience for my good. I never could have gotten to the palace without going through the betrayal that happened here."

Joseph noticed a pruning knife left on a nearby post. "I told you long ago about the need to cut these vines severely in order to make them bear much fruit," he said, taking the knife and cutting back a vine, "It was here in your vineyard that God pruned me for the work he has now brought me to in the land of Egypt."

"The branch that is to bear much fruit has to first feel the knife," Potiphar agreed, nodding. "Well, I'm pleased to inform you that you will taste the wine from your vineyard, which has borne much fruit. Come!"

Together they walked to the center of the vineyard to the grand arbor covered now with beautiful vines. The columns Joseph and Benipe had long ago set up and painted stood tall and majestic. Potiphar clapped his hands and all the guests gathered 'round.

Potiphar addressed the guests. "Tonight we celebrate the harvest. God has blessed us with a tremendous year of plenty. But we especially celebrate the firstfruits from my vineyard, planted and tended long ago by Joseph." The crowd applauded in celebration.

"It is my honor to welcome you back to my home, Joseph. May God's favor continue to flow over you now as you rule Egypt," Potiphar said.

Joseph replied, "And may God's favor never leave the house of Potiphar."

The crowd wildly applauded and cheered as the servants busily went around filling cups for everyone. Potiphar and Joseph stood and looked at the beautiful arbor.

"No music, Potiphar? I always remembered you having the finest musicians for these celebrations," Joseph said.

"I've saved the debut of one I believe to be the finest harpist in all Egypt," Potiphar said with a smile. He clapped his hands and a hush came over the crowd as everyone gathered around the grand arbor.

Joseph's heart leapt as he saw Mandisa lead Benipe up to the arbor. Benipe carried with him a beautiful harp. It was an ornately carved, ladle-shaped wooden harp with eleven strings. At its base the soundbox was colorfully painted in red, yellow, turquoise, and black, and it was supported by a slanting brace. Benipe sat down, placed the harp on his right shoulder, and placed his hands on both sides of the strings.

All the guests grew quiet as the blind harpist began to play.

Benipe held the harp close to his body, feeling the glorious vibrations as he plucked its sinewy strings, pulling his fingers back into a perfectly balled fist, just as Nigel had taught him. He started softly and slowly but gradually crescendoed into a symphony of exquisite sound as his hands cascaded up and down the strings. The beautiful music drifted off his harp, filling the air with an inexplicable euphoria.

The people could not only hear but they could also feel the notes as they were enveloped by something wonderful. The presence of God Himself drifted on the notes. And for Benipe, the peace of God so filled his spirit and moved his fingers he felt as if he were not even the one playing.

Benipe's blind eyes were closed as he played but he was swept away by the joyful vision he saw in his heart. A kaleidoscope of colors, places, and faces entered his vision as he played. He saw his beloved Mandisa, her dimples showing in her precious smile as she gazed at him.

Then suddenly Joseph's face entered Benipe's vision. He smiled as he thought back to their early days together. Scenes of them on the caravan to Egypt, in the market, and working together in Potiphar's house played over in his mind. But none of the sadness, despair, or harshness remained in his memory—only joy from a deep friendship shared and a long-held hope for purpose fulfilled.

It was as if Benipe were in a dream as he journeyed through time. But he was transported from the past to this moment and reveled in where he and Joseph now existed. The impossible deliverance for both of them from their individual injustices to revered status was overwhelming. It was like a dream—but better. What God had worked together for their good was more than they ever could have dreamed or imagined.

Benipe felt the words of a new song drifting up from his heart, and he began to sing about what he saw:

Let not your heart be troubled during your sojourn on earth
Seize the day as it passes
Spend your days joyfully and do not be weary with living
Be an upright person, a just and true person, a patient and kind person,
A person content with life, a person who can rejoice and not speak evil.
For something which we have seen in a dream is the earthly side of life.
Do not grieve whatever problems come, but let sweet music play before you.
Let sweet music play before you.

Tears of joy streamed from Joseph's eyes as he listened to his friend Benipe. Once a boy so abandoned, so hurt, so lost, and so angry, he was now a man so whole, so happy, and so fulfilled. Benipe's life had the clear imprint of the one, true God, for only God could bring such spiritual sight to one now blind.

Liz and Nigel were well hidden under the grand arbor where Benipe played. Nigel also wiped back the tears as he listened to the beautiful music of this one whom God had given him to teach. In all his years in Egypt, never had he felt more joy in an accomplishment than he did in helping this struggling soul find his way through music.

"Mon ami, how very proud I am of you. Look what you have done for Benipe," Liz whispered as she gently touched Nigel on the back.

Nigel smiled. "All I did was share, my dear. It was God who worked His way in this boy."

Time seemed to stand still as the audience listened with rapt attention to the blind harpist. When he finally finished and softly put his hands on the harp to still the strings, no one said a word or made a sound. It was as if they willed the music to continue. But then almost at once the people erupted in applause, cheering and calling for more.

Benipe smiled and bowed his head as he heard their applause. He gave a silent thank you to God and was then filled with irrepressible laughter. He threw his head back with joy as he hugged his beloved harp. Mandisa rushed up to Benipe and threw her arms around him. They were filled with love and joy from the evening, and tightly held on to each other.

After a moment the crowd began talking among themselves about the wonderful performance. Servants brought trays of food and drink, and the people continued the merriment of the evening.

Liz noticed Joseph pulling Potiphar aside. They spoke a moment and Potiphar nodded as Joseph placed his hand on Potiphar's shoulder. Potiphar smiled and then extended his arm in Benipe's direction. Joseph smiled and nodded, then walked over to place his hand on Benipe's arm.

"Benipe, it's Joseph. I'm so proud of you. You have brought joy to everyone here with your gift," he said. "Mandisa, it is good to see you. I know you are proud of your husband as well."

Mandisa smiled and bowed low before Joseph. "I am, my lord."

"Joseph! You're here!" Benipe said, placing his hand on Joseph's arm. "I'm proud of you, too—prime minister of Egypt! Who would have thought on that caravan long ago we'd someday be where we are today?"

"Indeed. It seems impossible, doesn't it?" Joseph said. "Benipe, I'm so sorry you lost your sight."

Benipe answered, "You may have thought I was not listening when you talked about your God, but I want you to know I heard every word. It just took me a while to understand. And I'm not sorry I'm blind."

Joseph raised his eyebrows in delightful surprise. "I never would have expected you to react this way after what happened to you. Why aren't you sorry?"

"I know it's hard to believe this is me talking after all the anger I held on to. But you see, it was in my blindness I could finally see what you had tried to tell me for so long. Your God gave me this gift," Benipe explained. "When I surrendered all my hurt and my blindness to Him, He gave me a *new* kind of sight. And Joseph, it's what I've always dreamed of! You told me that if God gave me a passion to do something, then he would help me do it. Well, He sent a messenger to teach me how to really play the harp."

Joseph nodded and squeezed Benipe's shoulder. "Nothing could make me happier than to hear you say these things, my friend. God's blessings come to us in unusual ways," he said. "But a messenger from God, you say? Who?"

"His name is Nigel," Benipe replied.

"Nigel? What an odd name. Where is he from?" Joseph asked.

"Somewhere up north, he says. His accent is even stranger than his name," Benipe told Joseph. "I wish he could have been here to hear me tonight."

Nigel was about to burst. He wanted to rush up to Benipe and tell him he *was* here. He wanted to celebrate with him and tell him how proud he was, not only of Benipe's playing, but of his heart, which resounded with every note.

Liz came out of the shadows to see Joseph and meowed, *Nigel is here!* She knew no one would understand her, but she couldn't remain silent.

"Why, hello, Bastet. I haven't seen you in so long," Joseph said, picking Liz up. "Did you enjoy the harp?" Then turning back to Benipe as he rubbed Liz under her chin, he announced, "We must reward this Nigel with recognition from the palace. Not only him, but you, Benipe. I want you to come play for me in the court of Pharaoh."

"Me?!" Benipe exclaimed.

Joseph laughed. "Yes, Benipe. And not just play in the palace, but live there, too. I've talked with Potiphar, and you and Mandisa will be released to come live with me. You are free."

Mandisa's hands went up to her face as she squeezed back tears of joy. She leaned over to wrap her arms around Benipe's neck.

"I don't know what to say, Joseph," Benipe said, overwhelmed.

C'est magnifique! Liz meowed. She was thrilled with what was happening.

"Say yes!" Joseph said with a laugh. "Bastet even approves."

"Okay—yes! Mandisa and I will be happy to live at the palace and serve you," Benipe exclaimed.

"Yes, but I will pay you both for your service, and I will pay you handsomely," Joseph said. "It's only appropriate the finest harpist in all Egypt be given the best of everything. You will never want for anything again, my friend."

"Thank you, my lord," Mandisa said, her dimples showing. "I always knew you were destined for greatness. But I never dreamed we would be sharing that with you."

"You both are more than welcome. Now gather your things tonight, for tomorrow you will come with me to your new life at the palace," Joseph said. "And Benipe, what was that line you sang about dreams and life?"

"For something we have seen in a dream is the earthly side of life," Benipe replied.

Joseph thought about all the dreams he had interpreted for the cupbearer, for the baker, and for Pharaoh. Those dreams had indeed been fulfilled in the earthly side of life. He thought next about his two dreams from long ago. Could it be that they, too, would come true this side of heaven? He was already in the position of being bowed to. All he missed was his brothers to fulfill the dreams. How that would ever happen he couldn't imagine. But he had seen the impossible happen in *his* life and in the life of his friend, Benipe. Joseph smiled.

"I want you to play that song frequently at the palace. I like the words," Joseph said.

"I'll put it at the top of your request list," Benipe said with a wide grin.

"Very well, until tomorrow, my friends," Joseph said.

"Good night, Joseph. We'll see you tomorrow, and thank you again," Benipe replied as he and Mandisa shared an excited embrace.

Joseph gave Liz a final caress. "I wish you could see that orange cat from the market, Bastet. Pharaoh named him 'Hapy' and he's quite the celebrity in the palace. You would love him, I'm sure."

But I do love him, Liz meowed.

Joseph smiled and held Liz close so he could whisper in her ear. "Thank you for helping me that day in the market. If you had not convinced Potiphar to buy me as his slave, I never would be where I am today. Just as God sent Nigel to help Benipe, I believe He sent you to help me."

Liz looked intensely into Joseph's eyes and meowed, *You're welcome, mon ami.* She then winked. Joseph smiled and winked back. He put her on the ground and turned to leave.

Mandisa led Benipe away to the slave quarters for their last night in the house of Potiphar. Nigel crept out of the shadows and he and Liz shared a smile as they watched the couple talking and laughing about their new life to come.

"I'd say our work here is finished, my dear," Nigel said.

"Oui, Nigel. If only I could go with them to live with Joseph," Liz replied. "I will miss Mandisa and Benipe."

"Chin up, my pet. I'm sure we will enjoy many concerts at the palace," Nigel chuckled. "Well hidden, that is."

CHAPTER 47

Seven Years of Plenty

Hya! Hya! Faster!" Joseph yelled as he snapped the reins on the horses pulling his chariot through the streets of Avaris.

Joseph pulled up to his house and jumped out of his chariot without even stopping the horses. His servants had to chase after the horses and empty chariot while Joseph bolted up the steps leading to his house. He was out of breath as he swung open the door to his bedchamber. The room was full of handmaidens fussing about with linens and bowls of water.

Asenath looked up at Joseph and smiled from their bed. Joseph rushed over to her side and kissed his wife on the forehead. He knelt on the floor next to her as she uncovered the bundle nestled in her arms.

"It's a boy," she said, wincing as she rolled over on her side.

Joseph blinked hard at the small baby his wife held out for him. "He's so tiny! Oh, but he's so beautiful," Joseph said, a worried look on his face as he carefully took the baby into his hands.

"It's okay, you won't break him," Asenath smiled and said.

Joseph's face eased as he held the baby up to his cheek and heard the soft coos he made. Joseph squeezed his eyes shut tight as he gently swayed back and forth, embracing his son.

"What shall we call him?" Asenath asked.

Joseph held the baby out to study his face. "We will call him Manasseh, for God has made me forget all my troubles and all my father's household."

"Manasseh. I love it," Asenath replied.

Joseph laid Manasseh next to her on the bed and together the new family snuggled with their heads together. It was a precious moment. "Thank you, my love, for giving me such a fine son." Joseph kissed his wife tenderly.

"I hope he will be the first of many," Asenath said with a smile.

Of all the riches Joseph had gained from his powerful position in Egypt, nothing could compare with the priceless bundle in front of him. He realized his new, fourth job in Egypt was to be father to this son, and he was determined to be the best dad he could possibly be. He prayed he would not in *this* family repeat the mistakes of his own father.

The curse of favoritism and deception would stop in the house of Joseph.

The town center of Tell Edfu was busy with farmers, scribes, and city officials transacting business for the day. A line of farmers waited with their carts filled to the brim with sacks of grain. Scribes were busily making records of the amount of grain deposited into each of the eight round silos. Donkeys were braying and the men shouted back and forth, laughing at the abundance pouring in from the land of Egypt.

Joseph, followed by his chief steward Imenand, walked along with the governor of the region. Joseph was pleased with how well his plan for storing the grain was working. Farmers brought in one-fifth of their harvest to each town center across Egypt. Tell Edfu was one of the larger collection points, and Joseph liked to make unannounced inspections to gauge the efficiency of the city. Things were going so well he decided to bring his two sons with him on this trip. Manasseh was now six years old and Ephraim five. Joseph wanted the boys to see the goodness God had brought to their land. He also wanted them to get a taste of the importance of their father's work.

"We've received more than twenty cartloads this morning alone, my lord," the governor said. "I've never seen farmers this eager to bring in the harvest. They have so much grain on their hands they are glad to be rid of it. Seven silos are completely full, with one left to go. We may have to build more if this keeps up."

Joseph looked up at the tall mudbrick silos, twenty feet in diameter. At the top of each silo was a rectangular storage container holding gray ash to protect the grain from pests. Staircases wound around to the top where the grain was poured. A square doorway at the bottom was in place to dispense the grain.

"These past seven years have produced more corn than we ever could have anticipated," Joseph told the governor. "The scribes of Egypt are exhausted from trying to keep up with the amounts, and have told me it is almost not worth counting anymore, as we have so much grain. I'm glad to see Tell Edfu so well supplied. Is the gray ash working to repel the rats?"

"The rats are under control for the most part, but we find them here and there," the governor replied. "Of course, with the rats come their predators like cobras and jackals, which have been an even greater concern. But we have a good cat population here that has helped with the rats and the snakes."

"Very well. I'm pleased with what I see," Joseph replied as the three men walked toward the governor's palace. He called to the boys, who were playing hide and seek with Max in the street. "Boys, you be careful and stay out of the way of the workers. I'll be right back."

"Yes, Father," Manasseh called back.

The boys were running around the tall silos, with Max chasing after them. Manasseh came to the empty silo and peeked inside the square door at the bottom, which was held open by a hook latch. He was excited to see a slide inside the silo where the grain was poured. The slide ran from the top of the silo to the floor. Since this was the last of the silos to be filled, the bottom door remained open.

"Hey, Ephraim, look at this!" Manasseh shouted as he went running up the outside block steps leading to the top of the silo.

"Wait for me!" Ephraim called after his big brother, his sidelock of hair bouncing as he followed.

Max came running around the corner and didn't notice that the boys had run up the steps. He kept going around the silo, barking, *Come out, come out, wher-r-rever ye ar-r-re!*

Together the two boys stood on the platform to climb onto the slide leading to the bottom of the round silo. "Jabari will never find us in here," Manasseh said. "I'll get on first and you can get on behind me."

"It's a long way down there," Ephraim said, hesitating.

"Come on, it will be fun. You can hold on to me. I'll take care of you," Manasseh insisted as he stepped onto the slide, sitting down and bracing against the sides with his feet. He patted the slide behind him. "Get on."

Ephraim frowned but did as his older brother said. He stepped over and sat behind Manasseh on the slide, wrapping his arms around his brother's waist. "Okay."

"Here we go!" Manasseh said as he pushed himself forward to slide down to the bottom. The slide stopped about three feet from the floor so they had a small fall near the end. Ephraim held on tight and closed his eyes until they were back on solid ground.

"Hey, that was fun!" Ephraim exclaimed once it was over. "Let's do it again!"

Together the boys crawled out the bottom door to the outside and ran back up the steps that wound around to the top of the silo.

About that time the scribe and the granary manager walked to the front of the silo. "The other seven silos are completely full. We can start filling this one right away," the manager said.

"Good, I'll begin a new page with entries for silo number 8," the scribe said.

The manager went over to the silo door and released the latch. The door slammed shut and he closed the latch tightly. "We're ready to begin. I'll tell the next farmer we'll unload his cart here," he said, tapping the silo wall. He called out instructions for the line of workers to form a chain up the steps. They would hand off bags of grain to unload onto the granary slide.

Max came running back around the silo and looked back and forth in the street. He didn't see the boys anywhere, and furrowed his brow. *Now where did those laddies r-r-run off ta?* He went trotting in the other direction to see if perhaps they had gone down the street toward the fruit market.

Manasseh and Ephraim were still unnoticed as they quickly got to the top platform of the silo and stepped onto the slide. Manasseh thought it looked darker inside than before, but figured his eyes had not yet adjusted from the bright sunlight. Once Ephraim was behind him they let go and squealed with delight as they slid down the slide.

The boys landed with a thud and noticed the bottom door was closed. It was so dark they couldn't see where it was.

"Where's the door?" Ephraim called out.

"I'm looking for it. Don't move," Manasseh said as he felt along the silo walls for the door. "They must have closed it while we were climbing the stairs."

Ephraim started to cry. "I'm scared! Don't leave me. I can't see you!"

"I'm right here, little brother. Just stay put while I find the door," Manasseh said, also getting scared but trying to be brave for his little brother.

Suddenly they heard a noise coming from the top of the slide. They soon felt pellets of grain dropping on them. Manasseh looked up in alarm at the small opening of light and could see the men rapidly unloading bags of grain onto the slide. The noise of the falling grain echoed in the silo.

"Help! Stop! We're in here! Help!" Manasseh screamed. His voice was drowned out by the sound of the grain and by the men up above shouting among themselves to keep the chain of bags coming. Manasseh frantically ran around the silo and finally found the outline of the door. His fingers felt all over the surface but there was no latch on the inside. He started banging on the door, calling out for someone to hear them.

"I wanna get out of here!" Ephraim began wailing and crying as he sat on the floor and hugged his knees. "Father! Father!"

"They can't hear us!" Manasseh yelled as he attempted to jump up to the bottom of the slide to crawl out. The grain was coming down so fast he couldn't get a grip to pull himself up.

Soon the grain started filling the bottom of the silo. Manasseh looked around, desperate for a way out. "Dear God, please help us," he prayed silently. His father had taught them to always turn to God for help. Joseph modeled prayer for his sons, so it was a natural response for Manasseh. He was only six years old, but he understood how to pray.

"Jabari! I know he can hear us if he's out there," Manasseh exclaimed, running back over to the door. He pounded on the door and called repeatedly for the dog to help. "Jabari! Jabari! We're in here! Get help! Jabari!" Ephraim came over and together they pounded and yelled for help.

Max backtracked to follow the boys' scent when he couldn't locate them by sight. His ears perked up and he stopped in the road. He heard the faint sound of the boys pounding and shouting and listened carefully to find their location. He looked up and saw the workers lined along the stairwell of the silo, busily depositing the grain. He walked over to the base of the silo, sniffing and smelling.

As Max reached the door, he heard the boys clearly calling his name and pounding. *The laddies be in the silo!* He immediately started barking in alarm, but no one paid him any attention.

"Dog must smell a rat," a man said to his friend as they walked by.

No! No! Listen ta me! Two wee lads be in the bottom of this silo! An' it's fillin' with gr-r-rain! Max barked, looking frantically up at the people passing by. Nothing. He ran back and forth in front of the door and then noticed the latch. He pushed on it with his nose but couldn't get it to budge. Max then went running up the stairs, barking at the men filling the silo, but they too told him to be quiet. No one would listen.

The boys were calling so loudly they didn't notice the cobra sneaking up behind them. It had been coiled and sitting in the shadows, but the noise and movement of the boys stirred the snake to move toward them. It stuck its tongue out to taste the air as it rose up off the floor.

Ephraim was crying. He stood up to put his arms on the wall of the silo and then he heard the snake hissing. "SNAKE! SNAKE! SNAKE!" he yelled, causing Manasseh to jump up and pull Ephraim away from the sound of the snake and the door. They ran to the other side of the silo, not knowing if the snake was following them or not. They couldn't see it.

When Max heard the word "snake," a fierce anger rose in his spirit. "Maker! I need a r-r-reed aboot now! I got ta save those laddies!" Just then he noticed a merchant walking by with a money pouch in his hand. Max ran up to the man and jumped to snatch the pouch away from him. The man resisted but Max's strong jaws clamped tight on the pouch and he pulled it out of the man's hand.

"You crazy dog!" the merchant yelled as Max ran back to the door of the silo. "Give me back my money!"

Joseph, the governor, and Imenand were walking from the governor's palace toward the silo when they heard the man yelling and saw Max running away. They picked up their pace. Imenand kept his eye on Max, who dropped the pouch by the door and proceeded to bark his head off.

As the angry merchant reached Max, he pulled his hand back to take a swipe at him. Imenand's strong fist wrapped around his arm, stopping the man from striking a blow to Max. "Listen!"

Joseph and the men listened and heard the boys screaming inside. Joseph's heart sank as he realized what was happening. He immediately grabbed the latch and opened the door. Grain started pouring out as he called to the boys.

"Manasseh! Ephraim! I'm here! Come out!" Joseph called, trying to see inside the small opening.

"Father! There's a snake!" Manasseh called.

Max immediately squeezed in front of Joseph to run inside and over to where the boys stood. He growled and blocked the snake's way. As he barked at the snake, the boys ran away and hurried out into Joseph's arms. Joseph dropped to his knees and tightly embraced the boys, both of whom were crying by now.

"Shhhhhhh. It's okay now. I have you," Joseph said. "What were you doing in there?"

Manasseh wiped his nose with the back of his arm. "I'm s-s-sorry, Father. It's my fault. We went in to play on the slide."

"Oh, Manasseh, I'm glad you and Ephraim are all right. But that was a dangerous thing to do," Joseph said. "Don't ever play in the silos again." Manasseh nodded in hearty agreement and sniffed.

"Father, what about Jabari?" Ephraim wailed, pointing back to the door.

"Don't worry. Jabari is a master at rounding up pests. Watch and see what he does," Imenand said as he poked his head in the door. He turned back around and smiled. "That snake doesn't stand a chance."

"Ye're not goin' ta str-r-rike me dead! Not this time, ye r-r-repulsive beast!" Max barked as he grabbed the snake by the tail and slammed it against the silo wall. He ran over and picked up the snake and again hurled it at the wall. Max picked it up a third time and tossed it right under the downpour of grain. The grain quickly covered the snake.

"Jabari! Good boy! Come!" Imenand called.

Max ran out and was embraced by Joseph and the boys.

"Thank you, Jabari. You saved my sons," Joseph said as he mussed Max's hair.

Ye're welcome, laddie, Max barked with a grin. *'Tis all in the line of duty.*

Imenand picked up the merchant's money pouch. "My lord's dog isn't a thief. He was trying to find someone to listen to my lord's boys screaming for help," he said as he tossed the money pouch back to the man.

The merchant bowed low before Joseph and Imenand. "Of course, of course! Great Zaphenath-Paneah, please forgive me. I'm grateful your children are safe." He bowed repeatedly as he quickly backed away. He didn't know if the prime minister of Egypt would have him arrested for almost hitting his dog.

Joseph ignored the merchant, slammed the granary door shut, and tightened the latch. He breathed a prayer of thanks to God for the double protection this dog had provided his children. Little did Joseph realize Max had not just saved his boys—he had just saved two future tribes of the nation of Israel who would come from these children.

"What a remarkable dog you have, my lord," Imenand said with a broad grin. "Clearly he is the finest dog in all Egypt."

The boys were hugging Max, and he was happily licking their cheeks, making the boys giggle. Joseph smiled at Max, now even more grateful to this dog than ever before. "He most certainly is."

CHAPTER 48

Death of the Nile

So the Egyptians no longer measure time by the moon but by the Nile? This is fascinating, no?" Liz exclaimed as she and Nigel stared up at the ceiling of an old tomb.

"Precisely, my pet!" Nigel said as he pointed up to the ceiling mural of a calendar. "The Egyptians used to use the lunar cycle, but more than a thousand years ago they developed a calendar based on the water levels of the Nile." Nigel carefully studied the beautifully painted symbols for the sun, the moon, and the stars. "I must say, this is an exquisite frieze of the old method. This mummy was given his own calendar to keep track of time in the afterlife."

"But how does the Nile tell time, Nigel?" Liz inquired.

"The Egyptians figured out that by making notch marks in reeds to measure the rise and fall of the Nile, they could track time. The Egyptian year has twelve months of thirty days each, marked into three seasons. Akhet is flood season, Peret is growing season, and Shemu is harvest season," Nigel lectured, adjusting his spectacles.

Liz thought a moment as she added in her head. "But how do they account for the other five days needed for the year?"

"Well, you know our Egyptians. Their gods must always get into the mix of everything somehow," Nigel chuckled. "So they add five days of birthdays for the gods Osiris, Horus, Seth, Isis, and Nephthys to complete the year."

Liz rolled her eyes. "And I'm sure there is a story of how these five gods defeated all the other gods in some calendar battle to determine who would get to have an official birthday."

"Not that I've seen, but I'm sure some scribe will write such a story one day," Nigel predicted with a grin. "But see here, the Nile has always been an extremely accurate calendar," Nigel said, growing serious. "That is, until now."

"Ah, *oui,* the flood has not come for two years, no?" Liz asked. "Instead of the Nile flood, the drought has come."

"Yes, and with the drought, the famine. It appears Joseph's interpretation of Pharaoh's dream will now be the most accurate calendar in Egypt, at least for the next five years."

Pharaoh stood holding Al on the bank of the Nile, rubbing the big orange cat's chin. Together with Joseph and Potiphar they observed the extremely dry riverbank. The river was not full and flowing as it once was, but was a narrow channel of water winding through the Egyptian countryside. A whirlwind of dust kicked up in their faces as the wind rustled the dry, crackling reeds that once had grown green and tall here. They saw one lone, gaunt cow wandering along the opposite bank, mooing sadly and barely able to stand.

"For two years the annual flooding of the Nile has not come to water the land and produce crops," Pharaoh said. "Zaphenath-Paneah, just as you foretold from my dreams, the famine is here to stay."

"Yes, my lord, five more years of famine will come," Joseph replied. "We are witnessing the death of the Nile."

Pharaoh held Al up. "Well, Hapy, did we do something to anger the Nile god after whom you are named? He has withdrawn his favor from our land."

I didn't do it, I promise! Al meowed. *I didn't make the Nile dry up. It weren't me!*

"Reports from the market this morning indicate the famine is so severe throughout the entire world that all nations are coming to Egypt for food," Potiphar interjected. "It appears we are the only country with grain."

"Thanks to Zaphenath-Paneah, the world will be saved from starvation," Pharaoh said with a smile and a strong hand on Joseph's shoulder. "I have instructed the people to go directly to you for food. I've told them to do whatever you tell them to do."

Joseph humbly bowed. "Thank you, my lord. I am pleased to report our supplies throughout the land will be sufficient to feed our people as well as the other nations. I have opened the storehouses as we had planned."

"Well done. I knew you were the right man for this task," Pharaoh said, motioning for his chariot. "It appears your God knew it, too," he added with a smile.

"Thank you, my lord," Joseph replied. "I am grateful my God has supplied all our needs."

Pharaoh nodded, "Indeed. Your God has met our needs while the Nile god Hapy has not. Carry on. I'm going back to the palace. Keep me informed." With that Pharaoh climbed into his chariot, setting Al on the shelf in front. Joseph and Potiphar bowed to show their respect as he drove off.

Potiphar stood with his arms folded as he gazed out over the narrow waters of the Nile. "Joseph, you have saved us all."

Joseph shook his head. "Not me, but . . ."

". . . your God," Potiphar finished his sentence. "Yes, I knew you would say that. Well, Pharaoh certainly gave you the right name for your job," he said with a smile that suddenly morphed into a frown. "I do have some bad news."

"What's wrong?" Joseph asked.

"My vineyard is dying along with the rest of the crops in Egypt. There is just not enough water to keep it healthy. And the rich silt of the Nile is gone," Potiphar explained. "I will miss the fruit and the beauty of my garden."

Joseph nodded. "Yes, I assumed this would happen. I'm sad to hear it is happening so soon. But don't worry, Potiphar. Your vineyard will come back one day. Trust me."

Potiphar looked at Joseph and smiled. "Have you ever given me a reason not to, my lord?"

Kate watched as Judah wearily pulled up the empty bucket from the cistern. He put the bucket on the stone wall and shook his head. He rubbed his hands in his hair and then rested them on the side of the well, lowering his head between his shoulders.

"He looks like he has the weight of the world on his shoulders," Kate said to Dodi, her donkey friend.

"Yes, he and the rest of the brothers, with this famine. But ever since Judah returned to Jacob's house, he walks around with such a burden in his eyes," Dodi replied.

"He doesn't sleep well," Kate said, watching Judah as he picked up his walking stick and made his way through the blowing dust back to the safe haven of the tent. "I think the lad sees Joseph's face when he dreams."

"Even after all this time?" Dodi asked.

"*Especially* after all this time," Kate replied.

Kate followed after Judah and slipped into the tent. She went over to snuggle with Benjamin, who sat next to Jacob. He smiled and put Kate onto his lap. All the brothers sat looking depressed and lost. They stared at each other and then at the meager plate of dried bread and a few pistachios that sat untouched in the center.

Jacob frowned as he looked at each one of them, picking up and cracking a pistachio before putting it in his mouth. "Why are you all just sitting here staring at each other?" he said as he chewed and swallowed the nut. "I've heard there is grain in Egypt. Go down there and buy some before we starve to death."

Judah sat up and said, "Yes, let's leave right away."

Kate looked at Judah and thought, *He's always so eager ta leave this place an' the memories that be here.*

Reuben nodded, "As you say, Father. We'll leave right away. All of us will go to have safety in numbers as we travel. Robbers are attacking travelers en route to Egypt."

Jacob placed his wrinkled, aged hand on Benjamin's arm. "Benjamin stays here. I don't want any harm to come to him."

The brothers looked at one another and then to their father, all nodding in agreement. They no longer expressed jealousy over the favoritism Jacob showed to the one he thought was Rachel's only remaining son. They wouldn't think of asking to take Benjamin away from their father. They had already caused him to age beyond his years from the grief of losing Joseph.

"You may take Amisa. She will provide protection as a watchdog," Jacob said. "I know she is old, but I think she can still make the journey. Her age doesn't seem to affect her like mine does me."

Kate's heart leaped. *Max! Max is in Egypt! Oh, will I be able ta see me love?*

Benjamin leaned forward and whispered in Kate's ear, "Come back to me, girl."

Kate licked Benjamin on the cheek and wagged her tail. Her emotions were ignited with anticipation. She was going to Egypt! Thoughts and questions raced through her mind. *Is Joseph still a slave? Maybe he will be a slave in the inn where we stay. How will the brothers act if they happen ta see him? Gillamon said Al would be in the palace with Pharaoh an' Liz would live with a man named Potiphar. But wha' aboot Max? Gillamon said his place would be hard, but worth it. Oh, ta see all that's happened in twenty years!*

Kate couldn't wait to get on the road. She hoped and prayed Max would be the first one she'd see when they arrived. Her heart ached to be united with him again. She couldn't believe she had made it so long without Max by her side.

Jacob drew a curious grin as he watched Amisa come alive with excitement. He hadn't seen her this lively in quite a while. He wondered how a dog could possibly live for more than twenty years, but was grateful to God for bringing her to them when they lost Joseph. She had saved Benjamin's life, and had been a source of joy and comfort over the years. He prayed she would keep his sons safe as they journeyed to a foreign land for food.

Kate wagged her tail and barked with joy as she followed the brothers out of the tent. As they loaded up their supplies for the journey, she looked to the southern horizon.

Hang on, me love! I'm comin' ta Egypt!

CHAPTER 49

Brothers and Spies

I HATE THIS PLACE! WHY DID WE HAVE TO COME BACK HERE?" Osahar yelled as he slowly walked to the entrance of the market.

"*Mon ami,* please calm down. No one will bother you. I asked Nigel to bring Albert and me here for an outing. I wish to see for myself the humans coming to Egypt from other countries," Liz said, softly petting Osahar's neck.

"Right! Just keep one of your disgusting spit wads handy, good fellow, in case one of the merchants tries to take you," Nigel reminded Osahar, pulling on the camel's ears to direct him behind an unused awning hanging from a high window.

"I'VE GOT ONE READY TO FIRE AT A MOMENT'S NOTICE," Osahar said, chewing his cud and grinning.

"I hope he doesn't have to use it," Al said, worried that he would be seen out in the daytime away from the palace. "What if someone recognizes me? Pharaoh's put me picture and statues all over the place."

Liz giggled. "*Mon cher* Albert, do not worry. We will keep your 'fans' away. It will be good for you to spend the day out of the palace. Besides," Liz said with her coy smile, "you get to spend the day with me. I am your biggest fan."

Al melted with his goofy grin. "Aye, me lass. What were I thinkin'?"

The colorful red awning flapped lazily in the breeze as it hung from one of the tall windows. Since it wasn't in use at the moment, the awning lacked support beams to stretch it out over the sunny street. Nigel thought it would be the perfect place to hide Osahar. He busied himself running up and down Osahar's humps to pull the awning over the camel so he wouldn't be seen.

"THAT TICKLES!" Osahar laughed.

"Sorry, old chap, almost done," Nigel said with one final pull of the awning over Osahar's tail. "Splendid. You're covered. Now, Liz and Al, shall we go?"

"Oui, Nigel. We are ready," Liz said as she and Al followed the mouse onto a nearby window ledge.

Together they ran along the ledge until they could jump up onto an adjacent roofline. They finally came to a spot that overlooked a large platform. "This is a perfect spot to view the buying and selling. It's the international zone, if you will," Nigel said as he adjusted his golden spectacles. "Buyers from all the other countries are directed to this spot."

"C'est magnifique!" Liz exclaimed. "Look at the different clothing they wear. There are so many foreigners."

Al squinted and looked closely at the market floor. "Aye, an' I see one all the way from Scotland. Look who's here."

Liz and Nigel followed Al's gaze. There, trotting among the bustling crowd, was Max.

"I say, this is utterly splendid! If Max is here, then Joseph must be as well!" Nigel exclaimed.

"MAX! MAX! Up here!" Al meowed as loud as he could.

Liz put her paw up to Al's mouth. "Shhhhhh, Albert. What if Joseph looked up and saw Pharaoh's cat waving to him from the roof?"

Al gulped and grinned weakly. "Oh, aye. I'll jest watch the laddie from here then."

"Here comes Joseph now, followed by his personal steward," Nigel observed. "I like that Imenand. He's always such a gentleman, I must say. And quite intelligent. He knows many of the languages of these foreigners, so Joseph brings him along to assist in translation."

Joseph and Imenand climbed the platform, followed by Max, who sat down and gazed across the crowd. A mad rush of foreigners came clamoring up to them, all yelling and holding out their hands to be heard. Joseph sat in a gilded chair and raised his hand to silence the crowd. He was dressed in his usual Egyptian attire: a fine white linen robe, blue and gold headdress, golden necklace, and heavy black kohl eye makeup. Liz had not seen Joseph this close in a long time. The Egyptian sun, coupled with the burden of many hard years, had darkened and matured his face.

"It is hard to believe this is the same Joseph who once stood in this market as a slave for sale. He doesn't look anything like he did then," Liz said.

Imenand stepped forward and called out, "Zaphenath-Paneah will listen to your requests one at a time. Wait until you are recognized and you may approach the platform."

He proceeded to repeat the instructions in several other languages. Liz raised her eyebrows and thought, *Oui, he is extremely intelligent for a human. He must be well traveled.*

Liz's thoughts were interrupted when she saw them. A pair of jackals was sneaking around the edge of the crowd. She sat up and her tail began twitching back and forth. "Albert? Nigel? Do you see those jackals?" Liz asked. Her hair stood on end as she remembered dodging the jackals at night in the cemetery.

Nigel frowned. "Now what would they be doing here in the market, out in the open, in the middle of the day?"

"Maybe they're hungry," Al proposed. "Maybe the famine's got them to takin' more chances to get food."

"Perhaps. But like I always say, jackals are not to be trusted. No telling what they're up to," Nigel said as he put his spectacles on top of his head to follow them through the crowd.

As Liz watched the jackals, they darted behind a group of shepherds. There were ten of them.

"Albert, Nigel . . . look, there in the back of the crowd. I am certain those are Joseph's brothers," Liz exclaimed, pointing to where the men stood. "The jackals just went to hide behind them."

Nigel and Al looked out and noticed a group of ten men all dressed in the travel-worn shepherds' robes of Canaanite Hebrews. They were not clean-shaven like the Egyptians, but wore long beards that were now caked with the dust of their journey. They looked around nervously, appearing uncomfortable in this strange land.

"I say, they are exactly how you've described them over the years, my dear," Nigel said.

Al sat staring at the men, not saying a word.

"Well, Albert? Do you think those are Joseph's brothers?" Liz asked.

A grin slowly grew on Al's face. "I don't know if that be the laddie's brothers, but I do recognize someone else," he said with a huge grin.

Hundreds of foreigners pushed and shoved to make their way to request food from the prime minister of Egypt. They pulled along carts and donkeys, and carried empty baskets on their heads. Every nationality in the known world had arrived in Egypt, creating a tapestry of colorful clothing and unusual languages throughout the market.

Joseph scanned the crowd of foreigners and his heart stopped when he saw Reuben, Judah, and Simeon. He sat up and quickly looked at the men huddled behind them and one by one recognized the faces of his other brothers. Dan, Asher, Naphtali, Zebulun, Levi, Gad, Issachar—all of them were here except Benjamin.

Joseph stood and calmly walked to the back of the platform, his back to the crowd. "Imenand, come here."

"My lord?" Imenand responded as he joined Joseph.

"They are here. My brothers from Canaan," Joseph said, perspiring from the shock of seeing them. "Ten of them in the back of the crowd."

Imenand turned to look for the brothers and spotted them. Joseph had long ago told his trusted steward about his brothers and what they had done to him. "Do you wish for me to have them arrested, my lord?"

Joseph paused and thought a moment. "No, not yet. Follow my lead as I speak Egyptian. Act as my interpreter. Let's see if they recognize me," Joseph said, taking a deep breath. "Okay, call them over."

Imenand walked to the front of the platform and called out to the brothers, waving them over. "You ten men, come. Approach Zaphenath-Paneah."

Reuben, Judah, and Simeon looked at one another and behind at the others and worked their way through the crowd. As they approached, Joseph slowly walked to the front of the platform and boldly stood in front of them. The sun glistened off his golden necklace. The ten brothers all bowed before him, putting their faces to the ground. When they turned their faces back up to gaze at Joseph, he instantly saw they showed no sign of recognition of their long-lost brother.

Joseph and Imenand shared a look, and Imenand gave a small nod.

"Where do you come from?" Joseph asked in Egyptian. Imenand translated.

"We've come from the land of Canaan to buy food," they answered.

Even though Joseph understood them, Imenand translated their words to keep Joseph's identity hidden. Suddenly Joseph was distracted by the memory of his dreams—his brothers' grain bundles bowing to his bundle; his brothers as stars bowing before him as he hovered in the heavens. Twenty-two years were instantly erased and he felt as if it were the same morning when he shared those dreams with this brothers. They had mocked him and hurled insults at him, calling him "Dreamer." But now those prophetic dreams were unfolding as reality before Joseph's eyes. It was his brothers who needed to be awakened to see it.

"You're spies. You've come to see where Egypt is weak," Joseph accused. He watched their expressions as Imenand translated. Fear. Shock. Denial. Anger.

"No, Master! We've come only to buy food. We're all the sons of the same man and we're honest men. Please! We are your servants, not spies!" they protested all at once.

Joseph remained cool and continued his accusation, waving his hand to dismiss their protests. "No, you are all spies. You've come to find out where we are weak from the famine so you can attack us and steal our food."

"He's got them right where he wants them," Liz said as she, Al, and Nigel listened to this exchange from the roof above.

The brothers looked desperately at one another and blurted out, "Please! Your servants are twelve brothers in all, sons of the same man who lives in Canaan. Our youngest brother is back home with our father, and one brother is . . . no longer with us."

Joseph clenched his jaw as Imenand translated for show. *One brother is no longer with you? He's right here and you can't even see him,* Joseph thought.

"It's just as I've said. You are all spies! This is how we'll get to the bottom of your story. By the life of Pharaoh, you will never leave Egypt unless your younger brother comes here!" the prime minister said with a harsh voice and pointing an angry finger. "Choose one among you to return home to get your brother while the rest of you remain in prison until we determine if your story holds true. If your younger brother doesn't come and stand here before me, then by the life of Pharaoh, we'll know that you are spies, the whole lot of you!"

Max walked over to the platform steps and looked over the brothers with a frown. A growl rumbled in his throat as he spotted the jackals hiding in the back of the crowd. The fur on his back stood on end.

Kate peeked out from around Judah's robe and saw Max standing on the platform. Her heart leaped with anticipation. "Max!" she barked, moving toward the platform.

Max forgot all about the jackals when he heard Kate. "Kate! Kate!" Max said as he immediately took off running down the steps.

Max and Kate quickly met and snuggled their heads together in a long-awaited embrace. They frolicked around, barking and jumping for joy.

"Kate, me love! I kin't believe ye're here! Ye look as beautiful as ever!" Max barked with glee.

"Oh, Max! I felt like these long years apart would never end!" Kate replied with tears of joy.

"How wonderful! Max and Kate are together again!" Liz exclaimed as she saw her friends reunited after twenty-two long years.

"I say, what a beautiful bride Max has!" Nigel observed.

"Can I wave now?!" Al begged. He was excited to see Kate as well.

Tears of joy entered Liz's eyes. She also longed to call out to Kate, but knew she must hold her celebration and hellos for later. "Later, dear Albert—we will celebrate later. For now, let Max and Kate have their moment."

Joseph observed Max and Kate and restrained a smile. Here

was another dog similar to his Jabari. Why not let him enjoy her company for a few days?

"Get these spies out of my sight!" Joseph demanded. "Throw them in jail now, but keep their dog with me."

Imenand clapped his hands and motioned for the guards to gather the men. Fear rushed over the brothers with crushing force as the guards roughly bound their hands in iron chains. They were speechless before the great Zaphenath-Paneah. Judah watched as their little dog Amisa joined the harsh prime minister of Egypt on the platform. Even their dog was looked on with greater favor than they.

"I say, is Joseph taking his revenge on his brothers?" Nigel said. "It seems a bit out of character for the dear boy."

"It *is* out of his character to take revenge," Liz said. She smiled, impressed with the mental game Joseph played with his scheming brothers. "He's getting them to reveal their secrets."

No sooner were the words out of her mouth than she remembered the words of Gillamon: "There will be a test given by the Revealer of Secrets that may appear to be a scheme, but you will see that it is actually a test to reveal true character and a change of heart."

"That's it! Joseph's new name! Nigel, what does Zaphenath-Paneah mean?" Liz asked.

"Well, the name has two meanings actually. The first meaning is 'Savior of the world,'" Nigel replied.

"And the second?" Liz eagerly asked.

"Why, my dear girl, it means 'Revealer of Secrets,'" Nigel replied with a grin.

"C'est bon! This is the test Gillamon spoke of! *Joseph* is the Revealer of Secrets," Liz said excitedly. She leaned over and kissed Al on the cheek.

"Utterly splendid! Max and Kate are finally reunited and you've uncovered another clue to your mystery mission," Nigel said, wiping back his whiskers excitedly. "I'm thrilled I was here to witness this."

"Aye, we must be gettin' close to the end o' our mission then," Al said. "Does that mean I don't have to live in the palace anymore?"

Liz put her dainty paw up to Al's cheek. *"Mon cher,* it will not be long. You must remain Hapy a while longer."

"That'll be hard to do," Al said watching Max and Kate happily playing together. "I'm tired o' bein' apart from me lass. Nothin' makes me sadder."

"Chin up, old boy. As long as the brothers pass this test, you'll be able to resume your life with your bride," Nigel said, wiping his brow from the hot sun. "And I'll be ready to retire and pack my bags to return to Wales."

Liz looked in alarm at Nigel. *"Mon ami,* you would leave Egypt?"

"I'm afraid so. I've been away from my homeland for too long. I wish to retire in a quiet little green meadow in the green countryside. I've spent a lifetime studying this place. I daresay I've seen enough, my dear," Nigel said with a smile. Suddenly he was saddened to think about saying farewell to Liz, Al, Max, and Joseph. "But I shall miss my favorite student. Perhaps we can travel north together?"

"Oui, Nigel. Of course," Liz said. "But first we must see if the brothers pass this test. And we must uncover another scheme."

"Plus another robe," Nigel said holding up one finger.

"Maybe we need to help the brothers pass the test," Al said. "Would that be cheatin'?"

Liz looked at her mate and smiled. "Albert, you are absolutely right. Nigel, go to the prison and observe the brothers. Al, you return to the palace to see what happens with Joseph. I will check Potiphar's desk and listen to his discussions for information about the brothers in prison." She stopped and watched Kate and Max trotting side by side behind Joseph and Imenand as they walked away from the platform. "And Nigel, we'll need to all meet in the palace to discuss what happens and of course to welcome Kate to Egypt."

"Right! We'll all meet at the palace tomorrow night," Nigel said. "The whole team!"

Everyone was so excited about seeing Kate and learning about Joseph's test they failed to notice the jackals darting in and out behind the market stalls.

The jackals followed the brothers all the way to the prison.

CHAPTER 50

The Awakening

Joseph pulled off his headdress and closed his eyes as he listened to the soothing sounds of Benipe's harp. Joseph, Imenand, and Benipe sat in Joseph's special room where he frequently came to be alone and pray. But today he needed these two friends by his side as he figured out how to proceed with his brothers. Max, Kate, and Al were also in the room, listening to every word.

Benipe and Imenand didn't say a word at first, but allowed Joseph to just rest awhile and think. Joseph took a deep breath and finally opened his eyes. He looked over at Max and Kate snuggled together on the floor and smiled. "It's like they know each other," Joseph said.

HA! Al meowed out. *Good one, laddie!*

Max and Kate grinned and gazed at one another. *If he only knew,* they thought.

Imenand smiled. "I'm sure Jabari is enjoying the company of another dog for a change."

"Yes, but I'll send her back with the brothers," Joseph replied.

Kate looked at Max with grief in her eyes at the thought of leaving him again. He whispered in her ear, "Steady, lass."

"You're sending them back?" Imenand asked. "I thought you were going to keep all but one brother locked up."

"I've prayed about it and feel that I only need to keep one brother here for a test. I don't want to cause undue grief for my father. This is going to be hard enough on him as it is. I'm sure he doesn't want to send Benjamin to Egypt. That's why Benjamin didn't come in the first place. Father is afraid of losing him as he believes he lost me," Joseph explained. "Plus, their families are starving. They need many men to transport enough grain back to meet their needs. So, I will release the others and tell them to choose the one who will stay in Egypt. Three days should be long enough for them to think about things."

"I see what you're doing, Joseph," Benipe said as he continued to play. "You're treating them the same way you were treated. They spoke harshly to you and threw you into a pit while they were deciding what to do with you."

Joseph nodded. "Yes, but not out of revenge. I'm trying to awaken my brothers' consciences. Before there can be any kind of restoration between us, they first must come to true repentance for what they've done. Otherwise they won't be able to accept that I forgive them."

"You are most wise, my lord. Memory is a powerful tool. If sins are forgiven, then they may truly be forgotten," Imenand said.

"But sins that are only forgotten and not forgiven must come to the surface with a rude awakening," Joseph pointed out as he paced around the room. "What I am about to do with my brothers may seem harsh, but I think these hard men require such handling. I know that nothing short of the nightmarish famine would ever have brought them here in the first place."

Joseph stopped and put his hand on Benipe's harp to feel the vibrations as the blind harpist struck the strings. "Only a strong blow to their conscience and memory will succeed in awakening both."

Nigel hid in the shadows to observe the brothers in the prison. It was not a pretty sight. They were arguing and yelling among themselves, accusing each other of causing their imprisonment.

"This is all your fault, Reuben!" Simeon accused. "Why did you have to tell the prime minister we had another brother back home?"

"Because it was the truth! If you hadn't started trouble like you always do, we wouldn't be in this mess! Your disrespectful tone disputing we were spies to such a powerful man made us look guilty!" Reuben shot back.

Nigel shook his head. No one seemed to want to take responsibility for his actions. The little white mouse couldn't help but think of the irony of this scene. These ten brothers sat in the same dank prison cell where Joseph had sat. But what a contrast between Joseph and his brothers! Joseph was innocent yet didn't utter a word. These brothers were guilty, yet all they could do was yell and blame others, denying their guilt. Nigel then noticed Judah sitting quietly with his back against the slimy stone wall. He wasn't saying a word.

Dan walked over to Judah and nudged his leg with his foot. "Well, Judah? What do you say about all this?"

Judah looked at his brothers, who were dirty, weary, and afraid. "We are getting what we deserve."

Nigel's ears perked up. *Splendid! Perhaps one of them is waking up!*

"Ah! *Mon amie* Kate! How good it is to see you!" Liz said as they shared an embrace.

Kate grinned her peppy grin and wagged her tail. "'Tis grand ta see ye, too, Liz! How did ye get here ta the palace?"

Liz stepped aside and revealed Nigel standing behind her. "I have the finest tour guide in all Egypt. I am pleased to introduce my dear friend and teacher, Nigel P. Monaco."

Nigel bowed low with his paw draped across his chest. "My dear Kate, it is indeed an honor to meet you."

"Hi, Nigel. Max told me all aboot ye an' how ye help everyone here," Kate said. "An' I'm impressed ye could teach Liz *anythin'*. She's so smart."

"It has been an honor to be of assistance, my dear. And Liz has proven to be a most excellent student of Egyptology," Nigel said, stroking back his whiskers. He was proud of his teacher's pet.

"Oui, I never could have learned so much if it weren't for Nigel," Liz replied with her dainty paw on Nigel's shoulder. "Well, now that we are all here, let's discuss where we are on the Joseph assignment."

"Aye, well, Joseph is sendin' all but one br-r-rother home in thr-r-ree days. He decided he'd jest keep one for the test," Max said. "Kate will be sent home with them."

Liz stared intently at Kate for a moment and saw her pain. "Do not fret, *mon amie.* You will return to Egypt, no?"

"If I may," Nigel said, "the brothers are quite the rambunctious group in the prison. They've been fighting among themselves all day. However, Judah has begun to show signs of admitting their guilt over Joseph."

"Isn't that what the laddie were lookin' for?" Al said, munching on a bowl of dates.

"Oui, Joseph wishes the brothers to remember and repent," Liz said. "And he plans to help them along by returning the money they used to pay for the grain. I saw a note to Potiphar from Joseph directing the palace guards to replace their money sacks just before they leave."

"What a crafty little fellow that Joseph is!" Nigel said admiringly. "How utterly clever!"

"So how do ye think we should help then, lass?" Max asked.

"We must keep an eye on things to see how they progress when the brothers leave. Be on the lookout for an unexpected scheme to stop the test," Liz said. "And Kate, be brave as you return to Canaan. We will all pray you come back to Egypt soon."

"Out! Out! All of you! Zaphenath-Paneah has called for you!" the prison guards said as they threw open the door of the cell holding the brothers. The guards unlocked their shackles and tossed the irons on the floor.

The brothers' faces showed relief as they rubbed their sore wrists and followed the guards down the corridor. Nigel scurried behind them, faithful to his role in the test-watching experiment. *My goodness, what an impression three days in a dark pit has made on these men. They are quiet as mice.*

The brothers were brought to Joseph at the palace and bowed before his gilded chair. Imenand stood by his side, ready to act again as interpreter. Max, Kate, and Al stood quietly in the corner. Nigel snuck up behind them and peeked around Al's back.

"This should be quite the scene," Nigel whispered. "I predict a confession based on what I've seen in the prison this morning."

Joseph showed no emotion and boldly spoke with authority in his Egyptian tongue. "If you do as I say, you will live. I am a God-fearing man. If you truly are honest men, choose now who among you will remain here in prison while the rest of you return to your starving families with grain from Egypt," Joseph instructed. "But, you must bring your younger brother back to me to prove you are telling the truth so you will not die."

While Imenand translated Joseph's demands, the brothers all nodded and bowed, agreeing with his instructions. Joseph then listened as they started talking among themselves.

"It's clear we're being punished for what we did to Joseph so long ago."

"We saw the anguish on his face when he pleaded for his life, but we wouldn't listen. That's why all this is happening to us."

"We alone are responsible."

"Didn't I tell you not to touch the boy?" Reuben asked. "Why wouldn't you listen to me? Now we must pay for his blood!"

Joseph suddenly felt vulnerable and quickly left the room. Max followed him. Joseph put his hands on the back of a chair and rocked his body as he stood in the hallway weeping. Max went over and nudged Joseph's leg, gazing up at him with understanding eyes.

"Jabari," Joseph said as he knelt down to embrace Max. "What a comfort you are. My heart is bursting as my brothers confess their wrongdoing against me. How I want to tell them I forgive them. But not yet."

Joseph stood and wiped his nose and eyes, standing tall. "They can't see this side of me now." He regained his composure and reentered the room with a vengeance.

Joseph wore a hard look on his face. "Time is up! You had your chance. Now *I* will choose! You!" he said, pointing to Simeon. "You will stay. Guards, bind this one and throw him in prison."

A look of terror came over Simeon's face as the guards once more placed the iron shackles on his hands and led him away. He looked back over his shoulder at his brothers. "Please! Come back for me!"

The other brothers looked at one another and knew they had better remain quiet before Zaphenath-Paneah in case he changed his mind again.

"Fill their sacks with grain and give them necessary supplies to return home. And they may take their dog," Joseph instructed Imenand, who nodded in reply. He then looked his brothers square in the eye. "Do not come to me again unless your younger brother is with you." He stormed out of the room.

Judah went over to pick Kate up and she gave Max a last nuzzle. "I will see ye soon, me love."

Max closed his eyes tight and nodded. "Until then, be str-r-rong, lass. Go with me love."

Imenand ushered the men out of the room and outside to their awaiting donkeys. They hurriedly packed up and left Avaris.

When the brothers stopped for the night, they were weary from the day of travel. But their hearts were even more burdened with worry about how they would tell their father about Simeon. No one spoke much as they went about the chore of feeding and watering the donkeys.

As Naphtali opened his sack to get some grain for his donkey, he saw his money pouch sitting on top of the grain. With trembling hands he picked it up and shouted to his brothers, "Look! My money was put back in my sack! Someone returned it!"

Immediately the other eight brothers opened their sacks and there each found that his money pouch had been returned to him. But rather than seeing this as a blessing, they saw it as a curse. Their hearts sank, and they trembled with fear.

"What is God doing to us?!"

CHAPTER 51

Not This One

"They're home, Father!" Benjamin exclaimed as he ran out of Jacob's tent.

Jacob slowly stood and opened the flap of his tent to gaze out at the caravan of his sons with their donkeys laden with grain. He closed his eyes and breathed a sigh of relief his sons had returned. And not too soon, for the camp of Jacob was hungry.

The wives and young children all ran out to meet the brothers, cheering and hugging them and marvelling over the bounty received from the land of Egypt. As Jacob watched them approach, he squinted to account for each son. He counted only nine. Jacob rubbed his tired eyes and counted again. Nine. Perhaps one brother was following along behind, having stopped to check on the small flock that still grazed in their pasture.

But as Reuben and the others drew close, Jacob saw their faces and he knew. The memory of that dark day when he lost Joseph came crashing back into his heart, and he stumbled back to sit on the ground. The brothers rushed to their father, helping him to stand. "Where is Simeon?" Jacob cried out weakly, looking everywhere for his second son.

"Father, come inside so we can tell you what has happened," Reuben said with a strong arm around his father's waist. "Simeon is alive."

"Oh, thank goodness," Jacob said as he took his seat. Benjamin sat next to his father. The other brothers and Kate all filed into the tent and sat around Jacob.

The brothers looked at each other nervously. Here they were again, faced with telling their father about another son in jeopardy. Their consciences were seared even more as they remembered Joseph.

"Father, we met the prime minister of Egypt. He was a harsh man, and he accused us of being spies," Reuben started. "We told him we weren't spies, but were all honest sons of the same man. We told him there were twelve brothers, with one being home in Canaan and one no longer with us."

Jacob's face turned sour as he frowned with concern. Judah jumped in to help Reuben.

"Then the man told us, 'This is how I'll find out if you're spies or not. One of you will stay here while the rest of you return home, taking grain for your starving families,'" Judah began, but paused and took a deep breath. "'But you must bring your younger brother back to me. Then I'll know you are honest men and not spies here to scout out the land. I'll release your brother, and you can trade freely in Egypt.'"

Naphtali pulled out the money pouches they had retrieved from the grain sacks. "And someone returned all our money by placing it in each of our sacks."

Jacob started shaking his head back and forth, terror and grief rising up in him. "NO! You are robbing me of my children!" Jacob cried as his hand hit away the money pouches in Naphtali's hand. Coins went flying out of one of the pouches. "Joseph is no more!

Simeon is no more! And you would ask me to lose Benjamin as well? All these things are against me!" Jacob sobbed in anguish as he fell to his knees.

Reuben ran over and knelt before his father. "You may kill my two sons if I don't bring Benjamin back to you. I'll take full responsibility for his safety. I promise I'll bring him back to you."

Jacob shook his head repeatedly. "No, my son will not go down with you to Egypt. Not this one. His brother Joseph is dead, and Benjamin is all I have left. If anything were to happen to him on your journey, you would see this old grieving white-haired man go to his grave."

Kate's heart dropped at the words Jacob used in front of his sons. *Does he realize how he hurts them?* she thought. *He's jest told them they don't matter. An' Simeon isn't worth savin'. Not at the cost of Benjamin.*

Reuben and Judah looked at each other. Nothing they said mattered. No one had anything more to say anyway. With heads hanging, they left Jacob's tent as he clung to Benjamin. When Joseph was lost, Kate had stayed next to Jacob to comfort him. But now she felt like she needed to comfort the other brothers. Kate could tell a change was taking place because of where her sympathies fell. She saw the change of heart in the brothers. They had tried to save their brother Simeon. But his fate was sealed. For now.

Joseph walked along the outside watch tower above his palace chambers.

"I thought I'd find you up here. It's late, love. Why don't you come to bed?" Asenath said, putting her hand on Joseph's shoulder.

"Is it late? I didn't realize," Joseph answered, kissing his wife's hand. "I keep hoping I'm going to see them return. It's been three months. I shouldn't have let them go like that, Asenath. I should have known this would be too hard for Father to bear."

"Don't give up, my husband. They will return if they get hungry enough," Asenath replied.

"How sad is that? My father is unwilling to rescue Simeon for fear of losing Benjamin, and might only give in if they are all starving," Joseph said, shaking his head as he sat down on a stone bench. "He's always been so pessimistic. My father is the patriarch of this family, chosen by God to lead us, but he's always wrestled with God and his faith. He once physically wrestled with God one night for His blessing, and it left him with a limp for life."

"It looks like he's again wrestling with God, but is missing the very blessing he desires," Asenath said, sitting down next to Joseph and placing her head on his shoulder.

Joseph wrapped his arm around his wife. "You're right. He's missing the blessing in disguise, for he is wrestling with the love of God," he said as he kissed Asenath on the head. "But I'll keep hoping. God eventually always has His way."

"You do have one brother here. Why don't you go to him?" Asenath suggested.

"I can't reveal myself to him yet," Joseph answered.

"Then don't," Asenath suggested with a smile.

Potiphar shook his head and laughed. "You want me to do *what,* my lord?"

"I want you to put me in the prison cell with Simeon. Only for an hour, and I will disguise myself with a foreigner's clothes and a dark wig. I want to see what has happened to my brother during his time there," Joseph explained. "I need to know."

"Very well. I understand. I will escort you into the cell myself," Potiphar said.

A while later Joseph was following Potiphar through the gates of the prison. He jumped when he heard the heavy door slam behind him. He could feel the walls closing in as he remembered the days when he was first thrown into this place. Potiphar led

Joseph down to the lower cells where Simeon was kept. The other prisoners had been moved out of the cell so Joseph could be alone with his brother.

As Potiphar unlocked the cell door and swung it open, he followed Joseph's orders and roughly pushed him into the darkened cell. "Get in there, you dog."

Joseph stumbled into the cell and yelled back, "You can't do this! I'm not the man!"

Potiphar played along. "We'll know soon, won't we?" he said as he locked the door tight.

Joseph picked up a rock on the prison floor and threw it at the door as Potiphar walked away. He sat down with a huff and noticed Simeon quietly sitting on the floor with his back up against the wall. "Why are you here?" Joseph asked in Hebrew, lowering his voice.

"Because of something I did long ago," Simeon replied calmly.

A lump grew in Joseph's throat. "What happened?"

Simeon hesitated before answering. "I betrayed someone very close to me. Someone I loved. But I was too jealous to realize what I was doing."

Joseph nodded. "Jealousy is a dangerous thing. It can lead to much evil. So you acted alone?"

Simeon again paused before he answered Joseph's probing question. "I acted. Alone or not doesn't matter. I chose, and now I'm paying for it."

Joseph felt the emotion welling up again in him. "Do you regret what you did?"

Simeon looked at Joseph, wanting to know who this nosy cellmate was. "Of course I regret it. I think I've always regretted it," he said, now looking at the floor. "But I'm just now realizing it. I don't regret these prison walls as much as I regret what I did, if that's your next question. I wish I could make it right, but that hope is long gone."

This brother was wide awake. Joseph's hope was restored. Maybe his other brothers were experiencing the same regret. Now Joseph hoped his father would soon be driven to desperation from the famine. "Thank you, God, for the blessing of the famine!" Joseph prayed in his heart. "And thank you that my brother Simeon is awake. Please, awaken the others, as well as my father."

Joseph stayed quiet and left Simeon alone until Potiphar returned a short while later. He peered inside and saw the two men sitting silently.

"It appears you aren't the man after all," Potiphar said to Joseph. "Come with me."

Joseph got up and replied, "I told you. I'm an honest man."

Those words echoed in Simeon's mind. He wondered if his brothers would get to say those very words before the great Zaphenath-Paneah, proving they weren't spies.

Joseph turned to Simeon. "I hope you get out of here, too. Don't give up. There's always hope."

Simeon smiled sadly. "Not for the likes of me. Not after what I've done."

Joseph longed to go over and embrace Simeon, but he could not. The test was not over. He turned without saying a word and left the cell. Potiphar closed the door and turned the key in the lock. Tears stung Joseph's eyes to leave Simeon in such despair. But he knew he must remain hidden. For now.

PART FIVE

THE HIDDEN ONE

CHAPTER 52

A Necessary Cup

Is this all that's left?" Jacob asked as Leah showed him a small basket of grain.

"This is all. If we don't get more food soon . . ." Leah said, shaking her head.

Jacob put his wrinkled hand on her arm and patted it. "Very well, make it go as far as you can for now."

Jacob left the food tent and called for his sons to join him in his tent. He cleared his throat and said, "Go back to Egypt and buy us a little food."

Judah immediately spoke up. "The prime minister was serious when he warned us that we would not see his face if we didn't bring our brother back. If you allow Benjamin to go with us to Egypt to buy more food, we'll go. Otherwise, there is no point to the journey."

"Why are you making life so hard for me?!" Jacob moaned. "Why did you have to tell the man you had another brother?"

Reuben stepped in. "The man kept asking us questions like 'Is your father alive? Do you have another brother?' So we told him the truth. How could we possibly know he would tell us to bring Benjamin back to him?"

Judah nodded and rushed over to look Jacob in the eye. "Let Benjamin go with me, and we'll leave immediately. Otherwise, we're all going to die of starvation—the entire family including you, the women, and the little ones," Judah reasoned. He put his hand over his heart and said, "I'll personally guarantee his safety and be totally responsible for him. If I don't bring him back to you, I alone will bear the guilt and take the blame. If we hadn't waited so long to do this, we could have been there and back twice already."

Jacob's shoulders slumped as he hung his head low. He breathed a heavy sigh and slowly raised his head. "If there's no other way, then at least take the man some of the finest gifts the land of Canaan has to offer. Take him balm, honey, gum, aromatic resin, pistachio nuts, and almonds. Also give him double the money to replace the pouches that were in your sacks. Maybe it was a mistake you can point out and correct as soon as you return."

Jacob stood up. "Take Benjamin and go back to the man. May our Father God grant you mercy before the man's eyes so he'll release Simeon and let Benjamin return home. If I lose my children, so be it," he said with a defeated tone of voice.

"Thank you, Father," Judah said, followed by Reuben and the others. Finally Benjamin went up to hug Jacob. "I will be all right, Father. I'll come back to you."

Jacob stared into Benjamin's eyes and nodded, unable to reply as he had a lump in his throat. They shared one last embrace and Benjamin left Jacob's tent to help the brothers pack their provisions.

Kate sat staring at Jacob after everyone had left him there alone. She watched him hobble over to his bed and pull something out from under the covering. It was Joseph's bloodied coat, the stains long ago dried and dark, but still visible. Jacob put the coat up to his chest and clutched it to his heart, sobbing as he rocked back and forth. Kate walked over and jumped up on the bed next to him. Jacob put his wrinkled hand on Kate's back and gently stroked her.

"Go with them, Amisa. Keep them safe," Jacob whispered. "Bring Benjamin back to me. Please."

Ye have me word, Kate thought as her soulful eyes looked into Jacob's. She put her chin on Jacob's knee and sat with him for a few minutes before going to follow the brothers as they left the tents of Jacob.

The market was bustling with activity. Whirlwinds of dust were kicked up by the brisk wind that swept through the dry streets. A long line of foreigners waited to plead with Joseph for grain. Joseph's brothers entered the market and made their way to the platform to join the throngs of hungry beggars. They shielded their eyes from the blowing dust and searched the platform eagerly for the prime minister.

Imenand saw them first and went over to whisper in Joseph's ear. "They have returned, my lord. Your brothers are here."

Joseph stood up immediately and scanned the crowd until he spotted the tired, dirty men. His heart leaped when he laid eyes on Benjamin. *Finally! My little brother! Look how he has matured!* he thought.

"Imenand, I will not meet with them now. Go to my brothers and take them to my house. They will eat with me at noon today, so have a big feast prepared," Joseph instructed. "I'm going to depart for the palace before they have a chance to talk with me. Assign my chief scribe and granary manager to handle things here for the day."

"It will be done as you say, my lord," Imenand replied.

Joseph stepped off the platform and got into his chariot. He purposely drove past the brothers, eyeing them but not saying a word. The brothers looked at one another and wondered what they were supposed to do now.

Imenand directed the men on the platform to continue the dispensing of grain while he left to follow Joseph's instructions. He made his way through the crowd and was met by Reuben and Judah, who acted as spokesmen for the brothers. They bowed in respect for the chief steward of the prime minister of Egypt. Kate peeked out from behind Judah's legs and locked eyes with Imenand. He smiled at her and she wagged her tail. She immediately felt at ease.

"We have returned, our master. See here, we have brought our youngest brother," Reuben said, pointing to Benjamin.

Imenand put his hands on his hips and nodded. "Welcome back to Avaris. My lord Zaphenath-Paneah has instructed me to take you to his residence. Follow me," Imenand said, not waiting for a reply.

Reuben and Judah looked at one another and then back at the other brothers. They followed behind Imenand until they reached the palace complex. They gazed up in awe at the towering statues of Pharaoh and his various hunting scenes carved in the walls of the palace entrance. Imenand led them through the gates and down the outside corridor toward Joseph's house.

A sinking feeling grew within the brothers as they were taken to the private home of the prime minister. "Wait here," Imenand said as he left them in the outer courtyard of the palace with their donkeys. Suddenly terror gripped them.

"What is going on?" Dan asked. "Something is not right here."

"It's got to be the money that was put in our sacks last time we were here! He'll pretend we stole it so he can make us slaves and take our donkeys," Naphtali predicted.

The brothers talked among themselves until Imenand returned. As he came out of Joseph's home, they rushed up to him and Reuben exclaimed, "Sir, when we came to Egypt last time, we bought grain and paid for it in good faith. But as we returned home, we stopped to rest for the night and discovered our money pouches were put in the top of our sacks. Look! We've brought the money back," he said as each man pulled out his money pouch to show Imenand.

"We've also brought additional money to buy more grain. Please, my master, we have no idea how that money got into our sacks or who would have put it there, but we want to make it right," Judah pleaded.

Imenand briefly closed his eyes, smiled, and held up his hand to silence the anxious men. "Relax, relax. *Shalom.* Don't be afraid. Your God, the God of your father, must have been the one who put the money in your sacks. I received your payment, so all is accounted for."

Relief filled the brothers and they smiled and bowed before Imenand. "Thank you, my master," they all murmured.

Kate studied Imenand and was curious about this Egyptian who treated the brothers with such kindness, using their special word for peace, *shalom.* He even spoke about the one, true God, not the Egyptian gods. Here was a pagan telling the chosen men of God it was their God who had given them a gift, for *they* couldn't see it. *Look at the influence Joseph's faith has had on this man,* she thought.

"Now, I have someone who wishes to see you," Imenand said with a smile.

Imenand opened the door to Joseph's palace and Simeon stood there, clean and wearing new clothes. Imenand stood aside so the brothers could be reunited. They rushed up to Simeon and all laughed, hugged, and backslapped him from the joy of seeing he was all right.

Imenand motioned for Kate to come, leaned over, and said, "Hello, little one. There's also someone who wishes to see you."

Imenand whistled and Max came running. Max and Kate barked, wagged their tails, and nuzzled their heads together in a warm embrace.

"Welcome back, me love," Max said.

"Oh, Max! I'm so happy ta *be* back," Kate replied.

Imenand clapped his hands to get everyone's attention. "Now if you'll please follow me."

He led the brothers into Joseph's house, where he gave them food for their donkeys and water to wash their feet. Max and Kate followed along.

"You will be eating with Zaphenath-Paneah at noon. Take care of your donkeys and please make yourselves clean. I will come to get you then," Imenand informed them, walking away to see to the banquet.

"Can you believe this? We're in the clear with the man!" Naphtali exclaimed.

"And we're to dine with him? The prime minister of Egypt!" Dan added.

"Not only that, our brother has been restored to us," Reuben said as he put his hand on Simeon's shoulder. "How did it go for you here while we were gone?"

Simeon looked at his brothers, relieved and almost in disbelief they were really here. "I was treated well, despite the prison where I was kept. No harm came to me. Thank you, Benjamin, for coming."

"Well, Father hesitated awhile, fearful as usual," Benjamin replied. "But finally he released me and eagerly waits to see you return home."

"Let's get ourselves clean and make ready the gifts Father sent with us for the man," Judah instructed.

A short while later, Imenand returned and led the brothers into Joseph's house. They carried their gifts and gazed silently at the splendor of this place. Imenand brought them to a grand dining room with marble floors, exquisite murals painted on the walls, potted palm plants, and several tables positioned around the room. One table would serve the brothers, one table would serve the prime minister, and another table would serve the Egyptians in his employ. Benipe softly played the harp, and the brothers immediately felt enveloped in the serenity and beauty here. Never had they been in such a magnificent place! They had only known the humble dwellings of the dusty tents of Canaan. Now they were welcomed into a palace.

Imenand clapped his hands and the servants lined up in preparation for the entrance of the prime minister. The brothers also stood up straight and quietly awaited his entrance. "Make way for the great Zaphenath-Paneah, whose word is like that of Pharaoh, and whose power is second only to him," Imenand said.

The grand doors opened and Joseph entered, walking swiftly and boldly into the room. He stood a short distance from the brothers and greeted them. "Welcome back," he said in Egyptian. Imenand interpreted again between Joseph and the brothers.

The brothers immediately brought out their gifts and placed them at Joseph's feet. They bowed low before Joseph. Max and Kate smiled as they realized this was the fulfillment of Joseph's dream.

Joseph opened the pouch of pistachios and grinned. They had always been his favorite treat at home. "Tell me, is your father alive?"

"Yes," they replied. "Our father, your servant, is alive and well." They bowed low before him again. Joseph was caught up in the wonder of watching his dream unfold into reality before him. He felt strong emotions rising up again inside him.

Joseph then lifted his eyes and looked at Benjamin. "Is this your younger brother, the one you told me about?" he said, his voice beginning to falter with the emotion of seeing his full blood brother. "May God be gracious to you, my son." With that, Joseph had to quickly leave the room to regain his composure.

After Imenand interpreted what Joseph had said, he held his stance in waiting for Joseph to return. Everyone followed his lead, acting as if there were nothing unusual about the prime minister's behavior. They all stood silently in the dining hall, waiting.

Max whispered in Kate's ear, "Stay here, love." He followed Joseph into his private room and once again saw him weeping.

Joseph took a few minutes, allowing his emotions to spill out of him here, away from everyone. He prayed, "Oh, God, give me the words and show me what to do. And please give me peace as I speak with them." Max went over to Joseph and nudged him with encouragement.

"Okay, Jabari. We're almost finished with the test," Joseph said as he petted Max. He then washed his face at the basin. He made sure he looked the part of the strong, unshakable prime minister of Egypt and left the room.

Max followed behind and came back to Kate. "The laddie has a tender heart. He needs str-r-rength ta do wha' he must do aboot the br-r-rothers."

"I'm sure the Maker will give him wha' he needs," Kate replied. Together she and Max sat down side by side on the cool floor to watch what would happen.

Joseph confidently entered the dining hall and ordered, "Bring out the food!"

Imenand clapped his hands and the servants scurried in with a bountiful feast and placed it on Joseph's table. Joseph took a seat at his table and then gave orders for where each brother should sit, starting with Reuben and ending with Benjamin. As each brother sat down, they suddenly realized they were being seated in order, from oldest to youngest.

"How could this be?" Judah whispered to Levi. "The odds of him placing us in order like this are just too unlikely."

"I don't know. Seems this man is full of mysterious behavior," Levi replied.

Joseph ordered the servants to fill the brothers' plates with food from his table. But for Benjamin's plate, he ordered five times as much food. When the bountiful plate was placed in front of Benjamin, he looked over at Joseph with surprise. Joseph nodded and lifted a hand, saying, "Enjoy!"

Benipe proceeded to fill the room with beautiful music from his harp, and sang Joseph's favorite song:

For something which we have seen in a dream is the earthly side of life.
Do not grieve whatever problems come, but let sweet music play before you.
Let sweet music play before you.

The brothers started to loosen up, and laughed as they all enjoyed the feast, which lasted several hours. Benipe continued to play and Joseph had other singers and dancers come in to entertain the brothers. Toward late afternoon, they held their cups up to Joseph in appreciation for the meal, and Joseph raised his silver cup in response. Joseph stared at his cup for a moment. His gaze then drifted to Benjamin as he twirled the cup in his hand. He knew what he needed to do.

Joseph got up and the brothers immediately stood out of respect for their host. "Please, continue your meal," Joseph instructed. Imenand interpreted and the brothers sat back down. They resumed celebrating their good fortune, talking about how they could now return to their father with all his sons and the bounty of Egypt.

Joseph motioned for Imenand to follow him. Max and Kate were sitting right under them as he whispered in Imenand's ear. "Take my brothers and fill each of their sacks with as much grain as they can carry. Allow them to lodge here tonight. After they have gone to bed, put each man's money back in his sack. Then put my silver cup in Benjamin's sack. I'll give you further instructions in the morning."

"As you wish, my lord," Imenand replied, bowing.

Joseph nodded and placed his hand on Imenand's shoulder. "Thank you for your good work today in preparing this feast for my brothers. Attend to their comfort tonight. I will see you in the morning."

He turned and walked away, not bidding the brothers farewell. They were laughing and feasting, and didn't realize he was gone. Imenand stepped out of the room to attend to the brothers' accommodations for the night.

Max and Kate looked at one another. "I best tell the others wha' is happenin'," Max said. "Nigel were comin' ta the palace tonight. I'll send word with him ta Liz. Stay with the brothers ta keep an eye out here. I don't know wha' Joseph is up ta with the cup, but somethin' tells me it's goin' ta be important for the mission."

"Aye, Max. I'll watch over things here. An' ye're right, me love. We'll see wha' it's all aboot in the mornin'," Kate replied.

"That's me lass," Max said as he gave Kate a kiss on the cheek. He then left and trotted down the corridor to Pharaoh's palace.

It wasn't long before Kate thought she heard wolves howling outside. "AHHRROO! AHHRROO!" She lifted her head and wondered why wolves would be here in the city. She had seen them out in the fields with the brothers as they herded their flocks, but wolves usually stayed away from the city. Those howls sounded like they were right outside the palace. Kate continued to listen for them, but all was now silent. They must have passed on by. No matter.

Imenand walked back into the room and picked up the silver cup sitting on Joseph's table, holding it firmly in his hand. He gave Kate a wink as he walked by. What would be so important about that cup? She shrugged her shoulders and sat back down on the cool marble floor. They would all find out in the morning. All she knew was that, somehow, this was a necessary cup.

CHAPTER 53

Opener of the Ways

"I say! His personal silver cup? It appears our dear Joseph is planting a final test item in Benjamin's sack," Nigel said as Max explained to him and Al what had happened at the feast. "What a clever one he is. Quite the rascal," Nigel chuckled.

"Aye, an' with puttin' the money back in their sacks, they'll have more explainin' ta do," Max added.

"I must go inform Liz about all this. I have a feeling she will want to come see this for herself tomorrow," Nigel said.

"Keep her well hidden when ye bring her to the palace," Al said, munching on a bowl of smelly fish. "I can't wait to see me lass, but I always worry when she ventures out in the day."

"Never fear, old boy! Your Liz is in safe hands, I assure you," Nigel said, wiping back his whiskers. "Very well, I'm off to Potiphar's house. The hour is late and I wish to inform Liz before she goes to sleep."

"See ye tomorrow, Mousie," Max said as Nigel scurried down the hallway.

Al swallowed a mouthful of fish and burped loudly, causing smelly fish breath to waft over Max.

"Ooooh, laddie! Ye best eat some mint then before ye see Liz. She loves ye but she won't want ye kissin' her with fish breath!" Max said, turning his nose away and squinting with one eye closed.

"Good idea, Max," Al said with a wide grin, using a fish bone to pick his teeth clean.

Just then they heard a noise in the kitchen. Something was pawing at the door.

"Now who could that be?" Max asked with a frown. "Are ye still feedin' them jackals?"

Al shook his head and sat up. "No, I promise. I haven't let them beasties in here for years!"

Then they heard a howl. It was a jackal.

"Well, it looks like they're back," Max said, growling as he approached the door. "Go ahead an' open the door."

Al jumped up on the counter and opened the latch. Max stood at attention, tail up and growling as the door opened. Wep stood there alone, looking worried.

"Wha' do ye want?" Max growled.

"Ummm, hi. Al, I know you told me to never come back here and I've done as you asked. But this time I'm not here because of me or food. It's about your wife, Liz," Wep explained, a look of deep concern on his face.

A frightened expression grew on Al's face. "Liz? What's wrong?" he demanded as he rushed up to Wep.

"Tef and I were in the pyramid and we started hearing a voice come from behind a wall, calling desperately for help. The voice is a French, female feline, and your wife is the only French, female feline I know of," Wep explained. "We called out to the voice, and she told us her name was Liz."

Max frowned and looked suspiciously at Wep as Al began to panic. "Liz be stuck in that big triangle? Max, we have to help her!" Al cried.

"It's not like Liz ta venture out ta the pyramid alone, an' without Nigel. Why would she be there?" Max wanted to know, suspicious of this jackal.

Wep nodded. "I know. I don't have the answer. All I know is what we've heard. Tef stayed behind to talk to her so she knows she is not alone. She must be stuck in a tunnel we don't know about. These humans build so many tunnels in their pyramids that even *we* haven't found them all."

Max realized that what the jackal was saying was true. Even Nigel had not discovered all the tunnels. But how did Liz get out there, and *why* was she out there? *That kitty an' her curiosity. I've always said it would be the death of her,* Max thought.

"Aye. He could be tellin' the tr-r-ruth," Max said. "But Nigel said never ta be tr-r-rustin' these beasties."

"I know you have no reason to trust me, but here I am. Al, you once considered me your friend," Wep said humbly. "I've come because Liz is in danger."

"Max, we have to go see if he's tellin' the truth! If Liz really be in trouble, we've got to help her," Al said. "Come on, Wep. I'm goin' with ye." Al started walking ahead of Wep out into the garden and in the direction of the pyramid. Wep followed Al, leaving Max standing there.

Max hesitated, but knew he had to follow. "Gr-r-reat. I best go along. No tellin' wha' could happen out there." Max trotted along behind Wep and Al, but his guard was up.

"One more thing," Nigel said as he scurried back into the kitchen. He had forgotten to ask Max about the time the brothers were expected to leave the palace. He wanted to make sure he had Liz there in time. "Max? Al?" he called as he looked around for them.

No answer. He walked over to the open kitchen door and frowned as he stood in the doorway.

"Now where have they gone?" Nigel asked out loud, his paws on his hips.

"I can anssssswer that," said the snake who slithered up to the bottom of the steps leading into the garden.

Nigel jumped as the hungry snake eyed him with an excited look. "You again?"

"Yesssss. And it looksssss like your friends have gone back to the pyramid with one of those jackals," the snake replied, slithering up the steps. "I'll keep you company until they get back," it said with a fake smile, sticking its forked tongue out in the air.

"Splendid of you to offer, but I think I'll be running along," Nigel said as he scurried back inside the kitchen and down the corridor of the palace.

Nigel's mind was racing. Why would Max and Al ever go with a jackal back to the pyramid? It made no sense. Unless . . .

"Oh, dear," Nigel exclaimed out loud. He ran out of the palace as quickly as he could, right to where Osahar was hidden down by the trickling Nile.

"HEY! WHAT'S UP?" Osahar yelled as Nigel ran up his legs and mounted the camel's head, tugging on his ear to get him moving.

"A scheme, I fear, is what's up," Nigel exclaimed. "HYA! We're off to the pyramid!"

Max couldn't believe the speed at which Al ran across the desert. He had never seen this cat move so fast, except possibly when he had been chased by wolves down the beach or by the angry bull Don Pedro across the meadow. But Max knew that nothing was more important to Al than his beloved Liz, and she was in trouble. Al was even the first one to run headlong into the dark pyramid, calling Liz's name as he entered.

"This way," Wep said as he led Al and Max down one of the many tunnels that snaked deep down into the pyramid.

The threesome went on through the maze of tunnels, turning up and down and left and right. Max and Al could barely keep up with Wep as he ran through the labyrinth of passages. They came to a dead end and Wep hit a lever on the wall. A secret door opened and dust flew everywhere. "Follow me," Wep instructed as he hurried into the secret passageway.

"I jest dunnot know why the humans have ta build so many tunnels," Max said with a growl. "Seems ta me they'd actually like ta know how ta find things, not get confused by all these false turns."

"Well, remember that Pharaoh wants to keep the living humans out once he's inside for eternity," Wep explained.

"Aye, an' I think his wish will be gr-r-ranted then," Max said with a huff.

Wep suddenly stopped, and Al bumped into his back with a thud. "Oh, sorry, lad. Do ye hear somethin'?" Al asked.

"Shhhhh. Listen," Wep said.

Sure enough, they could hear the faint voice of a French, female feline.

"LIZ! I be here, me love! Your Albert has come to save ye!" Al yelled as he put his ear up to the stone blocks of the tunnel wall.

"AL! Don't worry! Tef is here with me. He found the tunnel to reach me," a muted voice replied behind the wall. It sounded like Liz.

"Well, I'll be. The laddie were tellin' the tr-r-ruth," Max said. All of a sudden Max's stomach growled. He realized he hadn't eaten a thing since early morning and was hungry.

"Aye! I knew we could trust Wep! Max, yer stomach sounds aboot like mine then," Al said with a wide grin.

They heard the muffled sound of Tef's voice instructing them where to go. "Go down two levels and enter the food chamber. The passageway leads off a secret door that you'll see on the far wall. Look for the sign of the jackal."

"Okay, we'll be right there," Wep called back as he took off again down the corridor.

Soon they reached the food chamber and there before them was a massive display of every food imaginable. Max's and Al's mouths watered at the sight of the spread. Lanterns glowed all around the food, and the two looked at each other as Wep searched for the sign of the jackal.

"Go ahead and help yourselves to a bite while I look for the lever," Wep said as he scanned the wall. "That is some of the best food we've tasted in a while."

"Well, I guess since Liz be okay, it wouldn't hurt to take a nibble," Al said.

"Aye, lad. Don't mind if I do," Max said as he approached the table.

Al spotted a bowl of plump, delicious dates and nuts and grabbed a mouthful, chewing with delight. "Wep, ye're right, lad! Some o' the best dates I've tried. Max, have some."

Max took a bite of the dates and the delicious juicy flavor burst in his mouth. "Wha' a g-r-r-rand bowl of dates!" Max said as he took another mouthful.

"Got it!" Wep said as he found and hit the lever, opening a secret door on the far side of the food chamber.

"Mind if we take some dates to Liz?" Al said, picking up the bowl and placing it on top of his head.

"Not at all. Bring it in," Wep said as he walked into the secret passageway.

Max and Al trotted happily behind Wep and into another chamber lit with lanterns all over the room. Al placed the bowl of dates on a table and started calling for Liz.

"Liz! We're here! Where are ye, me love?" Al yelled. He grabbed his head as he suddenly felt dizzy.

Just then Max also began to feel woozy and looked at Al, who clearly felt the same way. Max tried to focus his eyes on Al but all he could see was a blurry, orange blob moving around. "Al, stand still so I kin see ye then," Max said, staggering as he tried to walk over to Al.

Al put his paw out in front of him, trying to swat away whatever he was imagining right in front of his face. "Max, th-th-there be th-th-three o' ye here. How'd ye do th-th-that?" Al said, slurring his voice. "Lizzz! Come out!" Al staggered over to what appeared to be a big, black statue. He put his paws on the statue and said, "Is th-th-that me black beauty?"

Max shook his head and squinted. The room was spinning. He looked over at Al and saw a big black statue. As his gaze drifted up the statue, he struggled to focus his eyes on the head. A dark jackal head came into view. It was the statue of Anubis! Alarm began to race through Max as he realized where they were. The jackal had led them right into the inner chamber of the temple of Anubis. He tried to think clearly, but something strange was happening to both him and Al. He could barely walk as he staggered over to Al, pulling him away from the statue.

"Lad, I th-th-think . . . we'vvve been tr-r-ricked," Max said, slurring his words.

"Usss? Tricksss? Are th-th-they magic tricks?" Al replied with a slur, his goofy grin getting goofier and his eyes rolling around as he attempted to focus. "I like magggic tricksss. Ph-ph-pharaoh's court magggicians do th-th-them," he said, trying to whisper, "but I can't ever figggure th-th-them out."

Suddenly Max and Al heard a low, sinister laugh. "Then you'll love this trick," came a deep voice as a third jackal entered the room. It walked over to Wep and Tef, who stood there snickering at Max and Al. "Let's show them who we are, boys."

As Max and Al sat there helpless, dizzy, and barely able to focus, the three jackals stood up on their hind legs and howled. They appeared blurry and Max thought it looked like a heat wave washed over the jackals, like the waves of intense heat he'd seen out in the desert rising off the sand.

Their wavy bodies twisted and turned, and they soon towered over Max and Al. Two of them were seven feet tall, and the third one rose to nine feet. Max blinked hard and shook his head. Suddenly the jackals formed human bodies, but kept their jackal heads that now looked like black masks. Only these weren't masks like they'd seen the humans wear. They were real. The eyes really moved. And the mouths opened and closed, showing real teeth and slimy tongues.

"Wha' were in th-th-those datesss?" Max slurred. "I must be dr-r-reamin'."

The tallest jackal-headed beast threw his head back and laughed. "Ah, and so you are Maximillian Braveheart the Bruce! But this dream is going to be your worst nightmare."

Al leaned over and with his slurred speech whispered to Max, "He'sss not verrry niccce. And wherrre did Wwwep go?"

Max attempted to talk to the beast. "Who arrre yyye?"

"You mean who are WE? Oh, where are my manners?" the tallest jackal beast sarcastically replied. "Allow us to introduce ourselves," he said as he pointed to the other two jackal beasts.

"I am Wepawet, Lord of Abydos and Opener of the Ways," the jackal-headed god laughed. His head was more grey than black, and in his hand he held a bow.

The taller jackal beast added, "You've always known him as 'Wep,' of course. Ah, yes, good old Wep who opened the way for you to leave the pyramid so long ago," he said with a sinister laugh, "and now the one who has opened the way for you to enter my temple. Did you know he was first known as a wolf god, accompanying Pharaoh on the hunt? Probably not. No, but I'm sure your beloved Liz would know. Well done, Wepawet," the jackal beast added. Wepawet bowed in respect.

"Nonnne of th-th-these look like mmme Lizzz," Al said, his eyes getting droopy.

"And I am Duamutef, son of Horus and protector of the stomachs of mummies," the second jackal beast said with a vengeful voice. His body looked like a wrapped mummy with a jackal head. He lifted the jackal-head topper from a canopic jar that sat by his feet and slammed it back on its jar with a laugh.

Max's fur crawled. Although he was in some sort of a drugged state, he realized he was in the presence of evil.

"Isn't it poetic? Tef guards the stomachs of those pitiful humans who think they can use them later," the tall jackal beast said with a laugh. "And by acting like a crazed hungry jackal he weaseled his way right into Pharaoh's palace for food, and used Al's ever-rumbling stomach to lure him out to the pyramid. Bananas!"

"Be th-th-there banananananasss here?" Al stammered. "I lovvve banananananasss!"

Max was trying hard to keep his thoughts straight, but it was a battle. *This kin't be happenin'. They kin't be real. They must have slipped some sort of drug in those dates that's makin' us see things.*

Then the tallest jackal beast rose up and held his hands out over the other two jackals, exclaiming, "And I am Anubis, god of the dead! Welcome to my temple! I've waited for this day for a long time."

"Ye . . . kinnn't . . . be . . ." Max tried to say, but he was becoming paralyzed. He couldn't speak and now he couldn't move. He looked over at Al, who was lying on the floor frozen, left with a goofy grin on his face.

Anubis laughed. "Oh good, the drug is taking full effect. Wepawet and Duamutef, I think they are ready for you now."

Wepawet and Duamutef snickered and moved in close to Max and Al, who lay there unable to move. Max could still see the jackals but he couldn't stop them. They opened a basket and removed yards and yards of linen strips. He watched in horror as they quickly started wrapping Al up as a mummy! They sloppily wrapped the strips of linen around Al's legs, head, and tummy, and he giggled as they tickled him.

Stop! Max yelled inside his head. But he could do nothing to stop this.

Soon the jackals turned and came to do the same to Max, wrapping him up in yards of linen. They were laughing and doing such a poor job that they left a peep hole for Max to see and air holes for him to breathe, as they had done for Al. But all he could do was lay there as they did their dirty work. Max's eye followed Anubis as he looked on and laughed.

"Ah, it is grand to finally wrap up all the loose ends with this Joseph business," Anubis said as he twirled something in his hand.

Max struggled to focus. Joseph's silver cup! Anubis held the same silver cup Joseph had ordered Imenand to put in Benjamin's sack. Anubis tossed eleven money bags on the floor, laughing. The brothers' money sacks were there, too! What was happening? Had Imenand betrayed Joseph? All Max could do was listen. He wondered if he would even be able to do *that* soon. The drug had shut down his ability to speak, move, and think.

"Well done, boys!" Anubis said as he looked over the wrapped shapes of a Scotty dog and a cat. "Of course, since we couldn't really mummify them, it does take away some of the fun of it all. But it will have to do."

Out of the corner of his eye, Anubis saw movement from a high stone block shelf. He turned his back and grinned as he heard Nigel gasp when the mouse saw what they had done to Max and Al.

This can't be happening! I have to get Liz and Kate! Nigel thought as he scurried out of the chamber.

"What now?" Wepawet asked Anubis, who studied Joseph's silver cup under a lantern.

"Oh, we wait. We've taken care of half of them. The other half will be here soon," Anubis replied. He started laughing wickedly. Wepawet and Duamutef added their wicked laughter that echoed throughout the chamber as Anubis shut the door behind Nigel.

"Looks like this cup won't be used for redemption after all," Anubis sneered. "But it will make for a splendid artifact to be found in a few thousand years."

CHAPTER 54

The Temple of Anubis

O sahar galloped at top speed. Nigel directed the camel to stop right in front of Potiphar's house. He hadn't had time to walk there to get Liz and then to Osahar's hiding place. He hoped the camel wouldn't be seen in the shadows outside Potiphar's gate.

"Just don't say a word, old boy, not even to me!" Nigel instructed as he jumped off Osahar's back and onto the roof line that took him to where Liz would be.

Liz was already curled up and sleeping when Nigel scurried up to her. "Liz! Liz! I'm sorry to wake you but this is most urgent," Nigel whispered in Liz's ear.

She was up immediately. "What is it, Nigel? What is wrong?"

"Something dreadful, horrible, unspeakable has happened! Max and Al have been taken captive in the pyramid," Nigel blurted out.

Liz stood up, alarmed. "By whom?"

"You will not believe this my dear, but I saw it tonight with my own eyes . . . Max and Al have been taken by the three jackal gods Wepawet, Duamutef, and . . . Anubis himself," Nigel answered.

Liz cocked her head. "Why, Nigel, how can this be? They are not real!"

Nigel shut his eyes and nodded quickly. "Yes, yes, yes—I know, my dear. But something strange is happening and we must leave immediately to rescue Max and Al. They apparently were drugged and . . . oh, dear, I'm sorry to say, wrapped up like mummies."

"No! Nigel! Not my dear Albert! He must be terrified!" Liz said as she and Nigel began running quietly down the hall to get outside to reach Osahar.

"Actually, the good news is that Albert is quite unaware of all that is happening to him. He and Max are in a daze," Nigel said. "Now we must go get Kate. She is the only one who can open the levers to the secret tunnels to reach them. Osahar, to the palace, old boy."

"Osahar, thank goodness we have you to help us," Liz said as she climbed onto the camel's back.

"HEY, LIZ! GLAD I'M HERE TO HELP. HANG ON TIGHT! NEXT STOP, THE PALACE!" Osahar yelled.

Nigel cringed but it didn't matter if the house of Potiphar heard the shouting camel now. They were off, headed down the road as Osahar kicked up dust behind them.

Liz stayed behind in the outer courtyard to keep Osahar quiet while Nigel crept into Joseph's house, where the brothers were sleeping. Kate was snuggled next to Benjamin, and Nigel frowned as he walked among the loudly snoring brothers to reach her. *How could they possibly sleep with all this racket?* Nigel wondered.

Nigel gently placed his hand on Kate's back and whispered, "Wake up, dear girl."

Kate sleepily opened her eyes. "Oh, hello, Nigel. What brings you here?"

"A bit of bad news I'm afraid. Hurry, follow me," Nigel said as he led Kate out of the room. Benjamin sleepily pulled a blanket onto his back when Kate's warmth left him.

When they were outside, Kate saw Liz and Osahar. "Wha' is this all aboot?" she wanted to know.

"Max and Al have been taken captive by some jackals in the pyramid. We have to rescue them," Liz explained as Kate climbed up onto Osahar's back. "I'll tell you everything on the way there."

Soon they were galloping up to the darkened pyramid, which loomed over them in the moonless Egyptian night. Osahar knelt down and Kate, Liz, and Nigel all jumped off.

"I must tell you, my dear, that we will be entering not just the pyramid. We will go deep inside the temple of Anubis," Nigel said as he stopped Liz. "But don't be afraid. I know the Maker will help us accomplish this mission."

"Oui, Nigel. I also know He will," Liz replied, feeling nervous in her stomach. She had said she never wanted to go near the temple of Anubis. Now she had no choice.

"Of course the Maker will see us through!" Kate added. "Where are they, Nigel?"

"Follow me," Nigel said as they entered the dark passage of the pyramid. He took them down the same path Wep had taken Max and Al down, for he had followed close behind them all the way into the pyramid. If Nigel had not been there to follow the jackal, he might never have found them.

They came to the first dead end. Kate was the only one heavy enough to put sufficient force on the lever. The door opened easily and they quietly made their way down to the food chamber. Liz could already feel the oppressive evil surrounding them in this room. This was food offered to the god Anubis. It turned her stomach to think of such an offering.

"Now this lever is up a bit higher, I'm afraid, Kate," Nigel explained, pointing to the sign of the jackal on the wall.

Kate frowned with determination, not knowing how she could jump that high. Liz studied the room and the distance from the table to the lever. "Kate, I believe that if you stand on this table, you might be able to jump and hit the lever."

"Aye, Liz. I'll give it a try," Kate replied. She jumped up on the table and took a flying leap, just missing the lever. She landed with a hard thud on the floor, nearly knocking the wind out of her. But being the stubborn Scottish lass she was, she immediately jumped back up on the table and tried again. This time she hit the lever and the secret door opened.

"Jolly good show!" Nigel said, clapping with excitement.

"Well done, Kate," Liz said, then took on a stalking pose. She slowly slinked toward the secret door and peeked her head inside the inner chamber.

There she saw Max and Al completely wrapped up as mummies. Anubis and the other two jackal gods were howling with victory, delirious with their apparent power. Liz took in a quick breath at the shock of seeing Max and Al. Anubis saw her and grinned.

"Do come in. We've been expecting you," Anubis said as the other jackals snickered and moved over to guard the Max and Al mummies.

A wave of fear washed over Liz, but as she walked in closer to see the mummy-wrapped shapes of a cat and a Scotty dog, anger welled up inside her. A group of canopic jars were placed next to Max and Al.

"What have you done!?" Liz screamed.

"I've finally beaten you, oh, smart one," Anubis replied.

Liz moved in closer, staring intently at the tall jackal-headed man. She felt a shiver go down her spine. "Who are you?"

An evil grin came across Anubis' face. "Why, don't you recognize the family resemblance? I believe you've met my father."

Liz squinted as she studied this Egyptian god now come to life. "I recognize you as Anubis, Egyptian god who oversees the dead . . . but you cannot . . . be real."

Anubis cackled and said, "Very good, oh, smart one!" Then he turned a sinister face to Liz. "I assure you, I am very real." Another cackle. "Please, do tell me more about myself. You know *so much* about Egyptian gods."

Kate, Nigel, and Liz shared a look of confusion. This couldn't be happening. This just couldn't be real. "Liz, how kin this be? There's only one God!" Kate whispered, shaking with fear.

Liz didn't answer but kept staring at this apparition before her. "Anubis is known in his funerary role as 'He who is upon his mountain' —meaning he is the protector of the deceased and the tombs," Liz said flatly, trying to keep the conversation going as she struggled to figure out who this was. Nigel nodded with approval as Liz identified him correctly.

Anubis grinned and walked over to where Liz sat. At nine feet, he towered over her. Liz's heart was racing with fear and confusion. How could she possibly defeat this monster, as small as she was?

"*Oui*, Lizette Brilliante. You are once again correct. Death is where I reign supreme," Anubis said as he walked over to the other two jackal gods guarding the mummy-wrapped bodies of Max and Al. "Oh, how rude of me. Let me introduce you to my assistants, Wepawet and Duamutef. I'm sure you know of them as well."

Liz immediately knew which gods these jackals were. "Wepawet – 'Opener of the ways,'" Liz replied. She then looked at the other jackal god, a mummy-looking figure with a jackal head. "Duamutef, protector of the stomachs of mummies," she said, swallowing hard.

"Very, very good! What a bright student you are. Wep here was the opener of the ways for your precious Albert," Anubis laughed. "Now Wepawet opens the ways for the spirits of the dead."

Wepawet gave a yelp of excitement. Anubis grinned. "Oh, and I was just sharing with Max and Al that Tef did well to keep your Albert's stomach occupied in Pharaoh's palace, didn't he? Fear him, for he has a vengeful spirit and the tendency to hunt."

Liz looked at the "mummies" of Max and Al. She then gazed at the limestone canopic jars topped with carved jackal heads sitting next to them. Anger began to stir inside her. Surely the jackals had not truly embalmed Max and Al. She had to know their fate.

"So, Duamutef, are you guarding the stomachs of Max and Al in those jars?" Liz said, trying to sound stronger than she was. Her gut was tied up in knots at the thought of it.

Duamutef gave a snorting laugh. "Oh, how I wish that were so, but embalming would do no good with these two. We know all about your little secret."

Anubis lifted the mummy-wrapped bodies of Max and Al. He held one in each hand and looked at them thoughtfully. "Yes, what a pity to not do a thorough embalming job here."

Anubis tossed Max and Al onto the stone floor. Their bodies rolled across it and came to rest by the table where Al had placed the drugged dates. Liz and Kate cringed as they saw their mates treated with such cruelty. But Liz also felt relief. She knew their bodies were intact—that they had only been drugged and wrapped.

"Ah, yes, we know you four are immortal. Killing you is impossible, but confining you for eternity is another matter entirely," Anubis said, gesturing over to the other jackals, who started surrounding Liz and Kate. "We'll keep you here for all time, wrapped up like good little mummies, locked away in a dark pyramid where no one will ever find you. No more missions, no more rescuing those worthless humans. It's over, oh, smart one."

Liz noticed a swarm of flies eating off the bowl of dates. She had to think fast and blurted out, "I don't believe you. You aren't real. There is only one God."

Anubis shuddered at the mention of God's name. Then Liz knew exactly who he was.

"You are wrong, cat! We are real! We are many gods!"

Anubis started throwing his head side to side, convulsing as his body twisted in a grotesque display. His arms disappeared into his side, and his legs melted together into one tall column. His jackal head bubbled as if it were melting and took on a rounded shape with a short snout. Fangs grew from his mouth and a forked tongue whipped from side to side. Scales zipped up and down his body and his menacing eyes glowed red, boring into Liz and Kate. Anubis was now a massive cobra.

Anubis spewed venom at Wepawet and Duamutef, who immediately took the same form of cobras. They hissed and spit out their forked tongues as they moved in closer to Kate and Liz. Kate closed her eyes and nuzzled up close to Liz. Nigel hid under Kate's arm.

"Do you recognize me now?" the cobra hissed in a female voice.

The blood drained out of Liz's face as she thought of her last encounter with the snake who had struck and killed her at Noah's Ark. Then it was Charlatan—the Evil One. The presence of evil engulfed them with such heaviness she could hardly breathe. Liz noticed a fly fall onto Al's still body. Suddenly she received the strength to defy this evil.

"Your father, you say? Yes, now I see the family resemblance. You must be Charlatan's minions, doing his bidding. So now you have taken the form of Wadjet, cobra goddess. Supposedly you can punish criminals with blindness or venom," Liz said smugly. "Well, Charlatan's venom didn't last at the ark, *n'est ce pas?* You are an impostor just like your evil father. There is only one GOD!"

The cobra recoiled at Liz's remarks. "Perhaps you need a greater demonstration," the snake hissed. Once again it spewed venom on the other two snakes.

All three snakes dropped to the floor and began convulsing again as their bodies grew fat and the scales popped up as bumps along their backs. Four short legs grew out their sides, and their heads lengthened and grew massive numbers of teeth. They were now part crocodile, part hippo, and part cheetah.

"Ammut," Liz said matter-of-factly, gazing up at the ceiling, looking unimpressed. "You're the beast who sits at the judgment hall where the Weighing of the Heart ceremony takes place."

The evil being slinked up to Liz and breathed out his smelly breath, which almost knocked her over. "You forgot my most important attribute," Ammut said with a low, gravelly voice. "I punish evildoers by devouring their hearts!"

Liz was getting bolder now. She said, "Pfft!" and turned around, catching Kate's eye. She motioned with her eyes for Kate to follow her. She walked over to the table with the bowl of dates. The flies were swarming all over them now.

"This is getting tiresome. All this . . . hocus-pocus of these fake Egyptian gods is just another of your father's deceptions. It isn't real." Liz stopped and turned, daring the Ammut beasts to come near. "There is only ONE TRUE GOD!"

The beasts all shut their eyes and shivered at the mention of God's name. The two lesser beasts looked almost docile. Ammut would have none of it.

"You are so naive. You think you have all the answers with your G . . ." Ammut couldn't even pronounce the name of God. "Yes, we serve the Original Impostor, and have once again helped him lead mankind away from the Maker. So much for the Maker's great idea of the flood to recreate a perfect world," Ammut laughed as he moved closer to Liz.

"You only have one god. We are all the other gods! And we have convinced the humans there are many! The humans can see, make, and worship gods made in whatever form they wish. We have allowed their creativity to run wild in creating their gods! So you see, it doesn't matter, really, does it, oh, smart one? As long as humans can be led away to believe in other gods, we can continue our work. But alas, the time for *your* work is at an end," Ammut maniacally raved.

Liz saw more flies swarming and dropping to land on the mummies of Max and Al. "Ah, *oui*, this is true, Ammut. God gives men free will to choose to believe in Him alone or to foolishly follow their man-made ideas of what a god should be. But I still don't believe you are all these gods. You've shown me the big, scary gods you claim to be. Surely the small gods don't hold the same power. Certainly you aren't behind the kinder, weaker gods, such as, say, Heqet, goddess of childbirth?"

The big Ammut beast grinned and began convulsing again. The other two beasts did the same. All three beasts shrunk in size and turned into small, slimy frogs.

"For once, perhaps I am mistaken. You are indeed *small,* aren't you?" Liz said as her eyes quickly darted to the flies on top of Max and Al.

With rapid instinct, the three frogs slapped their tongues out at the flies. Liz grinned.

"Yes, smart one! We can take whatever form . . . we . . . desire," Heqet the frog goddess said, starting to slur her words.

"I feel kind of . . . strrrrange," said the second frog.

"I dddooo . . . too," said the third frog.

Heget tried to scream at Liz, but was rapidly fading. The frog managed to get out, "YOU . . . YOU . . . TRRRICKED USSS . . ."

"Ah, *oui*, Heqet-Ammut-Wadjet-Anubis—whoever you are, minion. But like Charlatan, it is your pride that has tricked you!" Liz exclaimed triumphantly. The three frogs' eyelids drooped and their breathing became shallow.

Kate put her paw on Liz's shoulder. "Liz, wha' is happenin'?"

"I believe I can answer that," piped up Nigel. "The frogs ate the flies that had eaten the drugged food. The very poison they set for Max and Al ended up on their own lips!"

Liz grinned as the frogs were now totally still. "*Tres bien*, Nigel. Evil always goes too far, *n'est ce pas?*"

"Ye mean ta tell me they kin't hurt us then?" Kate said, smiling with relief.

Liz looked at Kate and then back at the frogs. "Not for now anyway. Quickly, we have to find some waking potion for Max and Al. I believe I read about these sleeping/waking potions in *The Book of the Dead.*"

"Why of course you did, my dear! There should be some waking potion over by the stone sarcophagus," Nigel exclaimed. "No good mummy would ever leave home without it!" He snickered as he scurried off.

"Kate, would you please release our mates from their mummy wraps? We have to get them loose and awake. There's still a mission to complete," Liz said.

"I say, I thought this might be the final scheme, my dear," Nigel said, bringing a vial of the waking potion over to Max and Al. Kate took it from him to pour into their mouths.

"When I saw that Anubis was holding Joseph's silver cup, and that he had the eleven money pouches, I knew he was trying to prevent Joseph's test from proceeding," Nigel explained, wiping back his whiskers. "That Anubis was such a cheeky fellow."

"*Oui,* and he attempted to confine us here so we couldn't do anything about it," Liz explained.

"Oh, me achin' head. What's all this cloth aboot?" Al asked as he sat up and finished pulling the linen strips from his back legs.

Liz rushed to Al's side and kissed him on the head. "*Mon cher* Albert! I'm glad you were not a true mummy."

He looked up and said, "Liz! I'm so glad to see ye're all right! But wait a minute. Are ye tellin' me those jackals tried to make mummies out o' me and Max?"

"Aye," Max said, shaking his head. "There were nothin' we could do ta stop it. Looks like our lassies saved the day," Max said with a grin.

"Oui, but it was Nigel and Osahar who brought us here, no?" Liz said. "It was a team effort."

Nigel stood on his hind legs and rocked back and forth on his heels. "It was an exhilarating experience, I must say." Nigel placed his paw over his heart and gave a low, humble bow. "I was happy to be of service."

"Way ta go, Mousie! An' that scr-r-reamin' camel saved the day, too. We'll have ta use him for one more part of this mission," Max said. "It'll be daybreak soon. If that silver cup an' those money pouches aren't in the brothers' sacks, Joseph's plan will fail."

CHAPTER 55

Redemption

That will do it!" Nigel hoarsely whispered as Al placed the last money pouch back into Reuben's sack. "Thank you, old girl," Nigel said as he patted Dodi the donkey on the neck.

"Don't mention it," Dodi replied. "You are much kinder than those nasty jackals who about knocked us over to get to the grain sacks last night."

Max stood guard while Nigel instructed Al to put the missing items back in the brothers' sacks. Al jumped from donkey to donkey, causing the animals to grunt with each pounce. Finally he placed Joseph's silver cup in Benjamin's sack.

"Aye! The laddie's silver cup is in place," Al said as he jumped off Benjamin's donkey.

"Gr-r-rand job, Al an' Mousie! An' not a moment too soon. I hear the br-r-rothers comin'," Max reported.

Max, Al, and Nigel slipped away undetected as the eleven brothers entered the courtyard to mount their waiting donkeys. Kate was with the brothers and winked at Max as she walked past. Liz remained hidden in the shadows, watching all this unfold.

"It's a great day for travel," Judah exclaimed with a smile.

"Any day would be great after that feast yesterday," Reuben added, patting his belly.

"And after that good night of sleep in the prime minister's house," Dan said. "I think we can make it *way* down the road today."

"I can't wait to get home," Simeon said as he mounted his donkey and looked up at the magnificent walls of this Egyptian palace compound. "This place is grand, but I miss the tents of our father."

Everyone felt great. They had plenty of food, they had Simeon back, and Benjamin was safe and sound. They couldn't wait to return to Jacob with the good news. What a change from their previous journey.

The Egyptian guards opened the gates and the brothers lifted their hands in farewell as they departed the palace grounds. The city of Avaris was beginning to stir as the sun brought light to another day. A rooster crowed in the distance. And up above the waking city stood Joseph and Imenand on top of the palace walls, watching the brothers depart. They watched the men laughing and joking as they rode along the road. Joseph stood there with arms folded, watching and waiting. When the brothers had cleared the city limits, he turned to Imenand.

"Now, Imenand. Go after my brothers. You know what you have to do," Joseph said.

"Indeed I do, my master. I'm on my way," Imenand replied with a bow.

Max, Al, Liz, and Nigel watched Imenand walk boldly past them and into the courtyard, where his chariot stood ready. He took his horses' reins and snapped them with a "HYA!" The palace guards opened the gate, and Imenand rode his chariot swiftly through in pursuit of the brothers.

"Do ye think Imenand had anythin' ta do with helpin' the jackals last night?" Max asked. "Could he be part of the scheme?"

Liz stared intently at Imenand as he drove off. "I do not believe so. Something tells me if he did play a part in the scheme, he was on the right side."

"My dear, that would only make sense if Imenand knew what the jackals were up to," Nigel said.

Liz smiled. "Precisely, old boy."

Kate looked behind and saw Imenand's chariot quickly catching up to their caravan. She grinned as Joseph's steward approached and pulled his horse up in front of the brothers, blocking their path with his chariot. He wore an angry look on his face as he jumped down from the chariot.

"Why have you repaid evil for good? Why have you stolen my master's silver cup, the one he uses to predict the future? What a wicked thing you have done!" Imenand yelled, just as Joseph had instructed.

The brothers boldly looked at Imenand in disbelief. They knew they hadn't done such a thing, and they all began to shout their replies. "What are you talking about?! We are your servants and would never do such a thing! Didn't we return the money that was placed in our sacks before? We brought it all the way back from Canaan, so why do you think we would steal silver or gold from your master's house? If you find such a cup with any one of us, kill that man immediately! And the rest of us will be your slaves!"

Imenand stood with his hands on his hips and told them, "That's fair. But only the one who stole the silver cup will be my slave. The rest of you may go free."

It was almost a race to see who could open his sack first. The brothers couldn't wait to prove their innocence. Imenand walked down the line of brothers, beginning with Reuben. Once again, the brothers' hearts dropped as each found his money pouch put in the top of his grain sack. The blood drained from their faces as Imenand stood in front of Benjamin opening his sack. The sun's rays hit the shining silver cup, and all the men had to shield their eyes from the bright reflection. The brothers dropped to their knees, tearing their clothes in despair, crying, "NO! NO! Not Benjamin!"

Tears welled up in Kate's eyes as she saw their anguish. *Jest hang on. It's not wha' ye think. All will be well,* she thought as she gazed lovingly at Benjamin.

The brothers mounted their donkeys and followed Imenand back to the city. They were all broken men.

Liz, Al, and Nigel snuck into Joseph's room and hid behind a row of potted palm plants. Joseph sat on his gilded chair, tapping his hands nervously on the chair arms. Max sat at his feet, and servants stood silently by. The tension was so thick in the room every breath taken felt like a disruption of the deafening silence.

The doors flew open and Imenand boldly entered the room, the eleven brothers following along behind. Imenand locked eyes with Joseph as he bowed, a slight grin on his face as he announced the brothers. "My lord, your silver cup was indeed found. It was in the sack of the youngest brother."

The brothers fell on their faces before Joseph, crying out in anguish to the powerful prime minister of Egypt.

Joseph stood and angrily accused them. "What have you done?! Don't you know a man such as me can predict the future?"

Judah lifted his head and answered, "Oh, my lord, what can we possibly say to explain this? How can we prove our innocence? God is punishing us for our sins," he said as he shook his head in deep conviction. "We have all returned to be your slaves—not just the one who had your cup in his sack—all of us."

"No," Joseph said as he waved his hand to dismiss Judah's idea.

"I would never do such a thing! Only the man who stole my silver cup will be my slave. The rest of you may go back to your father in peace."

Reuben was speechless. Benjamin looked frantically at his brothers. Simeon lowered his head, remaining silent. No one spoke a word. Judah looked at them and then boldly stood to approach Joseph.

"Please, my lord, let me say one thing to you. Please don't be angry with me, for I know your power is like that of Pharaoh. But I must speak," Judah pleaded.

"We are watching the brothers pass Joseph's test with flying colors," Liz whispered to Al and Nigel, smiling as she stared at Judah.

"My lord, you asked us before about our father and if we had any other brothers. We spoke the truth and told you of our father, who is an old man, and of our younger brother, who was born to him at an old age. We also told you of our brother who is no more, the full blood brother of the youngest one. Our youngest brother is all our father has left, and he loves him very much," Judah said with a sad smile. He looked back at Benjamin, gaining strength from remembering his promise to Jacob.

"You told us to bring our youngest brother to you so you could see him with your own eyes. We protested and told you our father could not bear it if his youngest son was taken from him. But you told us that unless we brought him before you, we would never see your face again," Judah continued.

"Brilliant for him to recount all the facts of their case," Liz whispered.

"Indeed. Utterly brilliant," Nigel whispered in agreement.

"So we returned to our father and told him what you had said. Later, when our father told us to return to Egypt to buy food, we reminded him of your words. We told him we couldn't go to Egypt without our youngest brother, or we would not be allowed to see your face," Judah explained. He clenched his jaw and took in a deep breath before continuing.

"Then my father said to us, 'As you know, my wife had two sons, and one of them went away and was never seen again. No doubt he was torn to pieces by a wild animal. Now if you take his brother away from me and any harm comes to him, you will send this grieving white-haired man to his grave,'" Judah said. His lip began to quiver at the thought of his father's words and the reality that they might come true.

"My lord, please, I cannot go back to my father without the boy. Our father's life is bound up in the boy's life. If he sees that the boy is not with us," Judah paused and swallowed back the tears, "our father will die. We are your servants and will all be responsible for sending that grieving man to his grave.

"Please," Judah begged as he once again dropped to his knees before Joseph. "Please, my lord, I guaranteed my father that I would take care of the boy. I told him I would forever bear the blame if I didn't bring him back safe and sound. So please, let me stay here in his place as your slave and allow the boy to return to our father. For how could I possibly return to my father without the boy? I couldn't . . . I couldn't bear to see his face." Judah collapsed with his face to the ground, sobbing.

Kate could hardly bear to hear such words of genuine love come out of Judah. He was the one who had so coldly suggested they sell Joseph into slavery. Now he was offering himself as a sacrificial slave to take Benjamin's place. Surely this meant the brothers had passed Joseph's test. Kate caught Max's eye and he nodded as if to say, *Steady, lass.*

Joseph stood with his jaw clenching and unclenching, squeezing his fists tightly as he fought to maintain control of his emotions. As he gazed down at his brothers, he saw them bowing low before him, just as in his dreams. He realized this final act was the complete fulfillment of those dreams, for they weren't just begging for grain. They were begging for grace. They were begging for forgiveness. And redemption.

Imenand looked around the room at the many servants and saw how uncomfortable this moment had grown for everyone here. But for none more so than his master. Joseph shook his head and looked over at Imenand, pleading for help. He couldn't bear it anymore. "Out! All of you!" Joseph cried as he spread his hands wide in dismissal.

Imenand clapped his hands and ordered everyone out of the room, bowing out of respect for Joseph. "As you wish, my lord." Everyone quickly filed out of the room, leaving Joseph alone with his eleven brothers. Max remained by Joseph's side, giving him emotional support simply with his presence.

The brothers looked fearfully at each other and huddled in close, wondering what was happening. Surely it was a bad sign for the prime minister to do this. Suddenly, the unthinkable happened. The second most powerful man in the land of Egypt began to weep.

The prime minister let loose a deep, heart-wrenching wail of such grief that it surpassed even that of their father the day he learned Joseph was gone. Tears streamed down his face as he shook his head side to side. He looked up at them and his eyes darted from one brother to the other. The brothers didn't know what to think, and the tension became unbearable.

The sound of Zaphenath-Paneah's weeping was so loud it carried through to the outer rooms of the palace. Word quickly spread throughout the palace that something was causing the prime minister terrible emotional pain. No one knew what to think of this. Imenand quickly instructed everyone to respect the privacy of Zaphenath-Paneah. He would inform Pharaoh of what was happening.

Joseph wiped his eyes, and through his tears and with a broken voice finally exclaimed in Hebrew, "*AAA-NEE YO-SAPHE!* I AM JOSEPH!"

The brothers looked at Joseph in shock, and at one another in wild confusion. He spoke to them in their own tongue. And he claimed to be their long-lost brother. They were speechless. And terrified.

"Is my father alive?" Joseph said, his words now spilling out almost giddy with joy.

The brothers didn't utter a word. Joseph had compassion on them when he realized their fear and confusion. He smiled and said, "Please, come close to me!" The brothers slowly drew closer to Joseph, staring in disbelief at this 'ghost' before them.

"I am Joseph, your brother, the one you sold into slavery in Egypt. But don't be upset and angry with yourselves for selling me to this place. You didn't really do this! God is the One who sent me here ahead of you to preserve your lives," Joseph said, so relieved to now make his confession to his brothers.

"Look, this famine has ravaged the land for two years and five more hard years are coming. There won't be any plowing or harvesting until this famine is through. God sent me ahead of you to keep you and your families alive—to preserve life. Don't you see?" Joseph pleaded. "It was *God* who sent me here, not you! And He was the one who made me advisor to Pharaoh and prime minister over the land of Egypt."

"Do you realize the depth of what Joseph is doing? He has truly forgiven these men for what they did to him," Liz observed as tears welled up in her eyes over this beautiful scene. "Joseph could not speak these words of reassurance if he had not truly forgiven them. What grace! *C'est magnifique!*"

"Hear, hear!" Nigel exclaimed. "Never have I witnessed such a magnanimous speech!"

Al scratched his head with confusion. "Magnanimous? Is that good?"

Liz sniffed with tears of joy. *"Oui, mon cher.* It means Joseph is a great man. A great man of God to extend such good to those who extended such evil to him."

"So Joseph sees that what these brothers meant for evil, God meant for good," Al observed. "Aye, magnanimous. I'll think of

Joseph every time I hear that word."

"Psst, listen up, you two," Nigel whispered. "Our dear Joseph is about to make his brothers an offer they can't refuse."

"Now hurry back to my father and tell him what has happened. Tell him God has made me master over all the land of Egypt. Tell him to come to me!" Joseph instructed his brothers excitedly. "Tell him I said, 'Come to me immediately to live in the land of Goshen. You can live near me with your children, your grandchildren, your flocks and herds, and everything you own. I'll take care of you, for there are still five years of famine ahead of us. Otherwise, you, your household, and all your animals will starve.'"

The brothers still were speechless. This was too much for them to take in. Not only was Joseph alive, but he forgave them and wanted to take care of them! Such goodness was beyond comprehension with the load of guilt most of them carried. Kate stood at the feet of Benjamin and gently nudged him, willing him to embrace such grace.

Joseph saw Kate and smiled. "Look! You can see for yourselves, and so can my brother Benjamin, that I really am Joseph!" he said as he pulled off his Egyptian headdress, showing his light brown locks that fell around his face. His eyes penetrated those of his brothers as he continued, "Go tell my father of my place of honor here in Egypt. Describe everything you have seen, and bring my father quickly back to me."

Joseph lifted his arms out to Benjamin, weeping with joy. He went over and embraced his little brother, tears rolling down his face as he kissed Benjamin. Benjamin returned Joseph's embrace, burying his face in his older brother's fine, white Egyptian robe. "Joseph! Joseph!" Benjamin said as he squeezed his eyes tightly and cried tears of joy as he clung to his brother.

The other brothers all began to weep with the wonder of this moment. Joseph went over to each one, saying his name and embracing him tightly, willing him to open his heart to the truth of the grace and love he was offering them. "Reuben, Judah, Levi, Dan, Asher, Naphtali, Zebulun, Issachar, Gad, Simeon."

Simeon laughed with joy as he embraced Joseph. He held Joseph by the shoulders and stared intently into his face. "You visited me in prison, didn't you? You were the nosy cellmate!"

Joseph laughed and nodded his head. "Yes, I had to know if you had changed. I needed some hope. And you passed the test," Joseph said, again wiping his eyes, looking around at all his brothers. "You all passed the test. I know now you have changed. Your hearts are no longer hard but broken and desiring forgiveness. Know that you have it. I've learned God can only use men who have first been broken and willingly offer themselves."

Kate and Max ran over to join Liz, Nigel, and Al. The brothers were so happy and eagerly talking with Joseph that they didn't notice the animals.

"Oh!" Liz exclaimed. "These are the men God is to use! We are looking at the nation of Israel today coming together in new birth! God can finally use these men, no? This whole test wasn't just about Joseph preserving their lives. It was about God getting the rest of the brothers in line so He could bless them as the nation of His chosen people!"

"I must say, my pet, you have just taught me more in one moment than I have taught you in twenty years in Egypt!" Nigel said, astounded by Liz's revelation.

"We've done it then! Our mission is complete!" Kate exclaimed, wagging her tail.

"Not quite, love. There still remains one robe," Max said.

"And one dream," Al said, drawing delightfully surprised looks from everyone. "What? I can count. Liz weren't the only kitty learnin' things in Egypt these past twenty years. I went to school with Pharaoh's laddies. What would ye like to know?"

Max, Kate, Liz, and Nigel erupted with laughter at the thought of the simple-minded Al being schooled in the palace of Pharaoh. Perhaps he now knew more than all of them combined.

CHAPTER 56

The Final Robe

This pleases me!" Pharaoh exclaimed. "Bring Zaphenath-Paneah to me immediately."

Imenand bowed in agreement, having explained to Pharaoh that Joseph's brothers had come to Egypt and that they had been reunited. He quickly left and brought Joseph back to Pharaoh. Joseph was all smiles as he entered the court of Pharaoh. As he approached the throne, there stood his old master and friend, Potiphar. A lump grew in Joseph's throat as he saw the happiness that covered Potiphar's face. He couldn't wait to introduce him to his brothers.

Pharaoh rushed over to Joseph and put his arms on his shoulders, smiling as well. "What great news! My heart and all Egypt's hearts are glad for you. Here is what I want you to tell your brothers: 'This is what you must do: Load your pack animals, and hurry back to the land of Canaan. Then get your father and all your families and return here to me. I will give you the very best of the land of Egypt, and you will eat from the best the land has to offer,'" Pharaoh dictated excitedly.

"My lord, thank you for such kindness to my family," Joseph said as he bowed in respect.

Pharaoh excitedly continued: "Tell your brothers to also take wagons from the land of Egypt to carry their little ones and wives, and to bring your father back here. Tell them not to worry about their possessions back in Canaan for the best of all the land of Egypt will be theirs."

"My lord," Joseph said as he bowed again with gratitude. "I don't know what to say."

"Yes, you do! I just told you! Now go and give your brothers the good word," Pharaoh said with a laugh.

Joseph smiled and left Pharaoh's court. He and Potiphar smiled as they walked out of the throne room. As Joseph reached the corridor, Imenand was there waiting for him. They shared a big smile before Joseph took off running down the corridor to see his brothers. Imenand followed along behind, clapping his hands for the servants to bring the provisions ordered by Pharaoh.

Benipe played with great joy, and the music of his harp filled the room with beautiful sound. No longer was there tension in Joseph's home. Now there was joy! Unspeakable joy. Servants brought in trays of fruit, nuts, and sweet delicacies. All the men ate and laughed together, still marveling at the miracle of the morning.

Imenand clapped his hands and in walked a long row of servants, carrying beautiful new clothes.

"*C'est bon!* Here we go," Liz said excitedly. "I think we shall see our final robe now."

"I do believe you're right, dear girl," Nigel added. Together all the animals remained hidden behind the palm plants but gazed out at the gifts Joseph was about to give his brothers.

"Ah, good!" Joseph said as he stood to take the clothes from the servants. "I'm sending you home in style!" Joseph laughed and tossed the colorful, fine Egyptian clothes over to each of his brothers. The brothers laughed and held up the beautiful garments to their chests. Never had they possessed such grand clothing.

Joseph approached Benjamin last. He slowly took a fine robe from one of the servants and held it out for Benjamin to put on. "Come on, little brother. Let's see how it fits," Joseph said with a grin.

Benjamin turned and happily slipped his arms into the soft linen robe, wrapping his arms around himself in the fineness of the fabric.

"It suits you," Joseph said. "And there are four more robes for you here," Joseph said as he patted the pile of robes left for Benjamin.

"Thank you, dear brother. It reminds me of the one Father gave you," Benjamin said.

Joseph looked around at the brothers for their reaction, but saw nothing but gratitude and happiness. He saw no jealousy. *Good,* Joseph thought. *Now one more item to test them.*

Joseph clapped his hands and Imenand brought over a small, golden box. Joseph took the box and handed it to Benjamin. "Go ahead. Open it," he said with a grin.

Benjamin's eyes lit up as he opened the box. His jaw dropped and he threw his head back, laughing. "You can't be serious, Joseph!"

"I am serious, little brother," Joseph said, putting his hand on Benjamin's shoulder.

"What is it?!" Judah demanded as the other brothers drew near.

"Three hundred pieces of silver," Joseph exclaimed. "Your little brother is rich!"

The brothers all applauded and slapped Benjamin on the back to celebrate with him.

"Utterly splendid!" Nigel exclaimed. "That rascal is really pushing his brothers to the limit with this final test!"

"Oui, he wants to see if any greed remains," Liz observed. "It appears not. The test is complete. The brothers all passed. And the final robe has been given."

"There's still one dream," Al said with his mouth full, chewing on a banana.

"Albert! Where did you get a banana?" Liz exclaimed.

"Oh, I grabbed it when we left the temple of Anubis and stuck it behind me necklace," Al explained. "I were savin' it for a special occasion."

"My dear boy, I certainly hope you didn't take it from the same table with the tainted dates," Nigel exclaimed.

Al suddenly held his head. "I don't feel sssso gggood."

"Daft kitty!" Max burst out laughing. "Sweet dreams then, laddie."

"Oh, Albert!" Liz exclaimed, helping Al as he lay down on the floor, falling asleep. "Nigel, we shall need more waking potion."

"Right! I'll go retrieve some now," Nigel said, laughing as he scurried off.

"I don't suppose Al's the one who has the final dream?" Kate exclaimed.

Max, Kate, and Liz looked at Al and then at one another. They would know the answer to that question soon, that much was certain.

Joseph escorted the brothers out to the courtyard where a huge caravan of gifts for Jacob awaited them: ten new male donkeys loaded with the finest products of Egypt and ten new female donkeys loaded with grain, bread, and other supplies Jacob would need for the journey. The brothers were smiling and laughing as they gazed at the bounty Joseph was sending with them.

Kate jumped into the back of one of the carts as the brothers loaded up their gifts, happy to escort the brothers home. She barked her farewell to Max, who stood next to Joseph: "See ye soon, me love!"

"Aye, lass! See ye soon," Max barked back.

Joseph smiled and called after his brothers. "God be with you as you travel. And no quarreling about all this along the way!"

Liz smiled from behind the shadow of a huge outdoor urn in the courtyard. *He knows his brothers so well,* she thought. *They may be changed men, but their tendency to argue is very much the same.*

Joseph then squatted to pet Max. "Jabari, I'm glad you were here for this big day."

Aye, laddie. I wouldn't have missed it for all the bad dates in Egypt, Max thought with a grin.

CHAPTER 57

The Schemer's Dream

The oppressive heat was bearing down on Jacob as he sat outside his tent alone. He had not wanted much company since Benjamin and his other sons had left for Egypt. Leah was worried sick about Jacob. For a man of 130 years he ate like a bird. It wasn't a matter of Jacob being valiant and eating less so his starving family could have more during this famine. He simply was not hungry. For food, that is.

Jacob scanned the horizon every day, hoping for a glimpse of his sons. And as the sun set on each day that did not bring their arrival, he wearily put himself to bed, praying to God for their safety. Jacob prayed continually throughout the day for his boys. He hadn't experienced such close communion with God in many years. These long days were therefore bittersweet. On the one hand he was in anguish over his sons. On the other hand, he felt enveloped by the presence of God.

Throughout these days with God, Jacob revisited his past. He thought of the story of his birth, the second twin born, grabbing the heel of his brother Esau. Jacob cringed as he thought of how he had later tricked Esau out of his birthright over a bowl of stew. *How could I have been so selfish?* Jacob thought to himself with regret.

Jacob's memories took him to the dark day when he schemed to trick his father into giving him Esau's blessing. He had disguised himself as Esau and prepared his father, Isaac, a meal, and Isaac had given Jacob his blessing. Jacob had actually lied and told his father he was Esau so he could steal the blessing! As Esau had pleaded with Isaac he said, "No wonder his name is Jacob, for now he has cheated me twice. First he took my rights as the firstborn and now he has stolen my blessing!" The grief and remorse over past schemes swept over Jacob.

Later he recalled how he had been on the receiving end of the schemes of his father-in-law Laban, who tricked him into marrying Leah. Jacob had worked seven long years to earn the right to marry Rachel, but on their wedding night, Laban had given Leah to him instead. Jacob had to work seven more years for Rachel's hand. Deception and schemes infiltrated his family from the moment of his birth. Yes, he knew he was aptly named. Jacob ("holder of the heel" or "supplanter") was a schemer, and he deserved the title.

But then God brought to Jacob's memory the night Jacob physically wrestled with Him. Jacob wouldn't let God go until He blessed him. And bless him, God did. "Your name will no longer be Jacob. From now on you will be called Israel because you have fought with God and men and have won." Jacob rubbed his sore hip as he remembered that God left it out of socket as a consequence for wrestling against Him. But despite his scheming and wrestling against God Himself, God still promised to bless Jacob by naming him Israel and fulfilling the promise He had long ago made to his grandfather Abraham. The nation of Israel would be as numerous as the sand on the seashore and as the stars in the sky.

Jacob thought about the scheme his sons had played on the men of Shechem, and the ways they acted out in the fields. Joseph told Jacob about the deceptive practices of Jacob's sons behind his back. But Jacob knew that it was he himself who modeled such behavior for his sons. He was to blame for the way he acted, and for the way he treated his sons. He had shown favoritism and he realized now how it must have hurt his other sons to the core. "I am a failure. I have failed my sons. And I have failed You, my Lord," Jacob prayed with regret. He heard the voice of God answer his spirit:

"I PROMISED TO MAKE YOU AS NUMEROUS AS THE SAND ON THE SHORE, AND I HAVE GIVEN YOU A LAND WHERE YOU ALL WILL LIVE AS MY CHOSEN PEOPLE."

"But how, God?" Jacob prayed. "How can this promise be fulfilled now, after I've lost one son, possibly two? Perhaps I've lost them all," Jacob said mournfully as he looked out at the vacant horizon. "My family who remain are starving. It looks hopeless that a nation of Israel will ever be as numerous as You say. Perhaps the sin of my schemes has made You change Your mind about the promise. If so, I understand. I deserve it for all I've done. Forgive me."

Jacob spent the morning in prayer, asking for God's forgiveness. And this time he didn't wrestle with God for a blessing. He simply asked for it. If God saw fit to give him a blessing, he would never again scheme his way through life. Peace entered Jacob's spirit as he settled matters in his heart with the Lord.

The children were the first to spot them. "Grandfather! Grandfather!" the children exclaimed as they ran over to Jacob's tent. "They're back! And there's a lot of them this time!"

Jacob shakily stood and squinted toward the horizon and sure enough, there was a long line of men, donkeys, and carts. He didn't understand, but he slowly began to count the number of men.

Seven, eight, nine, ten . . . eleven! All his sons were safely back home. Benjamin was back! Simeon was back! Gratitude filled Jacob's heart as he went out to greet his sons. *Where did they get those fine, new clothes? And look at Benjamin's robe!*

The brothers left their donkeys and carts and ran down the road to their father as fast as their legs would carry them. Their faces were no longer downcast, telling of tragic news. This homecoming was different, for the smiles and joy on their faces accompanied an unexpected message for their old, heartbroken father.

"Father! Father, we have good news!" Judah exclaimed as he reached Jacob. "Joseph is still alive! And he is prime minister of the land of Egypt!"

Jacob looked at his sons as if they were insane. This wasn't possible. He had grieved for Joseph for more than twenty years. Joseph couldn't be alive. He was dead. How cruel of his sons to give him such false hope. This just couldn't be . . . could it?

Kate looked up at the face of Jacob and saw his unbelief. *Please, Jacob! This time yer sons be tellin' ye the truth! Long ago they told ye a lie aboot Joseph an' ye believed them. Now they be tellin' ye the truth aboot Joseph an' ye don't believe them. Now is the time ta believe, even though it seems impossible,* she thought.

Reuben stepped up and said, "Father, what Judah says is true. Joseph is the second most powerful man in the land of Egypt. He is second only to Pharaoh himself! He was the man who dealt so harshly with us when we first went to Egypt. It was Joseph, Father!"

"He had to test us, Father," Simeon added with humility. "He wanted to see if we were truly men of God after so many years. That's why he sent for Benjamin and put us through such a hard test before he revealed himself to us."

"And look at what Joseph has sent you, Father! Twenty donkeys and food and provisions beyond what we've seen in years," Dan said, pointing at the bounty they carried with them.

Jacob looked at the carts and the donkeys laden with food and provisions, and he began to believe it was possible that what his sons were telling him could be true. "How could this be?" Jacob almost lost his balance with the impact of such hope and good news.

"Father," Benjamin said as he put his hand on his father's shoulder to steady him. "Joseph said to tell you to come to him quickly, for he longs to see you. Not only that, Pharaoh himself sent word to have you bring the entire family to live in the land of Goshen. Pharaoh sent carts to carry your little ones and the women back to Egypt. He will give us the best of the land and the best of the food of the land of Egypt. Joseph said five years of famine remain, as foretold to him in Pharaoh's dream. Unless we go to him, we will all starve here in the land of Canaan."

The brothers remained silent as Jacob tried to take in all they had told him. A moment ago he had been in remorse for his past, and had released the promise of God, realizing he was unworthy of such grace. Now he was told that not only was Joseph alive, but a way for all his family to be saved from the famine was before him as well. Not only was he forgiven for the schemes of his past that had harmed his family, but the promise of God came rushing back into Jacob's spirit.

"YOU INDEED ARE WORTHY OF MY GRACE AND MY BLESSING," Jacob heard the Lord say in his heart.

Jacob's spirit was immediately revived. A tear of joy spilled from his eye as he imagined embracing Joseph again. It was too good to be true. But in his heart, Jacob knew this wasn't a scheme. It was real.

A smile came over Jacob's face as he exclaimed, "I've heard enough. I believe you! I must get to Joseph and see him before I die. God be praised!"

The brothers embraced Jacob as they all laughed and shouted with joy over the miraculous turn of events. Their family was being restored. Their hope was being restored. And their future as the nation of Israel was being restored. Never could they have dreamed up such goodness.

Kate looked at the night sky and marveled at the abundance of stars. There were too many to count. She smiled as she thought about the promise of God to make the descendants of Israel more numerous than these stars.

They were camped underneath the stars on the road to Egypt, and had stopped in Beersheba for the night. Jacob had decided for his family to stop here, at the very southern border of the land of Canaan, before they entered Egypt. Before they left this land God had called the Promised Land, Jacob wanted to make sacrifices to the Lord to reaffirm His guiding providence. A change had come over Jacob. No longer did he barrel ahead with his strong will and schemes. He was entrusting himself entirely to the direction and will of God.

Everyone was asleep. Kate walked over to Jacob and nestled next to him to keep him warm. Suddenly she felt Jacob stir. Then every nerve in her body tingled as she heard a voice she had not heard audibly since the day they left Noah's ark. It was the voice of God.

"JACOB! JACOB!"

Jacob's eyes remained closed. God was speaking, but Jacob was dreaming.

"Here I am," Jacob answered out loud.

"I AM GOD, THE GOD OF YOUR FATHER; DO NOT BE AFRAID TO GO DOWN TO EGYPT, FOR I WILL MAKE YOU A GREAT NATION THERE. I WILL GO DOWN WITH YOU TO EGYPT, AND I WILL ALSO SURELY BRING YOU BACK HERE AGAIN; AND WHEN YOU DIE, JOSEPH WILL BE WITH YOU AND CLOSE YOUR EYES."

Jacob didn't respond, but smiled and rolled over. Kate then realized what she had just witnessed. *The eighth dream! The Maker Himself was the final dream!*

Kate felt such joy and excitement she couldn't get back to sleep. She knew they would be rising soon to depart anyway. She pondered what God had told Jacob. He said He would be with them in Egypt, and that Jacob would die with Joseph by his side. And someday, they would return to the land God had promised Israel. Kate wondered when that would be. For now, it didn't matter.

There was nothing to fear. God would be with them in Egypt and remain with them until they came home. This was not just a family on the move, but a nation.

God's nation.

CHAPTER 58

Reunion

Joseph stood in the doorway of his sons' bedroom and watched them sleeping. Asenath came up behind him and wrapped her arms around his waist.

"What are you thinking about?" Asenath asked.

Joseph squeezed her arm. "I'm thinking Ephraim and Manasseh are going to get to meet their grandfather soon. They'll also meet aunts, uncles, and cousins they never knew existed. Just think of that!" Joseph turned to embrace his wife.

"And I get to introduce my beautiful wife to my father. How happy he will be to see the fine daughter-in-law he has! And such fine grandsons. Oh, Asenath, I can't wait!" Joseph said as he picked her up and twirled her around in the hallway.

Asenath giggled. "You are just as giddy as the moment our sons were born! But you should be. This will be a happy moment. I can't wait to meet your family."

Joseph led his wife by the hand out to the terrace. They stood looking up at the star-filled sky. "I have scouts out looking for them each day. I want to know the minute they get near Goshen," Joseph said. Then a frown grew on Joseph's face.

"What's wrong, my love?" Asenath asked.

"What will I say to him when I see him? Where do I even begin after so much time and after all that's happened?" Joseph asked.

"How about, 'Hi, Father,' for starters?" Asenath replied with a grin. "That and a hug should be enough."

Joseph kissed her on the head and chuckled. *Hi, Father,* he thought. Then he remembered the word in Hebrew. *Abba. Hi, Abba.* What could be a better way to start the reunion? He would be a little boy embracing his father. How often Joseph had dreamed of such a meeting.

The dreaming little boy inside him had clung to this one dream for more than twenty years.

Early the next morning, a young man rushed up to the entrance of Joseph's house. Imenand greeted the young man and they spoke briefly. Max, Al, and Nigel watched from the outer court as Imenand quickly rushed up the steps leading to Joseph's chambers.

"Could be news of Jacob's caravan," Max said.

"I do say, I hope so. How splendid to finally see Joseph and his father reunited!" Nigel replied.

"Aye! And how happy Joseph will be to see his father again!" Al added, a goofy expression on his face.

"Remind me to give Al a vocabulary lesson," Nigel leaned over and whispered to Max. "It seems he missed a couple of days of school."

Max grinned. "Aye. Let's go see wha's happenin' then."

Together the threesome followed Imenand up to Joseph's chamber and listened to what was said.

"How many are there?!" Joseph said as he jumped up to put on his robe.

"The scout said there are at least sixty-six people, not including some of the women. They are nearing the land of Goshen," Imenand replied, smiling as he watched Joseph hurriedly get dressed.

Another servant called from the door. "My lord, your brother Judah is here. Your father sent him ahead to find out where they should go in Goshen."

Joseph ran out of the room and bounded down the stairs. Max, Al, and Nigel looked at one another and grinned. "Let's follow the lad back downstairs. I don't want ta miss a word of this," Max said as the animal friends followed along behind Joseph. Imenand clapped his hands for servants to attend to his instructions.

Judah stood waiting in the outer court. He smiled at Joseph as his brother rushed up to embrace him.

"Judah! It is so good to see you. Father and the others, are they here?" Joseph blurted out excitedly.

Judah held onto Joseph's arms. "Yes, brother! We are all here, safe and sound. Father can't wait to see you. He . . . he didn't believe it was possible you were alive after so many years. Joseph, how happy he is. How happy we all are." Judah's eyes filled with tears of joy.

Joseph teared up and smiled. "God is good, Judah. I've dreamed of this day for a long time."

"Well, Dreamer, it looks like all your dreams are coming true," Judah said as he and Joseph laughed and embraced again.

Max, Al, and Nigel hid behind a potted palm plant and cheered at the news. "I must depart to the house of Potiphar and tell Liz what is happening," Nigel said.

"Aye, the kitty lass will want ta know the good news. Al, ye best go back ta Pharaoh an' give us a report of wha' happens when they get the word. I'll go with Joseph as he leaves ta meet his family," Max said.

"And of course you'll get to be reunited with Kate as well," Nigel pointed out.

"Aye, Mousie," Max said with a grin. "Finally I get ta be together with me lass. We'll all meet up back at Joseph's house tonight."

Imenand walked up behind Joseph, carrying Joseph's headdress. "My lord, your headdress. I thought you would want to present yourself to your father in the full splendor of the prime minister of Egypt." He bowed and handed the headdress to Joseph. "I have your chariot and one for your brother at the ready outside."

"That be our cue," Max said. "I'm goin' ta r-r-run out ta the char-r-riot so Joseph doesn't leave me. Al, ye head ta Pharaoh. Nigel, ye best stay hidden until the humans be gone. See ye tonight!"

With that, Max ran out to the chariot and Al ran down the corridor to Pharaoh's throne room. Nigel stayed hidden a few minutes longer.

Joseph smiled and placed the blue and gold headdress on his head. "Thank you, Imenand. For everything. Any last words of wisdom for me?"

Imenand smiled. "Know that you are loved and that you are able," he replied.

Joseph smiled and nodded. He grabbed Judah by the shoulder and together they ran outside to jump into their chariots to go meet Jacob.

Nigel watched Imenand as he stood in the doorway and waved farewell to Joseph. He sat there cleaning his spectacles, thinking about what Imenand told Joseph. *I do say, that sounds very familiar. I believe I've heard someone say that before. Perhaps Max? Liz? Ah, well. Splendid words no matter who said them.*

Imenand turned and started walking back toward Joseph's chamber. Nigel would leave when he was gone. Suddenly Imenand stopped by the potted palm plant and leaned over and spied Nigel. Nigel's heart caught in his throat. He'd been seen! His whiskers started nervously twitching and he feared Imenand would capture him.

But Imenand just stood there smiling at the frightened mouse. With a twinkle in his eye he then said, "Don't be afraid, small one. Go on. Don't you have someone to see?"

Nigel wasted no time scurrying away while he had the chance. His mind raced with confusion as to what had just happened with this human. He had gone undetected in the palaces, prisons, and pyramids of Egypt for more than twenty-five years. Nigel frowned as he thought about things.

Yes, I certainly need to retire. If I've lost my ability to stay hidden, I must leave Egypt, he thought. On his way to Potiphar's house, he dodged a group of humans walking down the street. *Oh, dear, how sad I will be to say farewell to Liz, Max, Al, and Kate. Well, perhaps the joy of the reunion of Joseph with his father will offset the sadness of my departure. I shall tell Liz the news and be on my way. How dreadful! Parting is such sweet sorrow.*

"Hang on, Jabari! I see them!" Joseph yelled as he drove his chariot like a crazy man down the winding road leading to Goshen. Max was sliding around the floor of Joseph's chariot, barely able to hang on. Judah rode in another chariot next to Joseph, driven by one of Joseph's many guards.

Jacob looked up and saw two chariots racing toward him. He held up his hand and the caravan slowly came to a stop. Jacob slowly climbed out of the lead cart. He took his staff and started walking toward the charging chariots. Jacob's heart pounded in his chest. Kate also jumped down from the cart and walked respectfully behind him.

Joseph saw a frail, old, white-haired man walking toward him, followed by the little white dog. "Father!" he cried with joy. He pulled on the reins of his horses and brought his chariot to a complete stop before jumping out. Max shook his head and followed

Joseph as he ran toward his father. He was running so fast his headdress flew off his head.

Jacob stopped in the road and dropped his staff as he opened his arms wide, waiting for his son. Joseph ran headlong into his father's arms and together the two melted into one another's embrace, weeping.

"Abba! Abba! Abba!" Joseph cried as he wrapped his strong arms around his elderly father. He sunk his face into Jacob's robe and smelled the scent of home.

"My son! Oh, my precious son! You're alive!" Jacob shouted as he sobbed with tears of inexplicable joy. "You're alive! Are you real or am I dreaming?"

"You're not dreaming, Father. And finally, neither am I," Joseph exclaimed as he and Jacob shared the laughter of this reunion.

Father and son held on to each other for a long time in the middle of the dusty Egyptian road, embracing, weeping, and laughing. It was a moment of miracles for them. The entire family stood back, giving Joseph and Jacob as much time and space as they needed.

Max and Kate walked up to each other on the road and embraced.

"Oh, me love, how happy I be!" Kate exclaimed. "We made it. Finally we kin be together again."

"Aye, lass," Max said with a grin. "Mission accomplished."

Together Max and Kate stood by and watched the beautiful scene of Joseph and Jacob. Time seemed to stand still.

"'Tis a gr-r-rand day for r-r-reunions," Max said.

CHAPTER 59

The Hidden One

Max and Kate were curled up napping in the wicker bed next to Joseph's desk. Al had just finished a plate of fish and was happily dozing on the plush pillows by the low table, drool running out of the corner of his mouth. They were all exhausted from their mission and were enjoying a well-deserved rest. All, that is, except Liz and Nigel.

Liz and Nigel sat at Joseph's desk. Laid out before them were some blank papyrus, a reed, and black ink. Now that she was fluent in both hieroglyphs and hieratic script, Liz practiced reading and writing as much as she could, just as Nigel instructed. It fascinated her to see how the letters and symbols matched up with letters and words she knew. Cracking the Egyptian code was one of the most enjoyable discoveries this intelligent cat had made in a long time.

Liz decided to use her newfound knowledge to create a decipher document. Now that their mission was over, she assumed they would all be leaving Egypt. If she ever needed to help someone translate Egyptian writing, she figured it would be best to have a written code to make it as easy as possible. After all, it had taken Nigel years to learn the language, and several more years for Nigel to teach Liz.

"The lengthy process of learning Egyptian writing is simply unnecessary, Nigel," Liz explained. "A decipher document consisting of identical words written in at least three languages it will speed up the translation process."

"Utterly brilliant, my dear! I do say, why didn't I think of this before?" Nigel replied enthusiastically. "I propose we use the hieroglyphs, the hieratic script, and perhaps English as the three languages to start. Of course, you can always add your beloved French as well."

"Oui, I agree Nigel, but since English and French are not widely known at this point in time except by the animal kingdom, perhaps we should use another language that will be used more universally in this region," Liz responded.

Nigel and Liz sat a moment to think about how to proceed. A brisk breeze blew the white gauzy linen cloth that hung from the window near the desk where they sat. Liz lifted her head to feel the breeze and closed her eyes, enjoying the fragrant smell of flowers that accompanied the breeze. When she opened her eyes, there stood Imenand.

"May I suggest you use Greek?" Imenand said.

"*Monsieur* Gillamon, I presume," Liz said with her coy smile. "You posed quite the riddle at the beginning of our mission, no? That was very clever of you to have us look for 'the hidden one.' I had suspected it was you for a while, but not until Nigel told me of your words when you spotted him at Joseph's residence did I know for certain."

Imenand smiled. "I knew you would figure out I was Gillamon, being the intelligent creature you are, Liz," he said as he winked at Nigel. "Sometimes it is difficult going undercover for the Maker and taking other forms, especially when in the company of friends."

"*Merci,* Gillamon. But why did I not think about the meaning of the name 'Imenand' sooner?" Liz said, shaking her head. "When Nigel told me about his encounter with you at the palace compound, it all became very clear. The meaning of 'Imenand' is 'the hidden one.'"

"Ah, yes, it is amazing how the truth sits before us as clear as day, if we will but open our eyes to truly see it," Imenand said with a chuckle. "But there is still a greater Hidden One you must know about, for this One will impact your next mission. I will reveal this to you now, but first, it is time for me to resume my true form."

The brisk breeze picked up and swirled around the room. Imenand lifted his arms and looked up to the ceiling. Liz and Nigel had to sit on the papyrus to keep it from blowing away. A potted palm blew over, crashing onto the floor and waking Max and Kate.

"Wha' in the name of Pete were that?" growled Max.

He and Kate looked to see a whirlwind of light surrounding Imenand. As it picked up speed and enveloped the man, the light became so intense the animals had to shield their eyes. Max attempted to look at the whirlwind and saw glimpses of an unfathomable transformation taking place.

The form of Imenand grew long and vertical and became indistinguishable. Max squinted and finally saw the silhouette of Gillamon take shape as the mountain goat shook his head back and forth in the bright whirlwind. Suddenly the wind stopped and there stood Gillamon, tall and majestic as ever.

"By Jove! What an astounding feat, old boy! I say, how ever did you do it?!" Nigel exclaimed as he adjusted the spectacles on his nose.

"Anything is possible with the Maker, Nigel, as you will soon see," Gillamon explained.

"GILLAMON! YE? YE WERE IMENAND?" Max shouted in disbelief. Half of him was happy to see Gillamon, and the other half of him was almost angry he hadn't figured it out.

"Yes, Maximillian. Sorry to give you such a shock," Gillamon said with a grin. "You may wish to wake Al. I want you all to hear what I have to say before I depart."

Max got up and trotted over to Al, giving him a good shake. "Wake up, kitty! Gillamon is here an' has some things ta tell us then."

Al rubbed his head and smacked his lips as he slowly came to, blinking his eyes to get them open. "Good to see ye, Gillamon." He rubbed his eyes again and suddenly realized what he had said. "GILLAMON! When did ye get here?"

"Daft kitty," Max murmured. "So Gillamon, ye were with us all this time an' we didn't even know it! Ye were well hidden, laddie. But tell me, were ye also the Bedouin man who gave us the water on the r-r-road ta Egypt?"

Gillamon chuckled. "Yes, it was I. I also helped direct Joseph when he was looking for his brothers in Shechem. You never know where I might turn up," he said with a twinkle in his eyes.

"C'est magnifique! I am most impressed, Gillamon. But why did you not reveal yourself to us?" Liz asked.

"When I gave you your assignment, I told you the element of faith will always play a role if you choose to be on mission for the Maker. And how you choose to exercise your faith will affect the outcome of the mission," Gillamon explained. "Part of that faith exercise is working with those placed in your path. If you had known who I was, it might have impacted your decisions. Let this be a life lesson for you as you go on to new missions. I may not be there for future events. But you never know when you may have agents of God in your presence."

"You mentioned there was another Hidden One who will impact our next mission. Who is this?" Liz asked.

"The Hidden One was part of your first two missions, although you did not realize it. As time goes on, it will become clear to you He is in every mission. But this mission with Joseph, which you all so successfully fulfilled, is a unique foreshadowing of the Hidden One," Gillamon explained. He looked intently at each animal to make sure they listened carefully to what he was about to say.

"A favored Son will be sent by His Father to His brothers, seeking after them as a shepherd searches for lost sheep. But He will be rejected by His own brothers, who will desire and scheme to achieve His death, stripping Him of His robe. They will not be able to bring themselves to spill His blood with their own hands, so will hand Him over to another race of men, selling Him as did Joseph's brothers, for a few pieces of silver.

"He will be betrayed and abused as a common prisoner while remaining completely innocent of wrongdoing. But in a surprising turn of events, like Joseph, He will ascend the throne at the right hand of the most powerful One. He will provide salvation for all the nations by going before them and making a way to bring life to those who are dying. Most importantly . . ." Gillamon paused for a thoughtful reflection, ". . . He will offer grace and forgiveness to everyone needing redemption, especially those who were involved in His demise. For He will know that although His betrayal appears to be a scheme of men, in reality, it was planned all along by God for good."

The animals were silent and in awe of the description of the Hidden One. It was difficult to consider that another would have to endure a path similar to Joseph's. But somehow, the magnitude of this future story felt even greater.

"Who is he?" Liz asked softly, amazed by what she heard.

"Since you enjoy solving riddles, I will give you several names—for He goes by many—and let you decipher the code," Gillamon said with a wink. He walked over to the desk and picked up the reed with his mouth. On the papyrus he wrote:

"You are to share these names with a prophet on your next mission, for he will write about the Hidden One for the generations who eagerly await Him to be revealed. The prophet's name is: [illegible]."

Al watched Gillamon hold the reed with his teeth to write the secret code names and whispered to Kate, "I never knew goat beasties were so smart. Do ye think he might nibble on the reed when he's done?"

Kate rolled her eyes at Al. "This isn't jest any goat beastie, Al. It's Gillamon, after all!"

Liz and Nigel peered at the papyrus as Gillamon wrote. "I do say, he has some wonderful names and sounds like a most remarkable fellow. How I would love to meet him," Nigel said.

Gillamon finished writing and set the reed down on the table. "And so you shall, Nigel."

Nigel and Liz exchanged looks and wrinkled their brows. Then a smile grew on Liz's face. She knew exactly what this meant.

"Nigel, I believe you will not be able to retire soon—as you had hoped," she said.

"I'm not following you, dear girl. Whatever do you mean? I'm an old mouse and quite ready to put up my travel bags," Nigel said, taking off his spectacles to wipe them clean on the gauzy curtain that fluttered in the breeze next to the table.

"Liz is right, Nigel. But the Maker will allow you to choose of course," Gillamon said before lowering his gaze to stare into Nigel's eyes. "Retirement seldom works for those who are immortal."

"Immortal! I do say, do you mean ME?" Nigel said, fumbling to put his spectacles back on. "Am I to join your merry little band?"

"Aye! Mousie gets ta be one of us then, Gillamon?" Max said, wagging his tail excitedly.

"If he so chooses," Gillamon answered Max. Then, turning to Nigel, he said, "The Maker was greatly impressed with your work on this mission and how you immediately and willingly volunteered to help. Your small size will come in handy for assignments requiring movement in small places. But your splendid mind and jolly good heart have also proved you worthy to join the others as they serve the Maker through time."

Nigel looked at everyone gathered around him before answering.

"Oh, do join us, Nigel!" Kate exclaimed, wagging her tail.

"Aye, Mousie! We kin r-r-really use a wee beastie on our team," Max added with his big grin.

"Ah, *oui, mon ami.* But you must join us. I am sure there is much more you can teach me, and I may be able to teach you a thing or two as well, no?" Liz said as she placed her dainty paw on Nigel's back.

"And I promise never to try and eat ye again," Al finally added with a definitive nod of his head to emphasize his commitment.

"Well, Al, I must say your promise makes this offer most appealing, knowing I will not be ingested," Nigel quipped. He then humbly draped his paw over his chest, bowed low, and said, "Ladies and gentlemen, I accept."

Max, Kate, Al, and Liz erupted in cheers and Gillamon nodded his head in approval. "Very well then, Nigel. Welcome to immortality. I'm sure Max and the others can tell you what to expect. Now it is time for me to leave you."

"One more thing, old chap, if I may," Nigel interjected. "You suggested Liz and I use Greek as the language for our decipher document?"

"Yes, use Greek. Someday your document will inspire the creation of something quite important," Gillamon said with an almost mischievous look on his face. "Be sure to leave a copy behind when you leave Egypt."

"What will our decipher document inspire, Gillamon?" Liz inquired, her curiosity growing.

Gillamon gave Liz a knowing smile. "You'll have to wait about three thousand years for the answer to that question. Let's just say one of your fellow Frenchmen will find it while working for a fellow named Napoleon in a little Egyptian town called . . . Rosetta."

"Merci, Gillamon, I think. I find it very curious you would give me such details for future events when you wouldn't give me the details I desired for the Joseph mission," Liz replied.

"Consider it your reward for acting in blind faith with Joseph, *mon amie,"* Gillamon replied with a wink. "Oh, and speaking of blind, you'll be pleased to know that the spectacles you created for Nigel will be used by many humans in the future. There will be one special human who keeps his spectacles pushed up on his head when he's bothered and determined about things. You will find him to be quite the exceptional fellow."

Liz and Nigel smiled at one another as Nigel again adjusted his golden spectacles on his nose. They couldn't wait to get started on their deciphering project.

"Farewell, my friends. You all have been faithful in your mission, and the Maker is once again pleased with you. Now enjoy a time of rest . . . until I come to you again," Gillamon said.

"Bye, me old fr-r-riend. I'll miss ye, lad. An' I'll be thinkin' twice when I r-r-run into a mysterious beastie," Max said, giving Gillamon a nudge.

"Farewell, Max. Yes, you never know where I'll turn up," Gillamon said with that ever-present twinkle in his eye.

Kate blew Gillamon a kiss and Al walked over to say good-bye. "We'll be seein' ye then, Gillamon!" Al said as he yanked on Gillamon's goatee before Max could stop him.

As if that were his cue, Gillamon quickly disappeared from their presence as the breeze picked up speed and a vortex of light enveloped him. They all shielded their eyes for a moment until the breeze stopped. Everyone felt a bit sad to say farewell to Gillamon.

"Daft kitty!" Max said as he bonked Al on the head. "An' take that r-r-ridiculous r-r-ring out of yer nose then. Ye're not Hapy anymore."

"I'm not?" Al replied with a confused look on his face. "Sure, and I thought I were very happy."

Max, Kate, and Liz shook their heads and laughed at the ever-humorous Al. Thank goodness he was always there to lighten the mood.

Nigel was over on the table reading the coded names Gillamon had left them. He looked up with excitement. "How utterly splendid! I can't believe it! Do you realize who we're going to have the privilege of meeting?"

"Who, Mousie?" Max asked.

Nigel scribbled a code, turned with a broad grin, and held up the papyrus for everyone to see. It read:

A Word from the Author

Mysterious Egypt. It's been thousands of years since Joseph walked the halls of Pharaoh's palace, but we remain intrigued with this incredible civilization. Egyptologists have uncovered marvelous clues to help us understand the Egyptians' social structure, their religious beliefs, their building practices, their way of life, and their way of death, including mummification, pyramids, and magnificent tombs. I thoroughly enjoyed researching Egypt for this book.

The ancient Egyptian culture was full of beauty, intrigue, drama, engineering marvels, artistic masterpieces, and incredible inventions that have benefited mankind. I owe my career to the Egyptians—they invented writing! They also were pioneers in mathematics, medicine, glass technology, quarrying, surveying and construction, and irrigation and agriculture. Music played a major role for the Egyptians; more than likely, the harp originated in Egypt.

A note of interest about our character Osahar the camel and his one-humped cousins, the dromedaries. We imagine dromedaries walking by the pyramids of ancient Egypt, but this is not how it was, as these creatures did not come to be part of the Egyptian landscape until foreign conquerors (Assyrians, Persians, Alexander the Great) brought them en masse to Egypt. Horses and donkeys were used primarily for transport during pharaonic times. And yes, I did read that horses are frightened by camels.

One of the mysteries of Egypt and the Old Testament is time itself. There are gaps in the biblical accounts of specific times given for some events. We don't know exactly how many centuries passed between Noah and Joseph. It could be anywhere from six hundred to two thousand years. And we don't know exactly which Pharaoh appointed Joseph the second-highest ruler in Egypt. Some accounts place Joseph in the Twelfth Dynasty during the Middle Kingdom (1985–1795 BC), but others place him in the Fifteenth Dynasty during the Second Intermediate Period (1650–1550 BC), when the Hyksos kings ruled Egypt from their capital of Avaris. The Hyksos were not native Egyptians but were "shepherd king" foreigners who gradually became immersed in the Egyptian culture to the point of taking over the rule of Lower Egypt in the Nile delta for one hundred years.

A fascinating time-placement clue for me came from Genesis 41:43 when Pharaoh appoints Joseph second-highest ruler in the land, sending him out to ride in his second chariot. The Hyksos were the ones who brought the chariot to Egypt, so it would make sense Joseph would have had to come to Egypt either during or after the reign of the Hyksos.

Pinpointing Joseph's time in Egypt by counting back from Moses' time in Egypt is equally difficult, as we don't know for certain the identity of the pharaoh of the Exodus, although it is believed to be Ramses II (1279–1213 BC). Regardless of *when* it happened, the most important thing to know is that the story of Joseph *really* happened. God allowed His incredible plan for the birth of the Hebrew nation to unfold in the middle of the Egyptian empire.

For purposes of *The Dreamer, the Schemer, & the Robe*, I've taken a few liberties with time, place, fictional characters, and what could have happened when details are missing from the biblical text. But as always for books in The Amazing Tales of Max and Liz, know I stay true to the facts of the biblical events that took place in the life of Joseph. The world Joseph entered was full of the imagery and the culture I write about in these pages, and I use that world as the backdrop for the actual events that transpired in this incredible account.

I did not list Pharaoh by name, but I did set the story in the Hyksos capital of Avaris. I also gave our Pharaoh a pyramid, for how could you have a creative novel set in ancient Egypt without the intrigue of a pyramid? In actuality the last great pyramid was built by Amenemhat III (1855–1808 BC) at Hawara, long before Joseph. Beginning with the New Kingdom, Pharaohs abandoned building pyramids, shifting to elaborate tombs hidden in the Valley of the Kings in western Thebes (Middle Egypt), due primarily to grave robbers. But for the interplay of the characters, I needed a pyramid close to Avaris. I also wanted to give you a sense of how the Egyptians created these incredible structures and funerary complexes. *The Book of the Dead* did not actually appear in tombs until the New Kingdom, but I wove that object into this story.

Benipe and Mandisa were not real characters in the Bible story, nor was there mentioned a witness to Potiphar's wife's scheme against Joseph. The Scripture says Potiphar was furious at Joseph and threw him in prison, but my heart tells me he believed Joseph was innocent. If a powerful man like Potiphar had truly believed his wife's accusation, I think he would not have hesitated to execute Joseph. Perhaps he threw him in prison because he had to do something to save face while providing a way out for Joseph. I feel the anger he showed may have stemmed from knowing his wife had caused this terrible turn of events for Joseph. A relief on tomb walls depicting the iconic figure of the Blind Harpist captured my imagination, and I had to bring the character to life in the person of Benipe. The song Benipe sings is the real "Harper's Song" found on a tomb wall in Thebes.

Joseph was seventeen when his brothers sold him into slavery, and thirty when Pharaoh made him second-highest ruler in Egypt, so thirteen years passed between these events. We know that Joseph interpreted the dreams of the baker and the cupbearer two years before facing Pharaoh, but we don't know how long he was in prison before that event took place. For purposes of this book, I placed Joseph with Potiphar for six years and in prison for seven years.

I had fun portraying Gillamon as the man in the field of Shechem as well as Imenand (Joseph's steward), who are both real characters in the Joseph story but are nameless in the biblical text. Some readers may be disappointed by how I described Joseph's coat of many colors, portraying it as white with colored trim instead of a patchwork of colors. But according to F. B. Meyer in his excellent book *The Life of Joseph,* the reasons why it would have been white with rich, colored trim made sense to me. The actual look of Joseph's robe remains yet another mystery. All these unknowns will be fun things to ask Joseph someday.

The account of Joseph is my favorite from the Old Testament, and I hope you have learned some things about him in this fictional retelling with Max and Liz. He has been called "an Old Testament Christ," as the incredible parallels of his life with Jesus' are amazing. The lessons his story teaches on forgiveness and trusting God in spite of unjust, cruel circumstances are ones we all can apply to our own lives.

It was only fitting for a story set in mysterious Egypt that I leave you with a mystery to solve on your own. In order to crack Gillamon's hieroglyphic code in the last chapter, use the clues on the title pages of the chapters in the book. I hope you have fun figuring it out! I look forward to seeing you when Max and Liz return in *The Prophet, the Shepherd, and the Star.* Please visit www.maxandliz.com for updates on all things Max and Liz and to sign up for e-news. Max, Liz, and I love hearing from our readers, so please drop us a line.

Until then,

Jenny

Bibliography

Bright, John. *A History of Israel.* 4th ed. Louisville, KY: Westminster John Knox P, 2000.

Cowman, L.B. *Streams in the Desert: 366 Daily Devotional Readings.* Edited by James Reimann. Grand Rapids, MI: Zondervan Pub. House, 1997.

Crowder, Bill. *Overcoming Life's Challenges: Lessons from the Life of Joseph.* Grand Rapids, MI: Discovery House, 2007.

Faulkner, Raymond O., trans. *The Egyptian Book of the Dead.* Edited by Eva Von Dassow. New York: Chronicle Books, 2008.

Kamrin, Janice. *Ancient Egyptian Hieroglyphs: A Practical Guide - A Step-by-Step Approach to Learning Ancient Egyptian Hieroglyphs.* New York: Harry N. Abrams, 2004.

Meyer, F. B. *Life of Joseph: Beloved, Hated, and Exalted.* Lynnwood, WA: Emerald Books, 1995.

Peterson, Eugene H. *The Message: The Bible in Contemporary Language.* New York: Navpress Group, 2002.

Putnam, James. *Eyewitness Mummy*. London: DK Pub., 2004.
Sanctuary: A Devotional Bible for Women, New Living Translation. New York: Tyndale House, 2006.
Schulz, Regine, and Matthias Seidel, eds. *Egypt: The World of the Pharaohs*. Konigswinter: Tandem Verlag GmbH, 2007.
Strudwick, Helen, ed. *The Encyclopedia of Ancient Egypt*. London: Amber Books, 2006.
Sudell, Helen, ed. *Ancient Egypt*. London: Anness Ltd, 2007.
Swindoll, Charles R. *Joseph: Great Lives Series Volume 3*. Nashville: Thomas Nelson, 1998.
Zodhiates, Spiros. *Hebrew-Greek Key Word Study Bible, New American Standard Bible* edition. Chattanooga, TN: AMG Publishers, 2008.

Glossary of Characters and French Terms

Animals

Max/Jabari: "brave" in Egyptian	Scottish terrier
Liz/Bastet: Egyptian cat goddess	French cat
Al/Hapy: Egyptian god of the Nile	Irish cat
Kate/Amisa: "companion"	West Highland terrier
Gillamon	Mountain goat
Nigel P. Monaco	British mouse
Osahar: "God hears me"	Bactrian camel
Dodi: "Friend"	Donkey
Wep, Tef	Jackals

Joseph's Family

Joseph/Zaphenath-Paneah	Son, slave, Prime Minister of Egypt
Jacob	Father
Reuben, Judah, Levi, Dan, Asher, Naphtali, Zebulun, Issachar, Gad, Simeon, Benjamin	Joseph's brothers
Leah	Joseph's aunt
Kerra	Joseph's cousin
Asenath	Joseph's wife
Manasseh, Ephraim	Joseph's sons

Potiphar's House

Potiphar	Chief Executioner/Head of Staff for Pharaoh
Zuleika	Potiphar's wife
Ako	Potiphar's chief steward
Mandisa	House slave
Benipe	House slave/the Blind Harpist
Gardener	Potiphar's gardener

Egyptians/Others

Abu and his father	Caravan traders
Pharaoh	King of Egypt
Sadiki	Jailer
Imenand	Joseph's chief steward
Bakers	Pharaoh's bakers
Cupbearer	Pharaoh's cupbearer
Chibale, Rashidi	Egyptian students
Anubis	Egyptian jackal god of the dead
Duamutef	Egyptian jackal god/Protector of mummy stomachs

Wepawet	Egyptian jackal god/Opener of the Ways

French Translation

Adieu	*Farewell*
Allons-y!	*Let's go!*
Au contraire	*On the contrary*
Bon	*Good*
Bonjour	*Good day/hello*
Bonsoir	*Good evening*
C'est impossible!	*It is impossible*
C'est magnifique/ C'est bon	*It is great/good*
C'est ridicule!	*Nonsense*
Comprenez vous?	*Do you understand?*
Enchanté/ Enchantée	*Delighted to meet you*
Faux pas	*Social blunder*
Je comprends	*I understand*
Je t'aime	*I like/love you*
Mademoiselle/Madame	*Miss/Mrs.*
Mais oui	*But yes*
Merci beaucoup	*Thank you very much*
Mon ami/amie/Mes amis	*My friend/my friends*
Mon cher	*My dear*
Mon professeur	*My teacher*
Monsieur	*Mister*
N'est ce pas	*Isn't that so?*
Oooh la la!	*Oh my*
Oui	*Yes!*
Pardon	*Excuse me*
Petite dejeuner	*Breakfast*
S'il vous plaît	*Please*
Très bien	*Very well*
Voila!	*There you have it*